DEMIGODS ACADEMY

SEASON ONE

YEARS
1-2-3

To Giuseppe Amore who got the idea to fill the academy with Gods and Demigods.

DEMIGODS ACADEMY
YEAR ONE

CHAPTER ONE

MELANY

There were more than one hundred people at Callie's eighteenth birthday party milling about in the northwest great room, drinking from champagne flutes and eating pickled fig and ricotta canapés passed out by uniformed waiters and waitresses. They were friends from her prestigious private prep school, their parents, and members of her big Greek family. I stood among them, although I didn't belong to any of those groups. To my face, Callie would definitely call me a friend, sister even, as I'd lived in close proximity to her for the past five years, but I knew behind my back she whispered to her parents, her friends, even the staff who worked in the big house about how I didn't truly belong.

And the sad thing was she wouldn't be wrong.

I took a sip of champagne, as I leaned against the

white railing of the veranda, and stared out over the grounds of the Demos Estate. It was lit up by solar garden lamps lining the cobblestone pathways and winding around the various stone statues guarding the back entrance to the house, as well as out front near the drive. It was always beautiful here at night. I'd often go for long, secret walks through the garden after midnight, my adopted mother, Sophie, and the rest of the Demos household none the wiser. Well, the gardener, Bishop, knew of my late night outings, as he'd caught me a time or two sprinting through the grass and leaping over the stone benches peppered throughout—my own private obstacle course. But he'd never rat me out. We had an understanding. He wouldn't snitch on me about my clandestine night-time adventures, and I wouldn't tell anyone he smoked weed behind the garden shed with Rachel, who was one of the cooking staff.

"What are you doing out here?" Callie joined me at the railing, the sleeves of her elegant blue gown draping over the white wood. She looked like a queen. Her hair was wrapped in a complicated braid around her head, like the Greek Goddesses wore theirs. She even wore a tiny diamond-encrusted tiara for the occasion.

"You know, the usual. Hiding out. Keeping away from Cousin Leo's grabby hands." I made the motion to tweak one of Callie's boobs.

She laughed and slapped my hand away. "I know, he's terrible. He grabbed Kate's ass earlier."

I took another sip of champagne, feeling aware I wasn't even close to looking as beautiful and elegant as Callie did. I hadn't worn a fancy gown, instead opting for a classic black long-sleeved cape jumpsuit. It wasn't mine; Callie loaned it to me. I could never afford something like that. I also suspected it was chosen for me, so it would cover the tattoos on my arms and legs. Her parents were very traditional and uptight. They only put up with me because I was the daughter of their most trusted housekeeper.

"It's time to come in now." Callie turned and gestured to the large room bustling with people in tuxes and gowns beyond the open terrace doors, the din of conversation buzzing annoyingly in my ears. "I'm going to be opening my Shadowbox soon. You want to be there when I do."

"Sure. I'll be right in. Give me a minute."

"You better be. You won't want to miss seeing me get my invitation to the Gods' Army."

I smirked. "You know that's a million in one shot."

Her eyes narrowed into slits. "I didn't waste my life worshipping at the temples for nothing."

Callie walked back into the party. Her feet didn't appear like they touched the floor; her gown was so long it dragged on the immaculate, white-tiled floor. She seemed to float she was so graceful. Often people compared her to the Goddess Aphrodite—long, golden blonde hair, perfect, symmetrical facial features, glacial blue eyes, and the nose of an aristocrat. I thought she also possessed some of the Goddess's character traits as well: vain, sly, and just a little bit diabolical.

Well, maybe not diabolical. People often saved

that word to describe me. Not that I blamed them. My midnight blue hair, tattoos, piercings, and snarly attitude were a bit out of place in the upper class neighborhood of Pecunia, where the families were mostly Greek and devout to the Gods. It wasn't like I didn't believe in the Gods—I sort of had faith. I just didn't worship them like everyone else did. They'd done nothing for me in my life. In my opinion, they didn't deserve my patronage.

Every Thursday, the Demos family went to the Temple of Zeus with their offerings of wine, which they made here on the estate, and lamb sausage, which a butcher in the neighborhood made especially for religious ceremonies, and laid them at the stone feet of the statue of Zeus. Then they spent the day with the other worshippers, drinking and eating. I'd gone once with them years ago, but found the whole practice ridiculous and uncomfortable.

To me, the whole thing was just a story passed down from generation to generation, going on more than a hundred years now. A story we all grew up listening to and reading about in our children's books about the resurgence of the Gods during the New Dawn. I'd read about the 1906 and 1908 earthquakes that killed hundreds of thousands of people, supposedly caused by the escape of a Titan from their prison, and how the Gods fought him and returned him to Tartarus. Worshipping the Gods ensured no other Titan would escape. And the Shadowboxes delivered to every child turning eighteen was a gift from the Gods in return for that servitude. Ninety-nine percent of the boxes contained a simple birthday message, but there was that one percent that held a special invitation to join the demigods academy to train to be a soldier of the Gods.

I thought most of it was just a load of crap. I mean, the Gods' Army? That couldn't possibly be true. Where was this army? Who was part of it? No one in more than a hundred years had seen any evidence of it. It was just another way for companies to make a buck. The amount of Blessed Day birthday supplies designed and sold to the devout was ridiculous. Especially since the chances of someone being invited to join the Gods' Army was miniscule—if it was even real. I'd never known anyone to be chosen. For me, it was just as much a myth as the Gods themselves.

When I joined the others back in the party, the crowd had formed a semi-circle around Callie, while she stood near the baby grand piano at the front of the spacious room. Her parents stood beside her; her mother beamed with pride. Her father appeared stoic. In fact in all the years I'd lived on the estate, I didn't think I'd ever seen Mr. Demos smile. Or it could've been he never smiled at or around me.

I spotted a few of Callie's friends, who I despised, standing near her at the front. Her best friend, Ashley, looked in thrall with the festivities. On the other hand, Tyler appeared bored to tears. When our gazes locked, he gave me a giant, fake smile then lifted his hand and flipped me the middle finger.

I returned the gesture just as the lights flashed off, and a huge birthday cake was wheeled in on a serving table by two of the cooking staff. Someone in the back started singing Happy Birthday, and then it gained momentum through the crowd as the cake, with its eighteen tall, flickering candles, got closer to the birthday girl.

Callie plastered a fabricated smile on her face, as her guests' song reached a high-pitched fervor. Then she blew out the candles and everyone clapped. I knew what her wish would be: an invitation to the mystical Gods' Army. Knowing Callie, she'd probably get it, as she received everything she wanted.

As the cake was wheeled away to be surgically cut into the perfect triangle-shaped pieces, a triumphant horn blew from outside. A murmur rippled through the crowd. The Shadowbox had arrived.

As everyone held their breath in anticipation of the presentation of the famed metal box, I swallowed down my resentment. I hated all this pomp and ceremony. It was a bitter reminder that on my eighteenth birthday, I hadn't received a Shadowbox. Although the magic box was supposed to be delivered to every child across the world on their eighteenth birthday, that momentous, blessed event had missed me entirely. And I wasn't sure why.

A hush fell over the congregation, as a dignitary of the Gods dressed in a traditional Greek white robe carried the metal box in on a clay platter. Fig leaves were embroidered along the edges. I craned my neck and jostled for position with others to get a better view of the box as it made its way to the front of the room.

Even during my time at the orphanage, I'd heard about the boxes—no kid grew up without hearing about them—but the reality of one paled in comparison to any elaborate story. Maybe they weren't the myths I'd thought them to be. But just because the Shadowboxes were real, didn't mean the rest of it was.

The Shadowbox was breathtaking. Constructed from bronze and inlaid with gold and silver, it seemed to glow with its own radiance. Beside me, someone gasped as the dignitary stopped in front of Callie, presenting her with the gift.

Now that it was closer, I could see the motifs engraved with painstaking detail into the metal: symbols of the Gods. The lightning bolt of Zeus, the star of Hera, the rose of Aphrodite, the wolf of Ares. I could see those plain as day. I imagined on the other side would be the moon of Artemis and the sun of Apollo, along with another six symbols to round out the pantheon.

Callie looked at her mother and father to get their permission to open the box. They both nodded. Before she could open it though, she needed to give her thanks to the Gods. It was tradition.

"I thank Thee, mighty Gods. To those who dwell in Olympos, apart from man yet always a part of our lives. To those who dwell in city, forest, stream, river, sky, and ocean and guard all realms, I thank Thee for your blessings and hope to be worthy of the call." Her voice cracked as she spoke, and I almost felt sorry for her. Almost.

Slowly, she reached for the box. When she picked it up, many in the audience gasped. I wasn't sure what they were expecting; maybe for light to shoot out of it, but that wasn't what happened. It might've been Callie had been expecting that as well, because her face fell a little with disappointment.

Lifting the lid, she peered inside. Her hand gave a slight tremble as she reached inside and drew out the tiny rolled-up scroll fastened with a gold ribbon. I could see her throat working as she swallowed nervously while she untied the ribbon and unfurled the weathered, yellowing parchment.

As Callie read the message written on the scroll, her cheeks reddened. Obviously, she didn't receive the message she'd been expecting.

"What does it say, darling?" Her mother craned her long neck trying to read over her daughter's arm.

Callie nudged her mother away as she threw the box to the ground and ran out of the room. Some of the guest murmured at Callie's shocking behavior. Frankly, it didn't surprise me in the least. Smiling, Mrs. Demos nodded to the five-piece band set up in the corner, and music filled the room. She gestured to the partygoers.

"Let's get on the dance floor everyone. This is a party, for Dionysus's sake!"

She grabbed my arm, pulling me close. "Go find Callie and tell her to get her butt back in here and make her apologies. She doesn't want to offend the Gods." She gestured to the box on the ground near her feet. "Take that with you."

I snatched it up, shocked to feel an instant tingle on my fingers. I thought the metal would feel cool to the touch, but there was a heat radiating from it enveloping my fingers and creeping up my hands to my wrists.

I found Callie out on the terrace smoking. She didn't look at me as I stepped up beside her.

"Are you okay?"

She kept puffing. "I can't believe after all the offerings we've made to the temples, and all the charity work my parents do…" She shook her head. "And I get a stupid birthday blessing and not an invitation to the academy."

"Yeah, that totally sucks." I wanted to roll my eyes at her entitled behavior, but didn't want to invoke her rage.

She whipped around to glare at me. "I'm the perfect candidate. I'm everything they need at the academy. I would have been one of their best soldiers."

"Your mother told me to tell you to come back inside and apologize to your guests." I held the Shadowbox out to her. "Here's your box back."

She slapped it away, and I nearly dropped it. "I don't want it. You can fucking burn it for all I care. I don't ever want to see it again!"

She ground out her cigarette on the railing and then stormed back into the house. I watched her leave, feeling anger welling inside me. Callie acted like a spoiled child, which I supposed she was. And one of the cleaning staff was going to get in trouble over the damage she just did to the wooden railing. If it ended up being Sophie, I was most definitely going to say something.

Tired of the theatrics of the party, I snuck out of

the house with the box and crossed the garden to the small cottage on the edge of the estate where I lived with Sophie. Screw Callie. I wasn't going to burn the box. If anything, I could hock it and probably get thousands for it.

Careful not to wake Sophie, who was likely already asleep in bed, as she'd left the party early after working hard for three days to plan the celebration, I crept through the house to my small bedroom.

"You don't have to creep, I'm not sleeping."

Hiding the Shadowbox behind my back, I turned toward the small living room to see Sophie sitting in her chair near the window with knitting needles in her hands, and a ball of red wool in her lap.

"Why are you in the dark knitting?" I smiled at her.

"It relaxes me. There's too much going on in my head to go to asleep."

"Did you hear about Callie?"

She clucked her tongue. "Yes, I heard. Spoiled girl. Some days I don't know how Mrs. Demos puts up with her."

She gestured to the floor by her feet where I usually liked to sit and listen to her tell stories about her and my parents when they were children. "Come sit with me. Tell me everything you got up to today. Did you get a piece of cake? I heard it was delicious."

"No, I didn't get a piece. Not surprising with all the commotion going on." I feigned a yawn. "I'm going to go to bed. It's been a long night."

"Okay, my darling. Have sweet dreams."

"Sweet dreams." I took a few steps backward,

then whipped around with the box so I could duck into my room without her seeing it.

I quickly got out of the jumpsuit, careful not to get it dirty, and put on a pair of sweatpants and an old tank top that had several holes in it from wear and tear over the years. Money was tight for us, so I didn't spend it frivolously on clothing that didn't matter.

Once I was dressed comfortably, I sat cross-legged on the bed and held the box. Again, a strange heat emanated from it and rushed up my hands. Feeling unsettled, I set the box down in front of me. I'd been right about the symbols etched into the metal. There were definitely twelve of them, representing each powerful being.

As I studied the craftsmanship, I was in awe. I'd never seen anything as intricate and beautiful before in my life. With careful hands, I lifted the lid on the box, expecting it to be empty, as Callie had already taken out the scroll and her message from the Gods.

But it wasn't empty. Another small, rolled-up scroll nestled inside, white against the purple velvet.

Confusion crinkled my brow. Callie must've missed this scroll in her haste. She had been overly anxious, and there were so many people crowded around watching; she must've plucked one scroll out and totally missed the other.

I reached in and took it out. The second I touched the paper my fingers tingled. I knew I should just put the scroll back inside and return the box to Callie, but something told me to open and read it. So, I did.

I pulled the ribbon off and unrolled the parchment.

*Congratulations, recruit! You've been invited
to the Gods' Army.*

My heart picked up, revving like a motorcycle in my chest. An electrical shock went through my fingers, and I dropped the scroll. The paper fluttered in the air for a few seconds then landed gracefully onto my blanket.

I couldn't believe it. Callie missed this in her spoiled temper tantrum. The proper and moral thing to do was to roll the message back up, place it in the Shadowbox, and return it to Callie, so she could go to the demigods academy and train to be a righteous soldier for the Gods. But I didn't want to.

Callie had everything: loving parents, a good home, lots of money and possessions, friends. And she didn't appreciate any of it, not one morsel. She always complained to me about not having enough, or her parents not letting her run off to the Cayman Islands in the middle of a school term. She complained about not being pretty enough, or thin enough, gorging on caviar and macrons, while three neighborhoods over, people were homeless and starving.

A thought crossed my mind. What if I kept it for myself? No one would know. Callie already thought the Gods had rejected her, commanding me to destroy the beautiful Shadowbox. She'd never know. If the academy really existed, maybe it would give me true purpose—something I'd never been able to find.

For the last eighteen years, I'd felt lost, like a ship without an anchor, being tossed around in a storm. I'd been an outcast my entire life, not knowing my parents, wondering why they'd left me, always feeling like I was worthless. And now, I could finally become someone who had worth and direction.

It was a once-in-a-lifetime-chance, and it required a hard decision.

I stared down at the box, my heart and my head at war. I had done really bad things in my life but stealing Callie's opportunity to attend the Gods' Academy? It was going to be the worst.

I knew it was wrong, but my heart longed to find my place in the world. Was it at the academy? I couldn't know… but I had to find out.

CHAPTER TWO

MELANY

$\mathcal{I}$ picked up the parchment lying on my bed and flipped it around, looking for the rest. Rumor was that inside the box, along with the invitation to the academy, would be instructions on how to get to the famed but secret institution and the date and time. I didn't see any of those things scrawled on the paper.

Lifting the box, I peered inside it again, paying particular attention to any clever hiding spot for another scroll. I ran my fingers along the smooth edges and planes to find nothing. But when I touched the velvet inlay on the bottom, a tiny bit of the corner curled up. Maybe there was something underneath.

I gripped the velvet between my fingers and tore it away. It didn't come easily, and I had to remove it in strips. When it was gone, I squinted into the box and saw an inscription etched into the metal on the bottom. I held the box up to my lamp and read the words out loud.

"To reveal the secrets of the academy, you must use the thing that has no legs but dances, has no lungs but breathes, and has no life to live or die, but does all three."

A riddle. *Perfect.* I groaned.

It couldn't be too hard, or none of the recruits would make it to the designated time and place, but I supposed that was the point, as they'd only want the best of the best. I read it over again, trying to put the pieces together.

I rose from my bed and paced a little. I did all my best thinking while moving around. What could dance, breathe, and live or die? Humans, but that wasn't it, as we had legs and lungs and had a life. It couldn't be an animal because the same parameters existed. As I marched around my room, my gaze kept going back to the Shadowbox. Every now and then, it would flash from a direct beam of light reflecting off the metal as I moved around it. I thought about how it felt in my hands; the wave of heat that rushed over my skin. Halting, I picked up the box again and studied the symbols of the Gods etched on the exterior.

Zeus – lightning.
Hera – star.
Aphrodite – rose.
Ares – wolf.

Apollo – sun.
Artemis – moon.

I flipped it around and looked at the other six, something irritating my mind like a piece of a popcorn kernel stuck in my teeth.

Poseidon – trident.
Dionysus – chalice.
Hephaistos – fire.
Athena – owl.
Demeter – cornucopia.
Hermes – snake.

Frowning, I brushed my fingers over the box, feeling the metal. Again, heat enveloped my fingers. It was as if I'd set my hand over a burner on a stove. The craftsmanship of the metalwork was beyond anything earthly. It had to have been designed by one of the Gods. Heat, metal…

Fire.

That had to be it. Flames in a fire appeared like they were dancing, fire needed oxygen, like lungs did, to burn, and fire could be snuffed out, the flames dying. That had to be the answer. There was only one way to find out.

Since I didn't have a fireplace to make a fire in, I

gathered all the pillar candles I had in my room, set them in a cluster, and lit them. Then I held the Shadowbox up over the tiny individual flames, hoping I wasn't making a fool out of myself in thinking how clever I was.

I held the box over the candles for ten minutes at least before I could feel a temperature difference in the metal. After another few minutes, it started to become difficult to hold, as my fingers burned. Wincing at the sharp pain, I didn't know how much longer I could keep the box over the flames.

Reaching my threshold, I was about to drop it when thin curls of black smoke rippled out from inside the box. The vapors snaked around in the air, animated, as if blown by an unseen wind. I looked to my window to see if it was open; it wasn't. It was closed tight. At first, I thought the smoke nothing more than a result of melting metal, but then the tendrils started to make words and numbers in the air.

Cala.

3 a.m.

Pier…

I leaned forward, my breath hitching in my throat, as a number formed. But I couldn't decipher if it was a nine or a six. It looped around, set into a spin by either the unseen wind or my frantic breathing. It looked like a six, then a nine, then it stayed as a six. Then after it had all formed in front of me, as if someone had been writing it in the air with a quill and ink… it vanished.

The flames on the candles flared. I dropped the

box, as my fingers couldn't hold it any longer. I glanced down at my hands; the tips of my fingers were red, and a few tiny blisters had formed. It didn't matter, as I had my information.

Cala was the small town near the bay. There was a large dock there; Sophie had taken me there once to watch the huge cruise ships come in. I didn't know how many piers were there, but I only had to find the one—pier six. And it had to be at three a.m. I grabbed my cell phone and looked at the time. It was eleven. I had four hours to get to the right spot to find the academy.

It didn't give me much time to reconsider my decision or to think about the consequences of it, either. If I was going to go, it had to be now.

I jumped to my feet, went into my closet, and grabbed an old ratty duffle bag that I'd had since being in the orphanage. I opened dresser drawers and grabbed whatever I could—underwear, bras, socks, jeans, a couple of T-shirts—and stuffed them inside the bag. On top of that, I settled in the Shadowbox. I imagined I would need it as some sort of proof that I belonged.

After zipping up the bag, I put on my old weathered leather jacket, my combat boots, slid my phone in a pocket, and then peered out. Sophie wasn't in the living room and her bedroom was closed, so she'd obviously gone to bed. After stepping out from my bedroom, I stopped in front of Sophie's closed door. I wanted to leave her a note to let her know where I'd gone, but I knew that would confess what I'd done. No one could know that I'd stolen the invitation. Instead, I quietly opened her door and crept in.

My heart filled when I looked down at her, sleeping so soundly, her face relaxed and devoid of all the worry lines I knew I'd carved on her skin over the years. Leaning down, I pressed a kiss to her forehead and whispered, "I love you."

Fighting back tears, I left the cottage and crept silently across the garden, keeping to the dark shadows, until I reached the driveway. As far as I knew, there weren't any buses that came to this neighborhood, nor would any be running this late, anyway, so I needed a way to get to Cala, which was at least ninety miles away from Pecunia. I had only three and a half hours to get there on time. On foot, I'd never make it.

I heard voices nearby. It had to be party guests leaving. For a brief second, I considered hitching a ride with one of them, but they would definitely inform Callie. I couldn't have that. I needed to leave here undetected, at least until sunrise. In the morning, they could all think what they wanted. Most likely that I'd run away. According to them, I was that type of girl. Sophie wouldn't think it though, she'd worry that something nefarious had happened to me, or that I had a good reason to leave. It broke my heart to put her through the anguish of not knowing, but I had to do it.

Headlights swept over the spot of pavement I stood in, and I jumped back, breath hitching, into the shadows, so I wouldn't be seen. When I turned, I spotted a street motorcycle parked in the corner away from all the other vehicles. That had not been valet parked.

A smile crept over my face, and I sent up a small thanks to the Gods, although I knew they couldn't give a shit and weren't likely paying any attention to what I was doing. I was insignificant.

Ten minutes later, I raced down the driveway of the Demos Estate, thankful of the illegal skills I'd learned during my time in and out of foster homes. I turned left onto the main road and roared out of Pecunia. Although I was excited to have my past in the review mirror, I felt guilty for leaving Sophie. I hoped over time she'd understand why I left.

My heart raced as fast as the bike as I drove toward the coast. I couldn't believe what I was doing. I prayed it would work. I needed it to work. If it didn't and I was booted out before I could even begin, I wasn't sure I'd return to Pecunia. Maybe it would be a sign to just keep on going until the road ended, and I could have a new start.

I thought about that all the way to Cala.

It didn't take me long to find the dock, as the touristy town was fairly small, and all I needed to do was follow the sounds of the ocean. I parked the bike at the main boathouse and then climbed over the chain link fence.

As I made my way to pier six, the silence surprised me. Where were all the other recruits? Surely, I wasn't the only one who figured out the riddle and was able to get here. The rumors were that every four years the Gods recruited thirty-six teenagers to train in the army. I'm not sure why that particular number, but knowing the Gods, it likely had some significance. So, where was everybody?

I found pier six easily enough, despite the lack of overhead lights. As I walked out to the edge, the darkness smothering me with each step, an eerie quiet settled over everything. All I could hear was the soft lapping of the water at the metal posts holding the pier up and my heart thundering in my chest.

I gazed out over the rolling ocean and thought, now what? Did I need to wait for a boat or something? But that seemed almost too easy for the Gods. Knowing them, the way into the academy would be complicated and dangerous. It wasn't like Jason was just given the Golden Fleece; he had to complete three very complicated trials wrought with danger at every turn.

I wondered if I would get a chance to meet Jason at the academy and ask him how he escaped smashing onto the rocks when a school of sirens attacked the ship he'd been on. All my thoughts about ships and sirens made me speculate the entrance to the academy was going to be underwater.

Squinting, I looked out over the water and spotted a buoy floating about a hundred meters away. Every few seconds, it lit up. That was where I needed to go. Strapping my duffel to my back, I took in some deep breaths, wondering if I was really going to do this.

"One, two, three." I dove into the water.

I swam down into the darkness, expecting something to happen. A portal. A door. I'd even take a submarine at this point. But there was nothing but seaweed and the soul-sucking black of deep water. Lungs bursting, I started upwards, my arms aching with fatigue by the time I broke the surface. I sputtered out water and circled around toward the pier.

And that's when I heard the very male sounds of laughter and spotted the outline of someone on the end of the pier watching me. I didn't have to see him to know he was getting a right kick out of seeing me floundering around like a guppy.

"Little late for a midnight swim, don't you think?"

I swam to the pier. The closer I got, the more I could make out the person's features. He was definitely male, and young, my age I thought, square jaw, sharp cheekbones, golden waves swept back to frame striking blue eyes, and to my misfortune, he was exactly the type of guy I'd swoon over.

I reached up and grabbed the edge of the wooden dock so I could heft myself out of the water. He took a step forward, and I thought for sure he was going to crush my fingers under the thick tread of his combat boots, especially when he grinned down at me.

CHAPTER THREE

MELANY

I was about to drop back into the water to avoid having my fingers crushed when he crouched and grabbed hold of my arms, lugging me up onto the pier. I rolled onto my back, dragging hair out my face, and blinked up at him, unsure if he was friend or foe.

"You're on the wrong pier." He nodded toward the other piers, and I spotted several other teenagers my age making their way down the main dock, backpacks slung over their shoulders, or firmly affixed to their backs.

I sat up, trying to keep some of my dignity intact, although I suspected it was much too late for that considering I was sitting here sopping wet, my hair looking like blue seaweed, and I could just imagine my dark makeup had run down my cheeks. The gorgeous stranger probably thought I looked like some deranged raccoon.

"Maybe I just wanted to go swimming." I wiped at my face with the sleeve of my jacket, which didn't do much of anything since it was wet, too.

"Right." He offered his hand to help me to my feet, but I ignored it and stood my own. He lowered his hand, shaking his head a little. "It's pier nine, in case you're wondering. You must've misread the smoke." Picking up his pack, he walked away, joining the swarm of other people.

Before following him, I waited for a few minutes. I didn't want to seem eager or that he'd just saved me from a huge mistake, although, he totally did. I got in line with the others moving down the ramp to pier nine. There had to have been at least thirty people, maybe more, gathered on the dock.

No one was really talking to each other, except for my mysterious savior. He was near the front of the pack, chatting it up with another guy and a pretty girl with long, dark hair. She giggled a lot and kept touching his arm. I hated her on principle, alone.

I took out my phone, which of course was now wet, but I'd wrapped it in plastic before I left, so it wasn't completely damaged. The time said it was 2:55 a.m. We were all cutting it close. I wondered what everyone was waiting for. Maybe I had got it wrong, and there really was a boat coming for us, which would mean I made an even bigger fool out of myself then I needed to.

The guy standing next to me frowned. "Are you wet?"

"Yes. Do you have a problem with that?"

He shook his head. "Nope. Each to their own, I say." He said it with such conviction that I smiled. He returned my smile then it faded a bit. "Are you scared?"

"Hell no." I peered at him, taking in his lanky frame and perfectly coifed jet-black hair. "Are you?"

He scuffed his converse sneaker on the dock. "Nah, I'm ready for the academy."

Except he didn't look all that ready. In fact, none of the people on the dock looked ready. Except for maybe mystery guy. He seemed ready for anything; he had that kind of confidence about him.

Almost everyone flinched when twenty-some alarms sounded on twenty-some cell phones. It was three o'clock. One by one, people leapt off the pier and into the water. It was more like a mass exodus than single file. When I got to the edge, I dove in as well.

This time, I knew where to go. I just followed the swimmer in front of me, as we all dove down. It was dark and murky, extremely difficult to see anything in any direction. But then up ahead, I spied a soft white glow. Everyone's course adjusted, and they swam toward the light.

The closer I got to the light, I saw that it was a blue-white cylinder hovering in the middle of the vast dark ocean like a giant glowing worm. It was a portal. This was how we were all going to get to the academy.

Each person who reached the portal ahead of me breached the barrier and was swept up into it. It looked like they were being sucked up through a large, white straw. Maybe one of the Titans was having a delicious cool glass of water, and we were the dirt specks getting drunk along the way.

As I got nearer, my heart hammered in my throat and my lungs burned. I didn't know how much longer I could hold my breath. Slowly, I reached out to the portal. My fingers pushed through the barrier, and I could feel the suction on my hand. If I weren't careful, my fingers would be ripped off from the force.

Here goes nothing.

I kicked my legs harder, propelling myself forward, and was instantly engulfed by the whirlpool. I hurtled along inside the portal, my body spinning around and around. It was hard to focus on anything, as I was spun like cotton candy.

The guy who'd been standing beside me did a couple of somersaults in the water as he hurtled by me, a huge smile on his face. While I watched him, something just on the edge of the portal drew my attention. Squinting, I could see a dark form moving beside the portal, just outside of its boundaries. Was it some kind of ocean creature, curious about the whirling dervish of water?

Except it was moving too fast to be natural.

I kicked my legs to move a little closer to the edge of the spout. I peered out into the darkness, flinching backwards when the water seemed to gaze back at me. Coldness crept through me, as if something had sliced into my very soul. Someone was out there, moving as quickly as the portal. Curious, I reached out with a hand, the tips of my fingers piercing the veil between ocean and portal.

Then I was sucked out of the vortex. Tossed out like week old garbage.

Panicked, I thrashed around in the cold water, twisting to my left and right, trying to get my bearings. I couldn't see anything around me. The light had vanished. I was alone. My lungs burned. I couldn't hold my breath any longer. I was going to drown in the void of the ocean. No one would ever find my body. Sophie would never know what happened to me. I'd failed before I even got a chance to start.

My chest hurt so badly, I couldn't think beyond it. I had to open my mouth. I had to swallow in the water, let it absorb me. Maybe it wouldn't be too painful to drown; maybe it would all be over in a matter of minutes, if I just succumbed.

A split second before I opened my mouth, I felt strong hands on me. They whipped my body around until I came face to face with the guy who had pulled me out of the water at the pier. He cupped my face with his hands, then leaned in, and pressed his lips to mine. Confused, I didn't know what was happening until I felt the pressure in my head and chest alleviate as he blew oxygen into my body.

Then he grabbed my arm and kicked hard with his legs. A minute later, I was dragged out of the water and up onto a rocky shore. Sputtering and spitting out liquid, I rolled onto my side. Blinking back black spots, I saw we'd come up into a large cave. The rock walls sparkled with some kind of quartz. Thick, sharp looking green-stained stalagmites hung down from the ceiling, dripping water onto the stone floor near me. The plip-plop of the drops echoed off the walls and floor. Beyond them, I could see a large opening where blue and green light beams seemed to dance around.

"Wow, who let her in?"

I blinked away water to see the girl with the long, dark hair snickering at me. Her companion, a plump girl with short blonde hair, shook her head. There was no hiding her disdain. "Her face is as blue as her hair."

I tried to sit up, but my body wasn't behaving. All my limbs felt weighted down. They were too heavy to lift. It was like having swimmer's cramps everywhere at once. This time the guy didn't offer his hand to me, he just yanked me to my feet, none too gently, either.

"Don't look so sad, Blue, you're not dead." He bopped me on the nose with his finger. "Not yet, anyway." He tipped his head then joined the girl with the dark hair and her friend. Together, they walked deeper into the cave toward the opening.

For a split second, I thought about running after him to thank him for saving my life, but I was already mortified about what had happened. I didn't want to give his spite-filled companions an opportunity to run me down even further. So, I just got in line with everyone else as they trudged toward the cave opening. We all looked like drowned rats marching through a sewer.

The guy who had been standing beside me earlier fell in step with me. "Are you okay?"

"Oh yeah, peachy."

"I'm Ren, by the way."

"Melany." I offered him a small smile.

As the opening drew nearer, nerves started zinging through me. This was it. There was no turning back now. A few more steps and I would be completely committing to join the Gods' Army. And the only way out was either by expulsion or death. There was no leaving on one's own accord.

I stepped through the mouth of the cave and into a whole new world. Literally.

The sky was a color of blue I'd never seen before, as bright as a robin's egg. The only clouds in sight hovered in a perfect circle over the massive gray stone building that couldn't be anything other than the academy itself. Sharp spires rose into the sky from round turrets located at all four corners. Large arched windows peppered all three levels of the building. The stain-glassed windows cast beams of green and blue and yellow onto the ground, like lasers.

The wide cobblestone path leading up to the school was lined with spindly trees whose branches should've contained green foliage, but instead were bare. Nothing could possibly grow from the ashen limbs. To the right was a large hedge maze, the entrance guarded by two stone soldiers, their swords raised to fight.

While we walked up the path, Ren audibly swallowed, as he quickly glanced at the statues. "I heard all the stone statues around the academy were once people, turned to stone by the fierce gaze of Medusa. The rumor is if you hear the hiss of snakes, then she's nearby, and you'll be turned to stone next."

I frowned. "I think that's just a stupid story to scare people. Medusa may exist, but she isn't some scary woman walking around with snakes for hair."

"Move it or lose it, recruit."

Someone pushed Ren and me aside, so they could pass by on the path. Two someones. A centaur with long, flowing auburn hair that matched the hair on his horse body, and a tall, thin woman topping six feet, with green tendrils of hair. Hair that seemed to move around her head, as if it was floating in water. I squinted to get a closer look. Were there tiny little faces at the ends of that hair?

She turned to look at me, and her eyes were completely white, devoid of an iris or pupil. She had no eyelashes either, just almond-shaped pale orbs. She smiled, flashing razor-sharp, pointed teeth.

The centaur also glanced back at us, and there was no disguising his distaste in what he saw. "Can you believe the type of misfit they're letting into the academy nowadays? It wasn't like when we trained here."

"That was a few thousand years ago, Chiron. The world has changed."

They both turned back around and kept walking down the path to the academy.

Ren nudged me in the side. "What was that you were saying?"

I gaped, rubbing at my eyes. Was I hallucinating? Had I actually drowned in the ocean, and this was some kind of purgatory? Or were all the rumors and stories about the Gods and the demi-gods who were spawned from them as real as I was?

CHAPTER FOUR

MELANY

*S*till startled by the encounter with Medusa and Chiron, I kept my head down the rest of the way to the academy. I really didn't want to court any more trouble. Deep inside, I thought for sure they somehow knew I didn't belong, being demigods and all, and would out me right there and then before my peers. It hadn't happened, but now I was even more paranoid than before.

The closer we got to the school, the grander and loftier it loomed. From a distance, it had looked maybe three stories tall, but the reality of it when we neared the ornate, ten-foot high wooden doors was like peering up at a great Gothic cathedral or a castle from medieval England, built to withstand any battle siege. It was all dark stone and sharp edges. There was nothing comforting or warm about the place at all.

As the first recruit arrived—naturally it just happened to be the guy who had saved me and his little crew—the huge doors opened, as if on their own, and he and the rest of the recruits walked through, entering the building. When I passed under the high arch of the entrance, a strange vibration rippled over my body, and now I was suddenly dry and so were my clothes and my backpack. I looked around to see if others had felt it, but I couldn't tell, as either they had a look of rapture on their face or abject terror. I didn't think they even noticed they weren't sopping wet anymore.

I decided to stick to Ren's side as we all gathered in the antechamber. I was a mass of nervous energy, unsure of what to do or where to go. But then an excited murmur rippled through the group as a man with long, gray hair and a neatly clipped gray beard leisurely came down the wide stone staircase in front of us.

Beside me, a girl I didn't know grabbed my arm. "It's Zeus," she whispered. "Holy crap."

I craned my neck to get a better view of him as he stood on the steps and looked down at us with an amused quirk of his lips. He didn't look all-powerful or all-knowing. He looked like a tired old man out for a stroll, wearing baggy beige linen pants and a roomy linen tunic. Was he wearing a bathrobe on top?

"Welcome recruits." His voice boomed, echoing all around us. I actually could feel it vibrating against my heart. It was like being next to a huge speaker at a rave, and the DJ was spinning something bass heavy. I rubbed at my sternum, frowning, as he continued to speak.

"You have been invited to the academy because there is something special about you. You have been picked out of millions of young people because somewhere in your family lineage runs Gods' blood."

Oh shit. I'm going to get found out. I most definitely do not have Gods' blood running through my veins.

The girl beside me continued to squeeze my arm, as her excitement grew with his words. "I knew it," she whispered.

"You are stronger, smarter, healthier, more enhanced than the rest of the population, and that is why you are here." His eyes started to glow as his voice rumbled throughout the building. "To train to be the fiercest soldiers to ever set foot on the Earth."

Some of the group clapped, others cheered. I swallowed down the bile rising in my throat, knowing I shouldn't be here. I wondered how easy it would be for me to turn around and walk out of the academy. Would I be stopped?

"Your training will not be easy. It will be the most difficult thing you have ever done. You will be asked to push yourself beyond your limitations. There will be sweat and tears and blood spilled in the halls of this academy before your three years are finished."

I glanced around at all the people surrounding me. Some had glossy, wide eyes, enraptured with Zeus's speech, and others kept their gazes on their feet, maybe too afraid to even look at the God of all

Gods. One boy nearby licked his lips nervously. His hands shook at his sides.

My heart pounded so hard I could feel it in my throat, but it wasn't with fear. Exhilaration at the prospect of pushing myself beyond anything I could imagine made my head swim. Maybe here I could prove myself. Prove that I was worth all the cells that combined in complicated patterns to make me a person. Although I was afraid of being found out, I wasn't frightened of sweat, tears, or blood. I'd spilled them already just to get here.

"Your first year will be hard. You will be trained in all disciplines, both physical and mental, so that we may ascertain where your Gods' power and affiliation lies. At the end of the year, you will each have to face twelve harrowing trials. One for each of the Gods. *If* you survive, you will be placed into the corresponding God's clan that you are connected to."

That caused a murmur through the group. I heard various Gods' names spoken out loud. *Poseidon. Athena. Apollo.* I heard one girl near me say, "I'm most definitely in Aphrodite's clan." She was pretty and blonde, and it made me both angry and sad that she thought her look was what was special about her. Everyone was so enthralled with what clan they wanted to belong to they seemed to have missed the, "*If you survive,*" part of that sentence.

I didn't know which of the Gods I aspired to. I hadn't given it much thought over the years, since I never expected to be called to the academy.

A buzzing filled my ear, like a slight brushing of a

finger across the top, or a hushed whisper of words I couldn't quite decipher.

I whipped around to see who had spoken. Someone was messing around. The boy behind me gave me a funny look and then ignored me. I glanced at the girl beside him, but I didn't think she even noticed my presence she was so wrapped up in what Zeus was saying. Had I imagined the voice? It was possible, but it just had been so clear.

"Know this now, not every one of you will succeed here."

That made everyone shut up.

"Some of you will fail. And if you do, you will not just be sent back to your homes. In fact, you will never be able to go back home again. If you fail, you will be expelled from this academy and cursed to live the rest of your life in hardship and misery. No one will take pity on you. No one will help you. You will forever be *the lost*."

Silence consumed the room. I almost covered my mouth, so no one could hear my sharp intake of breath. I heard the ticking of someone's watch and was surprised they even wore one. Every tick got louder and louder until I thought my eardrums would burst.

Then Zeus smiled and clapped his hands together, the sound like thunder, rattling the stones of the foundation of the building. "Now, let's get you settled into your dorms. Also, there's going to be a big party for you in the great hall later, so you can eat, drink, and be merry." His smile grew even wider. "Because come tomorrow, your training will start."

Two other people appeared at the top of the stairs. A man who looked like he just walked off the front page of GQ magazine—short, thick dark hair swept up off his face, chiseled face, cheekbones that could cut glass, a full set of lips made for kissing, and piercing blue eyes framed by dark, square-shaped glasses. He wore a tight turtleneck accentuating all his muscles and simple dark jeans that I imagined hugged a perfect behind. Every girl, even a few guys, swooned at the sight of him. Me included. This had to be Eros.

His female counterpart was equally as attractive —long, dark beach waves, sultry brown eyes, full lips painted red, high cheekbones, regal nose. She wore a simple red dress hugging full breasts and shapely hips. Her long, sculpted legs were perfectly presented in red heels. I suspected she was named Psyche. Every male's gaze was riveted on her.

Smiling, she gestured with her hand to her left. "If the boys would please follow me, I will direct you to your dorm rooms."

There was a mad rush up the stairs. I got jostled by the two boys who had been standing behind me.

"Ladies, if you will come with me." Eros grinned. "I'll show you to your dorms."

Another mad rush up the stairs, this time with a bit of pushing and shoving as girls tried to get to the front of the line and closest to Eros. I was happy to follow along in the back of the pack. Although Eros definitely ticked all my attraction boxes, I wasn't here to fall in love, despite the fact that I couldn't get mystery guy's face out of my head.

As we walked through the long, wide corridors of the living quarters of the academy, Eros chatted casually about the party we would be attending later and how much fun it would be.

"There will be all kinds of amazing food there. And Dionysus is an epic DJ. He helped Daft Punk get their start years ago." He looked left to right suspiciously, then leaned in toward the group. "He used to party with Mozart way back when, but you didn't hear it from me."

One of the girls at the front giggled. "Are you going to be there?"

He gave her a disarming smile. "I might be. Maybe you can save me a dance?"

She giggled again, and I thought for sure she was going to pass out. The girl next to her had to put a hand on her arm to brace her from falling.

"So, here we are, ladies. Your dorm rooms. They aren't assigned, so pick a room as quickly as you can. You don't want to be the odd one out, or you'll have to share a room with Medusa. And she's not very friendly."

Everyone darted to their left or right and into the rooms on either side. There was some shoving near the rooms closest to the stairs, so I hightailed it down the hallway away from everyone else and dashed into a dark room, hoping maybe I'd luck out and not have a roommate. I immediately toppled over whatever it was sitting in the middle of the floor.

"What the fu—"

"Oh, goodness, I'm so sorry."

I sat up, squinting into the darkness. A shadowed

form moved about on the floor then stood. Light suddenly flooded the room, and I peered up at a petite girl with short red hair.

I scrambled to my feet. "What were you doing on the floor?"

"Talking to him." She held up a tiny brown mouse by the tail. "I was telling him he needed to find another place to live."

That was when I noticed the state of the room. Cobwebs covered each corner, both ceiling and floor. Dust coated everything else, including the small desk by the grimy window and the two beds that were stacked up on one another along one wall. And I didn't even want to identify the tiny pebbles on the floor. Considering this girl was holding up a tiny rodent, I didn't have to try too hard to figure it out.

She must've seen the disgust on my face. "It'll be nice once we clean it up and fix the beds." She held out her other hand to me. "I'm Georgina Thrace, by the way."

"Melany Richmond." After we shook hands, I took off my backpack and set it down on the floor, glancing around. "I wonder where we'll find a broom."

She smiled.

An hour later, we'd cleaned the room and made our respective beds. Georgina proved to be incredibly strong and pretty much did all the heavy lifting when it came to organizing where our beds were going to go. I was surprised, considering she looked more chubby than sturdy.

Once we were done, I felt my stomach growl. I

didn't even know what time it was, as my phone didn't seem to be working any longer. I didn't know if it was because it got water damaged or if it was this place. We sure weren't in Kansas anymore.

"I'm starving. Do you want to go down to this party and get some food?"

Georgina nodded. "I could most definitely eat."

We left our room and followed some of the other girls who looked like they were making their way to the great hall, wherever that was. Eros left out that detail when he was giving us the quick tour. But as soon as we went down the large stone staircase, we heard the thumping strains of dance music.

We wound our way through empty rooms and hallways toward the sound. The moment we turned the corner of one hallway, there was no mistaking where the party was. The end of the corridor opened up into a cavernous hall made from dark gray stone with a domed ceiling, held up by stone pillars with decorative inlays.

The hall was packed with people. Both new recruits and other students I assumed were second and third year, milled about, talking and laughing. I marveled at it all. I'd never experienced anything like it. Every big party Callie ever had at her house paled in comparison.

My stomach growled again, reminding me of my initial goal. To eat. I looked around for any tables that had food on them but didn't see any immediately. What I did see were small wooden robots rolling around the room on wheels. They each carried a tray with some kind of food on it. I made a bee-line straight for one that had tiny sandwiches.

In my haste, I nearly knocked it over, as I grabbed four sandwiches and shoved them into my mouth. I looked down at the wooden server. Its beady-eyed gaze was on me; I swore there was judgment in that look, which was impossible as it wasn't even alive. I made a grab for one more sandwich before it rolled away from me.

I walked through the party, taking in the people bouncing to the music. It wasn't what I normally liked; I usually went for something a bit more thrashy, a whole lot more metal, but it was decent. My social skills were non-existent, so I kept to the outskirts of the festivity, preferring to watch than do. But my gaze honed in on a pretty black girl being ruthlessly and relentlessly hit on in one of the corners of the room.

Her body language screamed, "Go away!" but the guy wasn't listening. And he was big, too. Muscular, tall, he loomed over her, leering like a creep, trying to touch her long, dark curls. I didn't like the situation one bit. I moved closer to gauge what was going on.

"Please, leave me alone. I told you I don't want to dance." She tried to step around him, but he got in her way.

"We could go out into the courtyard and make out then, if you don't want to dance."

She tried to push past him again, but this time he grabbed her arm. Hell no. Not on my watch.

"She told you to leave her alone." I moved in to stand beside the girl. "You either don't understand English or you're stupid."

"Mind your own business." As he scowled down at me, I realized just how big he was.

"Okay, so you speak English fine, so I guess you're just stupid then."

I saw his attack in my mind before he even moved.

He lunged forward, swinging his right arm at me. I leaned back out of his reach, grabbed his wrist with both hands, tugged him forward, and then swept his back leg with my right one. He was down on the floor in seconds. There were a few people around us, and they started to laugh, as the guy sputtered in surprise on the ground.

I took the girl's hand and pulled her away. We joined a bunch of people on the dance floor.

Smiling, she bent towards my ear. "Oh my Gods, thank you for coming to my rescue."

"Any time. I can't stand bullies."

"I'm Jasmine."

"Melany."

"Isn't this all nuts?" She gestured to the chaos happening all around us, and I imagined she was talking about the whole situation we'd stepped into.

The DJ, who had spiked up black hair and wore black eyeliner, jumped up onto one of the serving robots and rode it around in front of his set up, flailing his arms around. "Who's ready to get crazy?"

Everyone on the dance floor screamed in response. Then he did a backflip off the robot, ran back to his turntable, and dropped another thumping song sending everyone into a frenzy. I couldn't help but be swept up as well. The music was infectious, getting right into my muscles and bones.

I danced with Jasmine, moving my body to each oscillating pulse of music. I jumped up and down, turned, and nearly collided with my savior from earlier. He grinned at me, which made my belly flip flop.

"Having a good time, Blue?"

"Yes. Are you?"

"I'll let you know in a minute." He reached for my hand and was about to pull me close, when the dark-haired girl interrupted, getting right in between us. He dropped my hand.

"You're not slumming it, are you, Lucian?" She gave me a side-eye, clearly disgusted with everything about me. In lots of ways, she reminded me of Callie.

Anger swelled inside me, and I needed to get away before I did something I'd regret. I didn't need to get expelled from the academy before classes even started. I walked off the dance floor and searched for a place to sit away from the celebration. But everyone was in full party mode. The music, the smell of the food and drink, and the heat of so many people crushed together pushed down on me. I needed some air.

I left the great hall with the intention of finding a way outside, but the sound of footsteps approaching had me pressing up against a shadowed wall. I didn't want to get into trouble for leaving the celebration. I had a sense this place was big on rules with harsh punishments.

I peeked around the corner to see literally a

blonde Goddess walking down the empty corridor. She was tall, six feet at least, yards of golden waves trailing down her back to her tiny waist. The hem of her sheer white dress dragged behind her like the train of a wedding gown or a royal gown. She definitely was regal.

After she moved down the hallway a little farther away, she stopped and turned. Even from where I hid, I could see how stunning she was. Her face looked like it was sculpted from the whitest, hardest marble to ever exist, and her eyes were as blue as the hottest part of a flame. This had to be Aphrodite. The stories about her beauty didn't even come close to the reality of her.

I wasn't sure what she was doing, but I didn't have to wait long until another form stepped out from a different darkened corridor. It was a man, a mountainous muscular man with a shaved head. He looked like an army drill sergeant on steroids. They embraced, kissing. Obviously, there was something going on there. But the way she kept looking around, it was definitely a secret something.

"Were you followed?" Aphrodite asked her lover.

He shook his head. "Does Hephaistos suspect anything?"

"He wouldn't notice if I came home dipped in blood. All he cares about is his toys and contraptions."

"Then he'd never noticed the key was gone?"

I leaned around the corner, eager to get closer.

"Not for the time we'd need to open…" Pausing, she whipped her head around to where I hid.

I jerked backward, the heel of my boot squeaking against the polished tile floor. *Shit.*

I didn't wait to see if they heard me. I hightailed it out of there. The very last thing I needed was a couple of Gods thinking I'd overheard their clandestine meeting to discuss evil doings.

CHAPTER FIVE

MELANY

*T*he loudest, most resonant gong ever to exist literally knocked me out of bed in the morning.

From the spot I landed on the cold, hard floor, I could see through the dorm room window that it was still dark out. I swore I hadn't even been asleep for more than four hours.

"Time to rise and shine." Georgina's face loomed over me. In the predawn, I noticed she was already dressed in the official academy uniform, dark red polo and charcoal gray military style pants with side pockets. She looked sufficiently groomed and ready to attack the day.

I, on the other hand, still had sleep gluing my eyelashes together.

She offered her hand to me to help me up and I

took it. "Do you always look this bright-eyed in the morning?"

"Yes, pretty much. I love early mornings. I like to be productive."

I sat on the edge of my bed and rubbed at the crusty flakes in my eyes. "Back home, I wouldn't even be out of bed until noon."

"If I were you, I'd get your butt in gear and run to the showers before they fill up. Or you won't be able to have one before we need to be in our first class." She handed me a thick leather folder. "Here's your class schedule. I hope you don't mind that I organized it for you. I had an hour to kill this morning before the gong."

I opened it to see a calendar and detailed timetable noting my classes and which professors taught them. As I perused my schedule for the day, I shook my head. I couldn't believe this was happening. I couldn't believe I was here, at the academy, training to be in the Gods' Army.

8 a.m.
– History of the Gods – Hera
10 a.m. – Spear and Shield – Ares
12 p.m. – lunch
1 p.m. – Archery - Artemis
3 p.m. – Hand to Hand Combat – Heracles
5 p.m. – dinner
7 p.m. – Prophecy – Apollo
9 p.m. – free time
11 p.m. – lights out

I kept reading, marveling at the other classes during the week.

"Transformation class?" I looked up at Georgina, dumbfounded. "What the hell do we do in that class?"

"I guess we make one thing into another."

I looked back at the schedule. "Flying?' I shook my head. "Tomorrow, we have an elemental class with Zeus and Poseidon."

"I know, right? I'm so excited for that one. Demeter teaches in that class, too. I've wanted to meet her my entire life. My family has made offerings to her since I was a baby."

I wanted to tell her that most likely the Goddess never got them, but what did I know? For most of my life, I didn't even think the Gods were real. I'd been told they were real. I read about them in picture books for children, been instructed on how to worship them, and what to take to what temple to pray. But I never truly, honestly believed there were higher beings sitting around listening to the whining and bitching of mortals. And here I was in their school, training to fight for them in some war that didn't exist. At least none that I knew about.

A half hour later, I, along with Georgina and twenty other girls, streamed down the main stone staircase and into the foyer where we first had entered the academy. The boys came from the opposite way, where their dorms were, and joined us on the stairs. I saw Jasmine near the front of the group. Hopefully, I'd be able to catch up with her.

At the bottom of the steps, we were met by an assuming woman with curly brown hair up in a messy bun, a very plain dress, and sensible shoes. She looked like a librarian. She even had reading glasses hanging on a chain around her neck.

She smiled warmly at us. "Good morning. My name is Pandora, and I'll be your guide for the day. I will show you to your various classes and answer any questions you may have about the academy. I'm your TA for the year. If you need anything, you can come to me."

She led us down a very large, wide corridor—the whole academy seemed to consist of enormous corridors—to a set of gray stone doors with stars engraved into them.

"This is where your history of the Gods class will be. It's a very important class, as you will need to know everything you can about each of the primary Gods and Goddesses to prepare for your trial at the end of the year."

A tall girl with blond hair raised her hand.

Pandora smiled at her. "Yes?"

"Are the trials as bad as they say? I heard that a boy died during the trial of Zeus."

Others in the group looked around nervously.

Pandora gave us a tight-lipped smile. "Rumors don't do anyone any good." She gestured to the doors. "Have a good class, and I'll see you afterwards."

The doors swung open, and we all entered the dark room. I wondered if anyone else noticed Pandora didn't exactly answer the question. Probably not, as everyone was busy gawking at the domed ceiling above us. It was lit up with a thousand twinkling stars.

In the center of the room stood a rising platform, and around it were fifty desks and chairs. There was a scramble for the desks in the middle, but I opted for one farthest from the lectern. Georgina followed me to the back. As I slid behind my desk, I was pleasantly surprised to see Jasmine taking a desk in front of me. We smiled at each other.

Another door at the far end of the room opened and a woman entered. I assumed it was Hera, our professor. She walked to the center of the room and stepped up onto the dais. She wore a long, flowing dark blue dress, and her hair was wrapped up on top of her head with a string of flowers acting like a turban. Jewels sparkled around her throat, her ears, and her fingers, as she lifted her hands in front of her.

"Everything in the cosmos was created by Uranus and Gaia, Heaven and Earth." Between her hands, light formed. She twisted her hands around until a solid ball of blue erupted then she threw it up at the ceiling. The orb bounced from one star to the next and the next, sending them all spinning, until they were a spiraling mass of stars and light above us.

There were gasps around the room as the stars separated and rotated into position in the universe. Then one star grew ten times its initial size into a large globe. Land and sea formed on as it turned on its axis. It was the Earth.

"Heaven and Earth gave birth to twelve great, ferocious and ruthless Titans. Oceanus…"

The thundering sounds of crashing waves filled the room. Then a swirling blue maelstrom spouted from the floor. Some of the students nearest to it jumped out of their seats and screamed. It looked so real; I expected to be sprayed by water as it spun through the room, turning into a gigantic monster made of water, with eight whirlpool arms spinning around.

"…dominated all the seas and oceans and lakes and rivers, demolishing ships and drowning everyone he came in contact with.

"Hyperion, made of the sun itself…"

Out from the ceiling dropped a male form made of fire, with huge fiery wings. A wave of heat surged through the room with every flap of his wings. He lifted his arms, which were columns of fire, and shot out fireballs every direction. One fireball zoomed straight for my head and I ducked. I could actually feel the heat as it flew by, vanishing when it hit the stone wall.

"…scorched everything in his path…"

For the next hour, Hera introduced all twelve Titans and talked about how monstrous and destructive they were. Then she talked about Tartarus, the stinking, dark, frozen wasteland they were imprisoned in, a place far below the underworld, and how important it was for the Gods to make sure they stayed there.

"This is why you are being trained," she said, her voice rising to a crescendo. "You will be the Gods'

Army, to fight by our side in the event our enemies are unleashed on the Earth."

A chill ran through me, as I thought about the repercussions of any of the Titans being released from their prison, and why someone would ever want that to happen. It made me think about what I had overheard in the academy halls last night.

After history class, Jasmine and I met up.

"That class was crazy, huh?"

I nodded. "Yeah, seems so unreal."

Georgina came along my other side. "It's as real as you and me."

I introduced her to Jasmine, and the three of us followed Pandora and the rest of the group to our next class—Spear and Shield—which was outside behind the main academy building in an open grass field. As we lined up in a semi-circle, three men ran out onto the field, shouting and making shiver-inducing battle cries. All three carried a long spear with an arrowhead-like tip and a round shield. I assumed one of them had to be our professor, Ares.

Two of the men, dressed in black military fatigues, attacked the third man, who was older, and wearing red nylon shorts and a white tank top. His hair was cut short, much like an army general. I remembered him from the hallway last night. This had to be Ares.

As I watched him dance around the field, deflecting blows from the other men, he reminded me of my old gym teacher from high school who loved to play dodgeball. I swore it was his most favorite activity. He'd probably even slept with the dodgeball clutched tight in his hands, like a child with his little stuffed toy.

The image made me snicker. I put a hand up to my mouth to stifle it, but it was too late. It had already escaped, and a couple of the people around me noticed, and basically took a step away from me, singling me out.

After Ares made a sharp cutting motion with his hand, the other two men immediately stopped what they were doing and stood at attention with their shield held at chest height, and their spear held upright in their hand, eyes forward, chins lifted. Ares spun around and glared at me.

Obviously, he had also noticed my snicker.

He pointed right at me. "Step forward."

I gestured to myself. "Me?"

"Yes. Get out here. Now!"

I stepped out of the group and onto the field. Both Georgina and Jasmine looked horrified, while the dark-haired girl, whose name I discovered during history class was Revana, openly smirked.

Ares tossed his shield at me. I put my arm up just in time to catch it before it smashed me in the head. It was heavy, and I had a hard time keeping it balanced. Then he thrust his spear at me.

"Protect yourself!"

I raised the shield just in time, so the spear tip didn't pierce my face. It bounced off the metal. "What the hell?"

He thrust it toward me again, this time at my legs. I managed to move the big metal plate down in time, and the clang of metal hitting metal reverberated over my entire body. My arm shook, and I nearly dropped the shield.

"Do you find this funny?" he shouted at me.

"No!"

He lowered his spear and took a step back to address the entire group. "War is not funny." He tapped the spear onto the ground. "There will be no laughing in my class. Do you understand?"

"Yes," some of the group said.

"Do you understand?"

"Yes sir!"

He came back to me and tore the shield from my hand. "Get back in line."

Head down, I quickly walked back to the group, standing next to Georgina and Jasmine. Jasmine leaned in. "Are you okay?"

I rotated my right shoulder; it was starting to ache from holding the shield up. I nodded. "I'll live."

"Form two lines." Ares gestured with his hand where we should line up. "You are going to learn how to use a shield properly to defend yourself, so you don't get stuck in the gut with a spear and bleed out."

We all jumped into motion. I wanted to get in line with Georgina and Jasmine, but ended up getting jostled around, until I could squeeze into a line, which just happened to be beside Lucian. Perfect. This day was just getting worse and worse by the minute. I could just imagine the joke he was going to make at my expense.

He bent toward me. "Not bad, Blue."

I didn't look at him, keeping my eyes ahead. "Oh

yeah, I was a real hero there. I'll be defending the masses in no time."

"Hey, I know it's not easy holding one of those shields up."

When I turned to look at him, I noticed the long, thin scar along his jawline.

He rubbed his thumb across it, then he winked at me, and I couldn't stop the smile blossoming on my face.

Then a shadow loomed over me.

"I said no laughing during class." Ares glared at me, his scowl so deep it cut lines into his granite-like face.

"Technically, I wasn't laughing. I was smiling."

He got right into my face. I had to crane my neck to look up at him. He was so close I could smell his body odor.

"You need to check your attitude, Blue Belle, or I'm going to rip that nose ring right out of your face."

The intensity of his anger rippled over me. I didn't like how it felt on my skin. Like snakes, a thousand tiny snakes slithering over my body, every muscle quiver constricting me tighter and tighter.

"To help you with this lesson, I want you to go out in the middle of the field and do some pushups. You will keep doing them until I tell you to stop. Do you hear what I'm saying to you, recruit?"

"Yes, sir."

Revana, who was nearby, started to snicker.

"Sounds like someone else is laughing, sir."

Ares whipped around and glared at Revana. "You can join her."

I walked out onto the field and dropped down to my hands and knees. Revana followed me out and nearly stepped on my hand as she took up a position beside me. As we both did our first pushup, she glowered at me, her eyes like dark storm clouds.

"I know you're a fraud. When I find out how you got in here, I'm going straight to Zeus, and you'll be expelled from the academy and exiled from your life."

"Wow, girl, you really need to relax. You are much too tense."

As she did pushups, she continued to glare at me. I didn't know how one person could put so much effort into hating someone they didn't even know. It must be exhausting.

It was just another reason, in a long list of them, of why coming here was a bad idea, and one I was sure I was going to regret. I should've given the box back to Callie, and maybe she'd be the one on the ground doing pushups until she puked.

CHAPTER SIX

LUCIAN

*D*espite all my past training, the reality of the academy and what we were being put through paled in comparison. Walking into the gymnasium for hand-to-hand combat class and seeing Heracles, the giant of a man who stood seven feet tall and was built like a semi-truck, training us crushed any confidence I had going in. This was in no way going to be an easy class.

All my life, I'd been training for the possibility of being invited to join the Gods' Army. For my parents, it was inevitable since my older brother, Owen, had been called four years earlier by his eighteenth birthday Shadowbox. I hadn't seen or heard from him since the day he'd left, as recruits were cut off from the outside world. In the back of mind, I had hoped he'd be here at the academy when I arrived.

But that hope had been dashed when I realized that those who had completed the training and gone through the trials transcended to Olympus to await the Great War. Maybe I would see him again when I, too, transcended.

Since I was six years old, my father had started training me in various disciplines like archery, deep sea diving, and hand-to-hand combat. And my parents had placed offerings at the temple of Ares since I'd been born in the hopes I would become part of his clan. Like my brother had. Or at least, I assumed he had.

"Form a single line," Heracles bellowed, his voice echoing off the dark wooden floors and paneled walls.

Everyone rushed to get side by side. My friend, Diego, made sure to get next to me. Revana pushed another girl aside, so she could get in on my other side. The girl could be ruthless, which I didn't like, but I supposed a person had to be to get through this training.

I looked down the line and spotted Melany about ten people away. I wasn't sure what to make of her. She seemed so much out of her element, like she didn't truly belong. From misreading where the entrance to the academy was, to diving out of the portal and nearly drowning, to talking back to Ares. I'd never thought anyone with any kind of smarts would ever risk that. She intrigued me; that was for certain.

"The first thing we are going to learn in this class is stance, how to keep your center of gravity. If you perfect this, you will never be knocked off balance, no matter how you move or what hits you." He moved to the center of the floor and put his left leg forward, toe pointing straight, and his back foot pointing outwards. He bent his legs a little and then put up his hands to his chest, hugging his arms a little into his sides.

"Now, from here, I can perform any kind of maneuver." He did a jab, and then upper cut, then threw an elbow, then he spun on his foot and did a back kick, coming back to rest in the same position. He moved so quickly, his limbs blurred.

Beside me, Diego sucked in a breath. "Damn. I've never seen anyone move so fast."

"In this stance, nothing can knock me over."

From the far back corners of the room, two six-foot tall wooden dummy robots on wheels rolled toward Heracles. Both carried long wooden Bo staffs. One of the robots rolled in front of Heracles, lifted its arms, the staff reared back as far as it would go, then it swung with all its power.

Heracles lifted his arm, tight to his body; the staff smacked him across the shoulder, the cracking sound reverberating off every surface, and snapped in half. Splinters of wood rained down onto the floor.

He grinned, his whole demeanor changing, as the second staff hit him in the other side, and snapped into pieces from the force of the blow. He straightened and brushed off the small wood chips still clinging onto his shirt. "Ha!" He pumped his fist in the air. "I am invincible. Nothing can knock me off balance. Now, it's your turn."

I heard a snicker down the line. I didn't need to look to know it was Melany.

"You're seriously going to smack us with wooden staffs?" She had her hands on her hips and appeared indignant. Her lips were curled in disgust.

Heracles shook his head. "Of course not. It's only the first day. I don't do that until at least week four."

That got a round of laughs through the group.

"Take up your stances."

I put my left leg forward, and my back leg turned like I'd practiced over and over again since I was six. The others around me all did the same, as Heracles walked down the line and inspected us. He spoke to a couple of people, correcting them, and then when he got to me, he stopped. He looked me over and then shoved me hard.

I stumbled a couple of steps backward, but I didn't break my stance. I didn't lose my balance.

He nodded. "Good. Step forward."

I did.

"Name?"

"Lucian Remes."

Heracles's eyes narrowed. "You have a brother."

"Yes, Owen." My heart leapt a little, knowing that Owen had made some kind of impression. He would've done well in this class.

"I want you to go down the line and try to knock down every person." Heracles glanced at the rest of the group. "Your job is to not let him." He pointed to the far end of the room where a short blonde girl stood.

I walked down the line and stood in front of her.

Fear clouded her eyes, and I felt bad for doing what I had to. It didn't take much to knock her onto her ass.

One by one, I pushed and shoved my fellow recruits. Some stayed on their feet, most fell. When I got to Diego, I had a feeling he thought I'd go easy on him. I didn't. He lost his balance after one hard shove. Revana kept her feet, even after two hard pushes from different angles. She grinned at me in triumph.

When I reached Melany, she looked like she was already ready to go to war. The fierce expression in her eyes made my gut clench. But I didn't think it had anything to do with being afraid of her.

"You ready?"

"Take your best shot." She lifted her chin in defiance.

I came at her from the side and pushed on her shoulder. She stayed pretty much in place. I tried again from the front. As I stretched my arms toward her, she stepped into me and swept my leg. I ended up on my ass. A ripple of laughter went through the room.

Stunned, I gaped up at her. She shrugged and offered her hand to help me up. "He said to not let you knock me down. So I didn't."

I grabbed her hand, and she pulled me to my feet. I felt a buzz of something not entirely unpleasant on the palm of my hand. I quickly let her hand go and rubbed it on my pants. The skin still tingled.

"Oh, I like this one." Clapping, Heracles walked over. "Name?"

"Melany Richmond."

"Melany, the dark one. I love it." He looked at the rest of the group. "All right, everyone pair up. We're going to learn to spar." He pointed at me and Melany. "Congratulations, you two are now partners."

When he moved away, we gaped at each other.

"We are going to learn how to jab, cross, and uppercut properly. Three fundamental punches in your arsenal. One of you grab a pair of focus pads from the wall, then we will start."

I looked at Melany. She sighed. "I'll go get them." Then she jogged to the far wall and grabbed a couple of rectangular pads and came back.

I took them from her. "You can practice first." I slid my hands into the holders and lifted them up in front of my body.

"Get in your stances," Heracles instructed. "Then we will practice a jab, cross, jab." He demonstrated, smacking huge fists into pads that one of the wooden dummy robots held up. I was surprised he didn't break the robot with his punches.

Melany got into position, then jabbed my one pad, then did a cross punch with her left, then another jab. Her punches were solid, and I liked that she didn't seem to hold back.

I nodded. "Not bad, Blue."

"Thanks."

She did it again and again, landing every punch with power. I could feel the zing of her fists even through the pads. It was impressive.

"Switch!" Heracles shouted.

I took off the pads and handed them to her. She

slid them on and raised them up. I got into my stance and led with a jab. I may have not put all my weight behind it, and I think she must've known because she gave me a disgusted look.

"I'm not fragile. You're not going to break me into little pieces."

"Are you sure? You are kind of small."

She shook her head. "You really do have a big ego, don't you?"

I shrugged. "No bigger than most."

Her lips twitched, but she fought back the smile.

I took up my stance again and jabbed with full power. Her arm snapped back a little, but then she pushed it forward, so I could hit the pad again. I did. Then I was doing my sequence of punches without any hesitation.

By the time Heracles yelled to stop, sweat covered my face and rolled down my back. It was the same for Melany.

"Woe ho ho, looks like we got ourselves a dream team here." Heracles grinned at both of us. "Keep up the good work." He smacked me on the shoulder, and I stumbled backward, but not before I caught Melany snickering.

"Are you laughing at me?" I gave her a searching look.

"No, of course not." Sarcasm dripped off her like the sweat dripped off her brow.

At first I'd been hesitant to be paired up with her. I thought she would slow me down somehow. But the truth was we made kind of an awesome team. It was both surprising and unnerving. There was something about Melany that unsettled me. It was more than just her unconventional good looks, her dark blue hair begging me to touch it; it went deeper than that. She was different in many ways. In ways I think she didn't even realize.

I'd spent my entire life around true believers. I'd been training for the day I got invited to the army. There had never been a question whether I would or not. I was certain that I had Gods' blood in my veins. I suspected that my friends had Gods' blood as well.

And here was this girl, who looked completely and utterly out of place, and I wasn't sure she even truly believed she should be here, but out of every first year recruit, I was sure she had more reason to be at the academy than anyone.

CHAPTER SEVEN

MELANY

*T*here was a buzz of excitement and nervousness as we descended a large stone staircase into the deepest and darkest part of the academy. Everyone was psyched to go to metallurgy class with Hephaistos. Everyone except me. I just wanted to go back to my dorm room and hide under the covers. I'd had a day of embarrassing blunders and didn't really want to suffer through any more.

The morning's archery class with Artemis had been mortifying. I'd wanted to impress Artemis, as she was badass. During the demonstration, the way she moved, so gracefully, so flawlessly, as she sprinted across the training field and shot three arrows into a moving target, rendered me speechless. I wanted to do that. I wanted to be that skilled.

But as it turned out, I had no skill whatsoever for

the bow. During training, I couldn't even hit the static target. All my arrows had limply hit the ground in front of them. The first few I understood. I mean, not everyone had hit the target on the first few tries. But even after an hour of pulling back the bow, I still couldn't hit anything but grass, while almost the entire class had at least struck the target. Jasmine had gotten a bullseye and Artemis's praise.

The disparaging looks and cruel snickers I'd gotten from Revana and her crew had nearly reduced me to tears from frustration. I didn't cry, though. I refused to, especially in front of them.

Jasmine nudged me in the side as we walked down the stairs. She knew how upset I was. "You'll get it next time. No one is expecting you to be great the first week of training."

"You were."

"I guess it's just my thing." She shrugged. "Anyway, you more than kicked ass during hand-to-hand combat. And you made Heracles pump his fist and clap. From what I heard, he's not an easy person to impress."

"I had help," I wanted to say, as I spotted Lucian on the stairs in front of me. He was with his usual group, Diego, Revana, and a couple others I didn't know. Why did he hang around them? They were all kind of mean, and he wasn't. At least he wasn't with me. They were laughing about something, probably making fun of someone, then his head turned, and his gaze met mine and my belly clenched. I immediately turned away, but the sensation still lingered.

I peered down the long, winding staircase. It felt

like we'd been walking on them for an hour already. "How many floors down are we going?"

"I heard the forge is deep in the bowels of the earth." This from Georgina, who'd been quiet until now.

Jasmine and I snickered.

"Bowels of the earth?" I gave my roommate a look. "Seriously?"

She shrugged.

Mia, who was in the room one down from Georgina and I, came along Jasmine's other side. "You were so good in archery, Jasmine."

"Thank you." She dipped her head a little, as if she was embarrassed.

As Mia moved on down a couple of stairs from us, Jasmine watched her.

I nudged Jasmine. "So, what's going on there?"

"Nothing." She frowned.

"Looked like something."

"Oh, like the something you have with Lucian?"

I was about to sputter a protest when we finally reached the bottom of the stairs. I turned to look back from where we came. We were at least five or six stories below the main academy.

Pandora led us down a long corridor. It looked more like a tunnel carved into a mountain, as the sides and ceiling weren't smooth, but rough with pieces of rock jutting out. With each step forward, the air around me seemed to be getting warmer. I noticed beads of sweat on Georgina's forehead. Bright orange light flickered ahead in the distance. The sounds of machinery thundered all around as we neared Hephaistos's classroom.

There was a wave of gasps as the tunnel opened up, and we stepped into a cavernous space. I couldn't even call it a room, as it was way too expansive. Stone steps led to bridges hovering over rivers of what I assumed was molten metal, linking various large, circular platforms. Past the biggest platform, bellows puffed, fanning the flames in a forge; its opening mimicked that of a mouth of a black dragon.

Above on the nearest platform, a man stepped out from the steam and smoke of the churning foundry. "Welcome to the forge." His voice was as baritone and resonant as the huge gears turning nearby.

Beside me, Jasmine grabbed my hand. "I don't want to be here."

"It'll be fine. What's the worst that can happen?"

"Technically, you could fall off one of the bridges and into the fire."

I frowned at Georgina, letting her know she wasn't helping.

Carefully, as a group, as everyone seemed to be a bit on edge, we went up the stone stairs and over a bridge to the platform nearest the dragon furnace. I kept my eyes straight ahead; I didn't want to tempt fate by looking over the edge of the bridge. There were several long rectangular stone crafting tables and bowls of fire at the ends. On top of the tables were various sized hammers, iron tongs, and metal files. Near the bowls of fire were several anvils.

We lined up behind the tables, as our professor took up a spot in front of the dragon. On close inspection, I could see that Hephaistos wasn't a pleasant looking person. He appeared a bit misshapen, especially his face and head. Longish, curly brown hair couldn't hide the scar running along his scalp. And his thick mustache couldn't cover the cleft in his lip.

"In this class," he bellowed above the rumble of the foundry behind him, "you will be forging your own personal shield. This shield you will use in various classes and one day out on the battlefield. By third year, the crest of your assigned clan will be proudly embellished on the metal."

"Cool," one of the guys at the table said.

Hephaistos glared in his direction. "The first thing you will learn in this class is that I don't tolerate jokers. There will be no tomfoolery or shenanigans."

Diego, who was at the other table, chuckled.

Hephaistos picked up the closest thing to him, which looked like a blade for a spear, and launched it at Diego. "What did I just say?"

Diego ducked in time, and the spearhead stuck into the stone pillar behind him with a loud thwack.

"To get started, everyone look under the table top, and you will find a cubby hole. Inside, you will find a pair of leather gloves. Put them on or else you will burn your fingers off. And what use will you be without any fingers?"

Over the next hour, Hephaistos showed us how to heat up and bend metal, using the forge and an anvil. Then as a group from each table we got to approach the main forge, stick a hunk of metal into the fire with iron tongs, and then take it over to one of the anvils and hammer it until it bent in half. In theory, it looked and sounded pretty easy. But I couldn't seem to get it right. Like with archery, I didn't possess the right skills. Soon, someone was going to point this out and kick me out of the academy.

I hammered at the glowing part of the metal piece I had, but it didn't bend the way I wanted it to.

"What are you doing?" Hephaistos loomed over me.

"I'm doing what you showed us."

"Then you must be blind, stupid girl. You are doing it all wrong." He snatched the hammer from me, and the tongs holding my metal, and struck at it on the anvil. With three sharp blows, the metal bent in half. Glowering at me, he handed the hammer and tongs back. "Do it again."

I carried my piece of metal back to the fire. Holding it over the heat, I watched as it melted, creating the tell-tale orange glow. Before I moved back to the anvil, something beyond the foundry caught my eye. There were several shelves along one of the only walls in the room, stacked with various metallic objects. Objects I assumed Hephaistos had made—swords, daggers, a flail, a mace even… and Shadowboxes. There was one long shelf with them, each of them different in size and design.

"For Hades's sake girl, it's going to drip into the fire!"

I turned abruptly and nearly dropped the metal piece. As I passed by the other table of recruits, Revana smirked at me and mouthed, "Loser."

It took all I had not to go over there and shove these tongs right up her—

"Girl, get a move on."

I hustled back to the anvil and hammered at my metal piece. This time I got the hang of it, and it bent the way it should have. I looked up at Hephaistos for approval.

His brow furrowed. "I'm not your mother. I'm not going to tell you what a good job you've done."

Anger swelled inside me. I was tired of getting pushed around today. "My mother's dead."

Hephaistos's eyebrows went up, but he didn't say anything, and just moved on to another anvil, to berate another recruit.

When class was over, I shuffled along with the rest of the group out of the forge and back up the seemingly non-ending spiraling staircase. At the top, everyone scattered in different directions, as it was our free time slot.

"We're going to the dining hall," Jasmine said. "I heard pizza is on the menu tonight."

"I'll catch up with you. I need to get something from my room."

Jasmine's eyes narrowed at me. I thought for a moment she was going to tell me she'd go with me. "Okay, see you in a bit." She left with Georgina and a couple of the other girls.

When they were gone, and the front hall had cleared completely, I crept back down the stairs. I wanted to get a closer look at those Shadowboxes. I wanted to know how they were made. I needed to know their secrets.

When I reached the entrance to the foundry, I stopped and peered into the gloom, making sure Hephaistos was gone or at least in a place where he wouldn't see me. I waited for five minutes, and when I didn't see or hear him, I mounted the stone steps and rushed across the bridge.

In my haste, I didn't see the loose stone, and I tripped over it. My heart leapt into my throat as I nearly keeled over the bridge. At the last second, I pushed off with my legs and jumped, arms pinwheeling, praying to every God and Goddess I could recall in a few seconds that I didn't land in the molten metal.

I fell onto my knees on the next platform. Closing my eyes and counting my blessings, I took a few seconds to catch my breath. I opened my eyes and glanced over at the bridge. It had to have been no less than fifteen feet away. How the heck had I just jumped more than fifteen feet? I shook my head to clear it and then ran over to the shelves before I got caught.

My fingers ached to touch the Shadowboxes. They were so beautiful, so exquisite. I reached for one when I felt a presence behind me. I whipped around and came face to face with Hephaistos.

"What are you doing here?"

"I… I had to look at the boxes. They're so beautiful."

His face softened at little. "You're probably wondering how someone so grotesque made something so magnificent."

"No, I…"

"I think about that all the time." He picked up one of the boxes. "It is my curse, I suppose."

"Did you make all the Shadowboxes?"

He nodded. "Yes, every last one of them. I would've made the one that came to you."

"How do they work?"

He eyed me for a moment and then opened the box for me to see inside. "After you open the box, a scroll appears. On the scroll will be an invitation and etched inside the box a riddle for you to solve, so you can find the location of the portal to the academy." He snapped the box closed. "But of course, you know all that, since you're here."

I couldn't give myself away, but I had to know the truth. "Is there a way to trick the box? To come to the academy on someone else's invitation?"

He snorted. "Absolutely not. That would be impossible. The box will only respond to its intended recipient. One of the Gods couldn't even break the magic tied to the box."

I gnawed at my lip. The relief was so instant that tears welled in my eyes.

"Besides that, the portal only opens for those who are supposed to come to the academy. A person could swim to Atlantis and never find it."

I nodded to him, trying hard not to sob with elation at the fact that I was supposed to be here. That I was invited by the Gods to train in the Gods' Army. That they wanted me, Melany Richmond, poor orphan girl, rebel, troublemaker, and not Callie Demos, the perfect specimen of Greek devotion, to come to the legendary academy.

He set the box back onto the shelf.

"Thank you, Hephaistos, sir."

I couldn't stop the smile spreading on my face. I turned to head back to the stairs.

"I saw your leap earlier."

I froze, unsure of what to say.

"That was sixteen feet, give or take a few inches." He rubbed at his bulbous nose.

I stared at him, wondering if somehow I had broken even more rules or had broken something when I jumped.

"It was impressive." He gave me a dismissive wave of his meaty hand. "Now, get the hell out of my foundry, and if you ever come here unsupervised again, I'll have you expelled."

I almost ran out of there but was careful on the bridge this time. As I mounted the stairs, my heart was hammering as loud as the one I'd used earlier. I vibrated with excitement. I wasn't the outcast I thought I was. I had every right to be here. The knowledge of that propelled me up the stairs two at a time.

When I reached the top, I had a skip in my step and was going to go to the dining hall and eat as much pizza as I could fit into my mouth. As I came around the corner, a hand clamped over my mouth, and I was pushed up against the wall. Instinct took over and I lashed out, biting down on the hand over my lips.

"Ow, Blue. You didn't have to bite me so damn hard."

CHAPTER EIGHT

MELANY

*M*y heart still pounded in my chest as I stared Lucian in the face. I had to take in a big breath to try and calm down. My flight or fight instincts had kicked in, and unlucky for him I was a fighter. "Why did you grab me?"

Rubbing at his hand, I noticed a red mark on his palm where my teeth had sunk in. He shrugged. "I don't know. I saw you sneaking around and thought I'd surprise you."

"Well, you deserved that bite."

His eyes narrowed. "What were you doing, anyway?"

"Nothing."

"Were you coming from the forge?" He peered around the corner at the winding staircase.

"No." I started walking to the dining hall, hoping

our conversation was over, but he got in step with me. My stomach growled in reminder I hadn't eaten since breakfast, which was a bowl of oatmeal and an apple.

"You know, I can't figure you out, Blue."

"I didn't realize I was a math equation."

He laughed. "That's what I'm talking about. That surly attitude."

"You know what I think? You're not used to girls with brains. You like girls who fawn at your every word. Girls who swoon when you flex your biceps."

He flexed his arm. "I think it's pretty impressive."

I hated that it was impressive and wouldn't mind wrapping a hand over it. But I wasn't about to let him know that. I knew boys like Lucian. I'd seen them sniffing around Callie. One had sniffed around me once, thinking he could take advantage of the poor girl who lived in the housekeeper's cottage. That boy ended up with a broken nose and ice on his junk after I set him straight and taught him some manners and how consent actually worked.

When we reached the dining hall, I quickly spotted Jasmine and Georgina and fully intended to go sit with them and eat some pizza where it was safe. Standing here next to Lucian felt dangerous. We weren't touching, but I wanted us to. I hated that I thought about his full, soft-looking lips, and how they would feel on mine.

He leaned into me, taking advantage of our height difference. Did he know what I was thinking? The gleam in his eyes worried me. "You look like you want to jump out of your skin."

I licked my lips. "I'm just hungry. I look edgy when I'm hungry."

"I think I make you nervous."

I met his gaze head on. His green eyes had pretty gold flecks in them. "No. Why would you?"

His eyes traveled my face, lingering a bit too long on my mouth. "No reason. I look forward to our next sparring class." He tipped his head and walked into the dining hall to join his friends, who stared our way. I could just imagine what Revana was going to say to him about talking to me.

I quickly made my way to where Jasmine and Georgina sat. Both of them had lifted eyebrows when I sat down and grabbed the piece of pizza they'd gotten for me.

"What was that all about?" Jasmine asked.

"Nothing."

"You know, I think maybe you and I have a very different definition of nothing."

I shoved the pizza in my mouth, ending the conversation about Lucian. I didn't want to talk about him because there *was* something between us. Some kind of energy that sparked every time he was near. It unnerved me. And I couldn't afford to be unnerved. Now that I knew without a shadow of a doubt that I was supposed to be here, I had to concentrate on being the best. Failure wasn't an option for me.

Elemental class was the one class everyone had been waiting for. Not only was it an opportunity to learn how to control various elements like water and lightning, but it was a chance to impress the God of all Gods: Zeus. Just about everyone I knew hoped they had an affinity to lightning, everyone except Georgina. The only God she wished to impress was Demeter. And it's all she would talk about as we made our way across the courtyard to the huge training facility behind the academy.

"Did you know Demeter invented agriculture? Without her we wouldn't even be able to feed ourselves. We'd still be a bunch of Neanderthals eating meat for every meal."

I just nodded and made agreeing noises, as she listed off all the things that Demeter had done or said or discovered. It was a long list, but we made it to the building by the time she finished. The doors opened, and we all walked into a huge, open-air facility that had been separated into different areas. Some of the areas were raised on platforms connected by metal staircases. In each area, I assumed, stood one of the Gods.

I recognized Zeus, who stood on the highest level, three metal rods erected behind him, and Hephaistos, who stood on a lower level next to a large unlit fire pit.

Georgina grabbed my arm and squealed, "It's Demeter." She gestured to the woman with long, messy dark blonde hair, who sat on a huge rock in the middle of a small garden. She wore a long, gauzy skirt, a band T-shirt that I think it said Jefferson Airplane, and was shoeless.

The man standing near a small pool of water on

the lowest level had to be Poseidon. He had a similar face as Zeus, but his hair was dark brown in short waves. I supposed he would be called ruggedly handsome.

"I wonder who that is?" I gestured to the nearest area shrouded in darkness. Every once in a while, I could see a shimmer of movement.

Jasmine frowned. "Who?"

I pointed to the shadows. "There's someone moving around on that platform."

"You're seeing things, Mel. There's no one there."

I peered into the cloying black and spied eyes staring back at me. A shiver of dread rushed down my back.

"Welcome recruits!" Zeus held out his arms toward us. "Today, you will be working with five different elements. Water, fire, earth, shadow, and of course, lightning." White sparks emitted from his fingertips.

Shadow? My gaze tracked over to that area. Now, a man with long, black hair and pale eyes stood there. He dressed like a Victorian vampire. When he spotted me looking at him, he grinned. Goose bumps popped out all over my arms.

"Break out into five groups, eight or nine in each group."

Of course, Jasmine, Georgina, and I melded together. Mia and Ren joined our group. I locked gazes with Lucian. For a brief moment, I thought he was going to walk over to join our group, and I held my breath. But the moment passed, and he gathered with Diego, Revana, and Isobel, along with some others whose names I didn't know. Eventually, Jasmine's roommate, Hella, and her friends Marek and Quinn, asked to join with us.

Zeus assigned every group an element to start with. We got water.

Ren was bouncing on his toes when we gathered around the pool. He looked like a kid at Christmas.

"Water is life." Poseidon gestured to the pool. "Our bodies are made of it, seventy percent of the world is covered by it, and without it food would not grow." With his hand hovering over the water, slowly it began to swirl like the tide pool we'd used to come to the academy. Then it spouted out of the pool and touched the palm of his hand. There he held it, this swirling column of water.

"But not only can it give life, it can take it away." With a flick of his hand, the narrow waterspout quickly surged into a huge cyclone that towered over us threateningly. "The oceans and seas could rise with five hundred foot waves and drown cities in a matter of minutes." He made a fist, and the water sloshed back into the pool, surging over the edge and splashing our legs. "To control the water is to control life."

He looked at each of us. "Who would like to try first?"

Ren's hand shot up like a rocket. "I would, sir."

For the next half hour, we each tried to manipulate the water with our hands. The only two who got it immediately were Ren and Marek. They both were able to produce tiny cyclones. I could barely make the water ripple.

Next, we moved onto the fire station.

"I'm not going to regale you with some soppy story about how powerful fire is," Hephaistos grumbled. "It speaks for itself." He snapped his fingers over the fire pit, and flames jumped to life.

I immediately stepped closer to it, so I could dry off the bottoms of my pants and shoes.

"If you can control fire, you can raze cities to the ground. You can burn your enemies to ash." The light from the flames glowed in his eyes as he walked around behind us.

Jasmine's eyes widened, and it looked like she was shaking.

"But you can also provide warmth and comfort and even healing." He set his hand on her shoulder, and she immediately relaxed and even smiled. "First, you will learn to control the fire, then I will teach you how to create it. Put your hand up to the flames and call it to you."

I raised my hand toward the fire. The heat from it instantly warmed my palm. It reminded me a little of the sensation I'd received from touching the Shadowbox. Concentrating on the flames, I watched them dance. Smiling, I thought about dancing with them.

"Mel," Jasmine said beside me. "Good Gods."

Frowning, I turned to look at her. "What?"

"Your hand!"

I looked at my hand. Flames had completely encompassed it. My heart leapt into my throat. *Holy shit, I'm burning.* But I didn't feel like I was burning. There wasn't any discomfort, just a warm, soothing heat hovering above my skin. I noticed my pants and shoes were no longer wet.

"Whoa!" I moved my hand back and forth, and the flames flowed with me. It was pretty cool.

I glanced at Hephaistos, and he gave me a quick nod.

I figured it was the most praise I was going to get from him. I'd take it.

When we reached the garden, I thought I was going to have to restrain Georgina; she was so excited.

"Controlling the earth is really cool." Demeter climbed off the rock and sat cross-legged on the patch of grass we stood on. She gestured for all of us to sit like she did. "You can grow food and literally move mountains. During war, you can manipulate the plants around you to do whatever you want." She placed her hand flat to the ground, closing her eyes. A vine pushed out of the ground through the grass. It looped around in the air and then wrapped around one of Georgina's arms.

Her eyes widened. She went slack and slumped to the ground.

Demeter frowned. "Shit, man, did I just kill her?"

"No, I think she passed out." I shook Georgina awake.

She sat back up, with a huge smile on her face. "That was awesome."

Everyone laughed.

Demeter chuckled. "What's your name?"

"Georgina," she murmured.

"Well, Georgina, I think you're going to be my fave student."

She nearly passed out again, and I had to hold her up.

Throughout the class, Demeter had us touching the dirt and grass, to really feel it, to think about its construction, and to picture it growing and moving. By the end of the class, Jasmine and Quinn were able to roll a rock without touching it, and Georgina, to the delight of Demeter and everyone else, had grown a flower in her hand. There was no doubt which clan Georgina belonged in.

My group's next stop was at the shadow station. The moment I stepped into the darkness shrouding the area, my body started to vibrate. It was a strange sensation, as if I was a human tuning fork.

"I'm Erebus." From the darkest part of the room, a form stepped into view. Up close, he looked even more like a vampire, especially with those pale, almost translucent eyes. The longer I stared at him, though, the more ethereal he seemed. In fact, his body didn't stay solid. It undulated back and forth. He was part of the shadows.

"Here you will learn how to manipulate light and darkness. When you master it, you will be able to disappear." He faded into the shadows. "And reappear in a different place." His voice came from behind me, and I jumped and whipped around, coming face to face with him. Another rush of dread washed over me.

"I'm going to teach you how to refract light, to bend it around your body. It is a form of disguise, so you can move around without being seen." He put his arms up, slicing them through the air. He did it again and again until they disappeared. "The key is to move quickly. Everyone try it."

As I walked around in a circle, I moved my arms back and forth in front of me, karate chopping the air. I whipped my arms up and down as fast as I could, so focused I almost didn't see Ren as he nearly walked into me.

"Whoa, watch where you're going."

Ren froze. "Melany?"

"Ah, yeah, who else do you think I am?"

His head turned right then left, as if searching for me. "Where are you?"

My brow knitted together. "Right here. In front of you."

He swung around toward me, his eyes darting everywhere, but not on my face. "I can't see you."

Damn. I'd manipulated the light.

"You know, you're quite beautiful."

I whipped around to see Erebus standing behind me, his hands folded in front of him. "Excuse me? That's a bit creepy, don't you think?"

He took a step closer, his gaze scrutinizing me. I didn't like it. It made me feel vulnerable and exposed.

"You have shadows inside you." He put his hand up and moved it around in front of me. His flesh came apart and then flowed back together. It was like watching an object being refracted into pixels. "I can feel them. It's why you were able to manipulate the light so easily."

"How do I become visible again?"

"Stop moving."

"I'm not moving. I'm just standing here."

He pressed two fingers to my forehead. "Stop moving inside."

I wasn't exactly sure what he meant, but I concentrated on calming my body one part at a time. I started at my toes and made my way up to my head. When I finally took in a long, deep cleansing breath, I felt whole again.

"Dude." Ren's eyes bugged out. "You just appeared in front of me."

Both Jasmine and Georgina ran over to me. "That's so cool. You, like, totally disappeared."

I smiled as they congratulated me. The others gathered around me, too, and told me how awesome it was that I manipulated the light so quickly. No one else had been able to accomplish it. Pride filled me up inside but so did apprehension. I was a bit uneasy with what Erebus had told me—that shadows filled me.

The lightning station with Zeus was our last stop. Jasmine was really pumped for this training. Earlier she'd told me she hoped to be assigned to Zeus's clan. I could see her there; she was strong and bold, two traits of someone who could manipulate lightning.

Zeus had us gathering around what I assumed were lightning rods. The Demos Estate had one on the grounds to try and harness the electrical current whenever it stormed.

"Lightning is just an electrical current," he said, from his spot in the middle of the three rods. "It's in the air all around us, all the time." He clapped his hands together. The sound made everyone jump. He started to rub his palms together. "Rub your hands together. You are creating an electrical charge between them by creating friction."

I could feel heat building between my hands. My fingers started to tingle. I frowned, unsure if that was what was supposed to happen.

While he kept rubbing his hands together, he walked around the group. Then he stopped in front of me, opened his hands, and set them over my head. "We've now created static electricity."

I could feel some slight tingles above me, and then I felt my hair rise. Strands of blue stuck out all over, some of them reaching for Zeus's hands. Both Jasmine and Georgina laughed, as I became a human Troll Doll.

I smirked, amused by what I could imagine I looked like. Then something felt wrong. The tingles around my head increased. It no longer tickled but started to sting. A thousand pinpricks turned sharper, stronger. Painful.

Jasmine's face turned ashen. Georgina took a step back, her eyes widening.

"What? What's going on?" I demanded, panicking.

I could smell something burning, almost like plastic melting. Then I realized the odor emitted from me. Sparks erupted from my head.

"It's going to kill her!" Jasmine's voice echoed around me.

Then everything went black, as darkness took me under.

CHAPTER NINE

MELANY

*T*he smell of bacon and cheese tickled my nose, and I blinked open my eyes. I was in my bed, facing the wall. I rolled to see Georgina and Jasmine, Georgina sat on her bed, and Jasmine was in the desk chair, both eating bacon cheeseburgers and French fries. Saliva instantly pooled in my mouth.

"Yay, you're finally awake." Georgina put another fry into her mouth and happily chewed.

"What happened?" Slowly, I sat up, but my head ached something awful so I reconsidered it.

"You've been out for about four hours." Jasmine came to my side and helped me sit up. She plumped up the pillows behind me. "The healers checked you out, but said you could rest up here in your room instead of in the infirmary."

Georgina unwrapped another burger. "Are you hungry? Do you want to eat?"

I nodded. I was starving. I took the burger and had a big bite. Once I chewed and swallowed, I looked at my friends. "I'm still a bit fuzzy on what exactly happened. I remember being in elemental class with Zeus—"

"You died." Georgina bolted off her bed and wrapped an arm around me, hugging me tight.

I choked on the next bite of burger.

Jasmine gave Georgina a look. "We weren't supposed to tell her right away."

"I know, I'm sorry."

Scrambling out from Georgina's octopus arms, I got all the way out of bed and stared at my friends. "What do you mean, I died?"

"I guess for some reason, a lot of electricity went through your body and your heart stopped." Jasmine winced. "But Zeus got it started again with a little zap of his finger." She poked me in the chest.

"Well, it took two zaps," Georgina added. "And then it still took a few seconds before you came back."

I gaped at her. I had no idea what to say. What did one say after they'd died and had their heart restarted by a God? "Wow" just didn't seem to cut it.

"I need some air." I headed for the door.

"Do you want us to come with?" Georgina started to follow me.

"No. I just… need a walk and some time to digest what happened."

"Okay." Jasmine squeezed my shoulder. "We'll be here when you get back if you want to talk about it."

I left the room and went down the hall, unsure of exactly where I was going. All I knew was that the air inside the school felt thick and oppressive. Thankfully, I didn't run into anyone as I crossed the front foyer and out the main doors.

The second I was outside I took in a deep breath of air, held it, and then let it out. I repeated the process until I wasn't dizzy anymore. I needed to move. I hadn't been outside much on the grounds, so I didn't know where to go, but I knew there was a maze on the west side. I hopped onto the cobblestone path winding through the grounds and just started walking.

Before I came around the corner of the main academy building, I heard a voice. It sounded tinny and mechanical.

"Meteorologists don't know what to make of the strange weather in Pecunia. In some areas, there have been varying degrees of rain, wind, and hail. There have been some large ocean swells, and some are even saying that there has been high seismic activity where there shouldn't be any."

My immediate thought was of Sophie and if she was safe.

Curious, I came around the corner to see Demeter leaning up against the wall, watching a video on her cell phone, and smoking what smelled like weed. When she spotted me, she quickly pushed a button on the screen and slid the phone in her back pocket.

"Oh, hey, there." She smiled, smoke coming out of her mouth. "It's Melany, right?"

I nodded. "Yup."

She raised the joint in her hand. "You don't mind, do you? I can't smoke inside." She shrugged. "Rules suck sometimes."

I shook my head. "I don't mind."

"Good." She took another hit. "So, how are you feeling? You gave everyone quite the scare." She chuckled. "I don't think any of your fellow recruits saw someone die before."

I rubbed at my chest; it still burned where Zeus had zapped me. I was afraid to look under my shirt in case there was a burn mark. "I feel… okay, I guess."

"You'll be all right. Just give it a few days."

"Right." I gestured to her pocket. "Were you watching the news?"

She made a face. "I know I'm not supposed to have a cell phone, either, but sometimes I hate not knowing what's going on around in the world."

"What were they saying about Pecunia? That's where I'm from."

"Ah, nothing to worry about. Just a rainstorm." She patted me on the shoulder.

"Oh, okay." But I wasn't assured.

She took another puff and eyed me. "You're different, you know?"

"What do you mean?"

"Your aura. It's odd. It's not like the others."

I wasn't sure if that was a good thing or a bad thing. I didn't want to be an outcast. I needed to be like the others, so I could pass through the training.

"It's good being different," she said. "Being like

everyone else sucks. Embrace your differences. It'll help you survive."

I was about to say goodnight to her when someone else came stumbling toward us from around the corner. It was Dionysus, and he could barely stay upright. When he saw us, his smile was instant and took up his entire face.

"Heeeeeeeeyyyyy." He weaved toward Demeter and swung an arm around her shoulders. "What are you doing out here, Demi?"

"Just having a smoke. Talking to Melany."

He swung his head my way. "Hello, Melany." He drew out every consonant in my name. "Your aura is funny. It's black."

"She died today."

His eyes bugged out. "You did? How marvelous. What was it like?"

"Um, I don't really remember it."

He scrunched up his face. "Pity. I would've loved to hear all about it." He crushed Demeter to his body. "Let's go party. I made the most amazing hooch."

"Last time I drank your hooch, I had a rash for two weeks."

"No, this batch is good. Trust me. I already drank half of it and I'm fiiiine."

Demeter looked at me. "I'm going to take this one back to his place, so he can sleep it off. You should probably get back to your dorm before curfew. Oh, and I'd really appreciate it if you kept all this to yourself."

"Yeah, no problem. Good night." I turned to go

back to the main doors, when Dionysus grabbed my arm.

"Aren't you coming with us, luv?"

Demeter pulled him away. "She can't come with us. She's a first year recruit and has to get back to her dorm."

He nodded. "Riiiiiiight. I knew that."

They started to walk away when Dionysus swung back around toward me. "I know what it is about you. Your tattoos are dancing."

"I think it's just your eyes, Dion." Demeter waved at me to continue on, as she guided Dionysus around to the back of the school.

Freaked out by the encounter, I ran back to the main doors. There was something about the way Dionysus looked at me that made me uneasy. Not like he was creeping on me or anything, but he saw something odd about me. Both Demeter and Dionysus spotted something different about my aura. I didn't know much about auras, but I knew everyone had one, and different colors had different meaning.

I knew red indicated love and compassion and sometimes anger, yellow meant optimism and intelligence, green meant balance and nature, white, of course, indicated truth and purity. But black, black was not a color a person wanted in their aura. It could mean lots of things like pent up anger and grief, maybe some health problems. And death. Black was the color of shadow and darkness and the eternal abyss.

I hoped it was because I'd died but had come back, and whatever energy required for my resurrection still lingered over me. And not because Death hadn't finished what he'd started.

Once inside the academy, I dashed up the stone staircase and down the long corridor toward the dorm. The lights along the wall appeared dimmer. Every one of them flickered as I passed by. Darkness seemed to be growing along the floor and up the walls. I heard whispering from the shadows.

I stopped and peered into the darkened corners. "Are you playing some kind of game, Erebus? You're wasting your time if you are." A shiver rushed down my back.

A form flickered in the shadows. Someone was moving inside the darkness. I took a step closer. "I can see you. You're not scaring me."

More whispers sounded in my ears, prickling the back of my neck. I spun around, expecting someone to be standing behind me, but there wasn't anyone. I was still alone in the corridor. Except I didn't feel alone. I was being watched.

I turned back to the deep shadows along the wall and swore they had swelled farther along the ceiling and the floor. It was like a slicker of oil slowly rolling toward my shoes. A voice in my head told me to run, but there was also another presence urging me to step into the darkness.

Like a siren's song, I felt compelled to move forward. I stared even harder into the shadows, seeing a face forming from the ink. It was a nice face, a welcoming one. I smiled. Then I lifted my leg to take that step.

"Mel?"

I felt a tug on my hand.

"It's curfew. We need to get to our room."

There was another tug on my hand, and I was suddenly moving sideways.

The spell broke, and I turned to see Georgina leading me back to our room. Before she yanked me inside, I looked over at the shadows once more, and spotted a form standing in the dark, and he was smiling back at me.

CHAPTER TEN

MELANY

$\mathcal{T}$he next few weeks just floated by in a bit of a fuzzy haze. Ever since the accident in elemental class and the strange occurrence in the hallway, I'd felt different. Something had changed inside me, and I wasn't sure what it was. The one thing I did notice was that some of the classes became easier.

I no longer missed the targets in archery. In fact, I hit the bullseyes often now, to the delight of Artemis and chagrin of Revana. She'd made her loathing of me known on more than one occasion, especially if I excelled at something she didn't.

And I was getting the hang of metallurgy. It helped that I seemed to have an affinity to fire, which had showed itself in elemental class before I got electrocuted and died. The shield I was crafting in class looked the best out of the entire first years. Hephaistos had even gifted me with some praise in the form of a few non-guttural grunts and a hearty slap on the back that nearly toppled me over.

Spears and shield class still proved difficult, but I think it had more to do with the fact that Ares seemed to have it in for me. He took great pleasure in whenever I failed at something. I'd gotten stronger, though, so holding up the shield was a lot easier, and I was decent protecting myself with it. I still struggled a little with holding and maneuvering the spear. I suspected I was going to be much better at handling a sword, and was eager to prove that theory when we had swordplay class next term.

I also saw a jump in improvement with hand-to-hand combat training. Lucian had mentioned it during one class right after I flipped him over onto his back in one quick move that he hadn't seen coming. Heracles had laughed with delight after that, which embarrassed Lucian. His cheeks had flared red.

I thought for sure he'd be all sulky after that and maybe even be a jerk to me, as most boys would after being bested by a girl, but to my surprise and pleasure, he asked me to show him how to do the move. We even practiced it a few times after class until Heracles kicked us out.

During that time, I'd been ultra-aware of everything about Lucian, especially when our bodies pressed against each other during the actual flip, and after when he wouldn't release my wrist right away.

His touch continually made my body tingle and my head fuzzy, which was why I avoided him at all costs outside of the classroom.

When we weren't in classes, Georgina, Jasmine, and I spent our time together either in our rooms eating and playing cards, or down in the common room where once or twice Dionysus would show up with some new song he created and make us listen to it on repeat. Those were fun nights and made me forget about the odd sensation growing inside of me. Every now and then, I'd catch Dionysus looking at me funny, and I wondered if he still saw my tattoos dancing and a dark aura hovering around me. I never asked, though. I was too afraid to.

I yawned again, as we made our way through the academy to the Hall of Aphrodite for our transformation class. The word was that the Goddess never left her gilded hall. I knew that was a lie, as I'd seen her skulking around with Ares on my first night at the academy. But I kept that information to myself.

"Are you still not sleeping?" Georgina gave me a concerned look.

"I'm fine. Just woke up a little earlier than I wanted."

She didn't look convinced.

I'd woken up at three o'clock, again for the fifth day in a row. I had a feeling I was having bad dreams, but I couldn't remember them when I woke. All that lingered was a feeling of ominous dread. So, it proved difficult to get back to sleep after waking. Some mornings I would just lie there in bed, staring at the ceiling, so I didn't wake Georgina. Other times, I walked the dark hallways of the academy, and made it a game of not getting caught by the hall monitors. Pandora had almost busted me the other morning, but I'd managed to duck into the girls' shower room before she could spot me. I figured I was improving my stealth skills.

It was my first time in the Hall of Aphrodite, so I didn't know what to expect. I'd heard a few of the first years, like Revana and Lucian, had been invited for a private dinner party a week ago by Eros and Psyche to the hall. It bothered me that even here, money and power and good looks gave you advantages the rest of us didn't have. After reading about Aphrodite over the years and overhearing some of the other recruits talking about it, I expected splendor. The reality of the hall far surpassed anything I could ever imagine.

The floor was a labyrinth of gold and red and black tile, producing an optical illusion of boxes stacked on top of one another. It was polished to a shine, and I could see my reflection in it as clear as a mirror. The arched ceiling was embossed with gold and painted with frescos done in red and gold and of Aphrodite and her various companions like Eros, her son, and the three Graces—Aglaia, Euphrosyne, and Thalia. Everywhere you looked, there were carved pillars holding up the ceiling, also gold embossed, and the walls were wallpapered in red velvet. I'd never seen anything so gauche; it nearly hurt my eyes.

As a group, we entered the adjacent room to the lavish front entrance of the hall, which I assumed was the classroom. Thankfully, it wasn't as opulently deco-rated. I didn't think I could've handled all that gold and red for two hours. Fifty high-backed chairs were arranged around a raised pulpit. It reminded me of a church. The Church of Aphrodite.

While we all got seated—Jasmine, Georgina, and I sat together as usual—the door at the back of the room opened, and Aphrodite walked in, head high, breasts jutted, hips swaying. She was accompanied by three other women, two of them carried the train on her lavish gold gown, and the other carried a large, black leather case.

Everyone was transfixed as she stepped up onto the pulpit, especially the boys. I didn't blame them; she was stunning up close. It was almost difficult to look upon her, like looking into the hottest part of the sun. She was too bright.

She waited until she had everyone's rapt attention before she spoke. "Transformation. It is the act of changing into something else. A caterpillar into a butterfly." Her gaze swept the audience. "A tadpole into a frog. I will teach you how to change your look, your shape, so you can turn into someone else. It is a masterful skill to have in order to deceive your enemies or to even hide among them." She looked right at me.

For the next two hours, Aphrodite showed us how to alter the shape of our faces, which was the first step to transformation. At first I couldn't believe it was even possible, but after she demonstrated by changing her appearance into that of an old, with-ered hunchback hag, I became a true believer.

With the help of her assistants, who ended up being the three Graces, Aglaia, Euphrosyne, and Thalia, we each took turns either plumping up our faces or thinning them down. Georgina, Jasmine, and I couldn't stop giggling, as Georgina ended up fattening her face so much she looked like a tomato, especially with her red hair. By the end of the class, it was obvious she had a knack for changing. Jasmine and I didn't latch onto it as well. I think all I managed to do was to make my nose long and thin like Pinocchio, which made everyone around us laugh hysterically. Lucian included.

At the end of class, I was leaving with my friends when Aphrodite called me back.

"Melany, why don't you stay a minute?"

Both Georgina and Jasmine gave me funny looks. I shrugged and then walked back to where the Goddess stood waiting. "Did I do something wrong?"

She gave me an indulgent smile, but it didn't make me feel warm. A shiver actually rushed down my back. "On the contrary, I've only heard great things about you."

I grimaced. "Really?"

"Oh yes, you have made quite a stir around the academy."

She was probably referring to the incident in elemental class when I'd gotten electrocuted. Despite that, I was still surprised Aphrodite even knew my name. She didn't seem like the sort of person who even bothered with that trivial information.

"My husband talks quite fondly of you."

Now, I really did give her a look. There was no

way Hephaistos said anything complimentary about me to his wife. He wouldn't say anything nice like that to anyone. Maybe she heard from her lover, Ares, about what a pain in the ass I was.

"And because of that, I want you know, that if you ever need someone to talk to, you can come to me." Her gaze scrutinized me from toe to head. "I can imagine it must be hard for you here, considering you're… so different from everyone else."

I wondered if she meant my strange aura, or if she meant that I had blue hair, piercings, and tattoos, and didn't look as pampered and polished as everyone else, especially Revana and her crew.

"I, ah, appreciate that." I wasn't sure what else to say. As if I would confide in her, knowing full well that she was conspiring with Ares about something. Although she was breathtaking, there was something utterly deceptive about her. Maybe it was the fact that she could transform into anyone. If that wasn't the ultimate trickery, I didn't know what was.

She set her hand on my arm, and I felt a prickle of heat along my skin. "I was very concerned when I heard what had transpired in your elemental training. Zeus's lightning is very dangerous. I've told him time and time again that he shouldn't be teaching that so soon in a young one's training. Disastrous accidents can happen. Obviously." Her hand stayed on my arm, and my head started to feel a bit floaty. Like I'd drunk too much wine. "Do you remember anything about how you survived? Did someone help you?"

I frowned. "Zeus brought me back."

"That's not how I understand it. He said he tried to bring you back, but it didn't work."

I wanted to pull away from her. My face was flushed, and too much heat circulated in my body. I felt drunk. But not just on alcohol—on her. She smelled like wild flowers, and her hair was so shiny and soft looking, I wanted to reach out and twirl a tendril of it on my finger, like spinning gold.

"Can you remember who brought you back? Did someone whisper to you?"

I shook my head, trying to clear it. Her words were like a lullaby in my ears, lulling me into a daze. Seducing me into submission.

Fight her.

I heard the voice in my head. It was like the whispers I'd heard before. From the shadows. In my dreams.

Her hand tightened on my arm, like a snake. Constricting me. "Tell me what you know. Tell me—"

With everything I had, I pushed her away, both physically and mentally. I stumbled backwards and nearly fell onto my ass. I expected anger from her for assaulting her. But she just smiled, as if nothing had happened.

"You should run along my dear. Your friends will be missing you." Her grin widened. It almost appeared as if her teeth had sharpened, but that could've been my imagination. "Won't they?"

Without responding, I turned and ran out of the room then out of the hall. The big, heavy gold doors slammed shut behind me the second I was out. The sudden need to be with my friends spurred me on, and I ran through the academy halls to the dorms.

I didn't quite know what had just happened with Aphrodite, but a sense of dread tightened in my guts. I'd been in danger that much I grasped, but I didn't know why. How was I a threat to Aphrodite? And what was she willing to do to end it?

CHAPTER ELEVEN

MELANY

*P*itch black surrounded me. I felt like I was floating. I could see a pinpoint of light, and that was when I realized I was back inside the spiraling portal underwater. My lungs burned from lack of oxygen. A few more minutes and I would certainly die.

I looked past the portal to the dark waters beyond, and saw a shape hovering nearby. Watching me. I reached out toward the form, pleading for help. Suddenly I didn't know how to swim. I didn't know why I was here in this portal again, but I was going to die if I didn't get out.

My fingers breached the edge of the whirling spout. My hand reached for the form floating within inches of me. I wriggled my fingers, grasping for assistance. *"Help me!"* I tried to scream, but when I opened my mouth, water poured in. And now, I was choking on it.

My vision blurred. The pressure inside my head expanded. Pain pummeled at me. It wouldn't be long before I succumbed to the water and took it in.

Then a hand snatched mine and pulled me out.

Bolting straight up in bed, I coughed and sputtered, taking in greedy gulps of air. Whispers swirled around me, trying to penetrate my ears. But I didn't want to listen to them. They were telling me bad things. Asking me to do bad things.

I swatted at them, buzzing like stinging insects. "Stop it!"

Then I felt warm hands on top of mine. "Mel! You're okay. You're safe."

Slowly, my surroundings came into view. I was in my bed, in my dorm. And Georgina held me, talking me out of whatever fugue I'd been trapped inside.

She ran a hand over my head. "You're okay. You're here, with me."

I nodded, and took in a deep breath, trying to slow my heart rate, which thundered in my chest, each beat like a hammer against my rib cage.

"Same dream?" she asked.

I nodded.

For the past nine days, I'd been having the same horrible dream every night. It all started right after the incident with Aphrodite. It was almost like she'd sparked something inside me. Tried to force open some door inside my mind. And it was opening. I could hear it creaking inside my head and feel every small progression in my body. I feared what was inside.

After Georgina helped me calm down, we dressed and headed to the dining hall for breakfast. Jasmine caught up with us, and upon seeing me, immediately hugged me.

"Are you okay? You look so pale."

I gave her a look.

"Well, paler than usual."

"Bad dreams still," Georgina piped up, as she slopped oatmeal into a bowl and handed it to me.

We took our meals and sat at our usual spot at one of the long tables in the hall. Mia joined us, and I noticed the instant grin on Jasmine's face.

"Are they the same?" Jasmine asked.

"Yeah, I'm trapped in the portal underwater, and I'm going to drown, but someone who I can't see pulls me out right before." I played with my oatmeal, not hungry at all.

"Maybe it's just stress getting the best of you," Jasmine said. "That is sort of what happened to you getting here, wasn't it? I mean, Lucian saved you, didn't he?"

I nodded, just as my gaze landed on him two tables away, laughing with his friends. He glanced up from his meal and caught me looking at him. Before I could turn away, he gave me a soft smile that made my heart thump a little bit faster.

"Maybe you're stressed about the practice water trial today." Mia shrugged.

Georgina nodded. "I bet that's it. You did tell me

you weren't looking forward to it since you didn't do too well in water."

"Yeah, you're probably right." I smiled at my friends, knowing they all meant well and were only looking out for me. But they were wrong in this. It wasn't stress trying to burrow into my mind like a worm in dirt; it was something altogether more worrisome. Something sinister.

There was a buzz of excitement and apprehension during elemental class. After our lessons with the other elements, we were all going to be doing a practice water trial in the pool with Poseidon. Despite my attempts to deny it to myself, I was nervous about the trial. I wasn't all that good with water or in it. After six classes, I'd only been able to make a tiny cyclone in the water while some like Ren, Marek, and even Lucian, could make waves as high as the twenty foot ceiling. But the prep training wasn't about making water spouts and waves, it was about staying underwater for as long as possible and collecting rocks from the bottom of the pool. It seemed simple enough, but the catch was we had to do it while evading an attack from some water beast Poseidon was going to set loose. *Fun times at Poseidon's pool party.*

The whole thing was a distraction, and I nearly set Hella's pants on fire when a fireball I was making got away from me, bounced once, and exploded at her feet. Hephaistos rushed over with a bucket of water and doused her before it could do any damage.

"I'm so sorry." I rushed over to her, my hands still aflame.

"It's fine." She moved away from me.

But I could see it in her face that it was far from fine, and now she was afraid of me. I supposed I didn't blame her; I had come at her waving around my fire hands.

"What's wrong with you, girl?" Hephaistos growled at me, tossing the rest of the water from the bucket onto me to douse my hands. "You have to stay focused, or you're going to hurt someone."

That distraction followed me through shadow class, as I walked through the motions, dissipating at will, then to lightning where I was barely even allowed to touch the metal rods in case I got electrocuted again, then over to the garden, where we were practicing growing vines. I hadn't managed to do anything in this class. I knew it wasn't possible to be good at everything, but I had no affinity to the earth and plants whatsoever. The rest of my group had been able to at least coax a flower to open its petals and to move a huge boulder across the garden. Georgina was already growing fruits and vegetables with the touch of her hands and the intention in her heart.

After having completely given up, I sat on the ground and watched as the others tried to coax some vines to wrap around Demeter's legs. I laughed when Jasmine's vine went crazy and did a loop around her feet and tried to trip her.

I heard other laughter, and my gaze drifted over to where Lucian and his group were at the fire station. Revana and Isobel were huddled together, looking my way and snickering. When Revana spotted me watching them, she sneered.

I didn't know how one person could be so hateful. It wasn't just me who she looked down on, either; it was almost everyone except her immediate friends, although I had overheard her talking crap about Isobel behind her back to Diego.

As I stared at her, I got angrier and angrier. Gritting my teeth and pressing my hands down into the dirt, I thought someone needed to shut her up. She reminded me so much of Callie with her backhanded remarks, disdainful looks, and condescending manner. I'd put up with it for years, swallowing it down over the lump in my throat because I hadn't had a choice.

While Revana continued to smirk and sneer, probably remarking about how trashy I was, all I could picture was a gag in her mouth. It was such a vivid image that I grinned.

Then I was being shaken out of my stupor. "Snap out of it, Melany."

I looked up as Demeter squeezed my shoulder. "What? What's going on?"

"Let go of Revana."

I frowned, confused. My gaze swung over to the fire station and I gasped.

Revana had vines wrapped around her head, over her mouth in particular. Every time she struggled, the vines seemed to be pulling even tighter until her eyes bugged out. Then I noticed the vine had originated from a plant near my shoe. I jumped to my feet, and immediately the vine went slack, and she and Isobel were able to tear it off her face.

The second she was freed, Revana came at me like a freight train. "You bitch."

I managed to dodge her first punch before Demeter intervened.

"Enough."

"She tried to kill me!"

Demeter made a face. "I'm sure that's not true. It was totally an accident, wasn't it, Melany?"

I nodded.

Zeus peered down at us from overhead. "Everything all right down there?"

"Yup, just a little mishap." Demeter gave him the thumbs up. "Nothing to worry about."

"Should we discuss it in council chambers later this evening?" He narrowed his eyes at me.

Demeter shook her head. "No, I don't think that needs to happen." She glanced at Revana. "No one's hurt. Right?"

Revana glared at me but shook her head.

"You see, it's all good."

"Return to your training." Zeus turned and gestured to his class, who were all peering over the side.

Revana, accompanied by Isobel, returned to the fire station. Everyone else went back to what they were doing before chaos had ensued. Demeter put her hand on my shoulder.

"Where did that come from?"

I shook my head. "I don't know. I was just sitting there."

"Something happened."

"I got angry I think."

She nodded. "I have to say I've never seen anyone in all my years of teaching do that at this level." She winked and patted my shoulder. "Well done."

Finished at the other elemental stations, we all gathered around the pool to wait for instructions from Poseidon. The other professors had joined us as well to watch. Nerves zipped through me, and I couldn't stop fidgeting.

"The object of this exercise"—Poseidon leisurely walked behind us, handing each of us a small mesh bag—"is to stay underwater and collect as many rocks as you can. Sounds easy enough. Except for one thing... you will have to evade my adorable pet Charybdis." He pointed to the water.

I gazed down into the pool to see a three-foot long, serpent-like creature whipping around in the water. I'd never seen a Charybdis in person, but the rumor was they possessed nine eyes that circled a round mouth lined with razor sharp teeth. I swallowed the bile rising in my throat.

"Don't worry, a bite from a baby Charybdis isn't lethal, but it does sting a bit." He grinned. "The prize for gathering twenty or more rocks is the favor of the Gods, and you will enjoy a lavish dinner in Zeus's Great Hall with me and Zeus himself."

I saw a lot of excited faces at that prospect. I wasn't one of them.

"BEGIN!"

One by one, my fellow recruits dove into the pool. I watched them go under, frozen in spot, completely petrified, the images and sensations of my dreams holding me hostage. I couldn't do it. I couldn't jump in.

Then Poseidon shoved me in from behind.

As I plunged under the water, I nearly collided with Jasmine, as she grabbed a couple rocks and put them into her mesh bag. When she saw me, she gave me a thumbs up and pointed to the rocks. I nodded and kicked my legs to dive to the bottom.

I scooped up a handful and put them in my bag. Movement next to me drew my attention. I looked up just in time to get Revana's fist in my face. The viscosity of the water softened the blow, or I was sure that it would've knocked me out. Blood floated in front of my eyes. It was coming from my nose.

She reared back to hit me again, when Lucian swam in between us. He shook his head at her, pointing for her to go. She did, but reluctantly. When she was gone, he swirled around to me, pointed at me, then gave the okay sign.

I nodded to let him know I was fine. Smiling, he scooped up a couple more rocks and put them in my bag. I shook my head at him but couldn't stop the grin on my face. My stomach lurched, and my grin faded in an instant when I spotted the Charybdis swimming right toward us. It must've been attracted to my blood.

I shoved Lucian to the side just as the creature lunged. I kicked up with my legs, giving me leverage, and punched it right under its mouth. My stomach churned at the feeling of its fleshy mass on my skin. But it did the trick and it scuttled away.

Lucian looked wide-eyed at me. I gave the okay signal and pointed at him. He nodded. Together, we gathered more rocks. I looked around and noticed there were only about five others in the water with me and Lucian. Ren, of course, and Marek, Revana, and two others I didn't know well.

After another minute, my lungs started to burn. The incident with Revana had distracted me, but now that I was floating here, I was reminded of being back in the portal and not being able to breathe. Noticing my rising panic, Lucian swam close and grabbed my hand. It helped calm me down a little.

After another minute, one of the others kicked to the surface. Then Revana looked over at us, and I could see the anger on her face. She struggled to stay under. She started to thrash around, as I imagined the urge to open her mouth pounded at her. She flipped me the middle finger and then kicked hard up to the surface.

I, too, began to struggle. My head grew fuzzy. Black spots started to form in my vision. Then the whispers infiltrated the back of my mind.

Don't be afraid. Let go of the panic. You won't drown. I won't let you.

I didn't know who was talking to me but I listened. Lucian eventually let go of my hand, kicking up to the surface. Then Marek went up, and then the other girl who I didn't know. It was just Ren and I left. When he noticed, he swam over to me, smiling.

We happily floated in the water together. My lungs started to burn again, but Ren looked like he could stay down here forever. I wondered if he was half fish. He most definitely had Poseidon's blood swimming through his veins.

Knowing Ren would win the prize, I was more

than happy to give up and swim to the surface. I was about to when his face changed and his eyes widened. I could sense movement behind me. I spun around to see the Charybdis's mouth just about to clamp down on my head.

CHAPTER TWELVE

LUCIAN

I paced along the edge of the pool, trying hard not jump in, especially after I saw the Charybdis zip through the water toward Melany and Ren.

"She can take care of herself," Poseidon said at my distress.

Everyone watched the pool, waiting to see what would happen. Some were scared, like Melany's friends, Georgina and Jasmine, others, like Revana, looked on in glee, hoping for a lethal outcome.

I watched, my heart in my throat, at the erratic movement in the water, and then the Charybdis came shooting out like a cannon and landed at Poseidon's feet. The little creature looked unharmed, but definitely indignant at being tossed out of the pool.

Laughing, Poseidon picked up the sea slug and patted its head. A few moments later, Melany and Ren popped up out of the water to a round of cheers and clapping.

"Well done, you two are the winners of the competition."

I reached down and helped Ren out of the pool and then Melany. She was shivering, and I draped a big towel around her shoulders. There was still a trickle of blood coming from her nose.

"You still got a bit of blood." I gestured to her nose.

She pressed the edge of her towel to her face. "Thanks."

"Does it hurt?"

"Nah. She punches like a girl."

I laughed, which earned me a lethal glare from Revana, who was chatting with Isobel nearby.

"You should have seen her." Ren was talking to Poseidon and the others who gathered around. "She just reached out and grabbed that thing by the neck before it could bite her and just tossed it through the water like a missile. I've never seen anything like it." He chuckled.

"I don't think it was as cool as that." Melany rubbed at her hair with the towel.

"Oh, yeah it was." Grinning, Ren patted her on the shoulder. "You're hardcore."

Her cheeks flushed a little at the compliment, but I had to agree. Melany was hardcore. She'd saved me from getting bitten by that creepy water slug. And she was consistently kicking my ass in hand-to-hand combat training.

"He's right, Blue." I leaned down to her ear, as we all left the training facility. "You are a badass."

She gave me a look, and I thought she was going to say something, but her friends came up on her sides, pushing me out. I stepped away and joined Diego, Jonah, and Trevin; they were congratulating Ren for winning the competition and basically for being part fish.

Back at the dorms, I'd finished having a shower and was changing into regular clothes since classes were done for the day. I was anxious to get down to the dining hall and chill out. I was hungry, but I also realized it was because I wanted to see Melany. I didn't get a chance to thank her for saving me from getting bitten by the Charybdis, and I just wanted to hang out with her. I didn't know anything about her and I wanted to.

"Can you believe that bitch today?" Diego ran product into his hair. "I mean, Revana should've really kicked her ass."

"Don't talk about her like that." I pulled on my T-shirt.

Diego smirked. "Why are you sticking up for her? Revana's supposed to be your friend."

"She is, but sometimes she gets what she asks for."

"What does that supposed to mean?"

"She's not always a nice person." I sat on my bed to put on my shoes.

"Nice is overrated," Diego said. "It's not going to

get you anywhere in this place." He frowned at me.
"And since when were you nice to girls like Melany?"

I shrugged. "She's different. I like her."

"I'd like her, too, if she put out." He made a rude
gesture with his hips.

"Don't be an asshole."

I left the room without him. Diego and I had
been friends before the academy, same with Revana.
We all ran in the same affluent circles. We were all
from devout families, who had started our training
when we were young. Someone in each of our families had been called to the army in the past. For me, it
was my brother, Owen. Diego's uncle from Argentina
had been called thirty years ago. Revana's patronage
was even older—her maternal grandfather had
gotten the invitation mere months after her mother
had been born. So, I basically grew up around them,
but I was starting to realize that neither of them were
good people. If we hadn't known each other before, I
wasn't sure I'd go out of my way to know them now.

I hurried to the dining hall, grabbed some food,
and sat at a table near the main doors. I wanted to
see when Melany came in. Soon, Diego and the
others joined me.

"Why are you sitting here?" Revana set her tray
down beside mine.

"Change of pace." Taking my eyes off the main
door, I shoveled some food into my mouth.

Isobel stole a fry from Diego's tray. "I think it was
totally unfair Melany won along with Ren. It
should've just been Ren."

"She must've cheated," Revana said. "She hasn't

shown an affinity to water at all over the past few weeks. Last time, she couldn't even make a spout."

I sniffed and shook my head. "She didn't cheat."

She gave me a haughty look. "How do you know?"

"Because I was down there with her, and she was just better than everyone else. Me included."

Frowning, she turned to talk to Isobel, who was busy eating all the fries from Diego's tray. I didn't think he minded, though, because I was pretty sure he was crushing hard on her. He always looked at her like a clueless puppy.

"Hey, did you guys hear about New Athens, Kios, and Pecunia?" Trevin asked. "Supposedly, there have been some earthquakes around there."

"Where did you hear that?" Jonah frowned. I could hear the concern in his voice.

"Are you from there?" I asked.

"Around there. I'm from the town over, Histria."

"Someone snuck a cell phone in," Trevin said. "It's all over the news."

"Sounds like a bad rumor to me. No one would be able to sneak a phone in. No way," Isobel said. "Besides, they'd tell us if something like that happened to where we're from." She looked around at everyone. "Wouldn't they?"

"Of course they would." Revana patted Isobel's hand. The girl looked like she was about to cry.

When I spotted Georgina and Jasmine entering the dining hall, I got to my feet. "I'll catch up with you guys later."

"Where are you going?" Revana called after me.

I didn't stop until I reached Georgina and Jasmine. Surprise flashed across both their faces at seeing me at their table. I slid in beside Jasmine.

"What do you want?" she asked.

"Where's Blue?"

Georgina's eyebrows shot up. "She's back in the dorm, resting. The whole thing in the pool took its toll on her."

"What do you want with her?" Jasmine gave me a pointed look, which I didn't blame her for. I hadn't been the friendliest person over the last month or so.

"Nothing. I just want to see if she's okay."

"She's fine." Jasmine went back to her food and talking to Mia, who sat on her other side.

I guessed that was the end of that conversation.

I got up from the table, but I didn't want to go back and sit with Diego and the others, and I didn't want to return to my dorm room. I wanted to see Melany. After I did a drive by the food line and grabbed a couple of chocolate cupcakes, I headed out of the dining hall and toward the girls' dorm.

I didn't know how I was going to get past the dorm monitor, but I was going to give it a go. What was the worst that could happen?

I ran up the stairs and turned left toward the girls' dorm rooms. Before I entered the main corridor, I stopped and peered around the corner, planning my strategy. I could dissipate into the shadows like Erebus had taught us. I wasn't great at it, not like Melany, but I had improved. I just needed more shadows to move through; there was too much light in the hall.

I looked around on the ground and spied a small pebble. I picked it up, rubbing it between my fingers, gauging my aim at the light in the sconce along the wall. Taking a deep breath, I reared back and threw the rock. Like a targeted missile, it hit the light and broke the bulb. Shadows instantly filled that side of the corridor.

Before anyone could come investigate the sound, I streaked down the hallway, keeping to the darkness hugging the far wall. I concentrated on refracting the light, so if anyone peered out from one of the rooms, they wouldn't see me, not unless they really stared into the shadows hard, then they'd probably see some movement.

As I made my way through the dorm, I realized I had no idea which room was Melany's. All I knew was that she bunked with Georgina. But I did remember one time when Georgina mentioned that they were always the last ones out of the dorm in the morning. So I assumed they were one of the last rooms.

At the end of the hall, there were two rooms; one had the door open, and it was dark inside, and the other's door was shut, light spilling from underneath, and the sounds of some kind of thrash metal emanated from within. This had to be Melany's room. She was the only girl I knew who would listen to thrash metal.

I knocked on the door and waited, feeling nervous all of a sudden.

The door swung open to a scowly face. "What?" Then her eyes widened.

I held out my hand, a chocolate cupcake balanced on the palm. "I come bearing gifts."

She took a step out and glanced down the corridor. "What are you doing here?"

"I heard you weren't feeling all that well, so I thought you might need some sustenance."

She narrowed her eyes. "You know this is weird, right?"

I grimaced. "I guess. But we're at a school for demigods, I think weird is relative at this point."

"Good point." She plucked the cupcake from my hand.

I leaned in the doorway. "Can I come in?"

She opened the door wider and gestured with her arm. I entered, my shirt starting to feel a bit constricting at the collar. I pulled at it and looked around. Everything looked the same as my dorm room. I wasn't sure what I had expected. Maybe pink wallpaper and furry pillows, although Melany wasn't the pink and furry type at all.

I sat on the floor; I didn't want to be presumptuous and sit on her bed. She joined me, sitting cross-legged. She peeled off the cupcake wrap and took a big bite. Icing got on the tip of her nose, and I pressed my lips together to stop from laughing.

"What?" She gave me a funny look.

I reached over and wiped the icing off her nose, and then we ate in silence. It was nice to just sit with her and not have to make conversation. When she was done, she licked her fingers clean.

"That was delicious, thanks." She gave me a small smile.

As she fidgeted a bit, I took the moment to take her in. All of her. She was so different than the girls I was used to. The ones who I grew up with were poised and polished, cultured and refined, raised from day one to be a perfect specimen, devout to the Gods, loyal to family. I saw nothing like that in Melany.

I reached over and touched the dark tattoo winding around her arm. "What does this one mean?"

"How do you know it means something?"

"Because you don't seem like a girl who does things senselessly."

"The snake. It means rebirth, an awakening. It reminds me that I can be whatever I want to be. I'm in charge of my destiny."

"Says the girl invited by a mysterious metal box to train in an army for the Gods." I chuckled.

"Hey, I chose to come here. I didn't have to. The invitation is just that, isn't it? An invitation. It's up to every person whether to answer it or not."

I frowned at her. I'd never thought of it that way. Although in my family, there was no question about me coming to the academy. I didn't think I would've been allowed to say no.

I gestured to the others on her arms.

"It's two ravens intertwined. They're for my parents, who died when I was little. Some kind of accident I'm told."

"Oh, I'm sorry."

She shrugged. "It's fine. I was like maybe three or four. I was taken to an orphanage. Bounced around from foster home to foster home, until my mother's estranged sister, Sophie, discovered I existed. She adopted me when I was thirteen."

"That must've been hard."

"It is what it is. I try not to dwell on it." She ran her fingers over the last markings on her forearms. "And the skulls... well, I just think they look cool."

"That they do." I laughed. "What did your adopted mom say about them?"

"She was fine with them. It was the Demos family that hated them."

The name sounded familiar. "The Demos's?"

"Sophie worked for them. We lived on their estate."

"They have a daughter named... Callie, right?"

She gaped. "Yes. You know them?"

I shrugged. "A little. My father knew Mr. Demos. They did some business together."

She shook her head. "Wow. Maybe we crossed paths at one of their huge parties."

"I don't think so. I would've definitely remembered you."

She blushed a little, and I wanted to grab her leg, pull her closer, and kiss her. The urge raced through me like wildfire. I was surprised how potent it was, how potent she was.

Then another thought intruded. Something someone had said earlier in the dining hall.

"You lived in Pecunia?"

She nodded, her brow slowly furrowing. "Why?"

"It's probably nothing. I don't want to worry you."

"Well, you already have, so you might as well tell me."

"There's a rumor going around that Pecunia and a couple other places had an earthquake."

Her face paled, and I thought she was going to pass out.

CHAPTER THIRTEEN

MELANY

"*P*ecunia doesn't have earthquakes." I stared at him, hoping he had misspoke, and he was talking about some other town.

"I'm sure it was just a rumor."

I jumped to my feet, my mind going a mile a minute. All I could think about was if Sophie was safe. Who would be there to protect her if something happened? "You need to tell me everything you heard."

"Trevin said he overheard it from someone who had smuggled a phone in. That it was all over the news that Pecunia, New Athens, and Kios had suffered an earthquake." His brow knitted together. "I'm pretty sure it's not true."

"It's pretty random not to be true, don't you think?" My heart raced. I didn't know what to do, but

I had to do something. There had to be a way to confirm the information.

Demeter. She owed me one.

"C'mon." I slid on my boots, heading out the door.

"Where are we going?"

"To find out if it's true or not." I didn't wait for him to respond.

He caught up to me as I pushed through the main doors to the outside and rounded the corner of the building on the cobblestone path. Demeter was exactly where I'd seen her last time, leaning up against the wall and smoking some weed.

She shook her head when she spotted Lucian and I. "Pretty soon, my secret isn't going to be a secret."

"I need your phone."

She made a face. "Any particular reason?"

"I need to see the news."

Her face changed; it was subtle, but I'd seen it in the slight downward tilt of her lips. She knew what I was after.

"Is it true?" I asked her.

She shrugged. "Don't know what you're talking about."

"Look, I know you're a Goddess, and you could smite me in mere seconds, but I'm asking for you to be a human being right now and do me a favor."

I felt Lucian tense beside me. He probably thought I was insane to talk to one of the Gods like this, but I didn't feel like I had a choice.

"Besides, you do owe me one," I said as a last resort.

Sighing, Demeter reached into her back pants pocket and pulled out her cell phone. She handed it to me.

When I pressed the main button, a news video was paused on the home screen. I pushed play.

"The damage here in Pecunia is devastating. In all my years of news reporting, I have never seen destruction like this…"

The news reporter walked past destroyed buildings, half a cement wall still stood in one lot, debris surrounding it. Behind him downed powerlines sparked. He neared a street sign that was bent in half. I could read the sign though—Homer Avenue. I knew that avenue; I knew that corner block he was moving past. It was just down the hill from the Demos Estate. Callie and I had been there countless times to get iced coffees and cappuccinos.

Lucian set his hand on my arm; he'd been behind me, watching the video over my shoulder. "Are you okay, Blue?"

A sudden coldness hit my core. Was I okay? I didn't know.

I looked over at Demeter; she'd been watching me. "When did this happen?"

"Yesterday."

"Would you have told me? Told any of us?"

She looked me dead in the eyes. "What would have been the point? You can't do anything about it. It would have only interfered with your training."

I slapped the phone back into her hand, uncaring that she was a powerful being and could destroy me with a blink of her eye. "How do I get out of here?"

She shook her head. "You can't."

"I don't believe that. There has to be a way for us to leave."

"If you leave the academy, you'll be immediately expelled and have your memories erased, and you won't ever be able to go back to your home. You'll become one of the *lost*."

I made a face. "According to the news, I don't have a home to go to, anyway."

"Blue... she's right." Lucian rubbed his hand over my shoulder. "There's nothing—"

I pulled away from him. "I have to go. I have to make sure Sophie is okay. She doesn't have anyone but me." Tears welled in my eyes, but I wouldn't let them fall. I refused to appear weak in front of either of them.

Demeter pushed off the wall, grabbing me by the upper arms. "Listen to me, Melany. There is nothing you can do for her by going to Pecunia. The best thing you can do is to stay here and complete your training. Your training is more important than you can even imagine."

It was obvious she was keeping something to herself. The Gods weren't known for their forthcoming nature.

"Tell me why it's so important, and I'll forget about leaving."

She stared me for a long moment, then sighed, dropped her hands, and took a step back. She looked at Lucian. "Talk some sense into your girlfriend." She reached behind her ear, pulled out another joint, and lit it up. "I'd get back into the school before curfew." Puffing, she walked away toward the maze.

I wanted to go after her and demand to know what was going on, but I knew she wouldn't tell me the truth. The Gods worked in mysterious ways, my ass. They were just jerks.

"C'mon, let's go back," Lucian said.

When I didn't walk with him immediately, he grabbed my hand and pulled me with him to the main doors. He opened the door for me and we went inside. He took my hand again and I let him. It felt good to be touching him. It grounded me a little.

As we walked up the stone staircase to the dorms, Lucian stopped and turned me to him. "I might know a way out."

"How?"

"I need to know that you understand the consequences. That it is worth it to you."

"I have to know that Sophie made it out. She sacrificed a lot for me. I need to be willing to do the same for her."

He nodded. "I heard there is a network of deep underground tunnels under the academy leading to the mainland."

"Where's the entrance?"

"In the forge."

I frowned. "You mean in Hephaistos's lair?"

"No, like literally in the mouth of the dragon forge."

"Through the fire."

He nodded. "Yeah."

"This just gets better and better." I rubbed my

hands over my face. "Is this reliable intel? I don't want to be risking everything and find out I'm just going to set myself on fire."

"Dionysus mentioned it one night."

I grimaced. "Dionysus who makes poisonous potions and drinks them to see how they taste? That Dionysus?"

"He mentioned it one night when he was hanging out with some of the guys in our dorm. He told us it's how he gets out to visit his lady friends."

I shook my head.

"Hey, I wouldn't suggest it to you if I thought it wasn't going to work. You have to remember the Gods are trapped here, too. Of course they're going to know secret ways out of here."

"Okay, but I need to talk to him. I need to know exactly how to get out. Do you know where I can find him?"

Lucian shook his head. "I have no idea. He's not—"

Music suddenly blasted from the corridor leading to the great hall.

When we stepped into the hall, we were bombarded with the loudest, most heart-thumping bass. It actually brought tears to my eyes. Dionysus rolled toward us on one of Hephaistos's serving robots. He was perched on top of it like a crazed vulture with a black Mohawk and black eye-liner running down its face.

"Lucian!" He wheeled around us, laughing manically. "Melany!" He said both our names in long, drawn out syllables.

"I need to ask you something." I had to yell to be heard over the music.

"What?"

"Can you turn down the music, so we can have a conversation?"

"Sure." He snapped his fingers and the music died. "What do you want to talk about?"

"Is there a way out of the academy through the forge?"

His gaze whipped over to Lucian. "I thought we were bros. I told you that in confidence."

"It's important. I had to tell her." Lucian set his hand on my shoulder in solidarity.

"You know leaving the academy will get you an automatic expulsion."

"I know."

He eyed me for a long moment, rubbed at his nose, and then shrugged. "Fine, I'll tell you. But when you get expelled, I want your boots." He gestured to my feet. "They are rad." He reached into his jacket pocket and pulled out a small, dark purple glass vial. He handed it to me. "You'll need this."

After I got the directions from Dionysus, I wanted to stop at my dorm room to get my jacket and my backpack. Jasmine and Georgina ambushed us the moment we walked into the room. It was obvious they had been waiting.

"What's going on?" Jasmine asked. "Someone told us you were running out of the school." She eyed Lucian, as if he'd driven me to do something crazy.

I grabbed my bag and packed it with my stuff. "I'm leaving."

"What? Why?" Georgina grabbed my bag, so I couldn't pack anymore.

"There's something I need to do."

"You'll be expelled."

"I'm willing to face that." I yanked the bag back from her.

"Is it about the earthquakes?" Jasmine asked.

I didn't know how she knew, but obviously the rumors had been flying around. I nodded.

"Then I'm coming with you."

"No you're not. You're not risking your——"

"My family lives in New Athens. If they're…" She swallowed, not wanting to voice what we were all thinking since we heard the news. "I need to know."

"Give me your address. I'll find out for you. There's no reason for you to risk everything, too."

Georgina snatched the bag from me again. "If you want to truly sneak out, you can't take your bag with you. You have to go light and quick. And you can't go now while everyone is awake. You have to leave in the middle of the night. That way you'll have at least six hours before you're missed in class."

"Georgina's right." Lucian nodded. "It's too dangerous to go now."

I looked around at everyone then my eyes landed on Jasmine. "Fine. We'll go at midnight."

She nodded, leaving our room to return to hers. It was almost curfew, and Pandora would be doing her rounds soon.

I turned to Lucian. "You need to go."

"I'll meet you at the bottom of the stairs before the entrance to Hephaistos's foundry."

I shook my head. "You've already done enough, Lucian. I can't ask you to risk anything more."

"You don't need to ask. I'll meet you down there. I'll be your diversion if you need it." And he left before I could respond.

Sighing, I sunk onto my bed. Georgina sat on hers, opposite me. "Are you sure you know what you're doing?"

"No. But I have to go. I can't stay here, not knowing what happened. Earthquakes have never occurred in or around Pecunia before. Ever."

"You think it's something unnatural?"

I shrugged. "I don't know, but if something happened to Sophie and I could've done something about it, I wouldn't be able to live with myself."

She nodded, chewing on her thumbnail. "Do you think you can go and come back without being discovered?"

"I have to try."

She climbed off her bed, dropped to the floor, and pulled out a box from underneath. She opened it and took out a small wrapped bundle, handing it to me.

I unfolded the handkerchief to reveal a small, round, green mass, almost as big as a golf ball. The strong odor wafting from it made me wrinkle my nose. It smelled like moldy cheese. "What is it?"

"A pick-me-up. It's like drinking ten energy drinks without all the sugar. It'll give you a burst of energy and strength when you need it most."

"Did you make this?"

She nodded. "With Demeter's help. She says I have a real knack for handicraft."

"You definitely have a gift, and I thank you for this." I rolled it back into the handkerchief and stuffed it into my pants' pocket.

Georgina jumped onto my bed and hugged me so tight I couldn't breathe. "I'm scared for you."

"I'll be fine, Gina."

She pulled back and stared me in the eyes. "I had a vision during prophecy class. I realize now it was about you."

"What was it?"

"I was outside on the grounds near the maze with Jasmine and Ren and Lucian, even. A giant snake slithered out from the maze and chased us. It opened its mouth, showing razor sharp teeth that were black and dripping with poison, and tried to swallow us whole."

I ran my hand down her arm and chuckled. "I'm not going to be eaten up by a snake."

"No, Melany, I'm pretty sure the snake was you."

CHAPTER FOURTEEN

MELANY

I didn't sleep. I lay awake on my bed in the dark, not only thinking about what I needed to do to get out of the academy, but about what Georgina had said—that I was the snake that swallowed everyone up. I wasn't sure how to take that. It definitely wasn't a positive connotation. I knew visions weren't literal, but I couldn't see the positive in it at all.

At midnight, I rolled out of bed and got ready to go. I patted my pants pocket to make sure the energy ball from Georgina was there, and then checked my jacket pocket to make sure I still had the vial Dionysus gave me. My stomach churned, and nerves zipped through me. I wasn't sure I could do this. I might be leading Jasmine into the abyss. I might end up dooming both of us.

Georgina whispered to me in the dark, "Good luck. Don't die out there."

"I'll try not to."

I peeked out the door into the dark corridor. It was empty. Pandora normally did her rounds at ten, which was curfew, and two in the morning. So I had a two-hour leeway to get down to the foundry and find a way out through the forge. I hoped Hephaistos wasn't in his workshop. This whole mission might be for nothing.

Sticking close to the wall and the shadows wavering there, I crept down the hallway and out onto the landing before the stone staircase to wait for Jasmine. A couple minutes later, she ran out to join me. I grabbed her hand and squeezed it, and then we carefully crept down the stairs to the main foyer.

All was quiet. There was no one around, and I didn't hear anything out of the ordinary because of the ticking of the huge clock hanging over the main doors. On silent feet, we snuck around the corner and to the stairs leading down four levels to Hephaistos's forge.

It was pitch black down the stairs. There wasn't a trace of light. If we didn't have some kind of light, we'd definitely trip down the stairs and break something. I hadn't thought to bring a flashlight, since I didn't know where I would find one. This couldn't be what stopped us.

I looked down at my hands and considered them for a moment. Then I slapped them together, very aware of the sound it made, but it had to be done, and rubbed the palms together.

Jasmine gave me a wide-eyed look and mouthed, "What are you doing?"

But it soon became evident when a soft yellow glow blossomed between my hands. Slowly, I pulled them apart to create a small ball of fire. It was enough to guide our way.

Smiling, Jasmine gave me a thumbs up. We made our way down the stairs, each step illuminated by my homemade lantern I carried in my hand. At the bottom, we waited for a minute. Lucian said he'd be here, but I didn't want him to get into any trouble. He'd directed me to Dionysus; that had been enough.

I counted to three under my breath then tapped Jasmine's arm, indicating for us to continue on. We moved two steps before I saw a very faint glow coming from the stairs. Lucian joined us at the bottom, but he wasn't alone.

"What are you doing here?" I whispered, angry.

Ren made a face. "I'm coming with you. I have family in New Athens."

I shook my head. "No. I'm not going to be responsible for all of you getting expelled."

"You're not responsible," he said. "I'm perfectly capable of making a decision on my own. And I'm coming, whether it's with you or on my own. I'd prefer to go with you, though, because I'm pretty sure you know what you're doing."

Jasmine nodded in solidarity. "I'm with Ren."

I wanted to tell them I really had no idea what I was doing. Although Dionysus had given me directions, I didn't know what to do if they went astray. We could all end up trapped in the tunnels forever, for all I knew.

"Fine. Let's go."

We snuck up to the entrance to the foundry and peered inside. The eerie orange glow of the molten metal flowing through the narrow gutters throughout the room cast the only light. My gaze swept the area, searching for any movement. As far as I could tell, we were alone.

I looked at the dragon forge. It was a straight shot across one of the stone bridges and up a few rock steps onto the highest platform. "We need to go to the dragon forge. Follow me."

I hurried into the room, everyone following behind me. We made it across the bridge and were about to mount the steps to the platform when a clanging noise reverberated through the chamber. A voice trailed behind the metal clash; it was Hephaistos muttering to himself.

Jasmine stared at me. I stared back. She pointed to a rock jutting out of the floor where we could hide. She bolted behind it, followed by Ren, Lucian, then me. I peeked around the stone; if Hephaistos took the bridge, we would be spotted in a matter of seconds. Lucian must've realized the same thing because he grabbed my face, kissed me hard, then jumped out from behind the rock and ran down the bridge toward the fire God. My lips tingled from the kiss, and I ran my fingers over my mouth.

I went to follow him, but Jasmine grabbed my arm and jerked me back. She shook her head. I knew she was right. Lucian had provided us with a distraction that we couldn't squander.

"What are you doing here, boy?" Hephaistos's voice boomed.

"I have a question about blast cleaning and whether we're going to do that with our shields."

"It's midnight. Why are you asking me this now?"

I peered around the rock again to see Lucian guiding Hephaistos away from the bridge, getting his back turned to us. I gestured to the others to follow me on three. I put up my fingers... one, two three...

We dashed out from the rock, up the steps in two strides, and ran to the dragon forge. The heat from it seared my face. I suspected some of my eyelashes had burned away already. The acrid odor of burning hair filled my nose.

We didn't have much time. A few minutes at most. Taking in a deep breath, I put my hands out over the fire, having faith they wouldn't burn to a crisp. Fire and I had a deep understanding. I concentrated on lowering the flames. Slowly, the fire started to recede until there were only hot red glowing coals. Grabbing an iron rod hanging from the side of the force, I pushed the coals to the side to give us a clear path. We were going to have to crawl into the dragon's mouth. It was the only way.

I set the rod aside and clambered up into the iron forge. The heat was nearly unbearable, but I braced against it, and inched my way deep into the channel. I glanced over my shoulder to make sure Jasmine and Ren were behind me. They were, both their faces masks of discomfort. Ren looked pained, and I wondered if it was because he had an affinity to water and the heat and fire were contradicting that.

I kept moving, praying that Dionysus had given me good information. Another few feet and I saw an opening into the surrounding rock. That had to be the entrance to the tunnel. I crawled through the opening, and relief surged over me. It was a tunnel, tall enough that we could stand. For a few minutes, I'd feared we'd be crawling through the rock.

"Now what?" Jasmine asked.

"We walk through the tunnel, and then we should come to a V. We're supposed to go to the right."

"I hope Dionysus wasn't drunk when he gave you these directions."

I made of face. "Of course not." But he was. Disgustingly so. By the time he'd finished giving me instructions, he could barely stand up. Lucian and I had to help him back to his room. He sang some bawdy bar song the entire time.

We jogged through the tunnel; time was our enemy. We needed to get there and return in less than six hours. When we reached the V, we went to the right. The tunnel got narrower as we went. I wasn't claustrophobic, but my heart still picked up a few beats. After another fifteen minutes, I noticed my shoes sloshing in water, and I wondered if we were under the ocean. The thought made my heart race a bit faster.

Another fifty feet and the water rose to our ankles. Another fifty and it was to our knees.

"I don't like this, Mel." A tremor ran through Jasmine's voice.

"We'll be okay. We got Ren with us. He can make the water go away." I glanced over my shoulder at him. "Right?"

His eyes were wide, and he didn't look confident when he said, "Right."

Finally, the tunnel widened, and as we came out into a cave, the water receded. Now according to Dionysus, we had to climb some rocks to get to a door. To the right was a steep incline. I pointed to it.

"There. We have to climb."

I started up the slope thinking it was going to be easy, but it wasn't. There were a lot of loose rocks, and I slipped a few times. Jasmine almost slid all the way back down, but Ren grabbed her arm and hauled her back up. I scrambled the rest of the way up, relieved to see a small wooden door in the rock wall.

I turned the knob and opened the door. We all had to crouch down to go through it. Then we were inside a fairly narrow wooden structure. Tilting my head up, I saw there wasn't a ceiling, just a column of wood that went up one hundred feet. I reached out and touched the sides; they were rough against my fingers.

"We're in a tree."

"Are you sure?" Jasmine looked around.

Then the surface in front of us moved. A diminutive form emerged from the wood, its skin as rough and dark as tree bark, eyes the color of leaves. Tiny branches protruded from its head, almost like a set of deer antlers. It was a Dryad.

It blinked angrily at us and then spoke, its voice as

crackly as dried leaves. "Who are you, and what do you want?"

"I'm Melany, this is Jasmine and Ren. We're from the academy. We need to get to New Athens and Pecunia."

"No."

I frowned. "What do you mean, no? We've come a long way to get here."

"No. Go back. I won't let you pass. It's too dangerous."

Frustrated, I smacked my hands down on my jacket. Something hard jabbed into my palm. I reached into my pocket and pulled out the small glass vial. I held it up toward the Dryad.

"This is from Dionysus."

It plucked the bottle from my fingers, its eyes wide and hungry. "Ah, bless Dionysus. You may pass. But be careful, malevolent forces are at work." It stepped to one side to reveal another door.

I pushed it open and crawled out of the tree on my hands and knees into what was once a park. When I stood, I could see, even in the dark, the destruction the earthquake had caused. The grand oak was the only tree left standing whole and untouched. The rest had either been completely pushed out of the ground, roots splayed in every direction, or broken in half, branches lying haphazardly all over the place.

"Oh, my Gods." Jasmine swung around, taking in all the damage.

"Do either of you know where we are? I don't recognize it." I gazed toward the street running along the park to see if there was a street sign anywhere.

"I'm pretty sure it's Pan Park." Ren pointed to the left. "If we go that way, we'll run into Hegemone Lane, which will take us into the center of New Athens."

"Yes, I see it now." Jasmine moved that way, and Ren and I followed.

As we made our way through town, destruction surrounded us. It looked like a war zone. Buildings and houses were in shambles. Power lines hung from poles. Nothing sparked though, as the whole town had been shut down. There was no electricity. And as we moved quickly through the empty streets, we realized we were alone.

When we reached a gated neighborhood, the placard still stood, called Vista Heights, and Ren took off at a run. Jasmine and I ran after him. He stopped in front of a two-story house, or what should've been a two-story' there was only one level left. It was really dark and hard to see anything.

Jasmine found a discarded flashlight, but the batteries were dead. She held it tight, and I could tell she was doing something to it. A few minutes later, the light flashed on. She went up to Ren's side and held it up for him. He aimed the beam at the front door. Painted in red on the wooden door was a giant X. In the right quadrant, EVAC 5 was painted.

Ren let out a long breath of air. "They got out."

Jasmine put her arm around him, and they leaned into each other.

I was happy for Ren, but we needed to keep

going. We only have maybe five hours, and Pecunia was at least an hour away. "Jasmine, how far to your house?"

She shook her head. "Not sure. By car Vista Heights would've been maybe fifteen minutes from me. Walking? It will take over an hour."

"Okay, let's get going then."

As we headed out of the neighborhood, we came across a car that still looked in shape. It had a few dings, but all the tires were good. I checked inside and saw the key was still in the ignition. We piled in and I wrapped my hands around the steering wheel holding my breath that it started. It whirred a few times, my knuckles turning white from the tight grip I had, but then it kicked over. My sigh of relief was instant. I checked the gas gauge; it was near empty, but at least it would get us closer to Jasmine's.

Twenty minutes later, I pulled the car to a stop in front of a condominium complex that was partially intact. Jasmine sprang out of the car and ran around to the back of the building. The damage in the back was worse. Half of some of the condos were completely in rubble.

Jasmine dropped to her knees, her face in her hands. I could hear her sobs. I crouched beside her and wrapped my arms around her, my heart aching for her. "Don't give up, Jas. I bet your family got out. I saw red X's on a couple of the doors at the front."

"Jasmine?"

We looked up to see an elderly black woman with grey curls picking her way over the debris on the ground. Jasmine jumped to her feet and approached her.

"Lolly?" Jasmine hugged the woman. "What are you doing here?"

"I could ask you the same thing. I thought you were at some fancy school."

"I was. I am. But when I heard about the earthquake, I—"

Lolly rubbed Jasmine's back. "Your momma and daddy got out. Don't you worry about that."

Jasmine sagged in the older woman's arms, and my heart ached for her.

"What are you still doing here?"

"I'm on my way out. There's a van just up the street taking the last of us. I wasn't leaving without my Denzel."

I could see now the small dog squirming in her arms.

"What happened?" I asked her.

She looked over at me. Her face was haunted. "Still not too sure. I was in bed, when the whole building just shook. I got out, turned on the TV, and saw in some areas that the ground just cracked open. It almost looked like something big pushed out of the earth itself. It was the craziest thing I'd ever seen." She shook her head. "Then the building shook again. I guess it was aftershocks, at least that's what they said on the news. Then we were told to evacuate the building. I got out of my apartment just in time before it all come crashing down."

Jasmine hugged her again, little Denzel yapping from between them. "I'm glad you're safe."

"The van's just up the street. They'll take us all out of here."

Jasmine shook her head. "We can't come with you. We have to go to Pecunia then back to the academy. No one can know we were here, Lolly."

She patted Jasmine's face. "All right. I won't say I saw you, but I may just whisper in your momma's ear that you're okay."

We wished Lolly well, and then we got back in the car and drove out of the neighborhood and on to Pecunia. It was almost an hour drive between towns, and I wasn't sure we were going to make it ten miles with an empty gas tank. My gut clenched with worry.

I was right; soon, the car puttered then rolled to a stop on the side of the dark, empty highway. I slammed my fist against the steering wheel. "Shit."

"I guess we're walking." Ren got out of the back of the car.

I stayed put as despair took its hold on me. We weren't going to make it. There was no way we could get to Pecunia and then back to a portal in three hours. I questioned if I wanted to bother going back. They couldn't expel me if I wasn't there, could they? I mean, what would be the worst thing that could happen?

But I wanted to go back. I wanted to complete my training and become a demigod. I wanted to see Georgina. And I desperately wanted to see Lucian again. I rubbed my fingers over my lips, thinking about when he'd kissed me.

Frustrated, I leaned against the steering wheel. There had to be a way to get to Pecunia faster. As I leaned forward, the scent of old cheese wafted to my nose. The super energy ball in my pocket.

I reached in and pulled out the bundle. Georgina said it was like drinking ten Red Bulls. It was a pick-me-up. It had to be a worth a try. I unwrapped it and pinched it into three globs. I handed one to Jasmine.

She wrinkled her nose. "What is it?"

"Georgina made it. Supposed to give us a lot of energy and strength. Maybe we can run to Pecunia."

"Too bad we haven't had flying class yet. We could've flown there." She opened her mouth and plopped the wad of green dough inside. "Here goes nothing."

I got out of the car and walked over to Ren and gave him his piece. He put it in his mouth and chewed. He grimaced. "It's really gross."

I ate the last piece. It was gross. Tasted like dirt mixed with some dried grass. It was also gritty, as if it actually had some tiny bits of gravel in it. But almost instantaneously after swallowing it, I felt something inside my body. Spreading out from my stomach was a soothing heat. It soaked into every single muscle.

Ren grinned at me. "I feel pretty good."

Jasmine got out of the car. "Do you guys feel like you could bench press an elephant right about now?"

I nodded. I moved my legs up and down; they felt really strong. Energized. "I think we could run to Pecunia."

And we did. What would've taken us forty minutes to drive and hours to walk, we made it to my town in twenty-five minutes. Every muscle in my body tingled when we came to a stop in my neighborhood. It was amazing what Georgina had concocted. A superpower pellet.

As we approached the Demos estate, my guts churned. The front cast iron gate was still standing, but it hung open, holding on by one fastener. The beautiful trees lining the driveway were all broken and lying on their sides. I had faith the house would be somewhat intact. It was solidly built. But when we crested the hill, I saw I was wrong.

It was in shambles. Not one wall stood erect. It looked like a giant had taken his fist and smashed it. My heart leapt into my throat as I crossed the grounds toward the cottage. *I'm sure she got out with the rest of the family.* That thought spun around and around in my head like a carousel.

I was so anxious to get there I almost started to run, but I froze when I heard voices coming from the garden. I also heard the squawk of a police radio.

Ren and Jasmine came up beside me, and we all crept over to the hedge that was still in one piece, so we could see what was going on. There were three men dressed in black, and they had flashlights sweeping over the area. They were looking for survivors.

One of them walked over to the pile of stone and wood that would've been the cottage, casting his light over the debris. Then his light stilled as did my heart.

"I've found someone. I've found a body."

CHAPTER FIFTEEN

MELANY

*M*y knees buckled, and I would've fallen if Jasmine and Ren hadn't grabbed onto my arms and held me upright. Before I could form a coherent thought, a loud moan erupted from my throat.

"Noooo!"

Several flashlights swung toward the hedge we hid behind.

"Who's there?" one of the officers demanded as he walked toward us.

"We need to go." Jasmine pulled on my arm, but my legs weren't working. I wanted to beg her to just drop me and leave me here. She wasn't going to do that. Instead, she grabbed my hand and yanked me with her as she and Ren ran for the road.

The officers were in pursuit.

"Grab them!"

With a renewed energy, I made my legs obey me. We sprinted toward the main gate and the road.

Misjudging the debris on the ground, I tripped over a piece of one of the stone statues and fell hard to my knees. Scrambling up, I spied something shiny near my hand. I reached for it. It was a piece of a rope, a golden rope. I shoved it into my pocket as I clambered to my feet and continued to run.

Georgina's energy ball still lingered in my system, and I felt it powering up my muscles. I assumed it was the same for Jasmine and Ren, as it didn't take all of us long to dash through the iron gate and sprint down the road, the officers struggling behind us. They wouldn't be able to catch up on foot.

After we'd ran for twenty minutes, we stopped and took a breather near the destroyed strip mall I'd seen on the news report.

"Are you okay?" Jasmine put her hand on my shoulder.

I didn't know how to answer that. I wasn't okay, but I knew they both needed me to be if we were going to make it back to the academy. For now, while I didn't have time to process what had happened, I nodded. When I was alone, I knew I was going to fall apart.

Ren kept watch on the road. "Do you think they'll follow us?"

We got our answer when two armored cars came roaring down the road with a huge floodlight sweeping the area. We ducked into one of the shops that still had one wall standing.

"Damn it. What are we going to do? They're blocking the road to New Athens."

I gestured to another road, the one leading out of Pecunia. "We could go to Cala. It's closer. Maybe the portal's still open."

"Why would it be?" Jasmine asked.

"I don't know, but we have to do something."

Ren's brow furrowed ,as if he were deep in thought. "If it's not open, I might be able to create one. Poseidon's been teaching me."

We all agreed that was the best course of action, considering we didn't have many options and were running out of time. Although I was past believing we were going to get back to the academy undetected.

While the two vehicles drove slowly around, we kept to the dark shadows and were able to get out of the area and onto the road. Once on the open high-way, we ran as fast as we could, still powered by Georgina's superpower concoction. She'd make mad money if she ever decided to mass produce and sell it in the health food industry.

We made it to Cala as the sun stained the horizon pink. Dawn was fast approaching, and we didn't have much time. The first thing I noticed as we made our way to the pier was the town had been seemingly untouched by the earthquake. They still had elec-tricity and all the houses and buildings were undam-aged. Considering that Cala was only one hundred miles away from Pecunia and New Athens, it didn't seem possible they wouldn't feel the effects in some way.

The dock was eerily quiet when we arrived, not even the waves from the ocean seemed to be making noise. In fact when I stood at the end of pier nine and looked out over the water, it seemed unnaturally calm.

"Are we ready for this?" Ren asked.

"At this point, I don't think we have a choice."

Ren dove in first, Jasmine and I followed. The water was as cold as I remembered it from the night of the invitation—maybe even colder as it was the end of November. This time we didn't have a light in the water to guide us, so we were basically swimming blind. I hoped Ren knew approximately where he was going because I didn't have any sense of direction. We could be swimming in a circle for all I knew.

Eventually, Ren stopped swimming and just floated. Jasmine and I floated up next to him. It was obvious now the portal wasn't open for us, and Ren was going to need to try and create one. Even in the dark, I could see Jasmine start to panic. I reached over and grasped her hand to try and calm her down.

Ren moved his hands around in the water. It looked like he was conducting an orchestra. After a few minutes, a soft blue glow formed in front of him. It was working. He was doing it. But then the glow collapsed in on itself and vanished. Frustration marked Ren's face as he swirled his hands around again, in sharper, more precise movements.

Jasmine tugged on my hand. I turned to see her struggling in the water. I pulled her to me, put my mouth on hers, and blew oxygen into her. I drew back, and she gave me a thumbs up that she was okay now. I wanted to tell Ren to hurry because I knew it wouldn't last. My lungs were even starting to burn.

The blue light flared to life again, growing. A narrow whirlpool formed under the glow. Ren smiled as his creation came to be, but then his brow furrowed as his gaze darted everywhere, and his hands stopped moving. Something was wrong.

Suddenly, the whirlpool expanded until it had encompassed all three of us. Then we were violently thrust sideways through the water. The force of it sent all three of us spinning. We were being sucked through a portal, but I didn't think it was one that Ren had made.

After a few minutes of being catapulted through the portal, we came shooting up out of the water to land on the cold, hard rock of the cave. I knocked my head when I landed, making everything fade a little behind my eyes, then go sharp again. I rolled onto my back and blinked up into a few angry faces looming over me.

One of those faces belonged to Zeus. "Bring them to the auditorium. We will assemble the school for a tribunal."

Ares loomed over me and then yanked me to my feet by the back of my jacket.

The three of us were marched into the school like criminals. I was surprised someone didn't put shackles on our wrists and ankles. Jasmine shook so hard her teeth chattered. I reached over and grabbed her hand but was pulled away again. Ares looked positively gleeful with his role as jailer.

We didn't enter the academy through the front doors but around back to another entrance. Then we were led through several corridors I didn't recognize and through a set of wide double doors and into a spacious domed auditorium with 360 degree seating. It reminded me of an ancient coliseum where gladiators fought to the death for the amusement of the masses. And like those doomed gladiators, we were marched into the middle and left to stand there out in the open to await our fate.

"I'm scared."

This time I went and hugged Jasmine. "It's going to be okay."

"How?"

"I don't know, but I refuse to accept that this is the end."

Ren clenched his jaw, fighting back his fear. "I don't want to be expelled."

"Neither do I, but we all knew this could happen."

"How did they know?" Jasmine wiped at the tears welling in her eyes. "Someone told them. Do you think it was Lucian?"

I shook my head. "No. I refuse to believe that."

"It could've been, Mel," Ren said. "No one else knew."

Another set of doors opened, and all the Gods entered, lining up on the edge of the platform in a circle around us. Then through those same doors, our peers streamed into the stadium and sat in the raised rows.

I looked for Georgina and found her in the second row. Our gazes met, and she gave me a soft smile. She was probably beating herself up for letting me go on this ill-fated excursion. I wanted to tell her that it wasn't her fault. I would've gone no matter what she said or did. I was stubborn that way. She had to have known that by now.

My gaze then found Lucian. He sat not far from Georgina. His face was a mask of sadness and frustration, and it nearly broke my heart to see it. Someone had ratted us out, but I knew deep in my heart that it wasn't Lucian.

Zeus stepped forward into the center of the auditorium. "The three of you are charged with abandonment of your post. The punishment for such a crime is memory wipe and expulsion from the academy."

There was a collective gasp throughout the stadium. But I spotted one happy audience member. Revana couldn't stop smiling.

I stepped forward. "May I speak in our defense?"

"It's not a trial but go ahead." Zeus waved his hand toward me.

"The fault lies entirely with me. I convinced both Jasmine and Ren to come with me by telling them about the earthquakes in their hometowns. They wouldn't have ever known if it wasn't for me."

Jasmine bolted forward. "That's not true."

"Melany never forced us." Ren shook his head.

"I should be expelled, not them. They are great

soldiers. I've been nothing but a problem. You can ask any of the professors."

Ares nodded, as did Aphrodite.

"Not true!" Jasmine came up to my side. "Melany is the best of all of us. She can—"

Zeus put up his hand to stop us from talking. "I appreciate the strength you have to fight for your friends. You have won them a second chance."

Ren put his hands over his face and shook his head.

Jasmine was about to say something that I knew she shouldn't; I grabbed her hand and squeezed it. "It's okay."

"Nothing is okay, Mel. Nothing."

Zeus nodded to Ares, and he came over to me and Jasmine. He took her arm. "Let's go." He nodded to Ren.

Before she was led away, Jasmine wrapped her arms around me. "I'll never forget you. Ever."

I swallowed, not wanting to shed tears in front of everyone. No, I would shed my tears when I was alone. Which was going to be soon. I could handle the expulsion and never going back to Pecunia, but not being able to remember my friends or Lucian was a dagger to the heart. It was cruel and inhumane. I would do anything not to have that happen. I would suffer through any other punishment.

Ares led my friends off the platform and back into the crowd of recruits. Jasmine and Ren both took up seats by Georgina, who reached out and grabbed their hands. Solidarity. They were going to need it. I hoped they stuck together no matter what. They made a great team.

Once Ares returned to the circle of Gods, Zeus raised his hands, ready to pass my sentence. But I had one more thing to say before he condemned me.

"Those weren't earthquakes that destroyed Pecunia and New Athens."

A murmur rushed through the stadium. A few of the Gods glanced at each other.

"I saw the cracks in the ground. It looked like something pushed out of the earth. The damage was secluded to just those two towns and nowhere else. That's not how earthquakes behave."

I thought for sure Zeus was going to shut me up, but he actually looked interested in what I had to say. I reached into my pocket and pulled out the piece of golden rope. "I found this at my childhood home among the devastation." I held it up for everyone to see. There were some surprised whispers in the crowd. "It's not an ordinary piece of rope. It looks like something enchanted. Something magical. Something one of the Gods would possess."

That started a major stir.

Aphrodite stepped forward. "She's lying. She'll say anything to get out of her punishment."

"Why are we listening to this?" Ares bellowed. "She broke the rules. There isn't any room for discussion."

I noticed Hera, Apollo, and Athena nod in agreement. Demeter, Hephaistos, and Dionysus remained tight-lipped, which I appreciated. The other Gods looked beyond bored. Like they had a million other things to do today besides destroying my life and sending me into exile.

Zeus approached me and took the rope. He ran his fingers over it, frowning. "You found this in the earthquake zone?"

I nodded.

"It doesn't change anything, Zeus." Aphrodite approached him.

He met her gaze and it wasn't friendly. "I will decide whether it changes anything or not."

She returned to her spot in the circle with a pout.

"Melany Richmond, you have proven to be resourceful, resilient, and fearless. Three traits I admire, especially in a soldier. You have moved me to give you an opportunity to stay in the academy."

There was some clapping and cheers from my peers.

"You can't be serious?" Ares blurted.

Relief surged over me. I couldn't believe I'd convinced the almighty Zeus to give me a second chance. I met my friends' gazes and smiled.

"I will give you a choice." Zeus turned to the crowd as if to regale them. "Accept a bolt of my lightning, or be expelled and thrown into exile."

"No. She'll be killed!" Demeter bolted forward.

All the blood left my head, and I thought I was going to pass out.

I looked out at the crowd and saw Lucian on his feet. "Don't do it, Blue."

"No," Jasmine and Georgina both shouted. "Mel. It's not worth your life!"

I looked at my friends and Lucian. I never wanted

to forget them. The thought of it churned my stomach. What would I be without my memories of them, of this place? I'd be empty and alone for the rest of my life. What kind of life would that be? Not one worth living, that was for sure.

Swallowing down any fear I had, I lifted my head proudly. "I'll do it."

CHAPTER SIXTEEN

LUCIAN

I couldn't sit and watch this. It was wrong. I tried to dash out into the stadium—I wasn't sure what I was going to do, but I had to do something—but Heracles, who had been sitting in the rows with the students, grabbed me before I could.

"You can't stop it, Lucian."

"The lightning will kill her. She's not ready to control it."

"She's strong. Stronger than you think."

Zeus held his arms up toward the murmuring crowd, and a crack of thunder zipped in the air over head. "Silence."

That stopped everyone from talking.

"Everyone needs to witness the bravery of this girl, as she attempts the lightning trial."

Melany walked to the middle of the arena and

stood there waiting. She looked so courageous out there on her own, preparing to undergo the most dangerous and most difficult trial of the academy training. I wanted to go to her, hold her hand, hug her, and tell her how I truly felt for her before it was too late.

"During the trial, Melany will have to hold my greatest and most powerful weapon crafted for me by the great cyclops, Arges—the lightning bolt."

Zeus clapped his hands together causing a loud crash of thunder to reverberate through the stadium, making everyone jump. The floor shook from the power of it. Then he slowly drew his hands apart. In between them the air sparked and crackled, until he'd formed a five-foot long bolt of glowing white lightning.

I could feel the power of it, even from where I stood. The little hairs on my arms lifted, and I could taste ozone on my tongue.

Zeus stepped toward Melany, whose face paled with every step he took.

"She will need to pick it up and hold it for no less than two minutes. There have only been ten recruits in the past one hundred years able to complete this trial. And they have gone on to glory as part of my clan."

Rearing his hand back, Zeus stuck the lightning bolt into the floor in front of Melany. She jumped back in surprise. Zeus moved back and waved his hand toward her. "You may start."

A tense hush fell over the arena. I couldn't sit and watch, so I stood beside Heracles just on the edge of the main platform. I dug my fingernails into the palms of my hands to keep me grounded. Nerves rooted deep in my gut, and I felt nauseated as Melany took a step forward.

She closed her eyes for a moment, lifted her head, and I saw her lips move. Was she praying? I could've told her it was useless, as all the Gods were standing in this room, most of them indifferent to what was going on. No one was going to rescue her.

When she opened her eyes again, she took a wide stance, then wrapped her hands around the bolt, and picked it up. Her face instantly contorted in pain as the electricity shot through her. There were several shocked gasps in the audience. I looked over to see Georgina and Jasmine clutching hands, their eyes wide in horror as they watched their friend be tortured.

Seconds ticked by and Melany still held the lightning. Her whole body shook with the effort. Even from here, I could see her hands had turned red, burned from the heat of the electrical current pulsing through the bolt. I couldn't believe she still held it. By the looks on the Gods' faces, they couldn't believe it, either. Zeus looked practically gleeful.

After a minute, the glow of the lightning intensified, and sparks started to flare, and I wondered if Zeus had done that on purpose. But his face told me that what was happening wasn't anticipated. Frowning, he moved toward Melany. Was he going to put a stop to it?

Just as he went to reach for the bolt, zigzags of white lightning surged up Melany's arms. She opened her mouth and let out a blood-curdling scream as more waves wrapped around her body from head to toe until she was entombed in crackling white bolts.

People in the stands jumped to their feet.

"Stop it!"

"It's killing her!"

I tried to push past Heracles, but he held me firm. I watched in horror as Melany was consumed by the lightning. But then I saw something dark swirling around her; it was like black smoke curling up from the floor. It weaved in with the electrical current, surrounding her body.

Demeter broke ranks and ran toward the spectacle. "Put a stop to this. Now. You've proven your power."

Even Hephaistos and Dionysus rushed forward.

Zeus reached over and grasped the bolt in one hand and yanked it out of Melany's grip. The second that happened, she dropped to the floor like a puppet without strings.

Apollo moved out of the circle and crouched beside Melany. I could see him checking her pulse on her neck and then picking up her wrist.

I pressed against Heracles again. "Let me go." If Apollo said she was dead, I was going to hurt someone. I was going to make someone pay.

He nodded to Zeus. "She's alive."

"She did it," someone from the crowd yelled. "She held it for over two minutes."

There were a few cheers and some clapping, but for the most part, everyone was a bit stunned at what we'd just witnessed. I wasn't sure what to call it. It was supposedly a trial, but it felt like corporal punishment. Torture even.

Heracles smacked me on the back, but not as hard as he usually did it. "You see? She's strong."

"She could've died, Heracles."

His smile faded, and he bent toward my ear. "It was a message. You and your friends would do well by heeding it." He moved away from me.

"Take her to the infirmary," Zeus said, his voice no longer commanding.

Chiron pushed through the crowd that had started to gather around the platform, everyone craning their necks to get a glimpse of Melany on the floor. Once people saw him, they made room. Standing close to seven feet tall, the centaur was very imposing. Apollo gathered Melany in his arms and very gently draped her over Chiron's back, and then together they left the stadium.

"Classes are canceled today," Zeus said. "Everyone return to your dorms."

It was a bit of chaos as recruits and Gods and others streamed out of the auditorium. I caught up with Georgina, Jasmine, and Ren as they exited through the main doors.

"Do you think they'll let us see her?" Georgina asked.

Jasmine shook her head. She looked worn out. "I doubt it."

"I can't believe that just happened." Ren rubbed at his mouth, and then his voice went low. "It was almost like they wanted to kill her."

I looked at each of them, wondering if I should

tell them what Heracles had said to me. "I think we need to be careful from now on and don't trust anyone. Especially not any of the professors."

"Who do you think ratted us out?" Jasmine's gaze was pointed, and I assumed she suspected me.

"I don't know, but I'm definitely going to find out."

She nodded to me, and I hoped that meant she believed me. Because if she thought I had informed on them, then maybe Melany did, too, and I couldn't live with that. Especially not after what she'd just gone through.

"Jasmine!"

The voice came from behind us. Jasmine turned just as Mia shoved through a few people and launched herself at the other girl. She wrapped her arms around Jasmine and hugged her tight.

"I was so scared. I thought you were—"

"I'm fine, Mia." She gave Mia a soft smile.

We walked together through the corridor, and when we rounded the corner to head to the main foyer and the staircase to the dorms, Dionysus was there, leaning up against the wall.

"Lucian, mate, we need to have a little chit chat."

Ren gave me a look of concern, but I shrugged it off. "You guys go ahead. I'll catch up to you later."

"Let's go to my office."

I followed Dionysus down another hall, up some stairs, then down another empty corridor until he stopped in front of a very ornate wooden door. All the carvings were versions of him dancing, or singing, or engaging in some suggestive activities with what looked like wood nymphs. He opened the door and we went in.

His office was dark and cramped with all manner of things: velvet covered chairs, round wooden tables stacked with glass jars and small boxes, piles of books and scrolls, shelves crammed with bottles of different colored liquids, and herbs and other plant based things that smelled horrible. He gestured for me to sit in one of the chairs, and he sat behind a very heavy-looking mahogany desk. He leaned back in his chair and put his feet up on the desk. There was a hookah on the desk, and he took a puff. He offered it to me, but I shook my head.

"So, that was sure something."

"I didn't tell anyone about you, if that's what you're wondering."

He pointed at me. "That is what I was wondering. I'd hate to be tortured like your friend Melany." He made a face. "She did do well, though. Surprised the crap out of Zeus I'm sure."

"Someone did talk, though."

His eyes narrowed. "And you're wondering whether I did?" He drew his feet off the desk and leaned in toward me. "I can assure you, mate, that would be the last thing I would do. Do you honestly think we're not all ruled with the same iron fist? Zeus likes his power and likes to wield it on whomever he wants."

I sagged in the chair. Everything was starting to weigh on me, especially what had happened to Melany. I couldn't get the image of her suffering out of my mind. Her scream still echoed in my head. I knew it would haunt my dreams for a very long time.

"Look, I'm really sorry for what happened to your girlfriend. It was a terrible thing to watch. But she'll heal. Chiron is a fantastic medic. And with my potions, she'll be up and about in no time."

"I want to see her."

He put a hand to his chest. "I'm not sure how I can help you there."

I gave him a look. "How do I get into the infirmary?"

"You can go now, mate." He waved a hand toward the door.

"I'm not leaving until you tell me how I can see Melany."

He opened his mouth and made a sighing noise. "You're going to be the death of me."

"You're immortal. You can't die."

He waved a hand at me. "It's a figure of speech, saying just how annoying you are." He stood and walked to one of the shelves behind the desk. When he turned back, he had a silver flask in his hand. He gave it to me. "Give this to Chiron. It'll buy you a few minutes with her I'm sure."

I tucked the flask into my pocket and left his office. Before I went by the infirmary, I snuck by the kitchen and stole a chocolate cupcake. I wrapped it up carefully and put it in my front jacket pocket. When I arrived at the infirmary, there was a lot of activity nearby, so I had to wait. Zeus, Hephaistos, Demeter, Ares, and Aphrodite all came and went, bickering amongst themselves the whole time. After the corridor emptied, I quickly walked to the main door of the infirmary. I was about to slip inside when I felt a huge presence behind me.

I whipped around and came face to chest with Chiron.

"What are you doing here? You're supposed to be in your dorm. I'll give you five minutes to get lost before I—"

I thrust the flask toward him. "Dionysus sends his regards."

His eyes narrowed as he looked at me, then the flask. At first I didn't think he was going to take it, but then he snatched it from my fingers. He uncapped it, sniffing whatever was inside. "You have ten minutes."

I stepped into the gloomy room; the only light came from a couple of lamps flickered in sconces on the walls. There were twenty small beds in two rows, one on each side of the room. They were all empty, save one. I could see Melany's blue hair spread out over the white pillow.

She was on her back, and her eyes were closed when I approached. I took in the ashen pallor of her skin and the hollowness of her cheeks and my stomach clenched. As I settled on the edge of the bed, her eyes blinked open.

"Hey, Blue."

"Hey." Her voice was hoarse and she grimaced.

I picked up the cup of water on the table beside her bed and bent the straw for her, so she could take a sip. When she sat up, the sheet fell away from her neck and shoulder, and I saw the red puckered scars branching out across her skin. It looked like spiderwebbed lightning on her body. A wave of cold surged through me. I had trouble swallowing as I took the damage in.

"Oh, Blue…" I didn't have the words.

She lifted her arm to show me more of the scars that coiled from her shoulder to her wrist. "I'm told they'll be permanent." Her voice cracked a little, and she licked her lips. "I guess I'll fit right in with these Gods and monsters."

"You're not a monster." I wrapped a tendril of her hair around my finger and gave it a little playful tug. "You're still beautiful."

That made her smile.

"I'm sorry you had to go through that."

"Yeah, not how I thought my day was going to start." She snorted and then grimaced as her body shifted in the bed.

"Were you able to find out what happened to your adoptive mother?"

She swallowed, a few tears rolling down her cheeks. "She didn't make it out."

"Oh Blue, I'm so sorry."

I reached up and brushed her tears away with my thumb. I wished I could wipe away all her pain as easily. But I knew that it would be impossible.

I put my hand in my jacket pocket and took out the cupcake; it was all mushed now. I unwrapped it for her. "I know this isn't going to stop the pain, but it might help a little."

She took it from me. "Thank you. I'm starving." She took a big bite and icing stuck at the side of her mouth.

Chuckling, I wiped the chocolate icing off with my thumb, lingering a little longer than was probably wise. I licked it off my thumb, when what I wanted to do was kiss her long and hard.

We locked eyes, and for a moment everything fell away. I bent down to her mouth and was about to touch my lips to hers when someone coughed from the door.

"Time to go, Romeo."

Startled, I got to my feet and bumped her bed, jostling her a bit. She grimaced. I winced. "I'm sorry."

She chuckled. "It's fine."

"I'll see you later, okay?"

Melany grabbed my hand before I could walk away. "Thank you, Lucian. For the cupcake… and for helping me get out. It means a lot to me."

"You're welcome. Just get better. Hand-to-hand combat won't be the same without you to spar with."

I left the infirmary, feeling both joy and despair. My emotions were so mixed up about Melany I didn't know what to do. All I knew for certain was that I liked her. More than I ever thought was possible. And that was scarier than facing any of the Gods' trials.

CHAPTER SEVENTEEN

MELANY

J spent fourteen days in the infirmary before Chiron said I was fit enough to go back to my dorm and to resume my training. Fourteen days of extreme boredom and bland, unappetizing food. I was only allowed visitors for a few hours in the day, and I was thankful for the snacks my friends snuck in for me.

The first three days I spent lying in bed, unable to move much. I'd been mostly sedated during that time while Chiron tried to heal the scars networking across most of my body from the lightning. Pain had been my constant companion during those days. After that I'd been able to sit up, talk, eat, and accept visitors.

The first time Jasmine saw me with my brand new lightning scar, she cried. Georgina was a little bit more reserved, but not by much. Ren told me I looked badass. And Lucian, when he snuck in after hours, told me how beautiful I was.

I also received visits from Demeter; she brought me some books to read, and one time Hephaistos popped his head in, grunted at me, checked my hands to make sure they weren't too badly damaged and I could still work with fire, and then left just as quickly.

During the down time, I tried to get as much sleep as I could, as I was beyond exhausted, and my entire body ached. But it proved hard, especially since most times when I closed my eyes, I kept seeing the pile of rubble that used to be my cottage and hearing the voice of the police officer saying he'd found a body. Not being active gave me too much time to think. Too much time to cry.

By the time I went back to class, I was completely empty of tears.

My first class back was elemental. When I walked into the training facility, there were a lot of stares at my newly acquired, full-body network of scars and whispers behind hands. But to my surprise, there were also some high fives, even from a few people I was not expecting.

Diego approached me, a bit sheepishly, to my delight. "Hey Melany, I just want to say that what you did with that lightning was freaking hardcore."

"Thank you, Diego."

He held out his hand to me and I shook it. "And I dig your scar."

When he returned to his group at the water tank,

I caught Lucian's gaze, and I wondered if he had a little chat with his friend. He gave me a sly grin, and I returned it, with my heart fluttering a little bit extra.

"No time for making goo goo eyes, girl." I jumped back as Hephaistos poked me in the gut with the iron tongs. "It's your turn to make some fire balls; you're behind in the class."

I opened my mouth to say, "Hey, I was in the infirmary for fourteen days." But he shook his head. "I don't want to hear any of your excuses."

"Fine." I walked up to the main fire pit where the flames flickered up five feet in the air.

I lifted my hands, hesitant to spread them out toward the fire. Sometimes, they still hurt when I used them too much. Chiron had given me salve for them, and they were healing, but every now and then I got a sharp pain.

Taking in a deep breath, I opened my hands and thrust them toward the fire pit. The flames instantly danced toward me, as if they were greeting me. Saying hello, welcome back. I smiled and coaxed the flames to me, until tendrils actually wrapped around my fingers.

Jasmine and Georgina, who were nearby watching, gasped in surprise as I gathered the fire into my hands. I moved them around, caressing the flames, molding them into the shape I wanted. I kept at it until I had a sphere of fire between my palms about the size of a basketball. I looked at Hephaistos over the glowing red ball.

I saw his lips twitch up into a smile, but then he

immediately turned away and frowned at something someone else was doing. I couldn't win with him.

Pleased with the result of my firecraft, I bounced the ball in my hands, wishing I could toss it at something. Or someone. The prime target was glaring at me from across the facility. Revana was never going to be happy until I was either expelled or dead. I wanted to ask her, "Wasn't my torture enough for you?" Obviously it wasn't, as she still hate-stared at me like I'd stolen something from her.

My gaze then landed on Lucian. *Bingo. We have a winner.*

I didn't steal him, as he was a person and not a possession, but I was sure he wasn't her boyfriend. During one of his secret visits to the infirmary, I had asked him about Revana, and why he hung out with her. He'd told me because he didn't know better. But now he did. That had made me grin like a love-struck fool.

When we were switching stations to work with shadows, Lucian's group and mine passed each other. Lucian grabbed my arm and pulled me away from the group.

"I was going to mention this before, and I probably should have, but I didn't want to bring it up so soon after…"

"Go on. You got me curious now."

"When you were going through your trial and the lightning was wrapping around you, I saw… well, I think I saw a shadow protecting you. Putting some kind of barrier between you and the lightning."

I frowned. "You think Erebus protected me in some way?"

He shrugged. "I don't know. I'm just telling you what I saw." He ran his hand down my arm, then he returned to his group, and I went to mine.

Erebus materialized in front of us. Today, he wore a top hat and carried a silver-tipped, black cane to go with his gothic look.

"Welcome back, Melany." He gave a little bow.

I pressed my lips together in a facsimile of a smile. I wasn't sure if he was being sincere or patronizing. He had that arrogant air about him.

"Today, we are going to learn how to manipulate the shadows, to control them, not to just be able to camouflage inside them."

He held out his right hand, and after a few seconds, tendrils of darkness coiled around his fingers, then he circled his hand in front of him, and the black smoke made a loop in the air. Then he flicked his hand toward me, and that smoke loop wrapped around my wrist. Erebus flicked his hand backwards, and I was tugged forward by my arm. He'd lassoed me with a rope of shadow.

Everyone laughed as I stumbled forward.

Erebus closed his hand, and the shadow rope vanished, releasing me. "Get into pairs and practice. First, make the shadow rope, then try to catch your partner with it." Since we were only a mere foot apart, he turned to me. "You can be my partner, Melany, since the group is uneven."

I almost let out a disgruntled groan but kept it

bottled inside. I glanced over at Jasmine and Georgina. They both gave me concerned looks and I shrugged. Nothing I could do about it.

I faced off with Erebus. He gave me a creepy smile as I lifted my hand and moved it through the permanent shadows swirling around us. Within seconds, I was able to manipulate the darkness through my fingers, making a circle in the air.

Erebus nodded. "Not bad. You take to the shadows easily, I think."

Throwing it was a whole other matter. Every time I flung my hand forward, the smoke rope dissipated, and I had to start all over again.

Under Erebus's eagle eye, I created the smoke rope again, and this time when I threw it, I was able to get it around his arm. I almost threw a fist into the air. Instead, I yanked on the rope and moved Erebus forward.

He smiled and tapped his cane on the floor; we were completely cloaked in darkness, and he was only a couple of inches away. He grabbed my arm hard.

"Who saved you?"

"What? I don't know what you're talking about."

"During the trial. I saw the shadows shroud you. Without them, you would have certainly died."

I tried to pull away from him, but his grip was solid. His fingers dug into my flesh. "I don't know what you're talking about."

But I did. Lucian had mentioned the same thing. He had insinuated Erebus had been the one to save me, but obviously that wasn't the case. So who had?

"You're being protected, that much is obvious." His hand tightened around my arm. "But understand this, Melany Richmond, that kind of protection comes with a cost."

I managed to wrench myself out of his grip, then the shadows fell away, and we were visible again. Flustered, I looked around at the others, but they were busy engaged in lassoing each other. I didn't think they had even noticed we'd disappeared.

After class I wasn't sure if I should tell Jasmine and Georgina what had happened. I was definitely going to tell Lucian next chance we got to be alone, which wasn't going to be any time soon, as we were ushered to our next class. The art of flying, which was a special lesson of transformation training.

The training was going to take place outside, and the reason for it was immediate as Hermes flew in with large, golden wings flapping and landed on the field in front of us. As we all gaped in awe, he folded his wings behind him and walked toward us.

"Good afternoon. Welcome to flying class." Smiling, he looked at everyone. Out of all the Gods, Hermes was the most affable. He honestly didn't look much older than we were, and always wore a buttoned-up shirt tucked into khaki pants and a bowtie. His dark brown hair always looked a bit unruly, and he constantly tucked it behind his ears.

"Today, I'm going to teach you how to fly. I know this may seem like an impossible feat, but I assure you, it is possible for every single one of you. You are here at this academy for a reason. Because you all have Gods' blood running through your veins. And it's through that you will be able to fly."

Heracles joined us out on the field, and I got a little bit nervous.

"Now, learning to fly is really quite easy..." Hermes walked around then grabbed onto Diego, his wings unfurled, and they lifted into the sky.

Diego's face was comical, and I would've laughed if Hermes wasn't taking him up three hundred feet into the air. My stomach flipped over as I craned my neck and looked up at them, hovering in the sky. Nervous chatter rippled among the group.

"Vertigo ignites the fear of falling, hiding our will to fly." Hermes's voice boomed down to us. "So we must find our will to fly."

Then he dropped Diego.

Diego's screams echoed throughout the field as he fell. Before he hit the ground, Heracles was there. He caught him effortlessly and then set him onto his feet again. Diego leaned over and vomited.

Hermes fluttered back down to the ground. "Who wants to try?"

Everyone glanced nervously at each other. Then Lucian's arm shot up. "I'll go."

"Excellent."

Hermes grabbed Lucian, and they shot up into the air. My heart leapt into my throat, seeing him up so high. Then Hermes dropped him, and I put my hand over my mouth to stop the gasp.

Right before Lucian hit dirt, crimson wings popped out from his shoulder blades, and he hovered in midair. He hung there ten feet above us, looking like a God. A gorgeous, golden God who took my breath away.

Hermes flew down to hover beside him. "Well done, Lucian." He beamed at him. "Now, who wants to go next?"

Several hands shot up into the air.

One by one, each student went up into the sky with Hermes and came down with wings. It took a few people a couple of tries, but eventually everyone produced ruby-red wings, even Revana, who unfortunately looked like a stunning Goddess.

I was the last to go. I really didn't like heights.

Hermes stepped up to me. "Well, Miss Richmond, it's now or never."

Jasmine touched my shoulder. "You can do it, Mel. It's easier than it looks. Honestly."

I didn't want to disagree with her and tell her I didn't believe her one bit.

Hermes grabbed onto my arms, flying us up into the air. My stomach dropped, and for a moment I thought I might retch. But I kept it together, focusing my gaze on him and not the hard ground four hundred feet beneath us and sudden, crushing death.

"Are you ready?"

I shook my head. "No."

"Good. Then that's the perfect time to do something great."

He let me go. I plummeted to the earth.

I squeezed my eyes shut, not wanting to see the ground as it came up to meet me, and thought about flying. How cool it would be. How amazing I would be flying around. How I was made of the power of wind.

I thought it would take me mere seconds to reach the ground. But somehow I still wasn't there.

Then I heard loud gasps beneath me.

"Oh my Gods!"

"How is that possible?"

"Mel! You're breathtaking."

Slowly, I opened my eyes. I wasn't a pancake on the ground; I was floating in the air. I could feel the rush of wind coming from behind me, along my cheeks. I looked down at the faces gaping up at me, and wondered why everyone looked so stunned. Hadn't I produced wings like they had?

Hermes landed on the ground, reaching up and tugging on my foot. "Come down. Now."

Surprised by the concern in his voice, I flapped my wings once and then settled down onto the ground. He hurried behind me, touching my back.

I looked to Lucian. "What's going on?"

His smile nearly cracked his face. "Your wings, Blue. Look at your wings."

Twisting my head, I looked over my shoulder to see huge, luxurious black wings protruding from my shoulder blades. Black, not red like everyone else's.

"Uh, what the hell is going on?" I could hear the quaver in my voice.

Hermes lightly touched my shoulder. "You stay here." He turned to the group. "Everyone else, please return to the school."

Hermes then shot up into the sky and flew toward the outer building.

I looked at Jasmine, Georgina, Ren, and Lucian, pleading with them to stay with me, but they were herded away by Heracles. I heard a few people's remarks as they moved back into the school.

"What do black wings mean?"

"Means she's defective."

I recognized that voice easily. Revana was obviously getting a kick out of this.

A few minutes later, Hermes returned with Zeus and Aphrodite, who were all flying in on golden wings.

The moment Aphrodite saw me she sucked in a breath. "How grotesque."

Zeus walked around me, poked at my back, and ran his fingers over my feathers. That was a strange sensation that pulled at my belly. It didn't feel good and made me a bit queasy. It was probably going to take a bit to be comfortable with the fact that I had wings, let alone black ones.

After some more intrusive poking and prodding, Zeus stood in front of me. "You can pull your wings in now."

I did, the feeling of them receding into my body sending a shiver over the rest of me. "Do you know why I have black wings? Is it really bad? Am I diseased or something?"

He shook his head. "No, you're not diseased."

"Then why? Did I do something wrong?"

"We need to confer with the other Gods. I suggest you return to your dorm with your peers."

I walked toward the doors to the school, but instead turned left to go out into the school grounds. I didn't want to be bombarded with a million questions that I didn't have an answer to. I needed some time alone to figure it out. There had to be a logical reason why I had black wings and everyone else had red ones. Maybe it had something to do with what I'd endured during the lightning trials. Maybe it had literally burned inside my body.

CHAPTER EIGHTEEN

MELANY

I didn't really know where I was going until I rounded the corner of the academy and spotted the tall hedge maze. No one would think to find me in there. I'd gone through the maze once before with Georgina and Jasmine; it was a bit harder on my own. I ran into three dead ends before I found my way to the center.

The moment I saw the white wooden gazebo in the middle, I heard music playing, the strains of something classical. As I got closer, I spotted a man in a dark purple suit jacket and slacks sitting inside the gazebo, strumming a guitar.

He looked up and smiled when I approached. "Hello there, Melany."

"Hey?" I'd never seen him before. I would've definitely remembered, as he was strikingly good looking with sharp cheekbones, a strong jaw with a bit of scruff, and large, dark eyes under thick, dark eyebrows. He had dark hair that was swept back off his forehead and curled around his ears.

"How's your day been?"

I sat on the bench across from him. "Not so good. Been kind of weird." I tilted my head to study him. "Who are you, exactly?"

He stopped strumming and met my gaze. "Hades. Surely, you've heard of me."

Although I didn't want him to see my surprise, I couldn't stop my eyes from widening. A little rush of adrenaline spiked through my body. Hades was a legend. The ruler of the underworld had a bit of a reputation. I was surprised to see him here, as I didn't think he was welcome at the academy by the way I'd heard some of the Gods talk about him.

"What are you doing here?" I gestured to the gazebo.

"Playing a little guitar, chilling out a bit. I like to come here when no one is around." He ran his thumb over the strings. The sound vibrated against my skin, making me shiver. "What are you doing here? Running away?"

"I'm not running away. I just needed a little time to myself to think."

"About what?"

I snorted. "You ask a lot of questions."

"I'm a curious kind of guy." He grinned.

"Well, if you must know, I kind of sprouted black wings instead of red wings during flying with Hermes."

He laughed. "Oh, I bet Hermes lost his mind, didn't he?"

I smiled. "Maybe a little."

"Then he flew off to grab old Zeus and whoever else to confer about this shocking occurrence, I'll bet."

"Yeah, he did."

Hades shook his head. "Typical. And I imagine after a lot of poking and prodding and humming and hawing, they didn't tell you a damn thing, right?"

I nodded.

"That's why they don't like me around here, and why I've never been part of the academy. Because I tell the truth. I don't hide it away from you."

"And what's the truth?"

"That you're different. And it's awesome that you are" He played a few notes. "They're scared of different. Different upsets their status quo."

I eyed him, unsure if he was feeding me a bunch of crap. Although he'd have no motive to do so. He wasn't even part of the academy. And he was right. They definitely didn't like different.

"You should embrace your differences, Melany. It's what makes you special. It's what makes you powerful."

"Blue? You in here?"

I looked up to see Lucian heading toward the gazebo. I smiled as he approached. "How did you know I was in here?"

"I may have not gone back to the dorms and hung around waiting for you. I saw you run over to the maze."

I turned to introduce him to Hades but he was gone. I hadn't even seen him get up and leave. The only thing that indicated he'd even existed was a guitar pick lying on the stone bench he'd been sitting on.

"What are you doing out here?"

"I was just talking to Hades."

Frowning, Lucian's gaze swept the gazebo. "Hades?"

"Yeah, he was just sitting there, playing his guitar." I pointed to the bench. "We were talking about the academy and my black wings."

Lucian sat on the bench beside me. "Blue, I didn't see anyone else when I came around the corner toward the gazebo. Just you."

I grimaced. "No, he was right there." I pointed to the bench.

"I'm sorry, but it's impossible that Hades would be here. He's not allowed to step on school grounds. There are wards or something preventing him."

I got up and went over to the other bench and picked up the guitar pick. "Then how do you explain this?"

He shrugged. "Maybe it belongs to Dionysus. I've seen him around the academy carrying a guitar."

I shook my head. That couldn't be right. He'd been here. I'd talked to him. It wasn't a figment of my imagination. But maybe I shouldn't press the issue. I didn't want Lucian thinking I was any crazier then he probably already did.

"Maybe you're still tired from the trial. I can't believe you're actually walking around after that." He got to his feet and came toward me. "And today was—"

"Messed up?"

"I was going to say amazing. You have black wings. It's wicked cool."

I made a face. "It's not cool. It's weird. Zeus and the others poked at me like I was some science experiment."

He grabbed my hand. "It's not weird. You're not weird. You're... special."

Hades's words played in my head again. What was so special about me?

"I bet everyone else thinks I'm weird."

"Screw everyone else." He tugged me closer to him. I looked up into his face, enjoying the way the gold flecks in his eyes sparked. "I think your wings are sexy."

I made a face, pressing my lips together. My heart skipped a few beats. Flutters started low in my belly. "Sexy?"

"Yup." He ran his fingers over my shoulder. "I'd love to see them again."

I knew what he was doing. Making me feel better about my wings. Who knew Lucian was so damn sweet? I wouldn't have ever thought that upon our first meeting. I'd thought he was a bit of a jerk.

He pulled me out of the gazebo and into the open. "If you show me yours, I'll show you mine." His sly grin made every muscle in my body quiver.

"What if I can't do it without being dropped?"

"Just try."

I took a few steps away from because I couldn't

coherently standing next to him. I squared my shoulders, concentrated on what I wanted to do, and then closed my eyes. Within seconds I could feel ripples up and down my back, then a bit of pressure, then…

My wings unfurled out of my shoulder blades and spread until they neared touched the shrub wall. I grinned in triumph.

Lucian beamed at me. "They're commanding. Just like you."

"You think I'm commanding?"

He put up his fingers, spacing them an inch apart. "Just a bit."

Laughing, I pushed him. "Ha! You're a funny guy."

He took a step back, swirled around, and BAM! Out popped his wings. He flapped them once, and then they curled around him a little like a red shield.

I actually sighed at the sight of him. He looked more God-like then the Gods themselves. And I'm pretty sure he noticed because he grabbed my hand. "Let's go flying."

"What? I don't think we learned that part."

He shrugged, wings fluttering in the process. "How hard could it be?"

I hesitated for a moment, considering all the things I could've been doing. Sitting in my dorm room worrying about the implication of my black wings, or wondering why I saw Hades in the gazebo and Lucian didn't. And decided that being here with Lucian, about to fly together for the first time, was the most exciting moment of my life and one I shouldn't squander.

"Okay. Let's do it."

I spread my wings out as far as they could go and then flapped them once to get the hang of it. I flapped them again and again, and the power of it lifted me off the ground. Soon, I was hovering in midair over the gazebo. Lucian joined me.

Then I winked at him and was off like a shot. I could feel the power of flying surging through my body. It was euphoric. I did a quick glance over my shoulder to see Lucian easily catching up to me, a grin on his face.

I flew up as high as the spire on the main tower of the academy then zipped to the right and soared around the citadel, swooping down toward the training field, then up again. Lucian was right on my heels, never breaking form. He was gorgeous to watch, like a golden bird of prey, powerful and majestic.

He swooped in along my side, the very tips of our wings nearly touching. Together, we veered around the east wing of the school, past the dorms. If anyone had been looking out their windows, they would've seen Lucian spiral up into the air, like a blazing red and gold tornado. When he swooped down, he tapped my shoe, and then shot off toward one of the towers. *Tag. You're it.*

Laughing I caught up to him, as he landed on the upper most balcony of the academy. He folded in his wings just as I landed beside him. We leaned against the railing and looked out over the vast grounds surrounding the school. I spotted areas I didn't even know existed. There was an expansive wood over the horizon. The land looked like it went on forever.

"It's beautiful here."

"It is."

I turned my head slightly to see Lucian staring at me and not the view. My cheeks flushed at the avid attention he gave me.

"You're not even looking."

He reached up and stroked his fingers over my cheek. "Oh, believe me, I'm looking."

My belly flip-flopped and I swallowed nervously. It wasn't that I'd never been intimate with a boy before. I had back in Pecunia. But it wasn't anything like this. The boy wasn't anything like Lucian, and I never felt this kind of intensity just standing near him, with just his fingertips caressing my skin.

A shiver rushed down my body, and I trembled a little.

"Are you cold?" He took a step closer.

I shook my head.

He inched even closer, until we were just a breath apart. Slowly, he moved his fingers down and traced a line along my jaw. Then with one finger, he tilted my chin up and softly brushed his lips against mine.

I couldn't stop the tiny intake of breath, and he kissed me again, this time sweeping his tongue lightly against mine. The intensity of it, of him, took over, and I buried my hands in his golden waves and moved my mouth over his, tasting and teasing.

We kissed on that romantic balcony until the sun went down. It was positively perfect in every way.

CHAPTER NINETEEN

MELANY

For the next few weeks, we were pushed harder in our training than ever before, and also introduced to new classes like swordplay, war strategy, potions and poisons, earth science, healing, and animal handling. The start of the trials was only two months away, and we needed to be ready to endure them.

No one was sure what the trials would entail, but we knew they weren't going to be easy. I'd heard a rumor we would be pitted against one or two of the demigods in a battle situation, and we'd have to use our training to survive. Hephaistos had let it slip one night, when I'd stayed late in the forge to put the final touches on my shield, that I'd be using the shield during the trials.

Thankfully, I didn't need to do the twelfth trial—

Zeus's lightning—as I'd already suffered through a form of that one and passed—well, survived, would be a better term for what happened. I had daily reminders of that every time I looked in a mirror. Despite most everyone saying how cool the scars were, they reminded me of that night of the earthquakes and the devastation I'd seen. And my great loss.

During the weeks of training, I ducked outside to the maze every chance I got to see if Hades showed up again. But every time he wasn't there, more and more I came to the conclusion that Lucian had been right, and I'd imagined it due to overwork and stress. And I was definitely stressed, as we all were. Why my mind would conjure up the God of the underworld was beyond me. Why couldn't I imagine unicorns and rainbows?

"Oof." The blunted tip of Jasmine's sword struck me in the side. Again.

She frowned at me. "That's the third time I've gotten you. You're really distracted today."

Today? She was just being kind and not mentioning the day before when she'd knocked me on my ass with an overhead swing of the blunted sword. I'd moved too late and tripped over my own feet. Just about everyone in class had laughed at that. Including Ares. He laughed the loudest, as usual. His laugh was like a donkey's bray.

"Just thinking about the upcoming trials."

"Oh, I thought maybe you were thinking about the trips to the maze you make almost every day."

I pulled a face. "You know about that?"

"Yeah, Georgina and I followed you one time."

I should've known they would have.

"It always appears like you're looking for someone."

I shrugged. "No. Just taking some alone time."

Her eyebrows rose. "You sure you're not having romantic rendezvous with Lucian?"

She said his name loud enough that he turned and looked over at us.

My cheeks flared red. "I'm sure."

Except I was lying, and she likely knew I was lying, especially if she had followed me. Lucian and I had met up in the maze a few times and went flying together, always ending up on the balcony of the tallest tower to make out for an hour or so.

"Stop your chattering and do more sparring." Ares marched up to us, his brow furrowed in anger. "That's all you two do, talk, talk, talk." He made a flapping motion with his hand. "Talking isn't going to save you from a sword in the gut or a spear in the eye."

From nearby, I heard Revana's snicker.

"But it could save me from ever going to war in the first place." The moment I finished the last word, I knew I'd made a mistake.

Ares's face flushed beet red. He unsheathed the sword, his very real sword, at his waist and swung it toward my side. I drew up my shield just in time before his sword sliced off a nice thick chunk of my right flank. The tempered steel blade clashed against the metal of my shield. The sound reverberated through the gymnasium and vibrated over my skin.

He took a step back and swung quickly at my head. I blocked that blow, as well. Then he pivoted and thrust at me again. I blocked with my shield. The power of his blow traveled down my arm. He wasn't messing around.

Another thrust, jab, and overhead swing. I blocked them all, but barely. My arms ached from holding up the heavy shield and moving it to protect myself from being sliced in half. He came at me again and again, so hard and quick, that some of my peers were shouting at him to stop.

"Someone do something."

I heard Lucian's voice in the mix.

"Stop Ares! You're going to hurt her."

But he didn't stop. I'd obviously pushed him too far.

As he pivoted back on his foot to get another swing in, I dropped the shield to the side, formed a ball of fire in my hand, and threw it at him. He tried to duck out of the way, but the fire singed him across his arm. The sound of his skin crackling made my skin crawl. The stench filled my nose and my stomach roiled.

I stood there, gasping for breath, my heart pounding so hard my chest ached, glaring at him, and defying him to cut me down. I was through being a target of his vindictive anger.

But he didn't run me through with his sword. He met my gaze straight on and then gave me a curt nod. "Class dismissed."

I let out the breath I was holding, and nearly

collapsed onto my knees, but I didn't want to give him the satisfaction.

Jasmine and Georgina were instantly at my side. Georgina took my shield.

"Holy crap. Are you okay?" Jasmine put her arm around me.

I nodded but had a feeling when the adrenaline stopped pumping through me, I was going to crash big time.

Mia joined us. "I can't believe he can do that. He almost killed you."

"Well, there's not anyone we can tell." Georgina shrugged. "It's not like we can call our parents. We don't have families anymore."

I looked at her. "We're family now. We have to look out for each other."

She nodded. "Can you be like the father of this family? You're way more in charge then I ever could be."

That made all of us laugh, as we made our way out of the gymnasium and back to the dorms. I caught Lucian's gaze on the way out, and he gave me a soft smile. It made my belly flutter, as his smiles always did.

Before we reached the dorms, Ren caught us. "Hey, I heard Dionysus is putting on a show in the north hall. Should be quite the party."

"Is this an academy sanctioned party?" Georgina asked.

Ren smirked. "Probably not. Which is why it's going to be awesome." He slung an arm around my shoulders. "You of all people could use a good party. I mean, you almost died today. Again."

I snorted. "That's true."

After a quick shower and change of clothes, Georgina, Jasmine, and I met up with the others in the north hall. Music was already thumping before we even rounded the corner. As promised, Dionysus was DJing some epic beats, and there was food and drink a plenty, served by Hephaistos's little wooden robots on wheels. Laser lights danced around to the music.

I grabbed a plate of food and a drink and then commandeered a sitting area, which consisted of a sofa and bean-bag chair just off the makeshift dance-floor to eat. Georgina, Jasmine, Mia, Ren, and Marek joined me, all cramming in the space together. I looked around for Lucian but didn't see him. Disap-pointment flooded me. Despite our stolen moments in the maze, we hadn't had a lot of opportunity to socialize, especially in a group. I honestly didn't even know if he wanted people to know we were… I didn't even know what to call it. It's not like we were dating, the academy wasn't a place to date in. A relationship would've been too serious. I guess we were hanging out together. I really hoped he didn't want to hide that. I was already feeling pretty raw from the Ares incident I didn't want my whole heart torn out by Lucian's rejection.

After eating, Mia grabbed Jasmine's arm and pulled her out onto the dancefloor. I loved that Mia had been slowly urging Jasmine out of her shell.

She'd been guarded before, but with Mia she let those walls down.

After watching them dance for a song, I couldn't resist getting out there myself, and I pulled everyone out there with me. We all deserved a chance to just let go and have some fun. It wouldn't be long before things got really serious and after the trials, some of us might even be kicked out if we didn't pass. There were twelve of them, and everyone had to pass at least eight to be considered for placement in a clan.

On the floor, I closed my eyes and let the music take over. Every thump of the bass oscillated through my body. It was like the music originated inside me. It was vibrant and exciting, and I couldn't stop smiling as I moved to the beat. Bodies pressed against mine, as we all jumped and gyrated. Then I felt a hand on my waist. Opening my eyes, I twirled around to find Lucian swaying his body next to me.

My grin nearly split my face it was so wide. Overjoyed he was here, I moved in closer to him and wrapped my arms around his neck. He settled his hands at my waist, and we danced together, our bodies in perfect rhythm. I knew we were getting looks, but I didn't care, and he didn't seem to, either.

We danced and laughed into the late hours. It was the best night of my life. When he ran off with Ren and a few others to check out Dionysus's music collection, I decided to duck out to get some air. Dionysus had used too much dry ice in the smoke machine, and it had clogged in my nose and throat.

I left the hall and stepped out into the main lobby. There were a few students gathered here and there in small groups. I moved around them, heading toward a small alcove containing a stone bench. But when I neared it, I realized it was occupied by Jasmine and Mia. They were sharing an intimate kiss. They both looked up as I approached.

"Oops, sorry." I put up my hand to excuse myself, making an abrupt right turn and out into the dark corridor nearby, smiling to myself. I was so happy Jasmine had found someone in this place.

I kept walking until I was alone and found a bench to sit on. I'd been there no more than five minutes before I heard footsteps as someone approached. Revana stepped into a pool of moonlight that radiated through one of the big arched windows high above.

"Did you actually follow me out here? That's a bit creepy, don't you think?"

"You think you're so clever."

I got to my feet. I had a feeling this wasn't just going to be a social call. "Yeah, pretty much."

"Lucian just feels sorry for you, you know? That's the only reason he's slumming it with you."

"Maybe." I shrugged. "But he's still with me and not you."

"For now." Her eyes narrowed. "I've had him before. I'll have him again. We were meant to be together."

"Whatever, Revana." I was going to have to pass by her to return to the hall. "Have your little fantasy. Doesn't bother me any." I walked toward her with every intention of just brushing past her.

But she had other plans.

She grabbed my arm, turning me slightly. With her other hand, she tried to punch me in the face, but I sensed it coming and blocked her blow, countering with a strike to her midsection. It wasn't a hard blow, just a reminder to her that she shouldn't test me. I was better at hand to hand then she was.

"Walk away, Revana." I stepped back onto my left foot, preparing to fight if she provoked me any further. "This is a fight you won't win. I guarantee you that."

I thought for one moment, she was going to stand down, but then she flicked her wrist, and there was a small dagger in her hand. I didn't know where she'd had it stashed, but I knew she'd become proficient with knives, as she'd done some special training with Ares when he saw that she had an affinity to them.

"What? Are you going to kill me?"

"No, I'd get expelled for that." She spun the dagger expertly in her hand. "I'm just going to add to the ugly scars you already have."

She was skilled enough to wound me before I could disarm her. I had to find another way out of this. I cast my gaze around, sensing the shadows creeping along the walls and floor. I wasn't sure if I was doing it or someone else was, but soon we were cloaked in darkness.

"Coward!"

Revana's voice faded into the background, muffled by the thick murkiness of the air.

Not completely confident of where I was going, I took a few steps to the left, hoping to pass by Revana and escape the corridor. After another few steps, I realized the ground beneath my shoes felt different. I was no longer walking on tile, but spongey grass.

I took another few steps forward and waved my hands in front of me. The shadows dissipated to reveal I was out in the center of the maze and not in the academy at all.

"Well done. I didn't think you'd be able to transport through the shadows, but you've proven me wrong."

I whipped around to see Hades sitting on the stone bench in the gazebo, as nonchalant as could be.

I walked toward him. "Did you bring me here?"

"I merely sent the darkness to you. You decided what to do with it."

Another thought popped into my mind. I remembered something Lucian had said to me before. "Did you save me from being electrocuted by Zeus's lightning?"

He tilted his head as he regarded me. "And what if I did? What would you say?"

I shrugged. "Thank you, I guess."

He laughed. "Yes, perfect." He stood and came toward me. "I like you, Melany. You have a lot of feistiness. It'll serve you well in the days to come."

"What days? What do you mean?"

Before he could answer, he stepped into a circle of darkness and sunk into it, like quicksand, and vanished.

CHAPTER TWENTY

MELANY

I didn't tell anyone about the confrontation with Revana and the subsequent transporting through the shadows and talking with Hades in the maze. One, I didn't want to make the situation worse with Revana—besides that, I wasn't a snitch— and two, I didn't want to have to explain seeing Hades, a God who wasn't supposed to be allowed on school grounds. That would lead to too many questions, especially the one I didn't have an answer for— what was Hades's interest in me?

I put it all in the back of my mind as I buckled in for long, hard training. It was crunch time. We had only a couple of weeks until the trials.

Every day, I worked hard in my classes, even clocking in extra time in the evening before curfew, especially in animal handling class with Artemis and prophecy with Apollo, well, not directly with Apollo, but with Pythia, his assistant. I was having trouble wrangling and riding the fire-breathing horses in the stable. I'd had some luck with the griffin, and I once rode one of the unicorns, but the fire-breathing horses were the most powerful out of all the beasts. I wanted to learn how to tame them.

In prophecy class, Pythia helped me with divination. She told me that I'd never be able to do it until I learned to open myself up. During one extra practice, she'd tried to read into my past.

We sat across from one another in simple wooden chairs, knees touching. She held out her long, gnarled hands. "Take my hands."

I did, but not without wincing, as they felt like old, wrinkled leather. I felt bad, but I knew she couldn't see me. She was blind. She was self-conscious about her deformity, so she wore a gray blindfold around her face, where her eyes once were.

She clutched my hands, her twisted, claw-like nails digging into my skin. "You must learn to open your mind to others, so you in turn can see into theirs. You are too guarded."

I twisted my neck, the bones cracking from stiffness, and tried to relax. Closing my eyes, I attempted to empty my mind of all my worries, and there were many. I thought of calm water and light breezes. I imagined sitting in the garden back home listening to the chickadees chirp from the nearby trees.

"Relax your mind. If you can't, you will not pass the trial."

Her voice sounded far off as I started to drift. In

my mind, I was floating on a sea of white, fluffy clouds. It was so peaceful, and I wondered if I could stay there awhile. But those fluffy clouds turned dark, and I shot downwards, landing on the ground. It was day, hot; the land looked like a desert wasteland. Then I saw a woman, a tall, slender, pretty woman with purple eyes. Her face was a mask of fear as she ran from a mob of people who wore robes and carried large stones.

The mob yelled at her as they chased her, calling her monster and witch. Then they started to throw the stones. She was hit in the body and head and face. Eventually, she stopped running as her legs gave out. On the ground, she tried to protect her head, as more stones flew at her. But she couldn't stop them from hitting her face. Blood poured down her cheeks to drip on the sand beneath her.

Opening my eyes, I gasped, realizing what I'd witnessed. The woman had been Pythia, and this was how she'd lost her eyes.

She squeezed my hands. "Yes. Good. Now open for me."

I pulled away from her memory and tried to empty my mind again to let her in.

I watched as her face contorted and twisted. Her brow furrowed deeply, her whole body twitching. She squeezed my hands so tight they hurt.

Then she cried out and flinched backward, nearly falling out of her chair.

"What is it?"

She shook her head and put a trembling hand to her chest. "You must go."

"Why? What happened? What did you see?"

"Please, just go."

I stood, but I needed to know. "What did you see? Please tell me."

"I saw nothing. Just darkness…"

That couldn't be all that bad. Maybe she just couldn't get into my past.

"And death."

A shiver rushed down my back, as I left the classroom. I didn't know what Pythia meant when she said death, but maybe she'd seen the destruction I'd seen on the trip back to Pecunia. That would've been a very strong memory for me.

When I returned to my dorm room, Georgina was already asleep. I crawled into bed and lay there, staring up at the ceiling. The whole thing had unnerved me. I wasn't sure I could sleep without seeing Pythia's past. But eventually, I got so tired I just passed out.

One day blurred into the next until it was time for the trials. I was excited but scared that I wasn't going to pass enough of them to be able to stay at the academy. I did have a slight advantage though, in that I only needed to pass seven more trials, as I'd already went through the lightning ordeal. Despite not knowing what each trial entailed, I was confident I would pass anything to do with flying, fire, and hand-to-hand combat. I was pretty good with a bow now, and I could make a decent sleeping potion without killing anyone. I'd also proven myself in the water. It all depended on what we had to do in each trial. I suspected a few of them weren't going to be straight forward.

The night before the big day, we were allowed to spend it however we wanted to prepare. I spent it alone, walking through the maze. There was something about the place that settled my mind. It was like a kind of peace enveloped me. Maybe it was the darkness or the quiet. Whatever it was, I soaked it in as I sat inside the gazebo with my turbulent thoughts.

"So, I kind of feel like you're on my side somehow." I glanced around, hoping Hades would show. "Tomorrow is a huge day, and I'm... I'm afraid. I could really use a pep talk." I stood and walked over to the bench he'd perched on before. "Any words of wisdom? Any advice? A hug? I could use all of those things right about now." Laughing, I rubbed my hands over my face. "Mel, you are officially losing it."

"Who are you talking to?"

I whirled to see Lucian walking toward the gazebo. "No one. Myself, I guess." I shrugged.

He stepped up to me and grabbed my hand. "Do you want to go flying?"

"No." I shook my head. "Could you just hold me?"

He tugged me to him and wrapped his big arms around me, cuddling me close. I lay my head against his chest and inhaled, breathing the scent of him in. I was always surprised at how good he smelled. Like wood and pine, with just a touch of mint because of the gum he always chewed.

"You know, we might have to go against each other in the trials."

His hand on my back stilled. "I know."

"If given a choice, though, I won't fight against you. I'll pick someone else."

"Me too."

"I do hope I get a chance to fight Revana, though."

He chuckled and ran a hand over my head. "That I would love to see."

I raised my head to look at him. Going on my tiptoes, I brushed my lips against his. I couldn't think of a better way to spend the rest of the night—kissing Lucian until the sun started to pinken the sky and my lips got sore.

CHAPTER TWENTY-ONE

MELANY

*A*t 6 a.m., a trumpet-like horn sounded through the dorms.

It was a call to action.

I was already awake, having forgone sleep. I was wired and ready to go.

We all gathered in the great hall. Up on the dais, all twelve Gods looked out over their recruits. Zeus stepped forward to speak.

"Today marks the first day of the Trials. For the next twelve days, you will be engaged in the hardest tasks you've ever had to do thus far in your training. Each trial will last one day, and when you are not active in the trial, you will be in your dorm rooms resting. There will be no socializing, except with your dorm mates during the trials. Anyone caught outside of their dorm during rest time will be automatically expelled. No exceptions." His gaze landed directly on me.

He didn't have to worry; I had no plans to screw this up.

"These trials are created to best showcase the skills you've learned over the course of your training and to weed out the weak. Each trial is specialized to each God clan. How well you do in each of them will determine which clan you will be relegated to at the end of your first year here at the academy. To stay in the academy, you must pass no less than eight trials. Before each trial, you will be informed on what constitutes a pass and a failure. No two trials are the same in that regard."

Nerves vibrated through me. I hated I didn't know what to expect at each of the trials. It would be easier to know if we had to fight against each other, or against others. I could strategize better. As of right now, I didn't know what the hell I was going to do. But I supposed neither did anyone else. It put us all on a level playing field.

"You will be given specialized nourishment every day to keep your bodies strong and your minds sharp. I suggest you eat and drink what is given to you, as you will not have access to anything else throughout the twelve days.

"After your nourishment, which will be passed out shortly, meet out on the north training field at the sound of the horn.

"Good luck to all of you!"

He stepped back, and all of the Gods filed out of

the room, as several of the serving robots rolled in, accompanied by Chiron and Heracles.

"Form three lines," Heracles bellowed.

We scrambled to get in the lines, as a protein bar and bottle of water were passed to each of us. I looked at the small bar and thought, *This is all we get?* I ate the bar; it tasted horrible but had a hint of cinnamon to make it at least edible. Then I washed it down with the water, which had a bitter tang to it.

After about five minutes, I started to feel a heat spread throughout my body. Eventually, my muscles felt stronger and bigger. My mind felt clearer. I smiled at Jasmine and Georgina, whose faces lit up with the same sensation I'd experienced.

"Damn. That's better than drugs."

The horn sounded, and we all exited the academy and gathered on the north training field as instructed. Hephaistos was there, waiting for us. All of our shields were resting up against a wooden rack like the one in the forge. Artemis stood beside him, as did Ares, albeit on the other side of Artemis. It was the first time I'd seen Hephaistos and Ares in the same area together.

"I'm not going to make some grand speech. It's pointless." Hephaistos hobbled forward. "You've essentially been training for this trial the entire time you've been in the forge. The shields you have created will be the determining factor whether you pass or not."

That sent a concerned murmur through the group.

"Shut it. If you hadn't already figured that out, you're stupid."

I couldn't stop the bubble of laughter erupting. Both Jasmine and Georgina whipped their heads around and gaped at me.

"Melany Richmond," Hephaistos bellowed. "You may as well step forward and get this trial started."

Oh shit.

A path was made for me, and I stepped out from the group and onto the field.

Ares smirked and shook his head.

"Grab your shield."

I ran to the rack, found my shield, and attached it to my arm. I looked at Hephaistos for the rest of the instructions.

"Now don't get hit."

I looked around wildly. "From what?"

Artemis raised her arms, her bow strung with a long, sharp arrow. Fire erupted between Hephaistos's hands. Ares unsheathed his sword.

Oh shit.

"Start at the end of the field and run back here. If you can make it without being hit by an arrow, struck by a sword, or burned by fire, with your shield intact, you'll pass."

I ran as fast as I could down the field. Once I reached the end where a red flag was planted, I took a deep breath, made sure my shield was secure, and then ran toward the chaos.

I hadn't even taken two steps before two arrows rained down on me. I blocked them both, the arrow-

heads pinging off my shield, and continued on. A fireball came next. It hit my shield, exploded, but I was
safe behind it. All that sizzled were the ends of my hair.

I kept pressing forward. More arrows came; I
blocked them from hitting me in the legs and arms
and head. Other fireballs also soared through the air
toward me. Some hit the ground where I'd just been,
and others exploded over my shield. Then they came
at the same time, and I had to do some fancy maneuvering and dodging, so I didn't get an arrow through
the shoulder and a fireball at my head. Hearing my
friends cheering me on buoyed my step, and I kept
running even faster.

As I got closer to the finish line, Ares came
sprinting out toward me, his sword arched back. He
swung at me, and I blocked it with my shield. He
swung at me again, and again, and again. I had a
sense he was going a little harder on me.

I blocked his next hard overhead blow and then
pushed up with my shield, shoving him off balance. I
sprinted like a cheetah to the finish line. When I
crossed it, just about everyone cheered. Hephaistos
greeted me and took my shield to inspect it.

Ares stormed back, his face beet red. "She
cheated! She should fail!"

Hephaistos didn't even acknowledge him but
continued to inspect the integrity of the metal of my
shield. He nodded. "Not a dent. Congratulations, you
passed."

Ares sputtered. "She cheated. I'm going to bring
it up to—"

Hephaistos's large, beefy hand around Ares's

throat stopped his words. "Don't tell me how to run my trial." Then he shoved the God of War away.

Still red-faced, almost purple really, Ares stormed off the training field. I didn't know what stunned me more: that Hephaistos had moved so fast and bested Ares, or that Ares had left without a fight.

Hephaistos shrugged. "Guess someone else will be swinging the sword."

I laughed, as did a bunch of others. We were rewarded with a quick but potent grin from the craftsman God.

Breathing a sigh of relief that I'd finished and passed trial one, I stayed and cheered on my friends and the rest of my peers. I even lost myself and clapped when Revana made it through the gauntlet virtually unscathed. It was a good day, as no one failed the trial.

The next day, we all gathered in the garden near the hedge maze. Demeter welcomed us there in her usual laid-back manner. It was a nice reprieve from all the tension from the day before.

"I imagine y'all are thinking that I'm going to put you through some impossible feat." She shook her head. "Nah, man, I don't believe in all that bullshit."

There were some sighs of relief from people and some nervous giggles. I looked at Jasmine and Georgina and saw the same looks of relief on their faces. Especially Georgina. She'd passed through Hephaistos's trial, but it hadn't been easy for her, and she had suffered a bit of a burn on her arm from one of his fireballs.

"So, your task today is to get into teams of five and make it through the maze."

I laughed. This was going to be too easy. I could walk the maze with my eyes closed.

"But…" This quieted some of the excited murmurs. "I did redesign the maze. I mean, I wasn't going to make it *that* easy for you miscreants."

Everyone laughed at that.

"Oh, but you are being timed." Demeter grinned. "You'll have twenty minutes to get through it to the center. Get into groups!"

Jasmine, Georgina, and I stuck together. Ren jumped over to our group, and Jasmine grabbed Mia and pulled her in. I looked over at Lucian. He met my gaze and gave me a smile. I wasn't worried about him. He was smart, and he was in a driven, competitive group who wouldn't fail.

Lucian's group entered first. I was nervous waiting, hoping his team went through all right. After about fifteen minutes, Demeter clapped. "All right, who's next?"

We jumped to the front of the line.

"On your mark, get set, and go!"

We went into the maze together, took an immediate right, and kept walking. Then we came to an intersection. I was about to suggest right when a tiny arrow flashed on the ground, showing us the way. I laughed. Demeter really did hate all of this stuff, and I wondered if she would get in trouble from Zeus for it.

No more than fifteen minutes later, we came out into the middle of the maze. The other group was still there, and they were happily munching on pastries and cookies and all kinds of other tasty foods. When Lucian spotted me, he rushed over and offered me a plate of chocolate cupcakes.

"I was hoarding them for you."

I took one, peeled the wrapper, and shoved it into my mouth. I grinned at him around it.

For the rest of the day, we all chilled out in the middle of the giant hedge maze with our friends and peers and ate as many desserts as we could all fit into our mouths. Because we all knew we wouldn't get another reprieve like this. Things were just starting to get hard.

The next morning after eating the allocated protein bar and drinking the water, it was Dionysus's turn to challenge us. We met in his lab, where we'd been learning how to make different types of potions and tinctures, some of them for healing, others for more mischievous purposes.

"Good morning, my little apothecaries." His speech was a bit slurred, and I wondered if he was drunk already. Or hadn't stopped being drunk. Maybe drunk was his natural state of being. It was hard to tell.

"For this great trial, you will need to create three different potions." He ticked them off on his fingers. "Sleeping potion, super strength, and invisibility. Now since you've been learning to make these all term, you won't be provided with a recipe. You must make it on your own. All the ingredients for each potion can be found here in the workshop. You have two hours to complete your potions."

Before everyone could scatter to collect ingredients, Dionysus held up his finger.

"Once you've crafted your potions, you will be testing them on someone else. And I get to pick that someone else," he said with aplomb. "To pass this trial, at least two out of the three potions need to work properly. And if you end up poisoning someone, I won't be held responsible." He smiled and waved his hand in the air. "Begin."

While there was a mad rush for the valerian root —obviously everyone was starting with their sleeping potion, which was the easiest recipe to remember and to make—I opted for the ginseng. I was going to tackle the super strength potion first. Then for my sleeping potion, I was going to base it in lemon balm and not valerian, which was the more volatile herb.

I took my time making my potions, as quality was the important factor here. Every now and then, I peeked at my fellow recruits to see how they were fairing. I knew both Jasmine and Georgina were competent potion makers, so I didn't worry about them. Ren looked a bit flustered, as did Lucian. If either of them were going to fail at any trial, it would be this one or one of the other cerebral ones. I had no doubt that they would both excel in the more physically exerting trials.

Two hours passed quickly. Dionysus blew a whistle, and we all had to stop.

"Okay, now to test them." He walked around the workroom, peering at everyone's potions. He stopped at Jasmine's station. "You can test yours on…" His gaze traveled the room and then he grinned, pointing at me. "Melany. And vice versa."

Jasmine and I both picked up our individual vials and walked them to the front of the classroom to set them on the front table in the holders.

"Let's start with the super strength."

I handed Jasmine my potion and I took hers. I looked at her, and on the count of three, we both drank. It tasted like licorice, and I wondered if she'd added that for flavor.

"Now to test it." Dionysus pointed to the iron anvil sitting in the corner.

Jasmine and I walked over to it. "You first," she said.

I crouched, put my hands around it, and easily lifted the four hundred pound anvil. I grinned at Jasmine. Then it was her turn, and she also easily lifted it. That was one down, now onto the invisibility potion.

We drank at the same time, and within seconds we both faded from view. It was really cool to watch, knowing I'd brewed that. The effects only lasted for a few minutes; Dionysus had us design it that way. Later, we would learn how to make one that would last for hours.

"Now, technically, you both passed, but I want to see how you did with the sleeping potion." He pointed to two chairs in the corner.

We sat, and both of us downed the other's potion. I was happy to taste that Jasmine had used the lemon balm as well. That was the last coherent thought I had until sometime later Dionysus nudged us awake to find that Mia, Ren, and Diego hadn't passed. Ren's invisibility potion had turned Revana green. Literally. If I hadn't been sad that he hadn't passed the trial, I would've laughed my ass off at that.

Later that night, I lay in my bed and stared up at the ceiling, hoping I had the strength and fortitude to continue on. I'd passed four trials; I just needed to pass four more to stay at the academy. I couldn't be cast out. I wouldn't survive that. I was worried about tomorrow's trial, as it was with Apollo and Pythia. I hadn't done well in practice with Pythia. I hoped that it didn't hamper my performance.

Apollo paired us up the next day, with the intention of reading each other. I was hoping for someone I'd be comfortable with, someone I could open up to. I got Revana.

We sat in chairs facing each other, forced to touch knees.

"You must each read something from each other's past and say it out loud. Those who do not extract that information won't pass the trial." Apollo touched us both on the heads. "Clasp hands."

Resigned to my fate, I offered mine, and Revana slapped hers into my palms. I wrapped my fingers around her hands and squeezed. Probably harder than I needed to, but I didn't care. I wanted to pass this trial, and I wasn't going to let her mess with that.

I closed my eyes, took in a deep breath, and concentrated on Revana. I focused on her hands in mine, the sound of her breathing, the scent of vanilla she always carried on her. Then I shot into her mind, into one of her strongest memories. I hated that I had to speak it out loud. It was an invasion of privacy in the worst way.

"I'm at a track meet. Revana is racing; she looks maybe eleven or twelve."

Revana's hands tightened on mine, and I could feel her pulse thudding hard in her wrist.

"The gun goes off, and Revana sprints down the lane. She's running hard. she's passing the other girls. She's almost at the finish line, when another girl comes from behind and crosses first."

I didn't want to continue. Even in the memory, I could feel Revana's disappointment. Her despair. Her hatred at herself for losing the race.

"She's coming into her house, her parents entering behind her. She turns to look at her father. He doesn't smile at her. She tells him she's sorry. He scowls at her, and tells her she's stupid…"

Opening my eyes, I stopped and shook my head. I didn't want to go on.

"You have to tell us everything you see, Melany, if you want to pass this trial."

Revana glared at me and dug her fingernails into the backs of my hands. "Just do it."

"He tells her she's stupid and worthless. No one cares about second place. First place is the only thing in life that's important. She says she's sorry again. He slaps her across the face." I sighed. "That's it. That's the end of the memory."

Apollo nodded. "Good. Your turn, Revana."

I took in another cleansing breath, trying to relax and open for her. I hated that she was going to be poking around in my head, but it had to happen for the sake of the trial. I didn't have any way of blocking her. She was going to see what she was going to see. I had no control over what memory she plucked from my subconscious.

Revana stared into my eyes, as she squeezed my hands tighter. I was going to have divots in my skin. Her eyes narrowed, and her breathing picked up. "I can't see anything." She yanked on my hands. "Let me in."

"I am." And I was. Or at least, I think I was. I wasn't actively blocking her.

She snapped her eyes shut, and her face contorted in concentration.

"Try harder, Revana," Apollo said from next to us.

"I am."

"You only have a few more minutes to complete the task."

I wanted to tell him to shut up; he wasn't helping.

Finally, her eyes flicked open, and she pulled her hands away. "Nothing. I couldn't see anything."

Apollo frowned. "You couldn't capture one memory?"

"There was nothing there to capture. Her mind was just dark."

He glanced down at me. "Were you blocking her?"

I stood. "No, of course not. I wouldn't know how to do that, even if I wanted to."

"Okay, you pass, Melany. I'm afraid, Revana, you failed this trial."

"You bitch!" Revana bolted to her feet and sucker

punched me right in the mouth then she stomped out of the room.

Shaking his head, Apollo glanced at Pythia and shrugged. "I have a feeling this is going to be a long day."

The way Pythia looked at him, I thought for sure she was going to say something about the other day when the same thing had happened to her. But she didn't.

Later in the dorm room, Georgina asked me, "What did you do to Revana? She came out of the room with smoke blowing out of her nose. She said you were going to pay."

I shrugged. "I didn't do anything. She didn't pass the trial and blamed me for it." I collapsed onto my bed and turned toward the wall, tucking my legs up. I didn't want to talk about what had happened to anyone.

Today was a hard day, and I knew it was just going to get even harder. Right now, we weren't being pitted against each other much, but I knew it was coming. Today, it was Revana, what if tomorrow it was Georgina, or Jasmine, or even Lucian? Could I protect my friends while I protected myself? I really hoped so because I didn't want to face the alternative.

CHAPTER TWENTY-TWO

MELANY

*B*efore heading into the hall of Aphrodite for our next trial, Lucian caught me and pulled me aside.

"Are you okay?"

"Yeah, I'm good."

He lifted his hand and touched my puffy, sore lip. Revana's fist had split it open. "What happened? The rumor is you cheated or something, causing Revana to fail the trial."

I lifted an eyebrow. "And what do you think?"

"I think that's bullshit."

"Exactly." I beamed at him, happy he didn't believe the stupid rumor.

He smiled and tugged me close for a quick hug.

"How did you do in the trial?"

He hugged me tighter. "Not good. I didn't pass it."

I pulled back and looked him in the eyes. "I'm sorry."

He shrugged. "It's one fail. I don't plan on failing any others."

Aphrodite looked like a gold statue, as she stood on her little dais in her hall and addressed us. "My trial is one of deception. Over the past few months, you've learned how to transform your body into something else. From human to animal. For this trial, you will transform yourself into a goat."

That got a few snickers from the group.

"The object of this will be for your peers to pick you out of a herd of goats. If they do, you fail. In the old days, we would've slaughtered the goats one by one to reveal your identity, but we won't be doing that here."

I shared a horrified look with Jasmine. "Yikes."

Half of the group was escorted out of the room, while the rest of us stayed. So when the door opened again, and ten goats came scampering in, we didn't know whom it was that had transformed into a goat right away. It was smart to do that because it was possible that someone could still retain some defining feature, like a mole or a scar.

Our goal as a group was to examine each goat and then make a unanimous decision on which goat wasn't really a goat. I didn't have to voice my thoughts, but I was sure we all pretty much agreed not to out anyone if we spotted any obvious discrepancies in goats. This was one time when we could help out our peers.

After we all looked over the ten goats, we came together and made a decision. We agreed on picking the all-white goat. Jasmine was our spokes person.

She pointed to the white goat. "We think that one is an imposter."

Aphrodite nodded. "Very well."

She then snapped her fingers, and eight of the goats turned back into our peers, including the one we'd picked. The goat turned out to be Lucian.

My stomach churned. I stared at him in horror.

Aphrodite stepped off the dais and moved toward us. Her gaze flashed with blue fire. "Don't mess with me." She then gestured to the students picking themselves off the ground. "You all passed, except for you, dear." She pointed to Lucian. "You failed, thanks to your friends here."

Wow. Aphrodite was a real nasty piece of work. I was going to have to watch her more closely.

We took more care with the next group of goats that came in and thankfully didn't pick anyone. When it was my turn to transform, I did it as quick as I could, hoping that I did it well. There were no mirrors around, so I couldn't take a look at myself and fix any issues. Other goats joined me in the lobby; I didn't know if they were actually goats or my friends. The doors opened and we all ran into the room.

I tried to be as goat-like as I could. I made goat noises and butted my head into another goat, which I hoped was an actual animal and not one of my friends. Revana and her crew were part of the observing party. As she moved through the herd, she kicked at each animal. After seeing what I did from her past, I wanted to feel sorry for her, but the truth was she was not a good person.

When she neared me, she booted me in the side. Pain rippled over my body, and I wanted to whip my head around and nip her in the ass, but I didn't. Instead, I bleated at her and moved along to stand next to a little brown goat.

After a few tense moments of the group conferring, Revana pointed to a medium-sized black and white goat. "That's not a goat."

Aphrodite nodded and then snapped her fingers. Me, Jasmine, Georgina, Ren, and Mia all popped into existence. As did Ren's roommate Marek, but he'd been the one they'd pointed out. He'd failed the trial.

That night in the dorm, Georgina told me how scared she was for the rest of the trials.

"I've passed five of them, but I still need to pass three more, and I'm afraid I won't be able to as they're going to be the more physical ones."

"You're strong, Gina. Stronger than I think you even know." I grabbed her hand. "And if I can help you during any of the trials, you know I will."

Once more, my sleep wasn't all that good. I had dreams this time, of darkness and shadows. And I wondered if it was some kind of portent of things to come.

Hera's trial was very much like a locked room adventure. I'd done one with Callie and her friends. Everyone had spent the time arguing, so we never made it out. For the trial, we'd be in a group of five, and we had to use our knowledge of the Gods to uncover clues inside a room to discover another door, to move on to the next room. We had to clear three rooms in an hour. The team with the worst timed score failed the trial.

We got into our usual group, me, Jasmine, Georgina, and Mia. Ren decided to go into another group with Marek to make sure he didn't fail another trial, which made room for a new member to our group—Lucian. I was confident that our group would make it through the rooms in record time, as everyone had done well in history class. I was probably the weakest link this time.

Once we were locked in the room, I grabbed Lucian's hand. "I'm so sorry for yesterday."

He shook his head. "Don't be. It's okay."

"But you failed—"

"I won't fail anymore. Especially not this one." He gave me a soft smile.

Together, we worked through the puzzles in record time. At least we thought it was record time, as we didn't know the other teams' scores. After every group finished going through the rooms, we found out that we had come in second place. Ren's team had come in first, which I was very happy to hear. Revana's team came in last. That meant she had two fails so far. Not that I was celebrating. Okay, maybe I was just a little.

That night, I slept long and hard. I needed it to be fresh for Hermes's flying trial. I had no doubt that Lucian and I would do well, but I couldn't count out running into problems. Problems like Revana and her crew. It was no secret that the word in the halls was that they were out to get me. I had to watch my back.

Hermes met us out on the training field. He wore a blue polka dotted bow tie today, which I thought was really cute.

"This trial will be a race. Since flying is a fundamental part of your training as a soldier, only the first twenty-five flyers will pass this trial. The other half of the group will fail."

I glanced at Georgina and Jasmine. We all knew that the trials were going to get tougher. This was just an example of that. I was worried for Georgina. She was not a strong flyer.

"You will race in five heats of ten flyers. The best times will advance; the worst times will fail. I will pick the flyers for each heat."

I quickly moved away from my friends, hoping Hermes didn't just put a group together by proximity. I didn't want to race against them. Despite my tactic of moving around, I ended up in a group with Lucian, Ren, Marek, Mia, Revana, Diego, and three others I didn't know well.

After Hermes described the race route, we lined up on the starting line on the ground. Part of the trial was how fast we could produce our wings and shoot into the air. Thank the Gods, Lucian and I had a done a lot of practicing.

Hermes stood in front of us, his arms raised. Then he dropped them, shouting, "Go!"

My big, black wings popped out of my back in seconds, and I was air born. Lucian was right behind me, with Revana, Ren, and Mia shortly behind him. The others took a little longer to get their wings out, and then they flew into the air.

It was now a game of follow-the-leader, and I was in front. Lucian kept up but stayed a little behind me, and I wondered if he was protecting my back from Revana because I knew she was going to come for me given half the chance. In the air away from prying eyes was the perfect opportunity.

I soared past the first spire over the citadel and was swooping around the north towers when I risked taking glancing behind me. Lucian was still on my tail, but Revana had gained some ground. She was wing to wing beside Mia. Ren was a little bit behind them.

She must've known I was checking for her position because she edged in closer to Mia, her wing flapping against the other girl's. She was trying to knock Mia out to get my attention. Well, it was working. I slowed my pace a little, intending to drop back, but Lucian saw what I was planning and shook his head. He came up beside me.

"Don't play into her games. Keep flying."

I looked over my shoulder again to see Revana violently bumping into Mia. I wasn't having it.

"You take the lead." I could afford to fail a trial. I folded my wings in and dropped back like a shot to where Revana and Mia flew. Revana's eyes nearly bugged out when she saw me.

"You want to mess with me, mess with me, not with my friends." I shot out my wings and did a spin around her. The force of it knocked her off balance, and she fell behind. I nodded to Mia. "Get in front of me."

She did, and we flew in a triangle formation, Lucian in the lead, Mia, then me and Ren along the side. Revana was right on my tail, but my huge wing flaps were too forceful for her to fight against. She couldn't get any speed around me.

By the time we flew around the towers and back to the finish line, Lucian was already touching down. He crossed first, then Mia, Ren, me, and Diego had managed to come in alongside with Revana, and Laura, one of the girls I didn't know well. Marek came in then the other two.

I didn't know what our times were, but for sure Lucian and Mia had the fastest times. I was fairly certain I'd be okay, but it all depended on how the other heats went.

Nervously, we watched the other groups fly. Jasmine did really well in the second heat, and I was sure she'd pass. Georgina, on the other hand, came in seventh in her heat.

After all the races finished, Hermes had us line up again then he told us the results. I'd been right— Lucian and Mia had the fastest times. I'd passed, as did Ren, Jasmine, and Revana. But Georgina and Marek had failed the trial. I think that was number three for Marek and two for Georgina. I was going to have to keep an eye on her during the next few trials. There was no way I was going to let her get kicked out of the academy.

CHAPTER TWENTY-THREE

MELANY

*G*eorgina and I huddled in our room and talked for the rest of the afternoon and evening. She was upset she'd failed the flying trial, but I assured her that I wouldn't let her fail anymore. We talked about our pasts and our families and about boys. She told me about the boy back home that she'd left behind, and I told her about Lucian.

"Are you in love with him?" She nudged me playfully with her foot, as we sat on her bed.

"I honestly don't know." But I did know. And I was. I just didn't want to say it out loud because I didn't know what it truly meant here in the academy, especially during the trials. Love and friendship were complicated constructs, especially at a time when getting ahead meant leaving others behind.

In the morning as we assembled to get our meal for the day, I palmed my protein bar and when no one was looking, I gave it to Georgina.

Her eyes widened, and she shook her head. "I can't take this."

"Take it and eat it. I don't need it, Gina. I can afford to lose." I moved away from her, so she couldn't give it back. I peered over my shoulder and was satisfied to see she ate it.

Out on the south training field next to the stables, Artemis greeted us on top of one of the great fire-breathing horses that no one thus far had been able to ride. The beast snorted and stamped its big hooves against the dirt, making us all flinch backward.

"In this trial, you will wrangle one of the great beasts and ride them out here to the obstacle course." She gestured to the field, where a track had been created, including jumps and other hurdles. "There are ten targets. You must hit eight of them with your bow. Missing more than two is an automatic fail. You will also be timed, so even if you make all the required targets, you can't be slow. The best times and targets of the best twenty-five will pass. The rest will fail."

There were quite a few groans in the group, as well as a few very concerned looks. A couple of people were already sitting on their third fail.

"Get into two lines."

We all scrambled to do as she asked, but I didn't like it.

"I forgot to add that you will be racing against each other but through opposite ends of the course."

She pointed to the line I was in. "You head through the course from here." She pointed to the beginning of the track. "And this line will start from here." She gestured to the end.

I looked across from me to see whom I'd be racing against. Isobel glared at me. I nodded. It was a good choice. She was no threat to me. She could barely ride. During class, she'd fallen off every mount she tried.

I looked behind me to see who Georgina's opponent was and my heart sank. Revana would try everything she could to win. I wouldn't put it past her to cheat. I turned, grabbed Georgina, and switched places with her.

"Trust me," I whispered in her ear.

Artemis rode her horse in a path between our two lines. "Look across from you. This is whom you will be racing against."

I turned my head and gave Revana a huge, smug grin.

We were four back in line, so it was going to be an hour or more before we raced, but I knew the time would go by quick. And watching the others race wasn't at all boring. Lucian was two ahead of me. Before it was his turn, he turned around and gave me a quick smile. I returned it and gave him a lame thumbs up, which made him laugh. I checked to see whom he was racing against, Hella who wasn't very good at animal handling, and relaxed. Lucian was by far the most formidable one in the group.

When Artemis blew her whistle, Lucian grabbed the bow and quiver of arrows from the ground and sprinted into the stable. He was a millisecond behind his opponent. A few minutes later, Hella rode out on a unicorn. Unicorns were swift creatures; they could sprint faster than all the other horses. Another few seconds ticked by and I wondered what was taking Lucian so long.

Then he burst out through the large hole in the stable roof on Pegasus. Throughout our training, he'd been one of the only ones who the winged horse liked. Everyone else couldn't even get within a few feet of her.

Everyone broke out into cheers and whoops as the big beast swooped toward the obstacle course. Even Artemis grinned as Lucian made easy work of the course. He was back before Hella, missing only one target.

When he landed and dismounted, Artemis nodded to him. "Well done."

"Thank you." He awarded the group with an arrogant bow.

I shook my head and laughed. It felt good to laugh, especially now.

When it was my turn, my heart pounded so hard in my chest I could barely breathe. The whistle blew, and I picked up the bow and arrows and ran for the stable. Revana and I were neck and neck. She went straight for one of the griffins; I'd seen her practice with them, but along the way she kicked at all the other stall doors, which sent the occupants into a tizzy.

As she mounted her griffin, I couldn't even get near the other beasts. The unicorns were flailing their heads, their horns now a lethal weapon. The other griffins were stamping and snorting, clawing the air with their giant talons. I could forget about the Pegasus; she'd put her back to me, and I wasn't about to approach her. The fire-breathing horses were all skittish, some blowing smoke out of their nostrils. That left one beast—one of the fire-breathing horses, the biggest of them. His name was Aethon, and he was Ares's personal mount.

He stood there staring at me, his tail swishing back and forth, as if he didn't have a care in the world. He was huge; my head didn't even come up to his back.

"What do you think there, handsome? Want to go for a ride?"

He snorted, smoke curling out from his nostrils, but then he shifted just slightly, giving me access to his back. I couldn't believe it.

I ran toward him, jumped, grabbed a handful of long, black mane and mounted him. Then he was out of the stable like a thundering storm cloud. I heard a collective shout and gasp from the crowd, as I rode the huge beast to the obstacle course. We had some ground to cover, as Revana had already started through the course.

I sat up high on the horse, aimed and hit the first target, which was high in a tree, even before we entered the circuit. Aethon made short work of the jump over the logs then I hit the next target, which was low on the ground. As I rode through the sparsely wooded course, I could hear the squawks and wings flapping of Revana's griffin. Despite the griffin's speed and agility, I knew she was going to have a hard time because of its vast wingspan. It wouldn't be able to get as low as she'd want it to be for a few of the targets. Lucian wouldn't have had a problem with the Pegasus because she was also a horse and was comfortable on the ground, whereas the griffin was clumsier on the ground than in the air.

After hitting six targets straight on, we rounded the corner and ran into Revana and the griffin. It screeched at me, but Aethon wasn't concerned. He kept to the trail, thundering down it like a locomotive. I didn't think anything would stop him, let alone some angry griffin and an even angrier girl upon its back.

I hit the seventh target, which was precariously close to where Revana hovered.

"You could've hit me!"

"But I didn't."

She knocked her arrow in her bow, drew it, and swung around toward me. I looked around, but there was no target close to me.

"You're going to waste your arrow."

Her glare sharpened. "It won't be a waste." She let it fly.

The arrow whizzed by my head. I could feel the displacement of the air, and the sound of it buzzed in my ears. I knew she was angry. I knew she wanted to see me fail. But to actually want to kill me? I didn't think she had it in her. Obviously, I'd been wrong.

Aethon wasn't having it. That arrow could've hit him, too. He reared up, and blew a stream of fire from his mouth. Flames tickled the tips of the griffin's hooves, and he reared back, swooping to the right, and Revana nearly fell off his back.

As we galloped past her, I turned and flipped her the middle finger.

Aethon snorted, and I almost swore he chuckled.

I hit the last of the targets, not missing one, and then we thundered out of the course and back to the finish line. I was greeted to some claps and cheers. Revana flew in a few minutes behind.

After I dismounted, Aethon snorted then nuzzled my head from behind, knocking me off balance. Then he trotted back into the stables on his own.

Artemis brought her horse alongside me. "No one has ever ridden Aethon before."

"Don't tell Ares," I said.

She grinned. "I won't."

As Revana brushed past me, I grabbed her arm and leaned into her. "Don't push me, Revana. I'll let this one go because of what happened in prophecy, but next time… I will retaliate."

She jerked out of my grip and stomped away.

Georgina was next to race. I hugged her. "Good luck. Take a unicorn, the griffins are too hard to maneuver."

She nodded then the whistle blew. She sprinted into the stable. A minute later, she rode out on a unicorn, and it sprinted toward the course. She was ahead of Isobel by a few seconds, who came out on one of the griffins. Within seconds, she fell off and had to scramble up onto the beast's back. But the griffin wasn't having it, and it flew away to return to the stable.

Isobel let out an exasperated scream.

Artemis rode up to her. "Do you wish to try another mount?"

She shook her head. She knew it was pointless. Her time would've been bad and she'd fail anyway.

"You've forfeited. You're an automatic fail."

When Georgina rode back in, she was all smiles. I hugged her after she dismounted. "Yeah, I'm so proud of you."

"I wouldn't have done it without you."

Arm in arm, we stood back and watched as Jasmine made her run. She rode out of the stable on one of the fire-breathing horses and sped toward the course. When she returned in great time, she wasn't happy.

"I missed three targets."

"Oh, Jas, I'm sorry." I hugged her. "But it's only one trial. You got the rest." I gave her a reassuring smile, but I wasn't so sure about Poseidon's trial. She was pretty good in the water, but I'd heard rumors the water God was infamous for his difficult tests.

After everyone went through the course, Artemis let us know the results. I'd placed first, with Lucian a few seconds behind. Georgina, Ren, and Mia had passed. Revana had passed but barely. Isobel failed, and Diego was part of the twenty-five who had failed.

It was getting close to the end. We only had four trials left—Poseidon, Ares, Zeus, and the last one was for Athena. These ones were going to push us to the limits of our abilities. I was afraid, not for me, but for my friends. I didn't want to lose them. They were all I had left in this world.

CHAPTER TWENTY-FOUR

MELANY

*a*s I stood on the shore of the lake—that Lucian and I had discovered during one of our flights around the grounds—with my friends beside me, I couldn't stop shaking. I wasn't scared, well not entirely, but had adrenaline racing through me in anticipation of the trial. We all wore red and black wetsuits with the option of wearing goggles. I opted to wear them, as did Jasmine and Georgina. I noticed that both Ren and Lucian went without.

Poseidon stood proudly in front of us, the water of the lake lapping at his bare feet.

"This trial will test all your limits. This is a four-mile wide lake, and you will have three hours to swim from here to the opposite shore. There is a rest station in the middle for those who need it, but remember that you are competing against your peers. The first twenty-five swimmers to hit the opposite beach pass this trial. The rest will fail."

I glanced at my friends. This was it; this was going to be a real test. But I wasn't going to leave any of them behind. I reached for Lucian's hand and tugged him closer. Frowning, he looked down at me.

"No matter what, don't stop for me."

"Blue…"

"I mean it. You need to pass this trial. Please just concentrate on that." I squeezed his hand. "Promise me."

After a few seconds, he nodded. "Okay, I promise."

I let go of his hand, turning my attention back on Poseidon.

"You may use your skills however you see fit during this trial." A slow smile spread across his face. "But remember, you aren't alone in the water."

About fifteen feet out, the normally tranquil surface rippled. A small fin breeched the water, then another, then another, until there were nine small fins sticking out from the surface. There was more bubbling then the fins disappeared.

Jasmine grabbed my arm; her hands were trembling. "That's a hydra." Her voice was barely audible over the splashing of the lake water onto the beach.

"Are you sure? It didn't look very big."

"Those fins were just one of many on the tops of their heads."

I swallowed. Dealing with a baby Charybdis had been nothing compared to the possibility of a one hundred foot sea dragon with nine heads.

Taking Jasmine with me, I huddled in next to Georgina, Lucian, and Ren. Jasmine grabbed Mia and pulled her into the group. "We need to stay together as much as we can. I have a feeling there's going to be strength in numbers."

Everyone nodded. Then Poseidon blew into his shell horn to start the race.

We all entered the water, trying to stay close together. It was going to be a long swim, but I was sure if we grouped our strengths, we could all make it to the other beach and pass the trial. I knew Ren and Lucian had two fails, so I didn't expect or want them to sacrifice their time for us, well, for me in particular.

Once in the water, Ren and Lucian set the pace, and the rest of us followed behind. I sucked in air, then dived down to swish my body back and forth like a fish, propelling myself forward. Everyone else did the same; then we surfaced and did it again.

The next time I came up for air, I did quick look behind and saw we were making good time, and we were middle of the pack. It was a good position to be, as we could put on the speed at the end.

After about an hour of swimming, my muscles started to ache and fatigue was trying to settle into my body. I looked over at Georgina; she was struggling a bit. I swam over to her.

"Next time we dive down, hang onto my foot and just glide with me."

"Are you sure?"

"Yup."

She nodded, and we both took in air and dove. As instructed, she grabbed my foot, as I propelled my body forward like a dolphin. I didn't go as far or as fast, but it helped her conserve energy, so I considered it worthwhile. We did it again and again, until my legs started to seize up.

We swam close to the floating rest station. I saw a couple of people scramble up onto it to rest. In theory, it seemed like a good idea, but I knew from experience they couldn't rest enough to make a difference in their muscles when they got back into the water. Oxygen wise it was sound, but I suspected those people were going to suffer some severe cramps during the next half of the journey.

Halfway there and I felt optimistic. Ren and Lucian led the way, and they hadn't slowed. Like a flock of birds, we were conserving energy by swimming in the current they made with their bodies. I looked back. We'd pulled away a little from the pack. There were a few people swimming at our rate, and there was one person—I think it was Marek, judging by his black hair—who was ahead of us.

As the shore came into view, I started to smile, but a shout from someone nearby nearly froze me in place.

"I felt it under me!" It was Diego, and he thrashed about back and forth.

"Quit moving around," Revana shouted, as she moved away from Diego. "You'll draw it to us."

"It's not a shark. It's a freaking hydra. I think it's going to do what it wants."

Another shout came from another group of people.

Georgina started to thrash a little beside me. I

shook my head. "Don't panic. Just concentrate on your strokes. We're almost there."

Then Diego was yanked down into the water.

That made everyone within a ten-foot radius scream.

Georgina was one of them.

"Lucian!"

He stopped swimming and turned to me. "What happened?"

"Something happened to Diego."

Ren swam over. "What do you want to do?"

"Can you take Georgina, Jasmine, and Mia with you? Swim to the shore."

He frowned. "Mel… he wouldn't do it for you."

"I know."

He shook his head and looked at Lucian. "You take the girls. I'm going to go with Mel."

"No, he's my friend—"

"I can manipulate the water. Mel and I can hold our breath the longest."

I touched Lucian's cheek with my fingers. "Remember your promise."

He nodded then turned and swam hard toward the shore. Georgina, Jasmine, and Mia followed him in.

"Ready?" I asked Ren.

He nodded.

Then we both sucked in air and dove down deep in the water. It didn't take long to spot the hydra. It was huge. At this depth, it was creepy as hell to see this big, dangerous creature just hovering ten feet below a big group of swimmers. It looked like it was having a good time knowing it could pluck anyone of them at any time.

I spotted Diego, struggling to get out from between the jaws of one of its nine heads. There was no blood, so the creature hadn't bit into him. It was just playing around, probably instructed by Poseidon to detain, but not kill anyone.

We swam toward the beast. A couple of its heads took notice of us, but it didn't look worried in the least. As we got closer, Ren started to move his hands around in front of him until he formed a small cyclone. Then he sent it spinning toward the hydra's head, the one holding Diego.

As the cyclone hit, the head opened its mouth. I swooped in and grabbed Diego by the hand and dragged him to the surface. Another few minutes and I was pretty sure he would've drowned. When we came up for air, he gasped, taking in water. As he sputtered and coughed, I slapped him on the back.

"C'mon, we need to get swimming."

While I made my first strokes, I saw in the distance Lucian and the others were almost at the shore. Revana was close, as were most of the group. I looked behind me and spotted maybe ten or so still struggling in the water. We weren't going to make the top twenty-five. For me it didn't matter, but for Ren that meant three fails.

"Ren, you need to swim faster."

"What about you?"

"Don't worry about me. I'm good."

He nodded and dove down into the water. I knew he had the power and stamina to make it.

I kept swimming alongside Diego to make sure he didn't go under. He looked exhausted, barely able to swim. I was okay with failing this trial. It didn't matter to me.

As we kept swimming, I felt the water bubbling beneath me. I stopped and glanced around at the surface. It looked like we were floating in a pot of boiling water. It was the hydra, and it was obviously unhappy.

There was more bubbling under me, each bubble getting bigger, pushing me out of the water. Then it was like a huge wave growing underneath me, lifting me, Ren, and Diego higher and higher. I risked a peek behind me and saw the hydra emerge from the water like a volcanic eruption, rolling us on top of the wave. My stomach lurched into my throat as the wave sent us crashing into the beach.

I rolled onto my back, sputtering and coughing, and looked up as Poseidon loomed over me. His smile was broad and warm.

"You all made it. You passed the trial."

I blinked at him, shocked. "We did?" I sat up to see Lucian, Georgina, Jasmine, and Mia running down the beach toward us. I looked over at Ren, who seemed as dumfounded as I felt. Diego had yet to even register we were out of the water.

Lucian reached down for my arm and pulled me up. He hugged me. "You rolled in on the wave, beating the rest of the group."

I couldn't believe it. We'd passed, despite being almost dead last. We all shared hugs and stunned congratulations. Exhaustion started to settle on each of us. I could especially see it on Ren. I grabbed his hand and squeezed.

"Thanks for coming with me."

"You're welcome."

That night when I rolled into the dorm room intent on just unzipping my wetsuit and falling into bed, I found a small box on my bed. There was a note on top. It read: *For your bravery in the face of defeat. P.*

I opened it to find a large protein bar. Laughing, I picked it up and ate it in three bites. I was asleep by the time my head hit the pillow. And I didn't dream. I had the best sleep of my life.

In the morning, I felt invigorated. I was pumped, ready for the day. I needed that energy for Ares's trial. I braided my hair, put on shorts and a T-shirt, and figured I was ready for anything.

We gathered out on the south training field where Ares waited. Behind the God stood several warriors, including Heracles and Antiope, who was rumored to be one of the greatest female warriors to ever live.

"Today," Ares bellowed, "is about single combat. For this trial, you may choose what kind of battle. Sword, spear, or hand to hand. Depending on what you choose will determine which great warrior you will face." He gestured to those behind him. "In the old days, we would've fought to the death, but today you will fight until your opponent says otherwise. They will be the ones who determine whether you pass or fail."

One by one, everyone picked their poison. Jasmine picked the sword, Georgina chose the spear, and Lucian picked the sword. When it became my turn, I said, "Hand to hand."

Ares smiled at that, and I started to question why and whether I'd made a bad decision. "Your opponent will be Antiope."

The warrior woman stepped forward. She was no shorter than six and a half feet. Her long, golden hair was tied back in a braid, and she wore a tank top and shorts. Her muscles rippled as she walked toward me.

Ares laughed. "Have fun, Richmond. I'll inform Chiron to expect you in the infirmary later." He stepped away from the fight area.

I didn't let his smack talk rattle me. I didn't need to beat Antiope; I just needed to get her attention, let her know that I was a worthy opponent. I was quick, I was agile, and I could take a big person down. I'd taken Heracles down a few times during training.

When we were toe to toe, I nodded to her then pulled my stance back a few steps. She had a longer arm reach than I did, and I knew if she got a proper hold on me, it would be lights out, and I'd lose the match. My best defense was a strong offense. I needed to come in quick and strike her where it counted.

As soon as she put up her hands in a defensive position, I moved in. I ducked under her right hook, landing a solid jab to her midsection. It was like punching stone and my knuckles ached. I took a few steps back again, danced around her to the right, and hit her again in the side. This time she flinched; I'd found the sweet spot.

Before I could move around her again, she spun

to her right and struck me with a back hand to the face. Pain exploded across my cheek and mouth. I tasted blood. The blow had knocked me back a little, but I kept my balance and came at her again. I had to avoid getting hit in the head again. She was stronger, stronger than I was, and another blow would likely knock me on my ass. I had to be sneaky, I had to attack her in a way she'd least expect it.

As I took up my stance again, I spied a quick smile on Antiope's face. She was toying with me. I took a couple steps back, leapt into the air and spun, aiming my right foot at her face. She blocked me with her arm, then pushed, like she was swatting a fly away. I landed on my side on the ground, the impact knocking my teeth together. More blood erupted into my mouth.

I couldn't let her win. I refused to.

I flipped up back onto my feet, then moved around her to the right and hit her again in the flank. She dropped her elbow to protect that side. I moved around her and jumped onto her back. I wrapped an arm around her throat before she could get her chin down and pressed. Even a big opponent needed air.

I yanked on my arm as hard as I could, as her hands came up and tried to pull me off. I had my legs wrapped around her, my ankles locked at her navel. I was a spider clinging to its web; nothing was going to get me off. She'd have to drop onto the ground if she wanted me gone.

I could hear the cheers of my friends and peers.

"Keep at it, Blue. You got her!"

After a few more seconds, Antiope tapped my hand.

I couldn't believe it. I let her go and dropped to the ground. She turned to look at me, rubbing at her throat. A purple mark was starting to blossom there.

She offered her hand to me. I took it. "Good job. You passed this trial."

Jumping up into the air, I made a whooping sound. When I landed, Lucian was there to hug me. "You're freaking amazing, Blue." He kissed me, and it wasn't a simple peck on the lips. It was a full on proper kiss with tongue.

There were several "oooohs" and wolf whistles. Then Ares was beside us, pulling us apart.

"Let's go, lover boy, it's your turn."

"Good luck."

I watched as he walked out onto the battlefield, with a sword and his shield. His opponent was Achilles, the greatest warrior to ever live. Nerves zipped through me as he battled. But I didn't have to worry. Lucian fought like the warrior I knew he'd become.

At the end, even though he lost the battle with Achilles's blade tip pressed into his neck, Achilles told him he fought bravely and valiantly. He passed the trial.

In fact all my friends passed the trial. We only had two more trials to complete then it was over, and we'd be divided into our clans. Then the real training would start. Soon, we would all be part of the Gods' Army.

CHAPTER TWENTY-FIVE

MELANY

*E*veryone was nervous for Zeus's trial, and I didn't blame them. It wasn't going to be easy for anybody. After breakfast we were told to meet in the training facility where we did our elemental classes.

"Welcome to your trial by lightning." Zeus beamed at us, like an indulgent father. It made me want to punch him in his bearded, square jaw.

"This will be a difficult trial, and most of you will fail it." He clapped his hands together, and a boom of thunder shook the foundation of the building. The floor moved beneath our feet. Light sparked between his hands, and slowly he drew them out to create a bolt of lightning. The white glow was intense, difficult to look at.

"Each of you must grasp the bolt in both hands,

and throw it at the target. The majority of you won't even be able to hold the lightning, let alone throw it. But for those who do, you will pass this trial." He stuck the bolt into the floor.

I gaped at him. All they had to do was grab and throw it? What about holding it for two minutes while being electrocuted?

"Miss Richmond, why don't you come over here with me to observe since you already endured this task?"

I did a quick squeeze of my friends' hands before moving over to stand beside Zeus.

I held my breath as the first person stepped up to grasp the lightning.

One by one, I watched as person after person tried to pick up the bolt and hold it long enough to attempt to throw it across the room at the target. Each one failed. I grimaced every time a face contorted in pain as the electrical current zipped up their arms and burned their hands.

I watched Jasmine, Ren, and Mia all attempt and fail. My heart ached for each of them.

Then Georgina stepped up. I bit down on my lip as she leaned forward and wrapped her hands around the sizzling bolt. She winced, but she didn't drop it. In fact she looked in control. With it clutched in her hands, she turned, and with one arm, she balanced it, reared back, and tossed it across the room. She missed the target but it didn't matter. She'd done the impossible. When she turned back toward me and grinned, it was then I noticed her shoes were full of dirt.

I laughed. She was absolutely brilliant. She took her affinity to the earth and literally grounded herself. I thought maybe Zeus had noticed because his lips twitched up.

The last to go was Lucian. I figured he'd been biding his time and observing how everyone else did and figuring out an advantage.

He took in a deep breath, glancing over at me. I gave him an encouraging smile. He wrapped his hands around the lightning bolt and paused there. It looked like he was trying to acclimate himself to the electrical current shooting through his body. He then lifted the bolt, turned toward the target, and reared his hand back to throw it with everything he had. The bolt struck the target right in the bullseye.

The whole room erupted into cheers. Even Zeus clapped. But that caused the building to shake again. I ran to Lucian and hugged him. When he wrapped his arms around me, I noticed his hands weren't even red.

Because it was our last night before the final trial, Zeus let us gather in the dining hall for a couple of hours before curfew. He even allowed us a few special treats to snack on. The six of us sat together at our table and gorged on ice cream sundaes and banana splits. We talked and laughed, forgetting about what was in store for us tomorrow. Not once did we mention that it could be our last night together like this. As none of us knew what happened once we were divided into our clans. Maybe we'd never see each other again. At least not until there was a war the Gods needed us to fight.

I tried to push it from my mind and just enjoy the moment with my best friends and the boy I'd fallen in love with.

When I slept that night, my dreams were filled with darkness and shadows again. But this time, I sensed a presence in the darkness. It reached out to me, asking me for something. Asking me for permission to be with me. I didn't fear the shadows, as they'd always been kind to me, so I told the presence… *Yes.*

When I woke in the morning, I felt renewed and empowered. That feeling stayed with me as we made our way to the training field, which had been transformed into an ancient battlefield with stone walls to hide behind and trenches to jump into. The sun was bright in the sky, and it seemed to shine down on Athena as she walked out onto the field.

She wore traditional Greek robes and a gold band over her short, dark curls. Her dark skin was radiant against the white robes, and she truly looked like the Goddess she was. Ares may have been the God of War, but Athena had taught us more about the art of warfare than any other deity in the academy.

And now was our chance to show her what we'd learned. Her trial was going to be a battle, literally.

"In this trial, you will be fighting against some of the best warriors this academy has produced." She swung around and gestured to the people walking onto the field. "Heracles, Medusa, Achilles, Antiope, Helen of Troy, and Bellerophon." The six champions bowed toward us. It still unnerved me to see Medusa's hair swirl around on its own. "You will be having what you would call a game of capture the flag. The object is for your team to cross the field of battle to capture this team's flag."

I nodded. It seemed easy enough. Well, not easy, but definitely not complicated.

"Instead of paintball guns and paint pellets," she said, smiling, "you will be using bows and swords and whatever weapon you have at your disposal. Don't worry, though, those arrows are blunted, as are the swords, so you won't die on the field of battle, but you will most definitely be injured."

Great. Just what I needed. More scars.

"You will split into teams of ten and go against the champion team. If you capture their flag, you pass the trial, if they capture yours, you fail." She turned her head to look at each of us. "Just words of the wise… only two teams in seventy years have ever won."

We quickly formed a team consisting of me, Jasmine, Georgina, Mia, Lucian, Ren, Marek, Jasmine's roommate, Hella, Diego, whom Lucian had convinced to defect over to us, and a quiet girl named Rosie, who I knew was an ace with a bow. For a few of us, this trial was all or nothing. Ren, Georgina, Marek, and Diego's fates all hung on the wire. I vowed to make sure that we won this battle.

We all got outfitted with shield and weapons. I took a bow and a quiver of blunted arrows. I was better with it than a sword or spear. Lucian took a sword, of course. Once we were ready to go, we hunkered down in our home base to discuss strategy before the horn sounded.

"How in hell are we going to beat them?" Mia shook her head, already defeated. "You heard Athena —no one wins this trial."

"We don't have to beat them," I said. "Just have to distract them long enough for someone to sneak over and grab their flag."

"At least one of them will be guarding the flag." Lucian peered over at the champions, who weren't in huddle, but just standing by their home base. I noticed a couple of them even looked bored.

I wasn't so sure of that. They were demigods. They were used to winning. For them, this was child's play. It was more of a boring task in a long list of boring tasks they'd likely done over and over again for decades. Their arrogance would play against them. Or at least, we could make it play against them.

"I think this is what we should do." I picked up a stick and started to draw in the dirt.

When the horn blew, everyone but Georgina and Marek moved out from the home base. They were going to stay behind to spring the booby trap when it was needed. The rest of us split into two groups, going opposite ways. Lucian, Ren, and Rosie came with me, and Jasmine took charge of Diego, Mia, and Hella.

My team ran to the cover of a half-formed stone wall; some of the stones were broken, as if something chipped at them. It soon became obvious what had done the chipping. Arrows came sailing toward us. I could hear them ping off the rock. Through a tiny slit in the wall, I spotted Achilles standing on top of a slight rise, shooting at us. He didn't even have a shield. And he was smiling.

"What a dick." I shook my head. "We need to show this guy what we're made of."

"I agree." Lucian grinned at me.

"Rosie, I hear you're a great shot."

She shrugged. "I'm all right."

"Okay, on three, the three of us form a shield, and when we draw his fire, Rosie, take your shot. Aim for his legs."

She grinned.

"One, two, three…"

We ran out from the wall, Lucian, Ren, and I had our shields together, creating a wall. The sound of arrows pinging echoed around us. Crouching behind us, Rosie knocked two arrows and when I nodded, she came around the right side, fired, and then ducked back behind the shields. We heard an outraged shout.

"Bloody hell!"

I looked through the slot we'd created between shields to see Achilles with red splotches on his legs. It wasn't blood, but paint. Like paint pellets, our arrows, swords, and spears must've magically produced red paint to mimic wounds. It was perfect.

Now that we had their attention, we made a run for the next cover, while Rosie and I fired more arrows at Achilles. He dashed from his spot on the hill. One of my arrows struck him in the ass. While we regrouped, I heard a shout from the other side of the field.

"Finally. Worthy opponents!" It was Heracles, and he sounded positively joyful.

We were almost halfway across the field. More arrows rained down on our position. Achilles had found a better spot to fire from. I spied Antiope with her spear and shield. I found a hole in the wall and fired arrows back, but Antiope easily protected herself and Achilles. We needed a huge distraction to get farther down the field.

"I'm going to create a diversion. When it happens, you three run to the next cover." After affixing my shield to my back, I rubbed my hands together, an orange glow emerging. "One, two, three!"

I leapt out from behind the wall, hands thrust out. A wall of fire erupted from my palms, and I pushed it toward Achilles and Antiope. Lucian, Ren, and Rosie ran out around the other side toward the next wall of cover. The champions were so surprised by my fire-wall they didn't shoot any arrows.

I felt the power of the fire diminishing. Soon, I'd be exposed in the middle of the field. I spotted a cluster of fallen logs I could hide under. With one final push of the fire, I dropped my hands, snuffing the flames, sprinted to my left, and dove for cover. A couple of arrows whizzed over my head.

Being under the logs gave me a moment of reprieve, and I turned to look back toward our club-house. I was rewarded to see our plan had worked.

"What the hell is this?" Heracles and Bellerophon were both stuck in quick sand near our post.

I put my hand over my mouth to chuckle.

Georgina and Marek had combined their earth and water affinities and produced a wonderfully thick, impassable pool of quick sand, like a moat around a castle. And now, two of the champions were stuck in it. It gave me some time to get to their fort and get the flag.

Another arrow whizzed by me. Then one hit the logs I was under. They'd found my cover. I was about to pop up to find my next cover when a spear tip broke through one of the logs and nearly struck me in the arm.

"Found you." Antiope grinned down at me. She pulled back her spear, and I rolled to the right. She narrowly missed me, and then I was up on my feet, running as fast as I could.

An arrow struck the ground a sliver away from my right foot. I didn't know where I was running to, as there wasn't any good cover on this side. But I did spy a pool of shadows undulating near an outcropping of trees. I sprinted toward it, then dove into it, hoping beyond hope I wasn't making a huge mistake. An arrow zipped by me just as I sunk into the ground.

Darkness swallowed me up. It was like being in a void. My body felt floaty, like I was in a sea of salt water. Picturing their home base in my mind, I ran that way, hoping I wasn't just going deeper into the abyss with no way out. Finally, I reached my destination; the air felt lighter here, like I could easily move through it. Then I saw a pinprick of light. Eventually, that light swelled, and I stepped out of the shadow and into the field.

Medusa, who had been lounging nearby

inspecting her nails, startled when she spotted me pop out of nowhere. She raised her bow, but she was too slow. I'd already knocked my arrow and sent it sailing toward her. It hit her in the chest. Red paint splattered all over her white dress.

"You bitch." She lifted her head, removed her sunglasses, and I could see the her eyes start to glow.

I threw my shield over my face and made a run for their fort. As I ran, the flowers and the grass and the small bushes around me turned to stone. I nearly tripped on a petrified clutch of pansies, but I leapt over them and reached their home base. Now, I just had to clamber up to the top of their fort. But that was going to be impossible with Medusa on the rampage.

She cursed up a storm as she walked toward the fort. More things turned to stone as she neared. She was almost upon me. I risked a peek over my shield to see Lucian charging at her from behind, his sword raised.

He hit her across the back, more red splotched her dress, and she stumbled forward. I dashed up the fort steps, taking them two at a time. I reached the flagpole. With my heart nearly bursting, I grabbed that flag and tore it down.

The horn sounded.

We'd won.

I jumped up and down, waving the flag. "Wohoo!!" I looked over the side of the fort to see Lucian offering his hand to Medusa to help her up. Her eyes clamped closed, she swatted it away.

"I don't need your help, junior." She stood and

put on her sunglasses. She glanced up at me. "Well played."

"Thank you," I said as sweet as cherry pie.

Down the field, my team, my friends, celebrated. And it filled me with so much happiness, tears welled in my eyes. As I looked at each of them, I realized they had become my home, and I would do anything for them.

While the other teams went through their trial, we were whisked away back to our dorms to prepare for the ceremony. I wanted to celebrate with my friends, especially with Lucian, but I was assured there would be plenty of time and opportunity later to celebrate, as there was a big feast after the official dividing of the clans.

After we had all showered, a troupe of nine women came into the dorms, carrying cases and rolling in a hanger of white and gold robes. I was dumbstruck as each of the women looked exactly alike.

"They're the muses," Georgina said.

Two of the women made a beeline toward me and Georgina. They both grinned. Even the shape of their mouths and the whiteness of their teeth were identical.

"I'm Clio, this is Thalia. We're here to make you pretty."

I looked at Georgina, who shrugged. "Okay," we said in unison.

As we were being primped and polished, painted and styled, the word came in through the dorm that none of the other teams had passed the trial. I was happy we'd passed, but it saddened me to know that possibly some of the girls would be getting the boot from the academy. I may have prayed that one of those girls was Revana, but no such luck, as I saw her running around getting ready for the ceremony.

By the time Clio and Thalia had finished with us, we were both wearing the traditional white and gold robes, our makeup was flawless, our skin was dewy and glittered with the bronzer they slathered on. My hair was twisted up into a complicated braid on my head, a gold band wrapped around like a tiara. Georgina's short hair had been slicked up and pinned. Her gold band also looked like a tiara on her head. We slid our pedicured feet into sandals, and we were ready to go.

As we filed out of the dorm to head to the stadium where I'd endured the lightning trial, we caught up with Jasmine and Mia, who both looked like Goddesses. Together, united, we walked through the academy to accept our individual fates.

There was an electric energy humming through the arena when we arrived and filed into the rows of seats. I looked across the arena to find Lucian. I saw him in the third row, and he grinned when our gazes met.

All the Gods and Goddesses walked into the arena and took up positions on the edge of the circle. Like a pie, it was split into twelve pieces. Eventually, each of us would be standing in one of those slices, relegated to that for the rest of our lives. It was overwhelming when I thought about it. I wasn't sure if I truly wanted that fate.

Zeus stepped into the middle of the raised circular platform. "Welcome, recruits. You have all accomplished an amazing feat. You have successfully endured and passed enough trials to ascend to the next level of your training."

Everyone clapped and cheered.

"Now is the moment you will be divided into your blood clan. The choices are based on the skills you've developed, the affinity to certain elements and training, and the trials you've passed. We do not make these choices lightly, and we are never wrong. The clan you are assigned to will be yours for the rest of your life."

Jasmine reached for my hand. I took it, and we squeezed each other.

"After the grand celebration tonight, you will be moving to your clan's hall. There you will have your own room and be welcomed by your other clan brothers and sisters, who have gone through the same first year training as you have. You will become a family."

I looked across the arena at Lucian. I wanted him to know how I felt about him. There might never be another chance to tell him.

"When your name is called, get up and stand side by side with your God." Zeus waved a hand toward the others. "Jasmine Walker."

I squeezed her hand.

"Ares clan."

Jasmine stood, glancing down at me. "You're my best friend, Mel. I love you."

"I love you, too." A couple of tears rolled down my cheeks. I wiped them away.

She stepped down the rows and walked out into the arena and took her place near Ares.

More people were called. Every now and then, one of my friends stood and took their place in the circle.

"Ren Nakamura."

I watched as my first friend stood up.

"Poseidon clan."

I clapped hard and cheered as he moved down to the arena. He beamed as he took his spot in the circle.

Other friends were called.

Mia went to Hera clan. Rosie joined Artemis, and Diego ended up with Dionysus.

Revana landed in Aphrodite's clan, which didn't surprise me in the least, as she was as deceptive and mean as the Goddess herself. Isobel, I heard, didn't make it through the trials, and she'd already been evacuated out of the academy.

"Georgina Stewart."

I grabbed her hand. "I love you, Gina. You're going to be amazing."

"I know." She smiled.

"Demeter clan."

She stood and took her place. I was so proud of her. She deserved her place in the pantheon.

More people were called, and then my heart leapt into my throat.

"Lucian Perro."

He stood. His gaze captured mine, and I couldn't

look away from him. He was beautiful in his white robes and golden waves.

"Zeus clan."

His eyes widened. He was obviously surprised at his placing. He'd told me before that he'd expected to be in Ares's clan. Everyone cheered as he walked down into the arena and took his place next to the father of all Gods. He looked good there.

More people were called. One by one, they moved down into the circle. And then I was alone in the stands. Nerves zipped through me, and I didn't know what to do. I supposed someone had to be called last, and that someone was me.

"Melany Richmond." Zeus's voice boomed all around me. "Never in the history of this academy has one recruit ever passed all twelve trials."

That caused a ripple through everyone. Some of the Gods looked at each other, obviously not knowing that was the case.

"I am at a loss on exactly where to place you, where your skills will be most valued and nurtured."

Aphrodite spoke up. "That's not possible, Zeus. She must have cheated somewhere."

"Oh, shut up," Demeter said to the Goddess. "You always think someone is cheating because that's how you work."

As the Gods squawked and squabbled amongst themselves and my peers whispered about me, I stood and watched it all, unsure of what it all meant. Out of the corner of my eye, I saw the shadows along the stadium move. Wisps of darkness curled and snaked along the floor, then wound up the few steps to the platform. The black tendrils swirled around Hera then Artemis and Apollo. They whipped around, confusion on their faces.

Finally, the wisps swirled in the middle of the platform, making a dark tornado. Zeus took a step back, his eyes narrowing. Then the tornado just froze, the shadows evaporated, and Hades stood there, looking cool and hip in his purple suit and slicked-back, dark hair.

His appearance caused a stir, and every God gasped in shock.

Zeus pointed a finger at him. "You can't be here. It's impossible."

Smiling, Hades gave a deep bow. "It is possible, brother."

"What are you doing here? How dare you come."

Hades turned his head toward me and grinned. A shiver rushed down my back.

"I'm claiming her for my own."

DEMIGODS ACADEMY
YEAR TWO

CHAPTER ONE

MELANY

*S*tunned, I stood frozen in the second row of the arena, staring at the God of the Underworld and wondering if all of this was an elaborate joke. Hades was known for his trickery and deception. Maybe this was his idea of a prank to pull on the most important day of the year for the academy. The most important day for the first year recruits. The most important day for me.

Hades looked beyond pleased with himself. He even had the nerve to wink at me, like I'd been in on the whole thing.

Chaos erupted around me. I didn't know what to do.

"You are not welcome here," Hera shouted at Hades.

"Ah, but sis, it's been too long. Aren't you happy

to see me?" Hades gave a little bow, which just enraged her more.

"Where are the guards? Why aren't they here to apprehend him?" Hera asked of Zeus, but he looked just as confused as everyone else.

Revana stepped into the circle and pointed at me. "She cheated. Obviously, Hades helped her through the trials. She should be expelled for this and kicked out of the academy."

Of course she accused me of this stunt, anything to get rid of me. She couldn't stand I was just better than she was.

Others joined her in the cry that I had somehow cheated. They just looked for some lame excuse to implicate me in some nefarious plot. I wanted to yell at them that I didn't have anything to do with it, but I didn't think anyone would hear me. It was so loud in the arena with everyone talking at once, no one would listen to what I had to say.

While some of the Gods chose to be vocal about Hades's unexpected arrival, others attacked.

Ares waved his arms around in a panic. "Seize him!"

Armed with a sword, Heracles ran up on the platform and charged at Hades. Smiling, Hades waved his hand in the air, and a whip-like tendril of black smoke appeared and wrapped around Heracles's ankles, tripped him, and then hung him upside down over the platform. Heracles started shouting and cursing as he dangled over the cadets.

I pressed my lips together to stop from laughing; it was pretty funny.

Poseidon stepped out of the circle and created a huge cyclone of water around Hades. This started a panic among the recruits, who risked getting swept up into it. Screams echoed over the rush of water as recruits jumped down from the platform and fled toward the main door, which was still closed. Most of the other Gods got out of the way, too. Hermes hovered above the fray with his large, golden wings spread wide and powerful.

I saw Jasmine and Georgina running in that crowd, and I hurried down the rows of seats to meet them. Lucian had been on the other side of the stadium, so I didn't see where he went. But I couldn't get past the crush of other students who were all clamoring to get out.

The wall of water encircled Hades; I couldn't see him through the blue spray. Poseidon smiled as did Zeus, thinking they had captured their brother. They should've known better. Hades didn't have his fearsome reputation for nothing.

Fire flashed in the middle of the platform where Hades had been standing. Then the water just evaporated, and steam filled the arena like a giant sauna. I felt the mist on my cheeks. Once that cleared, I saw Hades standing there, the last remnants of flames disappearing from his fingertips. He wasn't even wet.

"Really?" Hades shook his head, a wry grin on his face. "Is that all you got? I expected more from you, baby brother." He lifted his hands toward Poseidon, but before he could do anything, Zeus clapped his hands together. White sparks erupted from between them and fell to the ground, sizzling the floor on impact. A crack of thunder shook the whole building. I grabbed the railing beside me, so I didn't fall over.

"ENOUGH!"

Silence filled the stadium, as the echoes of thunder faded.

Hades let his hands drop to his sides with a disappointed sigh.

"Open the door and release the recruits." Zeus nodded to Antiope and Achilles, who had been guarding the door. "Please assemble in the dining hall and wait for further instructions." The doors opened, and everyone started to stream out. I pushed into the crowd to follow. "Everyone may go but you, Miss Richmond."

My heart dropped into my gut. Of course. I locked eyes with Jasmine; she gave me a horrified look, as she was swept up in the crowd and out the door. Everyone else went, too, until I was the only student remaining in a room full of Gods and Demigods.

All eyes locked on me as I slowly made my way up onto the platform. I didn't know where to stand. Next to Hades, because he claimed me? Next to Zeus, because he made the decision about my fate? I ended up standing by myself, on the edge of the platform, in case I needed a quick exit strategy.

Ares and Aphrodite continued to grumble about Hades appearance.

"I'm here. Deal with it." Hades glared at both of them. "And like I said before everyone had a hissy fit, I'm here to claim Melany for my own clan. She belongs to me. She's in my charge, and I will train her as I see fit."

"You can't just claim a recruit," Zeus said. "That's not how it works. A recruit must show signs that they belong to your—"

"She's beyond proficient with fire, is she not?" Hades raised an eyebrow at Hephaistos.

After a slight hesitation, Hephaistos nodded. "Yes. She is gifted, but—"

"She has produced black wings." Hades looked at Hermes, who still hovered in the air.

He floated down to the platform, golden wings folding in behind him. "Yes, and it is an anomaly, but doesn't necessarily mean—"

With no effort, huge black wings unfurled from Hades's back. He gave everyone a pointed look, and then his wings folded in again and disappeared.

"And she has a mastery of the shadows." His gaze swept the stage and found Erebus, who had been almost hiding in the corner. "Come and tell them."

Erebus stepped onto the platform, swallowing. "Melany is very skilled in the shadow arts. She can manipulate the shadows to do her bidding. She can even tr… er…" He brought his hand up to cough, and then he started talking again. "She can use them as a p—" He coughed again. It was almost like he was choking.

I noticed Hades staring at him. Was he purposely stopping Erebus from saying something about me? If so, then why? What did he want kept secret about my abilities?

Every time he opened his mouth to talk about me,

he started to cough, and then he spit up something onto the ground. At first it looked like small stones, but they were reddish. After he did it a few more times, everyone stepped away from him; I saw that they were pomegranate seeds.

"Anyway," Hades said, turning away from Erebus. The shadow master sucked in a greedy breath of air. "The point is she possesses all the attributes belonging to me and my clan."

"She can also manipulate water and earth and lightning." Demeter stepped up beside Hades.

Hades's smile was slow and lazy, but vicious. "Yes, and so can I, to some extent."

Zeus glanced at Poseidon, who appeared a bit concerned, then back to Hades. "You don't have a clan here. You're not part of the academy."

"Yeah, and whose fault is that? You wouldn't let me be part of this." He gestured to the arena. "Besides, it's not really yours, is it?"

Everyone on stage glanced nervously at each other.

What did he mean the academy wasn't theirs? That didn't make any sense. The Gods had been recruiting for the academy for more than one hundred years. As a society, we reestablished all the temples of worship around the world, so we could make offerings to the Gods for their favor. If that wasn't for them, for the academy, then who was it for?

Zeus stepped forward, grabbed Hades's arm, and pulled him a foot away from everyone. They bent their heads close together to talk. I strained my ears but couldn't hear what they said.

I glanced around, unsure of what to do, searching for an ally, but I wasn't sure I had one here. Demeter had helped me in the past, and she did seem to be arguing in my favor here, as had Dionysus in his own way. Hephaistos was certainly less grumpy toward me than the others, and had worked with me on my shield after regular forging class. Or maybe I'd been stupidly mistaken, and none of the Gods cared about what happened here, or what happened to any of us. Maybe we were just pawns in some ancient family squabble.

After another few minutes of awkward waiting, Zeus and Hades walked back over to where me and the others stood. Zeus's expression wore frustration, his brow deeply furrowed, while Hades beamed.

"Melany will be under Hades's tutelage. She will go to live in Hades Hall outside of the academy, and train with him in whatever skills he sees fit to benefit the army."

Poseidon shook his head. "This is a mistake."

Hera threw up her hands and walked away.

Ares and Aphrodite expressed the most outrage.

"There should be a discussion and a vote," Aphrodite said. "This isn't fair."

I was curious as to why they were so adamantly against the presence of Hades at the academy.

Demeter, Dionysus, and Hephaistos all shared concerned looks but didn't say anything. Apollo, Artemis, Athena, and Hermes just shook their heads.

"Do I get a say in this? Since it is the rest of my life," I finally said, my voice a bit shaky.

Everyone turned toward me. I saw looks of

concern, whether for me or the situation I couldn't distinguish, and looks of disdain.

"No," Zeus and Hades said in unison.

Zeus addressed the others. "This matter is settled. There will be no more discussion about it. Not between you and definitely not with any of the recruits."

His gaze rested on me again, and I could feel the intensity of it right in my bones. "I trust we can expect discretion from you, Miss Richmond."

I nodded, although I knew I was going to have a hard time not discussing it with my friends. The second I saw them, they were going to bombard me with a million questions. And honestly, I wouldn't have any answers. Something monumental definitely happened here, but I had no real idea what it was.

"Okay, we have a celebration to prepare for," Zeus said. "The recruits will be expecting their reward for completing their trials."

"Am I allowed to leave and join my friends?" I asked, scared of the answer.

"Of course. You earned a celebration." Zeus gestured toward the open door of the arena.

Before I stepped off the platform, I glanced at Hades. He waved his fingers at me in dismissal. "I'll see you later, Melany. We're going to have a grand time together."

I swallowed, as I wasn't so sure.

CHAPTER TWO

MELANY

I joined the others in the dining hall. All the recruits sat at the long wooden tables in groups, talking. They all fell silent the moment I passed through the tall double doors. Jasmine, Georgina, and Lucian rushed toward me, all talking at once.

"What the hell just happened?" Jasmine put her hands on her hips and gave me a look. "You didn't have anything to do with that, did you?"

I frowned at Jasmine, surprised and hurt she'd ask me something like that. "Of course not."

"Are you okay? Did they do something to you?" Georgina grabbed my hand; she looked like she was going to cry.

"I'm okay. I swear."

Lucian pulled me into his arms. "What did Zeus

say? Surely, you won't have to go with Hades. The most logical place for you is in Zeus's clan. With me."

I drew back and gazed at my closest friends, wondering what all of this meant. Would we even see each other again? No one had been clear on exactly what happened to us after we were sorted into our clans. Maybe this was it. Our last goodbye.

"I, uh, I'm going to be training with Hades."

They all gaped at me as if I'd just grown a second head. Then the comments hit me like rapid fire and I felt attacked.

"You can't."

"Are you crazy?"

"There has to be another way."

I shook my head. Anger began to creep inside me at the implications that I had control over the situation. "I don't have a choice. Just like you guys don't. We are all stuck in the clan chosen for us."

Jasmine had the decency to look admonished for her earlier accusation. She sighed and reached for me to give me a hug. "I'm sorry if I came off as a bitch. I was just so scared for you. This is all so messed up."

I agreed it was messed up, but what could we do about it? This was our lives now. We survived our first year in the academy. This was what we signed up for. It was just that I hadn't expected Hades. No one did. He threw everything for a loop. And now, we were two years away from being active soldiers in the Gods Army. Maybe by then, I would have found out what happened to my town of Pecunia, to Sophie, and be able to exact my revenge with all the power of the Gods behind me.

"Look, I don't know what's going on, or what's going to happen to us in the future, but let's just go and enjoy the celebration together." What I didn't say was it might be the last time we were all together. By the troubled looks on their faces, they already knew that.

After another ten minutes or so of milling about in the dining hall, two ceremonial horns blew, echoing through the hall. Moments later a parade of champions marched in, led by Heracles and Hippolyta. Behind them were Achilles, Bellerophon, Antiope, Helen of Troy, Eros, Psyche, and a few others I didn't know or recognize. A buzz of excitement rippled through the room, and everyone got to their feet, watching and waiting in anticipation of what came next.

"Congratulations recruits," Heracles bellowed. "You have successfully completed your first year of training and have now achieved the rank of cadet."

A wave of clapping and cheering flowed through the room.

"Because of this great feat, you have been rewarded with a special position in one of the Gods' clans. You should be proud of this achievement. Not everyone who trains at the academy makes it through. You are the best of the elite selection of recruits." He beamed at us all. "Now it is time to celebrate."

More clapping and cheers. I didn't join in. I didn't feel rewarded, but like I was being punished. Others in the room gave me suspicious and cautious looks, like I was someone to be skeptical of, or even feared. I didn't like it. It made my stomach churn.

"We are here to escort you to your celebratory feast." Heracles gestured to the path that the champions made between them, and we all lined up. Some jostled for position to be at the front, but I, and my friends, including Mia, Ren, and Rosie, stayed back, so we were the last of the group to file out of the dining hall and into the main corridor.

As the procession wound its way through the stone corridors of the academy to the great hall, where even now I could hear the distant echoing thump of music, a rush of excitement circulated through the group. Jasmine and Georgina positively glowed with exhilaration. Lucian did, too. He walked with his head up, proud and jubilant about what he'd achieved. They all deserved to be praised, to feel triumphant in their achievements. I'd never want to take that away from them.

Despite my smiles and attempts at frivolity, I didn't share their eagerness and excitement for what was to come. I was filled with ominous dread.

There was something else, something nefarious, going on in the academy behind the scenes. I didn't know what it was, but I did know it revolved around Hades and his unexpected arrival... and around me.

When the front of the procession reached the towering double doors of the great hall, they slowly swung open, and golden light bathed us. Loud thunderous music swirled around us, so Dionysus must've been DJing again. One by one, in pairs, and in small groups, we entered the hall for our celebration.

Before I could enter, Heracles gently grabbed my arm and pulled me to the side, leaning down into my ear. "I just want you to know that I'm on your side. Others are as well. You have friends in the academy." Then as if remembering himself and where he was, he straightened and pushed me into the room. "Go have fun, cadet."

His words comforted me, as I stumbled into the great hall and caught up with Lucian and the others. We all paused for a moment, taking in the splendor of the gallery. Everything was gold and white and radiating with warm light. Hovering about six feet above us, like golden balloons, were candle filled lanterns immersing the room in a luxurious illumination. Tall gold vases of white flowers encircled each ivory pillar filling the air with a slightly sweet aroma. Long tables covered in gold cloth lined three walls and were stacked with every food imaginable. Roast chicken and duck, tiny sage stuffed partridges, roasted potatoes and root vegetables next to delicate pasta dishes. And the dessert table had its own chocolate fountain, which Diego was now shoving his face under. Students lined up, eager to fill up their plates.

Lucian glanced at me. "Hungry?"

"Oh, hell yes."

Laughing, we grabbed a fancy plate and got in line. After stacking our plates with mountains of food, we found seats at one of the round tables circumventing the dance floor and sat and shoveled food into our mouths. By the time my plate was empty, I didn't think I could move.

Jasmine patted her flat stomach. "I have a food belly."

I leaned in to peer at her washboard abs. "Where?" I poked her and she laughed.

It felt wonderful to sit with my friends and joke around after months of hard work, like we were just ordinary teenagers at spring formal, and not warriors training to one day risk our lives in war if needed. I soaked it all in knowing it wasn't going to last.

I looked over at the DJ platform where Dionysus had his turntables and sound system. His hair was spiked up every which way like a demented hedgehog, and he wore dark sunglasses and a black cape. He spotted me, grinned, and then grabbed the microphone. "This next song is for all the bad bitches out there."

Red laser lights cut through the air, rising from the ground to the roof, as the music dropped the beat. It rolled over me like a technicolor wave. I jumped to my feet and grabbed Lucian's hand, pulling him with me out onto the dance floor. Jasmine and Mia held hands on the floor. Ren and Rosie, even Georgina, all joined in until we were one massive group, jumping and bouncing to the music like pogo sticks.

"Put your hands up!" Dionysus shouted as the beat, that one glorious beat, dropped like a rock in water, rippling out to the entire room.

I closed my eyes, losing myself in the music. I swayed and gyrated, Lucian matching me with every move. I draped my arms around his neck, his around my waist, and we danced together, in synch, the heat of our bodies mingling as one entity.

Sweat slicked my skin, and I was so hot I wanted to tear off my robe, but I refrained, considering I only had on my underwear underneath. When the muses had come to dress us before the ceremony, Clio and Thalia wouldn't let me wear a bra, claiming it would ruin the elegant lines of my robe. It didn't matter now I supposed, as I wasn't about to undress, anyway. But I did want alone time with Lucian. My body was burning up for him.

I grabbed his hand and pulled him off the dance-floor and toward the main doors. He didn't say anything, didn't question me. By the wicked look in his eyes, I figured he was thinking about the same thing.

We found a dark alcove away from the noise and revelry of the celebration and embraced. His hands pressed against my bare back, sending a pleasant shiver over my skin, as he leaned down and kissed me. My sudden gasp emboldened him, and he moved his mouth over mine, tasting and teasing, making my heart thump so hard in my chest it was painful.

I dove my hands into the silky waves of his golden hair and hung on as he backed me up against the wall. His hands became bold and moved over my body, touching me gently. A slight caress along my hip made my belly flutter and then up to brush just under the swell of my breasts making me gasp again.

Breathing hard, Lucian pulled back and rested his forehead against mine. "I think we're nearing dangerous territory here. I don't want to do anything neither of us is ready for."

Should I tell him I was ready? That I was scared we wouldn't have any more time together, that this was it for us? That if we didn't indulge in each other, we'd never get another chance to do just that?

My heart raced so fast I couldn't catch my breath. I couldn't think beyond the way my body vibrated under his touch.

"I'm going to go get us some drinks." His voice was a bit ragged and rough.

I nodded, licking my lips; they still tingled from his kisses.

He pulled back, looked me in the eyes, then after a quick peck on the tip of my nose, he ventured out into the main corridor before heading back to the great hall. I stepped out of the alcove and casually paced around the area, trying to get my heartrate back to normal.

Leaning against the railing, I gazed down the huge staircase to the main foyer. It was dark down there, the only light radiating from one or two flickering lamps along the stone walls. I looked up at the glass dome ceiling. The moon was full, and its light seemed to beam right through me. It seemed to want to expose me for a fraud, or it could've been that was how it made me feel, as its light glared at me. I didn't know why I felt that way. I'd earned my place here in the academy. I'd passed every trial; I never cheated, despite the accusations from Revana and a few others. Still, that feeling lingered deep inside me. Uncomfortable, I stepped out of the moonlight and into the shadows.

The moment my foot touched the darkened floor, the shadows seemed to undulate playfully. Frowning, I watched as they moved across the white tile like wisps of black smoke to envelop my sandaled foot. I lifted my leg, and the tendrils clung to me like spider webs. A prickling sensation rushed over my body, and it made me feel cold and clammy.

I turned to walk away—to get away—but the shadows followed me. Now, they didn't seem so playful, but aggressive, purposeful. I kept walking, faster by the second, but I couldn't outrun the darkness. As I moved down the corridor toward the hall, I looked for firelight to step into, but each time I moved toward one of the lamps, the flames blew out, plunging me into even more darkness. I could see the golden glow of the great hall ahead, but I wasn't going to make it.

Running seemed pointless. I stopped and let the shadows swallow me up.

CHAPTER THREE

MELANY

J was pulled through the darkness, as if strings were fastened to my skin. It felt the same way as being sucked through the water portal to the academy, except decidedly more uncomfortable. My lungs didn't burn, but everything else seemed to. Eventually, the shadows dissipated around me, and I was left standing in a wide black stone corridor leading to several rooms, with high vaulted ceilings; there were four doors on each side.

It was dim in the hall. Firelight escaped from narrow slits in the juncture of the wall and floor and cast an eerie glow across the smooth black stone. I swung around in a circle, took note of the tall closed doors behind me, but I didn't recognize where I was. It was like no hall I'd ever been in.

"Hello?" My voice echoed off the walls.

I didn't expect an answer, so I jumped when I heard a deep male voice.

"I'm in the library. Last door on the right."

Cautious, I walked down the corridor to the last room on the right. It was the only one with an open door. I stepped into the room and hovered there in the doorway surveying my new surroundings. Two walls contained floor to ceiling shelves with meticulously organized books. Not one looked out of place. There were more books here than I'd ever seen in one spot. The other wall showcased several paintings— Renaissance paintings of old Greek myths. I'd seen some of them in books about the Gods.

At the far end of the room were a massive dark stone fireplace, fire crackling within, and two high-backed, decorative chairs sitting on either side, a mahogany round table by each. And Hades sat in one of those chairs, sipping red wine from a delicate wineglass, looking equally at home and on display in his sharp purple suit.

He smiled when our gazes locked. "Welcome." He gestured to the other chair. "Please sit and join me for a drink to celebrate."

I slowly moved across the room toward him. "Did you bring me here?"

"Technically, I just sent the shadows. You walked through them."

"It was kind of hard not to considering they swarmed me."

He chuckled. "Yeah, my shadows can get a tad aggressive from time to time." He pointed to the big chair. "Sit. Drink. Relax."

I considered not sitting but realized that was childish and a waste of my anger at being kidnapped. I sunk into the velvety cushioned chair. Beside me on the table, the wineglass magically filled with red wine as I watched.

I picked the glass up and peered into it suspiciously. I sniffed it.

Hades shook his head with amusement. "Do you really think I'd poison you? After all I've done to get you here?"

I took a tiny sip of wine, letting it linger on my tongue. I didn't normally enjoy red wine, but this was surprisingly sweet. "Where is here?"

"My hall, deep below the academy. This is where you'll live now. You'll have your own room with an en suite. The soaker tub is exquisite." He took a sip of his drink, watching me intently over the rim. "You will train with me to hone your skills. If you do everything I say, you could become the greatest warrior this army has ever seen." His lips twitched up in a sly, lopsided grin. "Besides me, of course."

"Of course." I smirked. "What makes you think I want to be some great warrior?"

"I've been watching you over the course of the year. You play to win, not to get some participation ribbon."

"How could you have been watching me? You were banned from the academy, or so the rumors said."

He shrugged. "I have my ways." There was a mischievous glint in his eyes.

The dark form outside of the portal. The whispers in the halls. The shadows that guided me. My dreams. He'd been there beside me from the moment I'd arrived at the academy. But why me? What was so special about me? I wasn't one hundred percent sure I wanted to know that answer, so I didn't ask. Although, I was sure he wouldn't tell me the truth anyway.

Hades intrigued me. But he also scared me. Because I felt drawn to him, and I didn't know why.

I set the glass on the table and got to me feet. "I want to go back to the party. I want to see my friends."

"There is no going back, Melany. That's not how it works anymore. You're in my charge now. You're my protégé."

That was what he said, but in my mind, I heard the words... *You're mine.*

Angry, I walked toward the door.

"Where are you going?" He sighed.

"I'm leaving."

"Okay, have fun with that."

Before I left, I glanced over my shoulder at him. He was still in his chair, casually drinking his wine, looking as if he didn't have a care in the world.

I marched back down the corridor to the towering main doors. At first I thought they were made of a dark wood, but they, too, were carved from stone. I reached for the large metal knob expecting it to be locked, but it turned in my hand, and I slowly pushed it open. As I walked through, the doors suddenly swung shut behind me, and I was in another corridor, which looked eerily the same as the last one.

I walked along the stone floor, my footsteps echoing off the walls. I passed three doors on either side, all closed except for one. When I peered inside, I saw it was the library—the same library—and Hades still sat in the chair near the fireplace.

When he saw me, he raised his glass. "Ready to see your room yet?"

I turned and ran down the corridor this time, pushed open the doors, crossed the threshold, and ended right back in the same hallway. It was an unending loop.

Frustrated, I ran to the first closed door on my left. I tried the handle; it was locked. I went to the next door, also locked. The third door wasn't locked, and I opened it, walked in, and had stepped into the library again. I whirled around to see the bookshelves behind me and no door.

Hades frowned. "Done running around yet?"

"No." I marched out of the library and tried the room next door. The door was locked. I banged on it, tried to push it open, but it wouldn't budge. The next door opened, and I walked in, popping out of the door across the hall back into the main corridor where it had all started.

I raised my hands into the air and screamed, "Are you freaking kidding me!"

When I was done, my throat dry and hoarse, I glanced up to see Hades strolling out of the library. "I'll show you to your room."

He crossed the corridor and approached the second closed door on the left side. It was one of the doors that had stayed locked when I'd tried it. He put his hand on the door handle and turned it. The door opened.

Of course it did. This was his world, and he was a God. And I was just some puppet he was playing with.

Flames in the wall sconces burst into life the second I followed him through and stepped into a huge suite dominated by a king-sized canopied bed, with indigo blue covers and pillows, and thick curtains tied up against the four tall posters. The stone walls had several paintings of what appeared to be fearsome beasts and pretty nymphs hung on them, and large, oval gilded mirrors with words etched on the glass. There was a navy settee and a cast iron table in one corner near the ornate hearth. In another corner near the closet was a dressing table with a large mirror and a decorative chair.

It was all very elegant and royal looking and gothic in shape and style. I could picture all the furniture as part of Dracula's castle from a book I'd once read. I looked so out of place with my white and gold robe, tiara, and sandals.

Hades gestured to an arched opening in one wall. "This is the en suite."

Inside the room were the toilet, sink, a waterfall like shower, and a claw-footed soaker tub.

He pointed to the drawers and cupboards near the sink. "Everything you need is in there. Soaps and shampoo and oils for your bath. I think there might even be a bag full of rose petals if that's what you prefer. Anything you want, just ask."

Rose petals? What did he take me for? A pampered princess?

I drank it all in. The room was bigger than the one Callie had had at the Demos estate. Although everything was all dark and stone and medieval like, it was still just as luxurious. In my lifetime, I never thought I'd have such a room to call my own. I couldn't stop my smile as I gazed around.

Hades must've spied my grin because he appeared positively pleased with himself as he went to the closet door and pulled it open. The lamp hanging from the ceiling flared to life as we walked inside. I gaped at the rows of clothes hanging along one wall and the rows of shoes and boots along another. The other wall was one giant mirror.

"Now that you're part of my clan, you should dress the part." He pulled a long plum-colored velvet dress off the rack and held it up for me. I ran my fingers over it; it was soft and subtle, and I noticed it had two slits in the skirt along the sides, so a girl could still perform a roundhouse kick. It was also in my exact size, as if it had been made specially just for me.

"It's pretty, but not really me."

He put it back, pulling something else off a hanger. "How about this?" He handed me a pair of black leather pants, also in my size, and a navy leather corset. Then he gestured to a long black leather duster. He flipped it open to show me the silky dark blue lining inside. There were skulls painted all along the fabric. "I think this would look good on you. You'd look kick-ass."

I gnawed on my bottom lip as I played my fingers over all the fine, expensive-looking clothes. "Why?"

"Why what?"

"Why all this?" I studied him. "Why me?"

He narrowed his eyes as he regarded me. "Because Melany, you have darkness running through your blood."

I winced. I didn't know what he meant. I wasn't a bad person. At least I didn't think I was.

"Darkness is not this bad thing as most people would have you believe. As the other Gods like to blather on about." He shook his head sadly. "Darkness is power and strength and stealth. With my help, you will be able to access that power and use it."

I frowned. I wasn't as thrilled as he was to know I had darkness inside me. All my life I'd been told I was different, an outcast. No matter how hard I tried, I knew I'd never be like Callie and her friends. Light didn't shine from inside me, as it seemed to shine from them.

Now, I supposed I knew why.

Was I born with this darkness inside of me? Did I get it from my parents?

Hades gestured for us to leave the closet. He walked to the table near the hearth and poured water into a glass. He carried it over to me. I took it gratefully, drinking it all down in a couple of swallows.

"I know this is a lot to take in."

"That's the understatement of the year."

He gave me a soft smile. "It's been a long, interesting day. I'm sure you're tired now."

I yawned. I was tired. It kind of snuck up on me

all of a sudden. Now that adrenaline wasn't coursing through my bloodstream, I was crashing down hard.

"You will find sleeping clothes in the closet and everything else you need in those drawers." He walked over to the bed and pointed to a silk cord hanging from the ceiling. "If you need anything at all, at any time, just pull on this, and Charon will get it for you."

"Who's Charon?"

"My butler. He's a bit of a grump, so don't be put off by his gruff manner. It's just how he is. He says it's from serving me for over a millennia, but I think it's just his low vitamin D levels. He doesn't get much sun." He winked.

And I giggled. I felt a bit drowsy. Almost tipsy. I stared at the water glass in my hand.

He took it from me and led me to the bed. "Get some sleep. We'll talk in the morning. Then we'll start your training."

"What if I want to leave?" My tongue felt fat in my mouth, and I wondered if I was mumbling my words. "Can I just open those big doors and go back to the academy?"

He looked at me a long moment. "No. You can't leave. That was part of the deal Zeus and I arranged."

I couldn't keep myself upright any longer. I fell back against the huge mattress, my eyes curling shut. Before I completely drifted away, I felt Hades hands as he positioned me on the bed and pulled the blanket up to my chin, tucking me in.

CHAPTER FOUR

LUCIAN

*A*ll I could think about as I walked back to the alcove with our drinks was how much I wanted to kiss Melany again. Her lips were so soft, her body so hot, especially in that toga. She'd probably kill me for saying it, but she looked like a Goddess with the gold eyeshadow and glitter on her cheeks. In my opinion, she was prettier than Aphrodite.

But when I returned to the alcove, Melany was gone. I wandered out into the main corridor to look for her.

"Blue?"

I glanced over the railing and down into the foyer. It was empty and dark, no indication anyone was down there. I checked in every corner and hiding spot but didn't find her sitting in the dark, waiting for me. I didn't think she'd go back to her dorm without telling me first. She knew, as we all did, this was likely our last night together for a while.

I made my way back into the great hall. Maybe she got bored waiting for me, and we'd missed each other coming and going.

After setting the drinks on a table, I headed over to the buffet to see if she was filling up another plate. Training as we did required a lot of calories, and that wasn't going to change any time soon. It was likely going to get a lot more strenuous now that we were in our respective clans.

She wasn't at the buffet, so I went to the dance-floor to see if she was dancing. I spotted Jasmine and Mia in the middle of the fray jumping up and down but didn't spy any blue hair in the crowd. I looked around and saw Georgina sitting at the table on the edge of the dance floor eating a large piece of choco-late cake. I approached her.

"Have you seen Mel?"

"No. I thought she was with you."

"She was. I left her out in the corridor to get us some drinks, and she was gone when I got back."

I didn't want to appear concerned. It was stupid to be worried in a place like this. We were all warriors in training, and I knew Melany could take care of herself and then some. But with Hades arrival in the academy and his claiming of Melany, everything no longer seemed safe and secure. I didn't know exactly what was going on, but it was clear Hades had a fixa-tion with her. And I didn't like it.

Georgina stood. "I'll help you look for her. I'll go

check our dorm room. Maybe she went back to change. I know she hated the robe she was wearing."

I nodded. "I'll ask Jasmine and Mia to be on the lookout for her, just in case." I went onto the dance floor to talk to them.

Jasmine took one look at my expression and frowned, leaning into my ear. "What's going on?"

"Have you see Mel?"

She shook her head. "Not since we were all on the floor together."

"She was waiting for me out in the main corridor near the stairs, but I can't find her."

"We'll look for her with you." Jasmine grabbed Mia's hand, and we moved off the floor.

Georgina and I went one way around the hall, Jasmine and Mia went the other way. My gaze swept the entire area, and I couldn't see her anywhere. Ren met up with us on the other side of the hall; he must've seen us doing the sweep.

"What's up?"

"Looking for Mel. She's missing."

"I haven't seen her." Ren grabbed Rosie as she walked by. "Have you seen Melany?"

Rosie shook her head. "No, not since we were all dancing."

Once we all met up again, we left the hall and made our way back to the girls' dorm. I didn't wait at the end of the hall like I normally would have, entering with Georgina to her room. It was dark when we got there, and when Georgina flicked on the light, we saw that Melany wasn't there, and all her stuff was gone. Panic swelled inside me. Had Hades already taken her?

"Are you sure her stuff is gone?"

She gestured to the empty closet on Melany's side of the room. "Oh yeah."

Jasmine lingered in the doorway. "What the hell does that mean? She wouldn't just leave. Not after all we've been through. Doesn't make sense."

"Well, we're all supposed to move to our clan halls by tomorrow," Georgina said. "Maybe she got moved early."

"Against her will, would be my guess." I ran a hand through my hair, concern making my guts clench. "She was less than happy to be forced into Hades clan."

"Where else would she go?" Jasmine asked. "Maybe she went somewhere to think."

"Let's try the maze."

Together, we left the academy and rounded the building to the hedge maze. The stone statues guarding the entrance appeared even more menacing than usual. Or it could've been the dread coursing through me.

Before we entered the dark maze, I created a small ball of fire in the palm of my hand to light our way. If Melany was here, that fireball would've been huge and bright. Her manipulation of fire was extraordinary. I'd even seen Hephaistos eye her with appreciation when she was creating something in the flames.

The maze was large, and it took us a bit to get through it, as the path had changed since I'd been through it last. When we reached the center and the gazebo, my dread increased as the strains of an acoustic guitar greeted us.

The four cauldrons around the gazebo were lit, the flames swaying to the music emanating from within. The orange glow created an unsettling display of light and dark over the stone pillars and roof of the gazebo. Shadows created by the flames seemed to dance in celebration.

I wasn't surprised to see Hades sitting on the stone bench strumming his guitar when I took the three steps up into the gazebo. Jasmine, Mia, Georgina, Ren, and Rosie all lined up behind me. When he saw us, he smiled, but kept playing his song with a bit more gusto.

"Where is she?"

His gaze fixed on me; it looked like there were flames crackling in his eyes, but it must've been the reflection of the fire in the cauldrons. He smacked his hand down on the strings of the guitar, letting go one last twang.

"Where is who? I think you should be a bit more specific."

I took a step toward him. "Don't play games with me, Hades. I know you did something to Melany."

He set his guitar aside onto the bench beside him and leaned back against the railing, as if he didn't have a care in the world. He grinned again, and it was cold and calculating and sent an icy shiver down my back. "Haven't you heard, boy, play time is over?"

I took another step forward.

"Lucian," Ren warned from behind me.

"Where is Melany?! What did you do to her?!" I demanded.

"What makes you think I'd do anything to her? She's my protégé now. She's special. Very special." He ran his fingers across his mouth. "But you obviously already know that about her."

He dripped with arrogance, and it got my blood up. Heat swelled in my hands, then sparks. Ropes of lightning encircled my fingers. One flick of my wrist and I could send a few bolts toward Hades. But before I could do anything drastic and stupid, Ren, Jasmine, and Georgina all grabbed me and kept me from charging toward the dark God. They probably saved my life.

Chuckling, Hades stood. He brushed at his pants and adjusted his shirt collar. "I admire your courage, Lucian. And it appears you have some ability." He lifted his hands and wiggled his fingers. Electrical sparks coiled around his hands, but it wasn't white lightning; it was as black as ink. "My brother must be pumped to have you in his clan."

I quickly snapped my hands closed, cutting off the flow of current. I sagged back against my friends, knowing I was foolish to think I could ever hope to go against a God as powerful as Hades.

"I understand your desire to fight me, Lucian. I like it. Shows great spunk." Hades shook his hands out, and black sparks bounced onto the ground then fizzled. "And Melany… is definitely worth fighting for."

He licked his lips, as if he was thinking about the most delicious meal he was set to devour.

I broke free of my friends' hands and rushed at him, my fists up to fight.

With a snap of his fingers, Hades dissolved into tendrils of black smoke, which swirled up into a dark tornado, blowing back my hair. Then the smoke vanished into thin air. All that remained was his acoustic guitar.

I picked it up and smashed it into a hundred pieces. It didn't do much to satisfy the rage coursing through me like wildfire.

"Lucian, stop!" Jasmine came to my side. She didn't touch me though, which was probably best.

Breathing hard, I sagged against the side of the gazebo. "He has her, Jasmine."

"I know. It'll be okay. Mel's tough. She can handle herself."

I nodded, but I wasn't so sure. Physically, I knew Melany could handle anything anyone threw at her, but I wasn't worried about Hades pushing her physical limits. I was worried he held some kind of mental thrall over her. I remembered how she'd sounded when she talked about Hades, about seeing him here in the gazebo, playing his guitar for her.

She sounded intrigued by him. Melany was a curious person, and it scared me to think what she'd do to satisfy that curiosity.

CHAPTER FIVE

MELANY

a sudden clanging sounded near my ear jolting me out of sleep. I blinked open my eyes to stare at the black canopy over top, trying to establish where the hell I was. I turned my head to see more dark things—the pillows, the blanket, the drapes clinging to the canopy, the round table near the bed. Then it came back in a heady rush, and I rolled over onto my side as nausea washed over me.

I was in Hades Hall with Hades.

But what the hell was that clanging noise?

Slowly, I sat up and stretched. That's when I spied the bell hanging on the wall near the canopy. It rattled back and forth setting my teeth on edge. Obviously, it was my new alarm clock.

I stretched again and stood. The bell kept ringing. "Argh. Okay, I'm up. Jeeze."

Instantly, the bell stopped. Well, that was creepy.

When I took a step forward toward the bathroom, something moved in the shadows in the corner near the closed door. I held my breath as a tall form in a hooded robe floated toward me. I clenched my hands, flames immediately engulfing them, and then raised them, ready to attack.

The form stopped, lifted long, bony hands, and drew back the hood to reveal a skeletal face, large rheumy eyes, and brown rotten teeth showing between pulled back thin, wrinkled lips. His long, white beard hung in a scraggly mess down his chest.

I screamed. I couldn't help it. It was a reflex.

"Good morning, miss." His voice was as brittle as yellowed old paper. "I hope you slept well."

Breathing hard with my heart hammering in my throat, I didn't lower my hands. "Who are you?"

"Charon, miss. Lord Hades has instructed me to inform you that breakfast will be served in the dining room promptly at seven and not to be late. Also, your training clothes are hanging in your closet."

Slowly, I lowered my hands and extinguished the flames sparking between my fingers. "Please tell me, Charon, that you're not going to be in my room every morning."

"Of course not, miss. That would be rude." He bowed his head then turned and floated toward the door, which opened on its own, and he sailed through, and the door shut behind him.

Once he was gone, I went into the bathroom, washed, and then went into the closet to get dressed. My training clothes consisted of black leggings and a long-sleeved, tight shirt, in a material that felt both lightweight and heavy. Almost like armor but without any bulk. I put on the black boots accompanying them.

I came out of my room, glanced around, and had no idea where the dining room was, so I checked all the doors. Two doors were locked, and when I tried the third, it opened into a large dining room, dominated by a long mahogany table with only two chairs, one at each end. Hades, dressed all in black, sat at the far end, sipping from a tea cup. There was another place setting of tea at the other chair.

"Good morning. You're on time. Good. Sit." He gestured to the end of the table. "Breakfast will be served shortly."

I sat and looked into the cup in front of me. I sniffed it, wrinkling my nose. Smelled gross.

"Drink it. It's good for you."

I met his gaze across the table, pissed. "Oh, like the water you drugged me with was good for me last night?"

He waved his hand at me. "I didn't drug you, Melany. You were tired; it had been a very long and stressful day. Even for me. Fighting with my brothers always wears me out. I zonked out the minute my head hit my pillow."

"Your butler scared the crap out of me this morning in my room. Does he always creep around?"

"Yes, I'm afraid that's his default state of being." Hades chuckled. "I'll make sure he doesn't pop in on you like that again. I think he was just excited to meet you. I haven't taken on a... recruit in a very long time."

"You used to teach here?"

"Don't look so surprised." His face scrunched up. "I'm a pretty decent teacher. I used to get all the apples." His grin was quick and sly and did funny things to my belly.

I swallowed, feeling a bit warmer than before. "Why were you banned from the academy?"

"It's a long story, and one you don't need to know right now."

The door behind Hades swung open and one of Hephaistos's little serving robots wheeled out with two plates of hot food. It stopped beside Hades and handed him a plate, then wheeled down to me. I took the plate of eggs, toast, sausage, and potatoes and set it down on the table in front of me. Then the little robot zoomed back through the door.

"Does Hephaistos know you have one of his robots?"

"Of course. He and I have an understanding. Now eat. You're going to have a long day of training, and you're going to need the energy."

After we ate, I followed Hades down the corridor to the closed door next to the library. Last time I checked, the door had been locked, but it naturally opened to Hades. I followed him in and was stunned. Of course every room in Hades Hall defied the laws of physics and form, and this room, although it seemed silly to call it merely that, was a glaring testament to the deception.

It was as spacious as the training studio in the

academy and reminded me a bit of a martial arts dojo, as one wall was covered in an array of weapons, from Bo staffs to long bows to ornate curved daggers. Close to that wall was a row of wooden training dummies. And across the room on the far side was an obstacle course, with hanging ropes to climb, narrow beams to walk, razor wire to crawl under, and a cement wall to scale.

Several tall torches lit the room, situated every few feet along the walls. It felt like we were in some ancient gladiator arena.

Hades spread his arms, gesturing to the room. "This is where you will train every day."

I walked to the weapon wall and ran my fingers over one of the broadsword's blade. I'd had some training with a few of the weapons on the wall, but not all of them, and I was eager to give them a try.

I spun around and looked him up and down. "And you're going to train me?"

His eyebrow arched. "Yes, in some of the combat tactics." He snatched a couple of the knives on the wall. One in each hand, he spun them around flaw- lessly, fluidly, and then with a flick of his wrists, they zipped across the room. One impaled a wooden dummy right in the middle, and the other dagger hit the next one in the same spot. It was impressive.

"But most of your training will be with my associates." There was a sly smile on his face as he looked up at the ceiling.

I followed his gaze and spotted three large forms moving about in the shadows on a ledge twenty-five feet above us. Then one by one, they swooped down and landed next to Hades. Their appearance startled me, and I took a few unsteady steps backward. I'd thought Medusa and Chiron had been unsettling to interact with.

But these creatures took things to a whole new level. I'd read about the Furies in a book about the Gods. They embodied anger, vengeance, and jealousy. The very air changed the moment they arrived. It was a chaotic energy, and it made the hairs on my arms and the back of my neck rise.

"Welcome ladies." Hades gestured to the first new arrival on his left, who towered over him. "This is Allecto."

She had long, bright red hair braided in two lines, one on each side of her angular face. Blood red eyes glared down at me, crimson lines running in tear stains down her face. Between her full, pale lips, I could see tiny, razor-sharp kitten teeth that looked more deadly than cute. Massive black leathery wings loomed behind her, the ends of them hooked much like those of a bat. Other than those oddities, she resembled a regular woman, except extremely muscular and tall. She would've loomed over Hippolyta.

"And this is Tisiphone and Megaera."

Beside Allecto stood her sister. I assumed it was as they shared the same facial features, but she had short, raven black hair. She also had red eyes with streaks of blood staining her cheeks, tiny fangs, and similar large, black wings. Although she wasn't as tall or as bulky, she was still intimidating and fierce looking, and she studied me like she wanted to dine on my blood and bones.

Next to her was a slighter, shorter woman; she was only a couple of inches taller than me, with long, stringy green hair. She shared all the same physical features, though, as her sisters. Her gaze was more pointed when she looked me up and down.

She smirked. "This is who you've chosen?" Her voice was high-pitched and shrill, making me shudder.

"She's tougher than she looks."

"She better be, or we'll break her within minutes of training." Allecto leaned down to scrutinize me. She sniffed the air around me and then snarled, "She reeks of fear."

I swallowed, taking a step forward. "I'm not afraid."

Although I was shaking inside, I wasn't going to let them intimidate me. I didn't go through hell in the twelve trials to be bullied around by three bat girls.

Tisiphone grinned, her teeth gnashing. "Yeah, we'll see about that."

Hades patted her on the shoulder. "Be nice, Tis. I need her to stay in one piece, okay?"

"I'll think about it." She sniffed and then flexed her wings. The hooked ends came very close to my face. Allecto and Megaera snorted and chuckled.

I couldn't let them push me around, especially since I was going to be training with them every day. I had to show them I wasn't scared, although I was a little, and that I wasn't someone to mess around with.

Puffing out my chest, I focused my mind. Seconds

later, my black feathery wings split through my shoulder blades and unfurled around me, twelve feet of wingspan. All three sisters' eyes widened in surprise.

Hades chuckled. "There's the fierce girl I saw in the trials."

Megaera sneered. "Fierce? We'll see about that."

Tisiphone bent toward me, reaching out to touch the tip of my wings. She pulled a face. "Not bad. They look good. Can you use them?"

Without hesitation, I shot up into the air, flapping once to gain velocity. I flew up to the ceiling, touched the crossbeams, and then swooped over to the ropes hanging down. I grabbed one and swung myself around, then let go, and flew off like a shot again to the other side of the training studio.

Laughing, Tisiphone clapped, cheering me on.

Hades's grin was instant and huge, and I felt a sort of pride swell in my heart.

Allecto just sneered.

Not to be out done, Megaera took to the air with a loud whoosh of her wings. As I hovered near the corner of the studio, she flew right at me. Folding my wings in, I dropped, then right before I reached the ground, I released them and soared just over Hades and the others' heads. I caught Hades's pleased chuckle as I swooped overhead.

Megaera came at me again, arms outstretched. I was about to dodge her and turn right, when two green whips snapped out of her wrists. The tips just brushed the top of my head, and it was then I realized, with sickening dread, that the whips were snakes. I heard their hiss as their open mouths snapped right by my face.

Shocked, my wings folded into my body, and I dropped like a sack of rocks to the floor. Before I could break my limbs in the fall, Hades caught me in his arms, and then set me back onto my feet. I wobbled a little but I didn't fall.

I couldn't believe what I just saw. I gaped at Megaera as she landed softly next to her red-headed sister. She rubbed at her wrists, and I saw painful looking red slashes across her skin where the snakes had broken through.

"There, I knew you'd all get along. Just like one big, happy family." Hades clapped his hands gleefully. He patted me on the shoulder. "Have fun. I'll leave you to your training. I'll see you at dinner."

Then he left the room, leaving me with three very strange and very unpleasant women, who I suspected had no intention of seeing me succeed.

CHAPTER SIX

MELANY

"Your flying's not bad." Tisiphone folded her wings behind her back. They didn't retreat into her body like mine had. "But we will teach you to be even better."

Megaera snorted. "She flies like a tiny chick."

"Now, now sister, don't be so harsh on the poor girl. She just got her wings while you've had yours for over a thousand years." Tisiphone patted her sister on top of her green head like a child.

Megaera batted her hand away. "Whatever."

"Stop bickering," Allecto snarled at her sisters then glared at me. "Are you ready to start training?"

I nodded. "Yes."

"Good." She walked toward the weapons wall. I rushed to her side to join her. "In combat you must be able to pick up any weapon and know how to kill with it."

I flinched at her bluntness, but the truth was I was a soldier training in an army. I not only needed to know how to defend myself and others, but how to kill. If someone or something was coming at me or those I loved, I couldn't hesitate to act.

She plucked a large mace with a spiked ball at the tip from the wall and handled it like it was made of plastic and not iron. She made her way to one of the wooden combat dummies, the one Hades had impaled with a knife, and swung the mace overhead. It came down on the dummy and broke it into pieces. With one mighty blow, she had demolished it, reducing it to toothpicks.

Turning her fierce gaze on me, she tossed me the mace. I caught it with both hands. It was heavy, but I'd been holding a sword for months now, so my muscles didn't shake.

She pointed to the other wooden dummy. "Let's see what you're made of."

"Won't Hades be angry we're breaking his things?"

Allecto's brow furrowed. "Do you really care?"

I couldn't stop the grin spreading across my face. "Nope." I hefted the mace over my head and brought it down. The wood cracked, one of the pegs broke off, but that was it. Despite the limited damage I'd inflicted, it still felt good.

She sucked on her teeth, looking at me with thinly veiled distaste. "You have some bulking up to do, so that next time you wield that mace, it will be lethal."

For the next seven hours, I trained harder than I ever had before. The three sisters put me through my paces challenging me at every turn.

Under Allecto's drill sergeant-like instruction, I did fifteen pullups on the metal bar (she wanted me to do fifty) thirty-five pushups (she expected one hundred), and then I had to run the obstacle course five times in a row. During the last run, I got a cut on my cheek from the barbed wire I had to crawl under, and I couldn't get over the cement wall. In fact I had a hard time holding my arms up, so I sort of shuffled around it, my arms hanging uselessly at my sides.

Tisiphone and Megaera had been on the sidelines, cheering and jeering me on, respectively.

"Yeah, you did it!"

"I've seen baby centaurs do better than you."

After a short break where I gulped down at least half a gallon of water and tended to my small cut, which I cleaned and dressed with a bandage—I had been shocked they had a first aid kit available in the room—I was handed off to Megaera for flying lessons.

"Unfurl your wings," she demanded roughly.

Concentrating hard, I pushed my wings out through my shoulder blades and spread them out wide around me.

"That took too long. In a combat situation, you'd be dead already."

"It was like a few seconds."

"A few seconds is all it takes for an arrow to pierce your eye." She thrust her fingers toward my eye. "Or Medusa to turn you to stone or one of my snakes to

bite your throat and inject you with lethal poison."
She rubbed her wrist when she said this, and I
wondered if she was fantasizing about just that. "In
combat your wings should already be out."

"You want me to fight while I'm winged?"

"Yes. Makes you ready for anything."

"But they're so heavy. I'm not sure I—"

She punched me in the chest. I staggered back a
step. "This is why you need to get stronger. Your
chest, shoulders, and back muscles need to be like
steel."

I nodded.

"Now, fold your wings back."

Using my back muscles, I pulled in my wings in as
tight as I could. I had a sense they still stuck out.
Megaera came around behind me, poking and prodding at my wings.

She folded them even more than I could. "There,
that will do for now." She came back around in front
of me. "We're going to practice taking off mid run.
In combat you could be exchanging sword volleys in
one second and flying the next to attack another
opponent. Watch me."

She nodded to Tisiphone. "Toss me a sword."

Tisiphone snatched a short sword off the wall and
threw it to Megaera. She caught it, spun it once
around with her wrist, thrust it out, and then started
to run. After a few long strides, she launched into the
air, and flew across the room in a few seconds. Then
she swooped down and landed lightly in front of me
again.

"You try." Megaera handed me the sword.

I held it up and sprinted across the room, stopping to spring into the air, my wings unfurling and flapping hard. I had only risen a few feet when she shouted at me to land.

She shook her head. "Horrible. You'd be dead by the time you got into the air."

"According to you, I'm going to die just by walking around." I smirked.

She didn't appreciate my humor and glowered at me with blood red eyes, which sent a shudder down my back.

"You could die right now…" She lifted a hand.

"Meg," Tisiphone warned. "Play nice. Hades has entrusted us with Melany's care. You don't want to disappoint him, do you?"

Megaera sighed and lowered her hand. "Whatever." She came to stand beside me, grabbing me around the hips. "When you are running, don't stop. Instead, bend your knees and tilt your pelvis. It will help you get power to launch into flight." She released me and then stood back. "Try it again."

Taking in a few quick breaths, I lifted the sword and ran full tilt across the room. I did what she said and bent my knees midstride, but I ended up tripping over my feet and falling face first onto the floor. Thank Gods, I had the forethought to thrust my sword to the side, or I would've fallen on it.

I heard someone laughing. I assumed it was Tisiphone, as she seemed like the only one who had a sense of humor.

"Get up. Do it again."

I did.

I fell two more times. On the third try, I stopped and jumped again. The fourth try I got off the ground, but my wings didn't unfurl in time, and I just fell back down. On the fifth try, I ran as hard as I could and sprang midstride, going air born. I flapped up and soared across the room, the tips of my wings brushing the ceiling arrogantly.

When I came back and landed near Megaera, she didn't smile, but she did nod. "Not bad."

Tisiphone smacked her sister on the back. "Pretty high praise from this one."

I tried to hide my smile, as I didn't want to draw Megaera's wrath again. Out of the three sisters, she was the one I worried most about. Not that I trusted any of them, but Megaera seemed like she'd have no trouble literally stabbing me in the back. I had a feeling she'd take great pleasure in it.

After another quick break, I started my stealth training with Tisiphone.

"I know you know how to use the shadows to cloak yourself and to move around. But to be truly invisible, you need to learn how to move around in darkness. Complete darkness without any sound." She smiled, and every torch in the room extinguished, and we were plunged into blackness.

I didn't know what to do, or what she wanted me to do, so I stood as still as possible and tried to control my breathing. Then a tap came on my right shoulder, and I spun that way, then a tap on my left, and I spun back around. I hadn't heard her move. There were no footsteps, no rustling of clothing or shoes. Mind you, the sisters didn't wear shoes.

"I am five feet behind you. Come and find me."
Her voice startled me and I flinched.

"I can't see, so how can I?"

"Focus on other things beside what you can see
with your eyes. Concentrate on what you hear. What
you can smell. The movement of the air on your
skin."

I obeyed and focused on the direction her voice
had come from. I took a hesitant step forward,
stopped, listened, and then took another step forward.
I tried to stop my heart from thundering in my ears,
so I could zero in on other sounds in the room.

There. I heard the slight crinkle, like paper
moving, of Tisiphone's wings shifting. I course
corrected and took another step forward. I stopped,
frowning, lifting my arm up to see if I could feel a
shift in the air. For a moment, I only felt my own puffs
of breath as they stirred the hair on my arms. Then I
felt something else. A whoosh of movement. Something approached my right side.

I whirled around. The flames sparked, and I was
face to face with Tisiphone. She had her dagger's tip
nearly pressed into my side.

She grinned. "Good job. I almost had you."

I knew she'd pulled back deliberately. She
could've slid that knife between my ribs any time she
wanted to. I appreciated that she didn't.

"Now, I'll teach you how to walk without making
a noise. Right now, you slap your foot down with
every step you take. I could hear you from a mile
away."

For the next hour, Tisiphone showed me how to

walk on the outer edge of my feet. Then she threw
down gravel over the floor and made me walk across
it. Every time I made a sound, she threw one of those
small pebbles at me. By the time I was done for the
day, my body felt like it had been stoned.

When my training was done, they all informed
me we'd be doing it all over again tomorrow. And the
next day and the next, and that I should probably
have a long, hot soak in the bath with some salts for
aches and pains. Tisiphone informed me there should
be a small bag of special salts in my bathroom,
brewed by Dionysus.

I walked across the corridor and to my room. My
legs and arms ached with every movement. A hot
bath sounded glorious. When I entered my room, I
found a long, sleeveless velvet black dress fanned out
on my bed, beneath it on the floor was a pair of black
heels. On the dress was a note:

*Spend the next two hours in the bath and resting, then put
on this dress and meet me in the dining hall for dinner. Hades*

I picked up the dress; it was pretty and elegant,
and so not something I would ever wear. I wondered
how angry he'd be when I showed up for dinner in
leather pants and a T-shirt instead. I set the dress
down and padded into the bathroom to start my
bath. I guess I was going to find out, because there
was no way I was wandering around in that dress for
anyone.

CHAPTER SEVEN

MELANY

I stayed in the bath until the water turned cold. I didn't know how long I stayed, as there wasn't a clock in the room, and I didn't have my cell phone, but it felt like hours. I grabbed the fluffy black robe that had been left for me in the bathroom, put it on, and wandered into the closet to get dressed for dinner.

The lamp automatically flared to life when I walked in—that was going to take some getting used to—and I immediately saw the closet was empty. Lonely hangers swung back and forth on the rod, and after I rushed to the drawers and pulled them open, I discovered there weren't any clothes folded neatly in there, either.

"What the hell?" I murmured.

I went back into the bedroom, my gaze focused

on the dress still spread out on the bed. When I neared it, I saw another note on the dress.

You will wear this dress tonight for dinner like I'd asked. Hades

Pissed, I crumpled up the note in my hand, and lit it on fire, until there were only bits of ash left in my palm. I opened my hand and let the ash float to the floor. I was uncaring if it made everything dusty and dirty. I shook my head. I couldn't believe he'd removed, or gotten Charon to do it, all my other clothes just so I'd wear this dress. How did he know I wasn't going to wear it? Was he spying on me? Did he hear my thoughts? Gods, they thought they could control everything.

I shuddered thinking about that possibility.

Without any other option, except for the robe I wore, I picked up the dress and put it on. There was a full-length mirror near the dressing table in the room, and I stood in front of it. I hated that the dress fit perfectly and accentuated my defined shoulders and arms and pale skin, along with exposing a healthy length of leg. I didn't want to consider what the plunging neckline did to my breasts, but the fact was I looked hot in this dress.

I did a spin, then a round house kick with my right leg, executing it flawlessly. I looked at myself in the mirror again.

Damn it. I also looked bad ass in this dress.

After doing my hair—I mean I had to because I was wearing this great dress—and putting on a little lip gloss I'd found in a drawer in bathroom, I made my way down the corridor to the dining room.

I opened the door to find the room lit by a bunch of tall candles on the table, and our meal already laid out. It smelled delicious and my stomach rumbled in response. Hades walked toward me, an unreadable look on his face as he gazed at me.

He gave me a little bow. "You look beautiful."

His compliment pleased me, and I felt my cheeks flush a little under his searching gaze. "Thank you."

"I knew the dress would look extraordinary on you."

"Well, you didn't really give me a choice. Cool trick making all my clothes vanish."

His smile came quickly. Again, my belly flipped a little over it. "I suspected you were going to come in a pair of jeans and T-shirt if given half the chance."

"Leather pants actually. Since there aren't any jeans in the closet."

He pulled out the chair for me to sit. "Jeans are for lazy people. And you are far from that."

I sat in the chair, and he pushed it up for me, and then he picked up a bottle of wine that had been chilling in a metal bucket of ice. He poured some into my wine glass, took it back to his side of the table, filled his glass, and then he sat.

He lifted his wine glass. "To the first day of a new chapter for the both of us."

Although I wasn't sure he was just talking about my training in his clan, I took up the glass and drank. The wine was sweet and delicious and surprisingly refreshing, something I desperately desired after the hard day of training. I took another sip before setting my glass down and digging into my food. I was starving.

As I shoveled food in my mouth, I sensed that he was watching me from across the table. I glanced up to see an impish lift of his mouth. "What? I'm hungry."

"I take it my assistants pushed you hard in your training."

"That's putting it mildly."

"Nothing you couldn't handle, I'm sure."

"I'm pretty sure Megaera would put a knife in my back if given half the chance."

He shrugged, taking a sip of wine. "Probably."

I set my fork down and wiped my mouth with the fancy linen napkin. "Why am I here?"

"To eat, obviously."

"No, why am I *here*?"

"To train for the Gods Army, to defend the world from—"

"This would all be a lot easier if you'd just be honest with me."

Amused, he leaned back in his chair. "That's why. Because you don't buy into all the bullshit. You're inquisitive, brash, and stubborn, to a fault quite possibly, but we'll see about that… Anyway, I like that you question things."

"Even you?"

His grin got bigger and predatory, and I swallowed, suddenly nervous. "Especially me. Makes it way more fun to have you around. I love a challenge. I've been so bored lately."

"I'm so happy I'm amusing you." Anger swelled

inside me. It burned as if my organs were on fire. I didn't want to be a prisoner here. That was exactly how I felt, and Hades was the warden. I stood, pushing the chair back with force. It nearly toppled over. "I'm not your play thing. You can't just dress me up and parade me around like I'm some doll."

"Are you finished having your temper tantrum? Can we continue on like adults?"

I whirled around and marched toward the door.

"I guess not." His voice followed me out of the room.

I clenched my fists. I hated his condescending attitude. I wasn't going to put up with it. I stomped down the corridor and back to my room. Slamming the door shut, I dragged one of the big, heavy chairs that stood near the hearth across the floor and jammed it up against the door handle. I knew if Hades wanted in, a stupid chair wasn't going to stop him, but it was the principle of the action that mattered.

I paced my room, so angry I couldn't sit still. I didn't like this situation. It wasn't normal, although at this point, normal didn't have the same connotation it had a year ago. I wanted to be with my friends. I missed them. They were probably worried about me, or at least I hoped they were. Lucian probably thought I had just up and left him without a word. It wasn't right.

I stomped into the closet. I wasn't going to wear this dress any longer. I didn't care if I didn't have anything else to wear. I'd go naked if I had to, but when I entered and the lamp flared, I saw that my entire wardrobe had conveniently returned.

After stripping off the dress, I put on a pair of leather pants and long-sleeved black shirt. I knew it was late, although I didn't know exactly what time it was, but I had no intention of putting on pajamas and going to bed like an obedient child. Screw the rules. I was going to find a way to get the hell out of here. Once I was out, I would beg Zeus to take me into his clan. Surely, passing all the trials for the first time in history gave me some kind of upper hand, or what was the freaking point?

I paced my room some more, waiting. I wasn't sure what I waited for. For Hades to go to sleep? Did the God even do something as mundane and human as that? All I knew was it felt right to wait. I did some jumping jacks and crunches to stay alert. I splashed water on my face to keep awake.

Finally, after I estimated two hours had passed, I decided to make my escape.

I pushed the chair away from the door, then opened it, and peered out. The corridor was empty and mostly dark except for the firelight emanating from the slats in the wall. I crept out, walking on the sides of my feet like Tisiphone had taught me. When I reached the closed main doors, I knew opening them and going through was pointless. I was just going to end up right back where I started.

But I knew another way to travel.

Because there was light nearby, there were also shadows. One didn't exist without the other. I stepped into one, concentrating on drawing the darkness to me. At first nothing happened, but then I could see the murkiness slowly draw along the floor and envelop my boots. I coaxed it up my legs and over my torso, until I was completely swallowed up by it.

Like before when I'd used the shadows to sneak up on Medusa during the twelfth trial, my body felt like it floated in salt water. I raised my hand, my arm weightless, and looked at it. It was attached to my body, but I didn't feel it. It was a strange sensation.

Concentrating on what I needed to do, I took a step forward in the darkness. It was like walking on air, there was no form and substance under my foot, or at least none I could sense. I took another step, then another. Back in the corridor, I would've walked right into the doors by now, but this shadowy world wasn't corporeal.

I kept walking, sensing I had bypassed Hades's looping trick, and headed in the right direction. After a few more steps, I felt a denseness under my boots. I was walking on something hard. A spot of light formed in the distance, and I moved toward it.

Another three steps and I emerged from the shadows. I felt the darkness fall away, like a snake shedding its skin. I looked around to get my bearings. Large, greenish rock masses hung down from a ceiling I couldn't see; it was too far up. More formations jutted out from the ground. I was in a huge cave, much like the one that had been at the end of the portal to the academy.

The air held the scent of water; it was also cool against my skin. Was I near the ocean again? Was this how I was going to get back to the academy? Was I going to need to swim? Maybe Hades Hall hadn't been under the academy like Hades had told me. It wouldn't have surprised me if he'd lied about that.

As I walked farther along the rugged and uneven rock floor, I could hear the rushing of water nearby. When I crested a slight slope, I saw it. It wasn't an ocean but a river flowing through the cavern. As I approached, I spotted a thick mist rolling over top of the water. Moonlight seemed to reflect off the surface, giving it an eerie glow, but when I looked up, I couldn't see any moon.

Okay, I just had to cross this. It was no big deal. I had the ability to manipulate water, and I could hold my breath for a long time. I wasn't an expert at it, not like Ren, but I had passed the trial easily enough, despite the attack of the hydra and nearly drowning in the waves it made.

Standing on the shore with the water lapping at the toe of my boot, I raised my hands over the river and concentrated on moving it. I wondered if I could part it like Moses had done in the Christian fables. Frowning, I put all my thought into shifting the water.

Seconds later, the mist hovering above the water began to swirl. Then the water beneath it bubbled. I smiled. I was doing it. A moment later, my smile faded, and my heart leapt into my throat when I realized I wasn't the one manipulating the river.

An enormous dark head rose from the water. Actually, it wasn't just one head, but three. Cerberus was as fearsome as I'd read in the books. Large eyes as red as blood and glowing like fire fixated on me. Three sets of jaws opened, razor sharp teeth as long as my forearm dripped with saliva, and thunderous growls emanated from within.

"Oh shit. Nice doggy."

The growls intensified, and the sound bounced off the rock. One stalactite broke from the ceiling and crashed down to the ground.

I whipped around and sprinted back the way I came.

I heard its giant paws scraping against the rock as it emerged from the river and into the cave. I kept running, as fast as I could, although I knew there was no way I could outrun it. Its one stride probably equaled ten of mine.

While I ran, fireballs formed in my hands. Without looking, I flung them over my shoulders, hoping to get lucky. I didn't. I formed some more and tossed them. Then I switched gears and tried to create lightning between my fingers. At first I only got a few sparks, but then I got a decent sized bolt. I stopped, turned, and hurled it at one of the stalactites hanging from above. My bolt hit one, it broke off, and fell, hitting Cerberus in its middle head. It yelped once, but it didn't stop.

"Shit." I spun and started running again.

Eventually, I came out of the cave and into a familiar looking hall. The ceilings were high, but I hoped it would be too short for the dog. I risked a quick glance over my shoulder. Nope. It was still coming; it just lowered its heads.

I searched for thick shadows along the wall, but every time I stepped into one, the firelight from the walls flared and vanquished the shadow. I wasn't going to find a way out. I was trapped. And that realization really smacked me down when I ran into the closed double doors leading to Hades Hall.

I tried the handles, but the doors were locked. I banged on them. "Let me in. Please!"

I felt Cerberus looming over me, and I slowly turned around to face it.

I craned my neck to look up into its three snarling faces. Their black lips pulled back, and they bared their teeth.

I couldn't believe this was how I was going to die. I thought for sure it was going to be in battle after doing something daring and heroic.

"All right, doggo, you got me. Do your worst."

I ignited my hands with fire, splaying them out to the side. If I was going down, I wasn't going to go without a fight.

Cerberus lowered its middle head toward me, hot breath bathing my face. My nose wrinkled at the smell.

I lifted my hands, intending to inflict some damage, when its tongue came out and slobbered all over my face. Then it pulled back and tilted its middle head inquisitively. The other two heads did the same.

I stared at it, stunned I was still alive. "Um, why aren't you eating me?"

All three heads made a whining noise, and then it sat its big butt down onto the floor. The action vibrated the floor a little.

Closing my hands, I extinguished the flames. Then after taking a shaky breath, I reached up toward its middle head. I didn't know what to expect, but it definitely wasn't the nuzzle of its wet, rubbery nose against the palm of my hand.

A bubble of laughter gushed out of me. "Holy crap. You're a nice pupper, aren't you?"

It seemed to like that because its tongue came out again and licked my face. Then I was attacked by three very enthusiastic doggy tongues drenching me in stinky saliva.

Giggling, I pushed at their heads. "Stop it. You're disgusting."

All three of them whined. Obviously, they could understand my words.

"Aww, you're not disgusting. You're good boys."

That made them happy. All three heads lifted their lips and gave me doggy smiles, their tongues hanging out.

"I wish I had three huge treats to give you."

They kept smiling and panting.

"I bet I could find you something, if you took me across the river and back to the academy."

They stopped panting. Then each head shook back and forth.

Well, I had to try at least.

"Okay, can you take me back to my room at least?"

All three heads nodded up and down, their ears flapping. Smiling, I shook my head. Then the middle head lowered until its muzzle rested on the floor. It was an offer of a ride.

Keeping the other two heads in my sights, just in case, I climbed onto the middle head. When it came up, I buried my hands into its ruff and held on.

Lifting a paw, Cerberus literally knocked on the door. It swung open.

I sighed, angry. "You're kidding me."

Cerberus carried me through the door and to my room. Hades casually leaned up against the wall. He smiled when we approached.

"Ah, thank you for retrieving Melany."

One of the heads lowered, and Hades scratched it behind the ears.

The middle head dipped and I jumped down.

Then Hades ruffled the fur on all three heads, as they nuzzled their faces into him. "Good boys. Charon has your supper ready for you."

Cerberus turned and padded back down the hall. It passed through the door, and the door closed and locked behind it.

"Did you have a nice outing?" His look of amusement set my teeth on edge.

Before Hades could lecture me, I marched into my room. "Good night." I shut the door and then leaned up against it.

There was obviously no way out for me. I was stuck here for however long Hades wanted. I just wished I knew how long that would be. A week, a month, a year? The rest of my life? My stomach roiled at that thought.

CHAPTER EIGHT

MELANY

For the next couple of days, I trained with the Furies. At least I think it was only a couple of days. I couldn't be sure, as I had no sense of time down here. I didn't know when it was morning or night. I didn't see the sun or the moon. The only thing I had to guide me was the ringing of the bell to wake me up, and the moment when the Furies told me I was done training. Then I would drag my ass back to my room, eat something, shower or bath, and then sleep. I assumed I trained during the day and slept through the night, but I didn't really know.

Hades never invited me for dinner again. In fact I hadn't seen him since that night I tried to escape. I was disappointed, which surprised me to no end. I hated that it bothered me so much. It was a distraction.

And that distraction awarded me with a hard blow to the shoulder pad I wore by Allecto, who wielded a broadsword. Pain rumbled down my arm as I stumbled sideways and nearly lost my balance.

"You're lucky you're wearing protection, or your arm would be dangling from your body right now held on only by a few tendons and some strips of muscle."

The image of that made my stomach churn.

"Gross." Tisiphone laughed from her perch on top of the climbing wall as she watched me and Allecto spar with swords.

Allecto was always very vivid about the carnage she would have been able to inflict on me due to my stupid misjudgments and mistakes. And those lately had been plenty.

"I don't know where your mind is, but it needs to be here, focused. If this was a real battle, you would already be dead." Allecto shook her head.

I rolled my eyes. According to her, I'd been dead ten times in the past two hours. I figured I looked pretty good for a zombie.

She raised her sword. "Let's go again."

I lifted my sword; my back ached from the movement. I'd been training with my wings out and folded against my back. It was surprising how much extra weight they put on me. But I felt stronger than I did the day before, so it was working.

I stood at an angle with my left foot in front, both hands on the hilt, elbows close to the body, just as I was taught. Allecto swung from her left. I took a step back to avoid her attack. Her sword brushed by me, the tip mere inches from my chest, and then I shuffled to my right, and brought my sword around to strike her in the flank. But she was quick and had her sword back over to defend. The clash of our steel blades echoed through the room.

Back and forth we went, striking and defending, striking and defending, until sweat dripped off my forehead and soaked the back of my shirt. By the time she called it quits, my arms shook with the strain of holding up and swinging around three pounds of forged steel.

I wondered if Hephaistos made all the weapons here. I assumed so, which then made me think about my friends back at the academy. I wondered what kind of training they were doing. I wondered if Georgina had already learned how to move the very Earth itself. I smiled, thinking if she hadn't, she would eventually.

Jasmine probably led cadets in weapons training. She had a knack for the spear. I'd seen her do the coolest spins with it. I imagined her being a giant pain in Ares's ass. At least I hoped she was.

And Lucian...

I sighed, thinking about him. I missed him. I missed the way his smile made my insides quiver, and I missed how his lips made mine tingle from the briefest touch. I missed sparring with him in Heracles's class and the stolen moments we took flying around the grounds together, finding secret places just for us.

"Think fast!" The bottled water Tisiphone threw at me nearly beaned me in the head. It clipped my shoulder and landed on the floor.

"What the hell?" I picked it up and unscrewed the cap.

The plastic bottles of water here always threw me off, considering it was the only modern item I'd seen in a long while. Despite Hades's slick purple and blue suits, the hall had a very medieval type vibe. Well, that and the iPod Tisiphone had strapped to her forearm. She'd sometimes fly around with earbuds in and her music playing. I discovered her favorite music was from the 80s. She thought Billy Idol was the hottest man on the planet.

I took a swig of water.

"What were you thinking about?" Tisiphone came and plunked herself down beside me on the floor. "You had that dreamy look reserved only for guys."

"My friends. I was just wondering what kind of training they are doing."

"I guarantee you they aren't training like this."

"You're going to be ten times the warrior." Megaera slid into the conversation after touching down from hovering nearby. I hadn't even noticed her flying around. "Everyone's going to be jealous of your skills."

I frowned. "I don't think so. They aren't like that."

Megaera pulled a face. "Everyone is like that. Believe me."

"Well, if I could see them and train with them,

then maybe I could put that to the test. But no, I'm stuck here like a freaking prisoner and Hades is my jailer." I drank the rest of the water, put on the cap, and then tossed the empty over my shoulder.

"Jailer is such a common term. I prefer guardian or overseer."

I bolted to my feet and whipped around to see Hades standing there, the empty water bottle clutched in his hand. He looked sleek and handsome in a tight black shirt and form fitting pants, similar to the training gear I wore. The shirt emphasized an extremely athletic chest and arms.

"How's the training going?" He glanced at Allecto as she joined us.

"Satisfactory. She has some skills but still lots to learn."

He then looked at me. "How do you think you are doing?"

I licked my lips, unsure of what to say. I felt like this was some sort of test, and if I said the wrong thing, I was going to be punished in some way. But I figured what was the worst that could happen that hadn't' already happened. I was locked away in a gilded prison like Rapunzel or some shit.

"Okay, but I'd do better if I could train with my peers. If I'm going to be a solider in the Gods Army, wouldn't it make sense that I learn how to fight with *that* army?"

His smile bloomed on his face, changing his demeanor completely. It was disarming when he did that.

"I'll make you a deal. If you beat me in a contest

of skill, I'll let you go to the academy to train with your… friends."

My heart dropped into my stomach. What the hell could I ever beat Hades at? It was all just to humor me.

"What skill?"

"You choose."

I thought about all the things I'd learned so far. I was good with a sword and spear and the bow, but I suspected he'd be better as he had thousands of years of extra training. Hand to hand combat was out; he was stronger than I was, and he was a God for Pete's sake. I was a great flyer, but again he was Hades; he was born with wings I suspected. There was no way I could out do him even on my best day.

Then I thought of something, and I had to fight from grinning.

"Can I choose absolutely anything?"

He pulled a suspicious face but shrugged. "Sure."

Half an hour later, Hades and I stood at the far end of the training arena.

"This is ridiculous." He shook his head.

"Hey, you said anything."

"But this is not a skill."

"Sure it is." I hefted up the enormous, meaty leg bone. I didn't even want to consider what kind of animal it came from. All I cared about was whether it helped me win this contest. "At the academy, Artemis trained us in how to handle various beasts. It is definitely a skill."

I looked down the length of the arena and prayed I hadn't overestimated my ability to entice a five hundred pound, twenty foot, three-headed puppy. Cerberus sat on the floor waiting for Tisiphone and Megaera to let go of his leash. His tail thumped so hard it vibrated the entire floor.

After that night I had tried to escape and met Hades's guard dog, I'd snuck out a few times and brought him treats. I was hoping that had endeared him to me. I was relying on an assumption that Hades didn't show the dog a lot of affection, whereas I had. I'd given him many head scratches and belly rubs.

Hades picked up another meaty bone, gave me a jeering look, and then moved farther down the room, away from me, so there could be a clear winner of Cerberus's affections.

Once we were both in position, Tisiphone and Megaera released their hold on the leash.

"C'mere boys," I said, as I tried to lift the bone up into the air. It was damn heavy.

Hades didn't have that problem, and he waved the bone around. "A nice big treat for you. Yummy."

I nearly burst into laughter at Hades saying the word yummy. He looked comical as well, waving the big bone around like a flag. Cerberus sniffed the air and then padded toward his master.

"Cerberus. Come here. Come to Melany." I hefted the big bone over my head like I was dead-lifting a hundred pound barbell.

He stopped for a moment, turned his heads toward me, sniffed the air, and whined.

"Boy! Come here right now!" Hades's voice was stern, echoing through the studio.

Cerberus ducked his heads down.

"I'll give you lots and lots of belly rubs!" I wriggled the bone. "And kisses!" I added.

That was the winner.

Cerberus bounded over to me, tongues hanging out. I set down the bone for him, but he wasn't ready to eat yet. I had to make good on my promises.

"Good boy." I scratched all three heads behind the ears, moved my hands down, and rubbed his big belly. He flopped over onto his back. I laughed as I ruffled his fur with my hands.

Hades walked over and shook his head, but I caught his smile. "Traitor." There was no malice in his tone.

He dropped the bone down next to the other.

Cerberus rolled onto his feet, and then two of the heads chomped down on the bones.

I couldn't wipe the smile from my face as I watched him devour the treat.

Hades sighed. "I suppose you won, although I feel like you cheated."

"Regardless, I won the bet. And you better keep your word."

He nodded. "You can go in a sennight." He moved toward the door.

"What the hell is a sennight?"

But he didn't answer me; he just left.

I walked over to Tisiphone and Megaera, who had been watching it all gleefully.

"What is a sennight? It better be like his version of tomorrow."

Tisiphone patted me on the shoulder. "It's a week.

I gaped at her. "A week? That's too long."

"Just be happy you're going at all." She extended her wings and flapped them. "C'mon, you still got training to do."

I should've been happy that I'd gotten the better of Hades, but in fact it was a moot point. I'd done nothing but showed myself to be a fool. To think I could get the upper hand on him. That was never going to happen no matter what I did. I hated that he had all this power over me. But he did, and I supposed I was just going to have to learn to live with it. Even if it made every atom of my being pulse with defiance.

CHAPTER NINE

LUCIAN

*T*he lake came into view as we flew up as high as we could while still being able to breathe. I led one of the six-member squads in the exercise with my wing mates Jasmine and Diego on my left and right, respectively. Like fighter jets, we were learning to fly in formation. Our goal, set by Hermes, was to reach around five hundred feet in the air, maintain it, and then descend to the lake's shore.

I loved flying. It was one of my favorite things to do at the academy. Deep down, I kind of wished I'd been called to Hermes's clan, so I could be in the air all the time. But I knew my love of it and my skill, along with my affinity to lightning, had gotten me into Zeus's clan, which was a good place to be. It was a clan of leaders.

I pushed a little more until I thought we had

reached our goal, and then checked over my shoulder at my team to make sure everyone was in proper formation. Mia, who flew behind Diego, struggled a little, but after a few moments she was able to get in line with Ren and Georgina. We flew like that for a few minutes.

Pride swelled inside me. We'd been working well together for the past two weeks. I was glad I had my friends in my squad. I didn't know what I would've done if Hermes had put me in Revana's squad. Although I'd have gone along with it, I imagined. I wasn't sure if I was cut out to be a rebel.

That made me think of Melany. She would've kicked, punched, and screamed her way out of that situation. Or she would've pushed herself to the front position of that squad and forced Revana out. I smiled, thinking about her, but it faded when I thought about how long it had been since she'd disappeared.

None of us knew if we'd ever see her again. Every time I asked anyone, like Zeus or Demeter or Hephaistos, anyone who would listen for a moment, I got the same answer: "I'm sure she's fine and will return soon."

Once we reached our target height, I gestured to the group to start our descent to the lake. With me in the lead, we dove down. I reveled in the way my body felt zipping through the air. Flying was so freeing.

As we swooped over the tall trees surrounding the lake, it reminded me of all the times Melany and I had escaped the academy and gone on several secret flights. One time we even followed Dionysus into these woods and crashed one of his strange but fun parties with a bunch of wood nymphs and a satyr or two.

Nearing the lake's shore, I heard the sounds of more flapping coming from behind my squad. I looked over to see Revana and her crew coming in fast to the same spot we'd planned on landing. Before I could react, Revana collided with Georgina and knocked her from the sky. Georgina crashed in a heap on the rocky shore of the lake.

The rest of us landed and immediately rushed to Georgina's aid. She was getting up but on shaky legs. Revana and her group landed a few feet away. Jasmine was up in Revana's face before I could do anything about it.

"You did that on purpose." Jasmine's hands clenched into fists.

Revana smirked. "Not likely. Your girl there just doesn't know how to fly. She should stick to what she knows best... gardening."

That had the others in her group snickering.

Now that Isobel had been punted from the academy, Revana had two other nasty little minions, Peyton and Klara, to laugh at her pettiness. I didn't know how I'd managed to stay friendly with her for so long. Before we came to the academy, she was snide and snobbish, but over the past few months, she'd just gotten petty and mean, really mean.

The ground beneath our feet started to rumble. A couple of vines burst through the rocks and wound their way toward Revana. One got very close to strangling her around the neck.

I stepped in. "Can we just put all this crap aside and work together? That's what we're supposed to be doing. We are not each other's enemies."

Revana smirked as the vines slunk back into the ground. I glanced over at Georgina, and she lowered her hands.

"Ever the peacekeeper." Revana took a few steps toward me, a finger twirling in her hair. "You know, Lucian, now that the trash is gone, there's no reason for you to stay on the lower-class side of the academy."

"You bitch." Jasmine went to charge at her, but I grabbed her before she could.

"Revana, every time you open your mouth you prove just how classless you are. You may have been born to money, but it certainly didn't buy you any common decency."

Jasmine laughed. "Oh snap."

"Whatever. You'll change your mind once I'm made overall squad leader. I mean, honestly, you're not really much without your pet. However much I hated her, I can't deny she was a fierce fighter. It's too bad she's not ever coming back. From what I hear, she's happy being shacked up with a God. I mean Hades is pretty easy on the eyes." Revana turned and walked away, her group following her.

I watched her go, her words drilling into me hard.

"Don't listen to her," Jasmine said.

"Mel would come back if she could," Georgina added.

"It's been over a month. What if she's right and—"

"She's full of shit, Lucian." Jasmine picked up a rock from the shore and skipped it across the water. "Mel will be back."

"I can't wait for that. Let's break her out."

Everyone gaped at me. "What do you mean, break her out?" Ren asked.

"Let's go to Hades Hall, break in, and bring Mel back here."

"There could be consequences," he said.

"I don't care."

"Do you even know where Hades Hall is?" Georgina asked.

"No, but I'm sure we can find someone who does."

The more I thought about it, the more determined I was. I couldn't stand that Melany had been gone so long. I knew she was probably sitting there wondering why we hadn't come to get her yet. I didn't want to disappoint her any longer.

"Tonight, we're going to rescue Mel and bring her home."

We agreed to meet just outside at the entrance to the maze at midnight. It wouldn't be easy for any of us to sneak out of our clan areas. Zeus Hall was in the highest tower of the academy, and the staircases were patrolled by various academy monitors. I called them guards, but I'd been assured that no one was stopping us from roaming the academy halls freely. Of course that was bullshit, as I'd been stopped before.

So instead of taking the stairs, I opened a window in my dorm room, and jumped out, my wings making an appearance before I plummeted to my death. I flew around the monstrous stone building that was the academy and landed in the gardens near the maze.

Jasmine, Georgina, and Ren were already there waiting. I'd told Diego and Mia not to come, as a smaller group would be less noticeable. Jasmine wasn't happy with me about that, as she didn't get a lot of time to spend with Mia.

"Okay, we're here. Now what?" Jasmine shrugged.

"Now, we wait."

"For what?" she asked.

A dark form stepped out of the maze. "For me, I imagine."

Dionysus lumbered into a pool of moonlight. He looked a bit unsteady; he was constantly leaning to his right.

Jasmine scowled. "Oh, you're joking, right?"

"Are you drunk?" I asked.

He shrugged. "That's a matter of perspective."

I shook my head, too anxious to find Melany to care. "You told me you could guide us to Hades Hall, so where do we go?"

"You need to find Hecate. She knows the way."

"Who the hell is Hecate?" Jasmine asked.

"She's the Goddess of witchcraft." Georgina's voice was so low she was almost whispering.

"Yes, but her disciples are the Lampades, who are

nymphs of the underworld. Hades Hall is in the underworld," Dionysus said.

"Where do we find Hecate?" I asked.

"In the woods. Near the lake's shore, look for the largest oak tree. You'll find Hecate nearby." He took out a flask from his jacket pocket and took a swig. "Now, if you'll excuse me, I have some serious drinking to do."

He gave me a curt nod, and then he stumbled away toward the back entrance of the academy, muttering to himself.

"Okay, let's go." I unfurled my wings to get ready to fly.

Georgina shivered. "Hecate is not someone we want to mess with."

"I'll deal with evil incarnate if it means getting to Melany." I flapped my wings, rising into the air. If the others didn't want to come, I was fine with that. But after a few seconds, Jasmine and Ren joined me. Then Georgina finally unfurled her wings and flew up next to us.

When we reached the lake, we touched down on the shore, not far from where we'd been earlier in the day during training. Jasmine created a small ball of fire in her hand for light, and then we walked along the edge of the woods looking for the biggest oak tree.

It didn't take us long to find it. It wasn't that it was tall, as much as it was wide. The trunk had to have been more than thirty feet in circumference, and its branches were so big and heavy that a few of them touched the ground, spreading out along the forest floor. From one angle, it looked like a giant spider with eight sprawling legs.

"Now what?" Jasmine asked.

Frowning, I walked around the tree, searching for something. I wasn't sure what, but there was something odd about the surface on one side of the trunk. There was a large crack down the bark, all the way to the ground. It didn't look natural.

I touched the trunk; it still felt like bark, but I couldn't help but think there was something different about it. I knocked my hand against it. There was a hollow echoing that resounded around me.

A cracking noise came from the tree. I took a step back as a portion of the trunk moved, swinging toward me. It was a door. Before I could remark on it, a tall, willowy woman with black hair hanging to her waist stepped out. She had a long wooden walking stick in her hand.

"Who knocks upon Hecate's door?" Her voice was lilting, musical, and very pleasant.

"Um, I do."

When she turned to look at me, the light from Jasmine's fireball fell upon her face. She was beautiful, with pale, flawless skin and ruby red lips.

"What is your name?"

"Lucian."

Her gaze then turned to the others. "What is it you want Lucian and companions?"

"We want to go to Hades Hall."

She frowned. "Why?"

"To save our friend," I said.

Her eyes narrowed. Then another voice spoke; it

was gravely, old sounding. "A girl. He wants to save his girl."

I didn't know where the voice came from, but it was close by. Behind her, maybe, from inside the tree?

"Who told you to come?"

"Dionysus. He said you'd help us."

"Liar. The boy lies!" The other voice came again.

Then Hecate started to shake and convulse.

"Are you okay?" For a brief second, I thought about reaching out to her.

Stunned, I watched as her head turned ninety degrees. The sound of her bones cracking and twisting made my stomach roil.

Jasmine, Georgina, and Ren all jumped back, as a different face glared at me.

This one was old and haggard with rheumy eyes, a crooked nose, and liver spots all over her sallow cheeks. And when she spoke, she revealed rotten brown teeth.

"You lie, boy. Dionysus would never send you here."

"He did." Jasmine stepped forward. "He said you'd know the way to the underworld, to Hades Hall. How else do you think we found you?"

"Shut up, girl. We are not talking to you." She lifted the walking stick and pointed it menacingly at Jasmine.

Hecate's body began to shake again, like she was having a seizure, and then her head twisted back. "I'm sorry about that." She smiled at me, and I was enchanted by her again. "For the path to Hades, you must pay a price."

"What price?" I asked, although I was leery about what she'd demand from us.

"Your blood."

Ren stepped forward and grabbed my arm to pull me away. "You can forget that, lady."

But I didn't move. "How much?"

She smiled again, and it was sweet and alluring, and I suddenly wanted to fall at her feet. "Not much, just an ounce, not more. I need the blood of a champion for my spells." She reached out a long, slim hand and caressed my face. "You look like a champion."

"Deal."

"This is stupid, Lucian." Jasmine shook her head. "You're stupid for agreeing to this."

"I'll do whatever it takes to find Melany. She'd do it for me."

For a moment, I thought Jasmine was going to say, "No she wouldn't," but she sighed and didn't say anything else.

"So, how do you take it? A knife?" I raised my arm toward Hecate.

She gently held my arm in both her hands. "You will need to be very still for this."

Her head twitched and spasmed again, and then it turned, but the opposite way from before. I didn't know what I was looking at, but it wasn't a face. It was some horrifying amalgamation of human and animal. Before I could react, its maw opened, revealing rows of long, pointy teeth, some of them like needles, then the jaws snapped shut on my arm and I screamed.

The pain was searing, burning through my skin

and flesh. I tried to pummel her head with my other hand, but it was to no avail. She was strong, gripping my arm tight in her claw-like hands. I felt my blood being sucked from my veins.

Ren, Jasmine, and Georgina all rushed toward Hecate, but she released my arm, took a step back, and I heard the squishy noise of her teeth coming out of my flesh. She raised her hands toward my friends, freezing them in place. They could no longer move. Only their eyes were left mobile to blink.

The creature snarled and growled, then it shook and spasmed, and Hecate's original pretty face came back into view. She reached into the clothes she wore, pulling out a small glass bottle. She put it to her lips and spit out my blood into the container. My stomach churned, and I nearly retched up the meager meal I'd had hours ago. When she was done regurgitating my blood, she wiped her mouth with her hand, streaks of red glaring against her pale skin, and slid the bottle back into a pocket in her robe.

"Thank you, Lucian." She bowed her head and then waved her hand in the air, releasing my friends from their frozen state.

I looked down at my arm, amazed as the holes she'd bitten into my skin knitted back together. There was no longer sharp pain, but a deep throb.

"What the hell was that?" Jasmine growled.

Hecate stepped aside from the tree and waved her hand toward the entrance. "Hades Hall is down the stairs and through the tunnel."

I frowned. What stairs?

"Come." She gestured for us to step into the tree.

Ren grabbed my shoulder. "This doesn't feel right."

I shook him off; I was determined to find Melany at any cost. I stepped through the door in the tree, uncaring if the others followed me. After some hesitation, they finally did.

Inside the tree defied the laws of physics. It was as spacious as my dorm room with a small bed and kitchen and table and chair. Curved along one wall were shelves crammed full with glass bottles and herbs and plants.

Hecate gestured to the floor in the corner. I stepped up to it and peered down into a hole. There were crudely built stairs in the wood and dirt spiraling down into darkness.

"The stairs will take you to a tunnel. There you will be greeted by Orphne, who will guide you the rest of the way."

"Thank you." I started down into the hole, cautious that I didn't slip on the stairs, as they weren't very sturdy. Jasmine followed me in, another ball of fire in her hand to light our way. Georgina came next, then Ren last.

I didn't know how far we descended, but I'd counted the steps in my mind. Eighty-five steps down into the Earth. When we reached the bottom it was, as Hecate had said, into a dirt tunnel. I was thankful it wasn't as narrow as I thought it was going to be, as the air down here was stale and thick, not pleasant to breathe in.

I looked at the others. "Anyone claustrophobic?"

They shook their heads.

"No, but I am thirsty," Georgina said. "And none of us thought to bring a canteen."

"Hold on." Ren reached into the air, bringing his hand down. Cupped inside his hand was a small pool of water. He brought it to Georgina's mouth. It was a bit awkward, but she managed to drink the water he'd captured. "Anyone else?"

I shook my head, as did Jasmine. Then I peered into the pitch black tunnel. "Looks like we're on our own." Before we could enter, I spied a yellow glow in the darkness, and it grew closer by the second.

Eventually, the glow manifested itself as a small, bald woman, warm yellow light shining through her translucent skin.

"Are you Orphne?"

She nodded and gestured for us to follow her into the tunnel.

I asked her a bunch of questions about Hades and his hall as we trudged through the tunnel, but she didn't answer. She either couldn't talk or wouldn't. Maybe Ren and Jasmine's reservations were warranted, and we were walking into some kind of trap. I wasn't sure I really cared; all I wanted was to see Melany. I needed to know she was okay.

After I didn't know how long—time seemed to be distorted down here, I could feel it move differently—Orphne led us out of the tunnel, which opened up into a huge underground cavern and into a marsh. Beyond that I could hear the rush of raging water.

"Where do we go?"

She pointed toward the sound of water, and then

she returned to the tunnel, which appeared to be dug out of the core of the Earth.

Out of nowhere, a sense of dread washed over me. Maybe it was just this place and getting nearer to Hades Hall and Hades himself. I didn't want to consider that we were walking into something ominous.

We crossed the marsh with ease. Moonlight illumined the way, or at least I thought it was moonlight, although when I looked up at the cavern ceiling, I didn't see any breaks in the rock. Then we stood on the shore of a dark raging river that I identified as the river Styx—the barrier between this world and the underworld. Between us and Melany.

"How do we cross it?" Jasmine asked, as she stood beside me and looked out over the turbulent water. "Can we swim it?"

I shook my head. "Too wild. We'd get swept downstream and end up Gods know where." I looked over at Ren. "What do you think? Could you create a path through it?"

"I can try." Ren took a few steps forward, so the toes of his boots touched the water's edge. Crouching, he thrust his hands into the river.

I watched him as he clamped his eyes shut, his brow furrowing, deeper and deeper, until his eyes snapped open again, and he glared out over the water. I didn't know what I expected, the bubbling of the river maybe, the parting of the water, but I didn't expect what we got—nothing.

Ren stood, shaking his head. "It won't respond to me."

I kicked at the rocks on the shore. "Damn it." I refused to be stopped. I had to get to Melany.

I thought about charging up my hands, but lightning wasn't going to do anything for us, except maybe get us all electrocuted. Electricity and water were a deadly mixture.

I glanced at Georgina. "Can you make us a bridge of some sort?"

She bent down and touched the pebbles lining the river's shore. She dug her fingers past them and into the ground. She kept digging, and her brow furrowed like Ren's had. Eventually, she stood. "I can't either. The ground won't talk to me."

I unfurled my wings out from my back and flapped them once. "We'll fly over." I flapped again, but the air felt different here. Thick and constricting. I couldn't get off the ground. It was like trying to fly through viscous liquid. I guessed we weren't flying anywhere. I folded my wings back.

"Shit!" I pounded my fists against my legs. How could we have come this far, only to be stopped from going any farther? It wasn't fair. "There has to be a way across."

Jasmine gripped my arm, gesturing with her head. "Look."

Across the river, I could see the mouth of a large cave, and something emerged from it. It was a large, black creature with three sets of glowing red eyes.

"It's Cerberus," Georgina said. "Hades's guard dog."

As the creature got closer, I could see someone rode on top of it. The three-headed dog stopped at the river's edge, and the person slid down onto the ground. It was Melany. I'd recognize that blue hair anywhere.

My heart jumped into my throat at the sight of her.

Smiling, she waved. "Hey." Her voice carried across the water, and it was like soothing music to my ears.

I waved back. "Blue, we're here to rescue you!"

"I don't need rescuing, Lucian."

Confused, I darted a quick glance at Jasmine. She was frowning just as hard as I was. "Mel, you've been gone for a long time. You should come back with us."

"I'm exactly where I need to be, Jas. I'm learning so much."

"Blue…?"

"I'm okay. I promise. Don't worry about me."

I didn't understand. Surely, she wanted to come back to the academy. To be with her friends, to be with me.

"I want to be here. I want to train with Hades. He's not who you think he is. Zeus and Poseidon lie about him."

I glanced at the others, wondering if they were buying this. The looks on their faces matched mine—confusion, sorrow.

"Go back to the academy. Don't come for me again," Melany said.

"Blue." I took a few steps forward, the river gushing over my boots. I could feel it pulling at me, trying to take me down. But I wouldn't let it. "I… I love you. Please come back with us."

I wasn't sure what I expected in return. A declaration of her love maybe, but all I got was a smile and another wave. Then she climbed back onto Cerberus and the big creature turned and lumbered back into the cave.

I felt Ren's hand on my shoulder. "Come on, let's go back."

I didn't say anything, just stared out over the river at Cerberus's retreating back.

Jasmine put her hand on my arm and tugged me out of the water. "She's made her choice, Lucian. I don't understand it, but she probably has a reason for it."

I stepped away from the river and turned around, starting across the marsh. The others fell in step with me. No one spoke, which I was grateful for. I had no words for this crushing feeling inside. I didn't think I could explain it to anyone so I didn't try.

Head down, I concentrated on my steps and not on the despair rolling over me.

CHAPTER TEN

MELANY

I bolted straight up in bed, sweat covering my body and my heart hammering in my chest. I took in a few gasping breaths as the remnants of my nightmare still lingered in my mind. I scrubbed at my face with my hands, trying to brush the horrifying images away.

I'd dreamt about Lucian, Jasmine, Georgina, and Ren. They'd stood on the opposite shore of the Styx River, shouting my name. Then the dark water started to bubble and boil. From the swirling river, a large black creature emerged. It had been Cerberus. Growling and gnashing his teeth, he'd leaned down and tore at my friends. Blood and body parts had spewed into the air. I'd seen Lucian's throat torn open. Their collective screams still echoed in my ears and I shuddered violently.

The worst part of the nightmare was I'd ridden on top of Cerberus, laughing at it all. My stomach sloshed, and I thought I might get sick.

I tossed aside the blanket, rolling out of bed. When I stood, my legs wobbled a little, but I forced myself to walk into the bathroom. At the sink, I filled the basin with ice cold water then dunked my face into it. I stayed submersed until my skin stung from the biting cold, and I could no longer hold my breath.

I refused to stay a prisoner any longer. I wanted to see my friends.

After I dried my face, I threw on a black robe over my pajamas and marched out of my room and down the corridor. I was going to find Hades and demand to be allowed to return to the academy. The thing was I had no idea which door led to his room.

I checked the library first but he wasn't there. Then I looked in the dining room, also empty. Just in case, I checked the training studio. It was also empty, or at least I think it was. I heard some rustling up near the ceiling, so it was highly possible the Furies were perched up on a ledge. Did they sleep there? Weird.

That left two rooms to check.

I tried the door right across from my bedroom. It was locked. I jiggled the handle over and over, hoping if he was in there, he'd get annoyed enough to come open the door. But that didn't work and it stayed locked. I marched across the corridor to the other closed door. I tried it and it, too, was locked.

"Damn it." But I refused to give up.

If using the shadows to get past the main doors

worked, I could do it here. Looking for a deep shadow near the door, I found one, and quickly stepped into it before I lost my nerve. I reached out with my hands and gathered more of the darkness around me, until I was completely shrouded in the gloom and the corridor faded.

I could feel the change in the air, the buoyancy of it, like floating in salt water. Taking in a breath, I moved through the darkness trusting I was going the right way. After a few steps, I searched the shadows for a pinpoint of light. I found it, moved toward it, and then stepped out into another room.

It was a bedroom suite similar to mine, but twice the size. Of course Hades would have a bedroom the size of an entire floor in a castle. The room was dimly lit by a low fire crackling in the hearth. It cast a warm orange glow over all the furniture and bookshelves and the canopied bed on the far side.

I marched over to it. The dark curtains were drawn around the bed, so I didn't know for sure if he was there, but I thought it was safe to make the assumption. I felt odd confronting him in his bedroom. I felt a bit uncomfortable with the fact that he could be sleeping naked or even have a companion under the sheets with him.

But it still didn't stop me from gripping one of the drapes and yanking it aside.

He was there, lying on the bed, fully clothed thank the Gods, eyes closed, his hands resting on top of his chest. He looked dead. Like Dracula asleep in his coffin. It was a bit unsettling looking down at him.

Then his eyes blinked open and I jumped back.

"If you had a bad dream, you can't sleep with me. It would be inappropriate." He sat up and swung his legs over the side of the bed.

"That's not why I'm here."

"Then why are you here? In my bedroom at this late hour?" One eyebrow rose with amused curiosity.

Something pricked at my mind, and I frowned at him. "How did you know I had a bad dream?"

"Lucky guess." He got to his feet and scratched at the stubble on his chin. "Is that why you're here then?"

"I demand to return to the academy."

He brushed past me and walked over to the wooden stand near the fireplace. He picked up a glass decanter of what I assumed was water and poured some in a glass. Lifting the decanter, he glanced at me. "Do you want some water?"

"No." Then remembering myself, I added, "Thank you."

He drank the water and then turned to me. "You woke me up to demand to return to the academy?"

"Yes."

"Do you wish to go now in the middle of the night while everyone is sleeping?"

"No. But I didn't want to wait until you disappeared somewhere like you do sometimes when I'm training. I thought it was best to catch you by surprise, so I could tell you what I wanted."

He made a face. "Okay, you've told me. Now, can I go back to bed?" He yawned and stretched.

I took a couple steps toward him. We were a mere foot apart. I could smell the spiced cologne he always wore. It was light and subtle and pleasant. He grinned as if he knew what I was thinking. The light from the fire danced in his dark eyes and I shivered.

I cleared my suddenly clogged throat. "I want your word that you'll let me return to the academy tomorrow."

His gaze travelled my face, spent too much time lingering on my mouth for my liking, then came back to my eyes, gazing deep inside. "You can return to train. They are doing a mock war game tomorrow, and then you must come back here."

"Why can't I stay up top for a few days? I could stay in—"

"No. It's out of the question. It's not how it works, Melany." He moved to the fire, picked the poker, and stoked the flames. "Every cadet must stay in their assigned clan."

"Why? What's going to happen if we don't? Is the world going to fall apart?" I knew I was pushing him, but I was tired of the rules. I hated rules.

"It's how it's done. In a past age, it wasn't like that, but now under Zeus's lightning fist..." He poked the fire again. "If we want to stay, we have to play."

"What do you mean a past age? How old is the academy? I thought it was just over a hundred years old."

"Too many questions. You're giving me a headache." He put the poker away and turned to look at me. "You can have your day at the academy with your friends. Be happy with that." His eyes flashed again, but it wasn't from the fire in the hearth.

He frightened me. I wasn't going to lie to myself

and say he didn't. But I wasn't going to let him continually push me around, so I didn't back up when he moved toward me, knowing he wanted me to. I stood my ground.

"Don't push me, Melany. I've given you a lot of leeway since your arrival. Don't make me put on the restraints."

"Fine. You can go back to sleep now." I turned and marched toward the door.

"Good night, Melany. Have sweet dreams."

I froze in the doorway, swiveling to look at him. He gave me a wink, and my blood ran cold.

I continued out of his room, hurrying to mine. I climbed into bed and pulled the blankets up to my chin. Although I was still tired, I didn't think I could go back to sleep. Hades had sent me that dream; I was sure of it. And now that I'd gotten in his face, I feared what he'd send me next.

CHAPTER ELEVEN

MELANY

*W*hen the wake-up bell rang, I was already awake, sitting up in bed and staring into the darkness, anxious to see my friends. I jumped out of bed, did all my washing, and then went into my closet to get dressed. It shouldn't have surprised me to see only one outfit hanging in my closet; all the rest of the clothes had vanished. Hades was obviously very concerned about appearances and didn't trust me to make the best decision about that.

I took the pieces off the hangers—black leather pants, black leather waist harness, dark purple shirt made with that same armored material as my training outfit, black cowl, and hooded cape. Included were heavy-duty, ankle-length black boots that had dark purple stitching. I put everything on and looked at myself in the mirror. I resembled a post-apocalyptic Robin Hood. I grinned. I was completely badass.

After I finished dressing, I made my way to the dining room for breakfast. Hades wasn't there, just the little serving robot to keep me company, but he left me a note next to my plate of eggs and sausage.

I will meet you in the library to show you how to get back to the academy. Hades
    P.S. Don't choke on your eggs from eating too fast.

I chuckled as I ate. Not only was he starting to know me pretty well, but I was starting to appreciate his sense of humor. And I wasn't sure how I felt about that.

"Too bad you can't talk, little dude," I said to the robot. "Then we could gossip about Hades."

The robot just blinked at me, but I imagined if it had a mouth, it would be smiling right now.

Despite Hades's warning, I did eat quickly but didn't choke on anything. I hurried across the corridor to the library eager to get to the academy. I spotted Hades near one of the bookcases, reading from one of the old books. When I stepped into the room, he turned and his face lit up.

The way he looked at me made me uncomfortable. Partly because he was my teacher, and partly because it made my insides tingle, and my belly performed a little flip flop. Which could become problematic.

He shut the book, slid it back onto the shelf, and then turned his attention on me. "I see I chose well. You look totally worthy of my clan."

"I thought I was worthy because of my skills."

He waved a hand at me. "Yes, of course, but it doesn't hurt to look fierce and capable of breaking a person in two now, does it?"

I couldn't stop the smile. "I suppose."

The surprised looks on my friends; faces was going to be so worth it. Especially Lucian. Oh, and I couldn't wait to see Revana's reaction. She was going to gag with jealousy.

"Right." He stepped close to me. "So, what I'm going to show you is secret. It's something only I know, and I'm going to trust you enough to share it."

I nodded, surprised by his comment, as I didn't think he trusted me at all. At least he hadn't acted like it over the past week, or couple of weeks? I wasn't even sure what day it was.

"Don't make me regret it."

"I won't."

"Disappearing into the shadows is the first step. I know you know how to walk through the shadows, short distances anyway, like from here to the river." He gave me a sidelong glance, obviously knowing I had tried to escape the hall the other night.

"What I'm going to show you is a way to transport yourself from one place to another through the darkness. Like from here to the academy."

"Like a portal?"

He nodded. "It's a powerful ability, and one you

will only possess. None of your fellow cadets will ever learn to do this."

"Can the other Gods do it?"

"Of course, but not through darkness. They use other methods, which is why they can't just pop into my hall."

"You mean Zeus can't just come here?"

"That's right. He has to cross the river and knock on the door just like everyone else."

I smiled at that.

He caught my smile and returned it.

Then he reached into his pants pocket and pulled out a black disc on a chain. He held it up toward me. It was a silver necklace with a black wooden amulet on it. "You must wear this at all times." He slipped it over my head.

The amulet felt warm as it fell between my breasts. My hand came up to touch it.

"It's made of ebony, from the giant tree in the hall. It makes a connection to this place. It will help you move around easily."

"It's beautiful."

He glanced at the amulet, then up at my face. "Yes, it is."

I frowned, confused if he was referring to the necklace or me.

"Now, stand here." He pointed to a spot right next to him. I obeyed. "Together, we will gather the darkness."

I felt uncomfortable doing this with Hades. I mean, he was the God of Darkness essentially. He could do all of this in his sleep and probably did. But

I figured I could just suck it up and do it, or stay in this hall forever.

Concentrating on the shadows around us, I reached out and drew them closer. A prickling sensation rippled over my skin as the gloom shrouded us. I shivered at how quickly I could do it now. Maybe it was because I stood beside the master of the dark, or because I was starting to become like him. Either way, I smiled.

"Good," Hades said from beside me. I could see him there, but it was like looking at someone through a filter. A really hazy, dark filter. "Now, the next thing you need to do is to picture where you want to go."

"The dining hall," I blurted. "That's where I imagine everyone will be."

"Okay, so imagine it in your mind. Picture it clearly."

I shut my eyes and thought about the academy and the dining hall. I could see the dark wooden tables, polished to a shine. The immaculate white tiled floors. The huge open doors that had intricate carvings in the wooden frames. I imagined Lucian and Jasmine and Georgina sitting at one of those tables together, eating pancakes with fruit and whipped cream, and the huge cup of coffee Lucian always had.

"I can see it."

"Good. Now, keep it in your mind and start walking. It'll feel weird at first, like you're marching through liquid honey. There will be some resistance, but push through it."

I felt the viscosity almost immediately. The air

surrounding us was thick and cloying, almost sticky on my skin. It proved difficult to lift my leg and put it down to step forward. But I pushed through. Hades walked beside me with almost no effort at all.

He must've sensed my thoughts because he commented, "It'll stop being hard after you've done it a million times like I have."

Eventually, I was able to garner a decent walking pace, and then the air didn't feel so heavy.

"How will I know that I'm going in the right direction, and that I've arrived at my destination?"

"Practice."

I smirked. "That's not really helpful. What if I end up in some random closet in some random room I don't recognize or outside, a hundred miles away from where I want to be?"

"You can only go to places you've been before. There has to be some kind of connection." He pointed ahead of him. "Concentrate and you'll soon start to hear and see where you want to be."

I raised my head and looked forward. He was right. There was distant light up ahead, and I could hear the faint sounds of voices and laughter. That spurred me on, and I moved faster, determined to get out of the shadows and into the dining hall.

After a few more steps, the shadows started to wane, and it wasn't so difficult to move. I glanced at Hades, a smile creeping across my face.

"Remember, you have to return to the hall this evening. Hold the amulet in your hand, and it will take you there quickly." He stopped walking as I continued on.

Finally, I could see the light blossoming, and I aimed right for that growing circle. Then I stepped out onto the tiled floor of the dining hall. To those in the room, it would've looked like I just appeared out of nowhere.

The reactions I received didn't disappoint. And my ego just got stroked really hard.

"Holy shit!" I heard someone gasp.

I looked toward one of the voices and saw Diego's eyes bugging out. "Damn girl, you look like an assassin."

That made me grin.

"Blue!"

"Mel!"

Lucian, Jasmine, and Georgina rushed toward me. They all tried to hug me at once, so it became an awkward group pile on, making me laugh.

Jasmine eyed me up and down. "What the hell are you wearing?" She poked her finger against my leather corset.

"Armor."

She frowned. "Really?"

I nodded. "Everything I'm wearing can deflect a blade."

"Wow." Jasmine touched my cape.

"I think you look amazing." Georgina smiled.

"You do look amazing." Lucian grinned.

"Gods, it's been so long since we've seen you." Georgina shook her head.

Lucian hugged me again. "I can't believe you're here."

I giggled. "You are all acting like I've been gone for months. It's only been a week or two."

I caught the look between Jasmine and Georgina. Lucian's brow furrowed.

I looked to each of them.

Lucian swallowed. "Mel, you've been in Hades Hall for two months."

"What?" I flinched. "You're messing with me."

"We're not." Jasmine shook her head. "It's been two months since the celebration when you disappeared. Two weeks since we saw you at the river."

My head started to swim and my knees buckled. Lucian caught me before I could collapse onto the floor. He helped me to the table nearby and sat me down, settling in beside me. His knee touched mine, and it helped me feel more grounded.

I shook my head, trying to rectify my experience to what they were telling me. "I swear it's been maybe two weeks for me. Time did feel different down there, as I didn't have a watch and had no access to the outside, but two months? I can't believe it." Then it hit me what Jasmine had said. Frowning, I looked up at her. "And what do you mean at the river? I haven't' seen any of you since the big celebration."

They all shared a concerned look again. I hated that it made me feel like an outsider. They'd had two months together without me, making new memories that I'd never be privy to.

Lucian grabbed my hand. "I knew it wasn't you."

"Explain what's going on," I demanded.

Jasmine sighed. "About two weeks ago, we found

a way down to the underworld. We planned on breaking you out of Hades Hall…"

Georgina picked up the story. "But when we got to the river Styx, we couldn't get across. None of our powers would work."

"Then across the river we saw Cerberus. And you were riding it, and you told us to go back and to forget about you. That you were happy where you were." Lucian squeezed my hand. "But I knew it wasn't you."

My stomach churned. I gripped the table, my fingers digging in until my knuckles turned white. Anger surged through me. I couldn't believe Hades would do that to me. And here I was starting to like my training, starting to like him even. Why would he do that? Why was it so important to keep me away from my friends, away from the academy?

CHAPTER TWELVE

MELANY

"*W*as it Hades?" Lucian asked. The look in his eyes was a mixture of anger and sorrow. And it pained me to see it there. I knew I hadn't betrayed him, but I still felt responsible.

I nodded. "He really doesn't want me to be here. I had to jump through hoops just to get a day pass."

"That sonofabitch." Lucian clenched his hand into a fist. I saw a few white sparks flying off his fingers. "Why?"

"I don't know." But I sort of did, didn't I? It was becoming evident that maybe Hades looked at me as more than a student. I felt his gaze on me sometimes. It was a searching look, curiosity definitely, and something more maybe. The distressing thing was I liked it. But I'd never say it out loud, not to anyone, especially not Lucian.

Jasmine gave me side-eye, as if she knew the answer and didn't approve.

Before we could discuss it further, a loud horn blast echoed through the halls of the academy, making everyone jump. Lucian stood.

"What was that?" I watched as cadets started to stream out of the dining hall.

"The call to battle." He grabbed my hand and pulled me up. "It's part of our training today. It's a mock battle, executed as if it was really happening." Together, we moved toward the exit.

"What's the goal?"

"To not get killed." Jasmine snorted.

"We're supposed to band together as a group and keep the enemy from reaching the academy."

"Who's the enemy?" As we walked, my gaze caught Revana glaring at me, her eye daggers were lethal.

Lucian shook his head. "Don't know. Could be anyone. Gods, demigods. We have to be prepared for anything."

All forty or so of us gathered just outside the main door to the academy. A makeshift armory had been set up on the grounds. Rows of weapons including swords, spears, axes, hammers, and bows and arrows leaned up against one wooden stand. All of them were blunted, so we didn't actually kill anyone. I imagined it would be similar to the mock battle we had for the twelfth trial, like a really big brutal game of paint ball. Another stand held our shields that we'd forged with Hephaistos. There was also a stable of a few animals. I spied the wings of a

Pegasus as it stamped impatiently around the grounds.

The buzzing of voices filled the air, along with a bit of confusion, then the group split in two, half settling around Lucian, and the other around Revana. It didn't seem planned but just a natural separation.

Then Lucian just took charge, and I watched as everyone in our group turned their attention to him. I was pleased to see it, as he was a born leader. Deep down, there was a little dagger of envy stabbing me in the gut. I tried to bury it, angry at myself for its existence.

"We need to organize into two squads. One on the ground and the other in the air. We need those with good elemental skills on the ground. The best flyers should be in the air."

Georgina and Ren moved off to the side along with Marek.

"Jasmine, can you lead our ground troops?"

"Yes." Jasmine gave my hand a quick squeeze then moved over with them.

"Blue," Lucian said, nodding to me. "You're the best flyer here. You'll be with me, Quinn, and Hella."

I saluted him. "Aye, aye, Captain." Then I chuckled, but no one else laughed. I guess they didn't think I was funny. Lucian didn't crack a smile, either. Oops.

"Suit up then into formation."

While everyone went over to the armory to get their preferred weapon, I watched as Lucian made his way to talk to Revana. She'd arranged her group into similar squads. I hated that my gut churned at seeing them together. When Revana smiled at something Lucian said, my hands clenched into tight fists. Jealously was a bitch.

"You okay?" Jasmine asked, as she fastened a scabbard and sword to her back.

"Yup." I reached for a long bow and quiver of arrows.

Her brow furrowed. "You seem different."

"In what way?"

"You seem harder. Closed off." My eyebrows rose and I scowled as she added, "Defensive."

"I've been locked away for two months, Jas. My only companions have been the dark God of the Underworld and three bat-like women who take training to a whole other level of difficult."

Her eyes widened. "You've been training with the Furies?"

"Yup. They're as harsh as you've read about." I lifted my head to show her another scar on my neck to go with my lightning ones that I'd picked up along the way. I ran my fingers over it. "Courtesy of Allec, during weapons training. She likes to play with knives."

"I'm sorry, Mel." She wrapped her arms around me and hugged me tight. It was a bit awkward, as the hilt of her sword nearly smacked me in the forehead.

"It's okay."

We broke apart when Lucian returned to grab a sword and back scabbard. He looked from me to her. "Everything all right?"

I nodded.

Another horn sounded, this one was louder and

longer, and I suspected signaled the beginning of the melee. A wave of excitement and nerves rippled through the group. I found I was eager to get into the air and fight.

Lucian lifted his sword into the air. "Follow me!" His wings unfurled, and he flapped them a couple of times to stretch them out.

Thankful for the way my outfit was designed, my wings came out quickly and unhindered. I shot up into the air almost immediately. I hovered over the group, knowing full well I made a savage picture. Like a giant, black raven, a human-sized bird of prey. Lucian joined me in the air, as did Quinn and Hella.

I had to resist the urge to shoot forward and lead the charge, allowing Lucian to go first. I flew on his right side, Hella on his left, and Quinn brought up the rear. Down below, I saw Jasmine mounted on one of the giant, black fire horses, galloping across the field, the others, weapons drawn, running behind her. The scene nearly brought me to tears it was so powerful. She was glorious.

As we flew toward the rise before the woods, Revana and her squad of four flyers came alongside our formation. From below, I imagined we looked like two stealth jet fighters going in for the kill. Or at least, I hoped that's what we looked like.

I didn't know what to expect, but as we came over the rise, I gasped at what we encountered.

Helen of Troy flew up from the cover of the woods on the back of Pegasus. She had on gold armor and held a long bow much like mine. Beside her flew a giant in black armor and bull-like helmet.

His gold wings extended the breadth of two of us. His sword glinted in the sunlight nearly blinding me.

"Veer right," Lucian shouted.

As one, we swerved right. I nocked an arrow and turned to fire while the others kept flying. I fired, aiming at Helen. I hit Pegasus with the blunted tip. The beast let out an angry snort, as red blossomed across its chest.

The rules of the game dictated that Helen had to drop to the ground as her mount was injured. I saw the fury on her face and heard the string of curses coming out of her mouth. I couldn't stop the bubble of laughter as I flew closer to her, nocking another arrow.

There were no referees in this game, so she could've stayed in the air and attacked me, but valor got the best of her, and after letting one of her own arrows go at me, she dropped to the ground. I easily dodged the arrow.

The demigod in the black armor swooped toward me. Lucian and the others flew up beside me just as his long sword made a dangerous arc at my face. I didn't have my shield, as it was too cumbersome to fly with so, I couldn't block the attack. I folded my wings in so I'd drop, but before I could act, the clang of metal reverberated in the air as Lucian's sword blocked the parlay, protecting me from injury. It was so loud it vibrated over my skin.

This gave me an opportunity to nock another arrow and let it fly. The demigod's armor deflected the arrow and didn't make a blood splatter, but it did make him think twice about attacking all four of us, and he spun away from us, his wings like razors cutting through the air.

I was about to pursue him when Lucian grabbed my arm. "We don't split up, Blue."

I shrugged his hand off. "He's retreating. We could bring him down if we all attacked him at once."

"Together, okay? That's how we'll win."

I nodded. "Sure. You're in charge."

He frowned, obviously not liking my tone of voice. But I couldn't keep my annoyance and frustration out of it. I had that guy in my sights. I knew I could take him on my own.

Together, we swooped down into the battle raging on the ground. I could see Georgina wrapping vines around a raging demigod who used her fire to burn away the plants just as fast. Ren had Heracles locked in a water tornado. Jasmine traded sword blows with Helen, who had replaced her bow and arrow with a short sword and shield.

I spotted a large, bare-chested man with huge curved horns sprouting from his head standing on the ridge, shooting arrows into the group. When he moved, I saw his bottom half was that of a goat, hooves and fur and all. I nocked an arrow and aimed it at him as I flew down toward the ground.

A high-pitched shriek drew my attention, as a fierce female warrior with spiked armored shoulder plates and long, flaming red hair flowing out from under a Trojan helmet shot through the air and ploughed Hella right in the back, knocking her down to the ground. Hella landed in a heap on a bunch of rocks. There wasn't any blood, but she definitely wasn't moving.

Stopping on a dime, I spun around, and nocking an arrow, I let it rip at the redhead. She smacked it away with her sword, letting out another shriek as she dove at me. I grinned, eager for a worthy challenge.

Lucian flew up to me. "We need to head toward the field. There's a break in ranks. Revana needs us there to protect the academy."

"But I can take this bitch out right here and now."

"Mel." His voice was filled with anger, which in turn made me angry. I really didn't need his lecture right now. "We need to work together as a team if we're going to win this battle."

"You guys go ahead and I'll catch up. This won't take me long."

Lucian shook his head but nodded to Quinn, and they flew off toward the field. Once they were gone, the redhead hovered closer to me.

"I'm Enyo," she said. "Goddess of War and Destruction."

"Melany. Human of rebellion and pissing people off."

She laughed. "I like your scars. They're very pretty."

"I like yours, too." She had white lines down her cheeks and down her arms, like tiger stripes.

"Each scar represents a kill I've made."

I did a quick count of the scars that I could see, and it came to more than fifty. She was trying to scare me. And maybe if I hadn't spent the last two months sparring with the Furies, the three most frightening women I'd ever met, I might have been.

"Good for you."

She grinned, and I saw that her teeth had been filed down into points. She looked like a shark. "You are the one who Hades chose."

"I guess."

"I can see why. You have an air of fearlessness."

"It's a gift." I shrugged.

She laughed. "Let's see how long that lasts." Lifting her sword, she flew toward me like a bullet.

My bow was ineffectual at this close range, so I let it drop to the ground, and reaching around my waist, I unsheathed the two daggers I had strapped to my back underneath my cloak. I veered to the left and spinning to the side, I swiped my knives. One blade caught her across the arm.

I'd forgotten that my weapons weren't blunted. They were real lethal weapons made to wound, and blood ran in rivulets across her pale skin. Shocked, she hovered in midair and looked down at the gaping gash in her flesh.

"You will pay for that."

The horn sounded, ending the battle. I didn't know if it was because the enemy had breached our battle lines and reached the academy, or if I had been caught breaking the rules of combat.

Enyo folded her wings in, and she dropped to the ground. I watched as she landed, and the warrior in the black armor came to her side to inspect her wound. Others came to her as well, both demigod and my fellow cadets.

Lucian looked up at me. Even from here, I could see the disappointment on his face.

I floated down to the ground, folding my wings onto my back.

Everyone gathered around me but didn't come too close. I saw looks of anger and fear on some faces. Before I could catch it, gratification swelled in my chest at the terror I'd invoked. Allec, Tis, and Meg would be proud of me. I couldn't wait to return home to tell them.

Heracles pushed through the murmuring crowd toward me. "You broke the rules, Melany. You disqualified the entire group from the battle."

I glanced around at the faces staring at me. Jasmine and Georgina both looked at me like I was a monster. My stomach roiled at what I'd done. What the hell had come over me?

I shook my head, trying to cast off the clinging anger that seemed to be wrapping itself tighter and tighter around me.

"I'm... I don't... I'm sorry." I licked my lips, suddenly feeling sick.

"You risked getting expelled." His voice was low as he spoke to me. I could see he didn't want to punish me.

"I understand."

"Next time, you will be."

Revana stepped out of the group. "That's bullshit. She should be tossed out! Why are you always sticking up for her? She doesn't belong here. She's trash. Everyone knows it. Just look at her."

A savage heat flared in my chest and rushed over

my limbs. Hatred, pure and blazing hot, filled me. All I could see was a red haze before my eyes. Before I could stop myself, my hand clenched into a fist, and I punched Revana in the face. Blood spewed from her nose as she stumbled sideways.

And Gods help me, but I liked seeing her bleed.

Gasps sounded all around me. I spotted Georgina's horrified face as she stared at me.

"Jesus, Mel." Jasmine's voice came from behind me.

I didn't turn around to face her. I couldn't.

I wrapped my hand over the amulet around my neck, stepped into a shadow on the ground, and vanished.

CHAPTER THIRTEEN

MELANY

I didn't know if it was my swirling mass of conflicted emotions that fueled my travel through the shadows, but I stepped out into the library in a matter of seconds. The trip was so quick, zipping through the ether, I ended up nauseated. I had to bend over and take in some deep breaths or vomit all over the nice, clean hardwood floor of Hades's library.

"Back so soon? I thought for sure I was going to have to come get you at the end of the day."

I glanced up as Hades strolled across the dimly lit room toward me, an air of extreme superiority wafting off him like too much cologne. He was haughty and entitled, behaving like he hadn't stolen me away against my will for two months, lying to me the entire time.

And in that moment, I hated him with every fiber of my being.

Hands ablaze with fire, I launched at him, trying to wrap those fiery appendages around his throat. But he was quick, and I suspected he had anticipated my attack. He dodged out of the way, as he pushed me to the side.

I stumbled into the drinks table, knocking over a decanter of water and two glasses. They shattered on the floor, sending shards of glass sliding across the wood. Water splashed over me and doused the fire from my hands. I turned and dove at him again, this time with electricity coiling around my fingers. One touch and I would shock him.

He dodged away from me again, this time pushing me into the wall. I bonked my head against the wood paneling, which just made me angrier. Incensed, I flung my hands toward him, intending to send a bolt of lightning at him, but the sparks fizzled, landing on the ground with little ping sounds. It was like one of those sparklers that people lit on birthday cakes or during the Fourth of July.

"I'm getting tired of this game." He cocked an eyebrow at me as if he was bored to tears with my outrage.

I glared at him, focusing on the shadows all around the room. I imagined them moving and swirling toward us. I pictured a rope of darkness twisting around Hades, squeezing. Squeezing until he couldn't move.

With a flick of his hand, a tendril of shadow coiled around me instead. It wrapped around my throat, my wrists and ankles, pulling tight, and I was flung backwards. I hit the wall, the back of my head hitting the wood hard enough I saw stars. I was yanked upwards until my feet dangled three feet off the ground.

Hades strolled across the room until he stood right in front of me. "I admire your spunk. It's one of the reasons I picked you. But did you really think you could use the shadows against me? I am the shadows, darling."

I struggled against the restraints on my arms and legs, but it was to no avail. I wasn't going anywhere until Hades decided to let me go. I was at his mercy. Again. Always.

"Why are you so angry?" he asked, and I heard a genuine interest to know.

"You've had me locked down here for two months!"

He nodded. "Ah. I see. I was sure I explained how time worked down here. Every day here is like two of them topside."

"You didn't explain it. You let me believe I'd only been here for a few weeks when in fact I've been gone for months."

He tapped his lips with a finger. "Hmm. I can understand why that would be upsetting. I apologize for not explaining the rules."

I glared at him some more, trying to muster up some witty comeback, but I could feel my anger dissipating like mist in the morning sunshine.

"Is there anything else you wish to yell at me about? You might as well get it all out in one fell swoop. It's not good to bottle these things up. I heard it can cause stress related illness."

I knew he was making fun of me. It was in his tone and the way he tilted his head to regard me with a slight upturn at the side of his mouth, like a parent indulging a child having a rip-roaring tantrum.

I sagged into the shadows pinning me up against the wall. There wasn't any more point to fighting. Hades was too strong; I was never going to win. Besides that, I wasn't entirely sure I wanted to hurt him. Maybe I'd just wanted that apology he gave. Some acknowledgement that this situation sucked for me.

With a wave of his hand, the shadow bonds evaporated, and I dropped to the floor. I put out my hand to brace against the wall, so I didn't fall onto my knees. He reached for me. I shied away from his hand, but he persisted and grabbed my arm and led me to one of the chairs in front of the giant fireplace. A fire crackled pleasantly inside. Heat washed over me.

He poured two glasses of wine, set it on the table between the chairs, and then sat in the other chair. "Now, tell me what's really upsetting you."

Sinking into the chair, I smirked. "As if you care."

"Of course I care, Melany. You're important to me."

I looked at him wondering if that was really true. He met my gaze, and I wasn't one hundred percent sure what I saw in the dark depths. Could a God like Hades truly care? About the world? About me? I wanted it to be true because at the moment, I felt truly alone.

"I think the others are scared of me." I was surprised by my confession. It wasn't something I was sure I could talk about, especially not with him.

"Of course they are." He picked up one of the glasses of wine and took a sip, watching me over the rim. "You're fierce. You're strong. You're better trained. They'd be stupid to not fear you."

I was startled to find his compliments pleased me. I picked up the other wine glass and took a sip. The second the wine hit my tongue, my stomach growled, reminding me I hadn't eaten since breakfast.

Hades smiled. "Shall we eat?"

I returned his smile.

In the dining hall, the little wooden robots served us roasted duck and a warm beet salad. At first I wasn't too sure about the meal, but after the first few bites my taste buds were in heaven. I finished it all in record time, which made Hades chuckle.

"I like that you have such a hearty appetite. A lot of young women worry so needlessly about overeating. It's stupid. Food, drink… these things should be enjoyed."

I eyed him across the table, wondering if there were a few other things that should be enjoyed that he purposely left out. Maybe it was inappropriate of me to consider those things, but I couldn't help it. Hades piqued several of my interests.

"Did you eat like this when you lived at the Demos estate?"

The question took me by surprise, and I nearly

dropped my fork that was halfway to my mouth. I hadn't realized he knew anything about me besides I'd passed the twelve trials, a feat no one else had ever achieved in the history of the academy.

"Don't look surprised. Of course I know everything about you."

"Why?"

"I don't invest in something that I don't know anything about. So I did my research on you." He sat back in his chair. "Melany Richmond, eighteen, parents Andrew and Joanna Richmond, orphaned at age three and a half, lived in an orphanage until the age of thirteen when your mother's estranged sister, Sophie, found you and adopted you. You came to live on the Demos estate where Sophie worked… I imagine living with Callie Demos was hellish. I bet she was furious when her shadowbox contained nothing but a simple birthday message and not the invitation she'd been expecting." He chuckled to himself. "Such a vain girl."

My heart squeezed painfully at the mention of my adopted mother, and I threw my napkin onto my plate. "I don't want to hear anymore."

"I know what happened to her."

My eyes narrowed, and I glared at him. The image of the pale hand I saw in the rubble of the guest house still haunted my dreams. I'd worked hard at diminishing the pain of that moment; I didn't need it brought up all over again to torture me.

"She died in an earthquake," I said through gritted teeth.

"Are you sure it was an earthquake?"

"I saw it. I saw the damage it did to the estate."

"Did you ever think it was odd that there was an earthquake in Pecunia?"

I had thought it was strange at the time. I'd questioned it even. There was no fault line near that part of the country. I'd found that piece of gold rope at the site of all that destruction. I'd mentioned it to Zeus and was basically electrocuted nearly to death for it.

He stood and walked over to my side of the table. He pulled out the chair next to me and sat. "You know what I'm talking about."

I frowned. "I'm not sure I do."

"Someone released one of the Titans from Tartarus. Probably Atlas." He waved a hand. "He likes to dig in the dirt."

I leaned toward him. "Why would someone do that? And who would do that?"

"Why does anyone do anything? For power, of course." He rubbed a finger over his lips. "You found that piece of golden rope?"

I nodded.

"The golden rope controls whoever or whatever it's wrapped around. And it could only come from one person…"

I knew the name he was going to speak before he said it. I'd had my suspicions from day one of being at the academy.

"Aphrodite."

"She's totally in cahoots with Ares," I blurted.

Hades's eyes narrowed. "I know they're having an

affair and have been for centuries, but what do you mean 'in cahoots?'"

"The first night at the academy, I saw them sneaking around the halls, and I heard her mention something about a key, stealing it or something."

Pressing his lips together, Hades nodded. "Just as I suspected."

"Why would they release a Titan? Why destroy Pecunia and those other towns?"

"I suspect it was a test run for something bigger."

"Like what?"

"That I don't know." His lips lifted into a sly smile. "Yet."

"How are you going to find out?"

He pointed at me. "You're going to find out. I've taught you how to travel through the shadows. You can use them to move around the academy. You can get into places that I can't."

I shook my head. "They'll see me. It's not like I'm invisible."

"But you can be."

"How?"

"I'll show you." He stood and offered his hand to me. I took it, and he pulled me to my feet. My skin tingled where he touched me. Licking my lips, unsure if I liked that feeling, I tugged my hand away and rubbed it against my leg. It did nothing to diminish the pleasant sensation of touching him.

I followed him out of the dining hall, across the expanse of the corridor, and into his personal suite. He led me to the far wall where a six-foot high painting dominated the space. It depicted a nearly naked, muscular man with longish black hair and a rigid face. He had horns curling from the sides of his head and fire shooting from his mouth. On the ground, cowering in front of him was a beautiful young woman with long black hair and pale skin, wearing a long blue dress. It slipped down to reveal her shoulder. It was a powerful picture, and it made me shiver.

"I don't think the artist did me much justice. I look like I should be in an eighties hair band."

I glanced at Hades as he gazed up at the painting.

"Mind you, it was a different time then. I was different guy in the 1500s." He chuckled. "And no matter what you're thinking, I definitely didn't pose for that. The artist took a lot of liberties. I haven't breathed fire in a millennia."

"Who's the woman?"

"No one you know."

The look on his face darkened; he obviously didn't want to discuss it. So I stopped asking questions.

He slid his hand along the frame of the painting, and then he pulled it forward, like opening a door. Behind it, imbedded in the wall was a metal door. It looked like a safe, with a numbered knob and a metal crank.

Hades spun the knob to the right, then to the left, then to the right again. He pulled on the lever, but the safe didn't open. Frowning, he tried the combination again, but it still didn't unlock.

He sighed, and then shouted, "Charon!"

Seconds later, the decrepit-looking butler floated into the room. "Yes, my Lord."

"What is the Gods damned combo? You didn't change it on me, did you?"

"Of course not, my Lord." Charon reached for the knob, flicked it quickly one way then the other. He cranked on the lever; there was a distinctive clicking sound, and he pulled the safe door open.

"Ah, thank you, Charon."

The butler tipped his skull-head and then floated out of the room.

"Why didn't you just snap your fingers and open it? What's the point of being a God if you can't just snap things into existence?"

He shrugged. "Where's the fun in that? After a few thousand years, things like that get boring. Besides that, Hephaistos forged this for me with special metal to prevent something like that happening. No one can open this without the combo. Not even me, obviously." He chuckled.

"But what if Charon hadn't been here? What would you have done?"

"Charon is always here. Even death hasn't stopped him." Hades pulled the door wide open. Inside the safe sat a horned helmet made from the blackest of metals. The front face plate had openings for the eyes and mouth, and a nose guard only. And it sported horns that were similar to that of a big horned sheep. He reached in and drew it out. "It's called the Helm of Darkness." He set it on top of his head.

In an instant, he vanished from sight.

I stared at the spot he'd been in then swung around searching for him, anxious that he would pop up behind me and scare me. I heard his distinctive chuckle next to me, and then I felt a slight brush of air on my cheek as he moved positions. Curious, I raised my hand to touch him, my fingers brushing up against the metal of the helm covering his face.

Then he reappeared in front of me as he removed the helmet and set it under his arm. "Ta da. Pretty cool, right?"

I snickered. "Yeah, it's cool." I reached for it. "Can I try it on?"

He pulled it away from my grasp. "No."

"Then why show it to me?" I shook my head as I turned to leave. "You're frustrating, you know that?"

"I showed it to you, so you know what it looks like when you make your own."

"What do you mean when I make my own? I can't make something like that."

"Sure you can. You made your shield. One of the best ones from what Hephaistos says."

Frowning, I studied him. "He said that?" I found that almost impossible to believe. Hephaistos didn't do praise. He was the sternest, grumpiest man I'd ever met.

Hades nodded. "He likes you."

I pulled a face. "Bullshit. Hephaistos doesn't like anyone."

"He didn't smack you with a hammer, did he?"

"No."

"And he worked with you after class, didn't he?"

"I suppose." I shrugged.

"Then he likes you."

I still wasn't so sure that meant he liked me. Tolerated was more like it. "He's not going to let me come into his forge to make an invisibility helmet. I mean, where do I even start? Does he know how to make one? Who made that for you?"

"Brontes, a cyclops who was a good friend way back when. Brontes and his brothers taught Hephaistos how to forge, so I'm sure he has the knowledge."

"And why would he even help me?"

"Because Hephaistos has a stake in this. I mean, Aphrodite is his wife, and she's been cheating on him for hundreds of years. And I know he detests Ares. Who doesn't, honestly?"

"Then why hasn't he just divorced her?"

"Because divorce is the mortal way of doing things. We Gods... we get revenge instead." He grinned, and that fire inside his eyes ignited.

CHAPTER FOURTEEN

MELANY

Over the next couple days while I trained, I thought about what Hades wanted me to do. Sneak back into the academy and spy on the other Gods. But first I had to sneak into the forge and make myself an invisibility helmet. I didn't know why I couldn't just borrow his. I mean, it wasn't like he was using it. When I brought it up the next evening at dinner, he refused to answer and just changed the subject, preferring to discuss how social media was making people stupid.

I considered just ignoring his request. It wasn't like he could make me do it, but he knew I would, anyway. Hades knew I wanted to find out who was responsible for Sophie's death and make them pay. Revenge was an exceptional motivator.

But it was also a distraction, and I got hit in the shoulder by Allecto's sword during training. The blade wasn't blunted, but thankfully I wore light armor or else my arm probably would've been dangling from my side as I bled out all over the floor.

"Where's your head, girl?"

I shook it, trying to clear it, so next time I didn't get a sword through the gut. "Sorry."

"Sorry?" She sneered. "Sorry is for cowards and weaklings. Are you a coward or a weakling?"

"No."

"Then quit acting like it." She took a few steps back and raised her sword. "Let's go again."

I shook my head again, rolled my shoulders, then went into my defensive stance, my sword lifted and ready to parry.

I trained with Allecto for another hour and then did flying tactics with Tisiphone. After that, Megaera put me through my paces through the obstacle course over and over again until my legs were rubber, and my abdominals quivered from exertion. Honestly, it felt like I'd been punched in the gut with an iron fist repeatedly.

After eating, Hades was noticeably absent. I sat in my room and paced. I couldn't relax, despite training for eight hours. I had too many thoughts about the supposed earthquake that killed Sophie. What if what Hades had said was true, and that Aphrodite and Ares were somehow responsible? What if they were planning something else? I had to do something.

Dressing in my best stealthy black clothes, I stood

in my room and concentrated on the shadows lurking in every corner. I gathered them to me, pictured the door outside of Hephaistos's forge, and then dissolved into the darkness to make the trip.

It wasn't as long or hard as my first trip to the dining hall, but it still had its problems. I'd almost gotten lost and ended up walking out into the crowded corridor near the dining hall. I'd heard Jasmine's voice, so it was really difficult not to just walk out of the shadows instead. I wanted to explain to her about what had happened before, about the anger that seemed to be growing inside of me. But I wasn't sure she'd understand. I didn't fully understand.

When I materialized right outside the forge, I was thankfully alone. It was late, so I didn't think anyone would be inside working. Not any of my fellow cadets, anyway. I crept inside, the heat of the fires blowing over me. It never failed to literally take my breath away. It was as if all the oxygen in my lungs was being sucked out to feed the flames.

I moved across the room, over the bridge, and up to the main forge. The bellows pumped hard keeping the fire high and hot. I didn't know exactly what I was planning to do. I mean, how the hell did a person create an invisibility helmet? But Hades had told me there should be a mold there and the right type of metal. After that, all it needed to work was a piece of shadow weaved into it. Hades said he'd show me how to do that.

I found where Hephaistos stacked the clay molds.

I discovered a mold for an ax blade and a mace, and then I found one for what looked like a war helmet. I took it and placed it on the forging table. I needed to pour molten metal into it.

I went to the storage units and found a hunk of black metal that appeared similar to what Hades's helm was made from. Now, how the heck did I get it over to the mold? Thinking back to my time in the forge when we made our shields, I remembered how Hephaistos moved the giant blocks of metal around with ropes and pulleys. I looked up to see a contraption hanging above the storage units.

I hooked it up to the hunk of metal then using the ropes, I raised it up and pulled it along the track on the ceiling to the table across the forge. As the block of metal hung over the mold, I realized I didn't know what the hell I was doing. I should've taken the metal to the tank to be melted then used the gutters to transport it to the mold. But I didn't have that kind of time. I had to be innovative.

I lifted my hands and flicked my fingers back and forth until flames erupted. I focused on the fire until it was so hot, it turned blue-white. Hoping for the best, I set my hands onto the hunk of metal and coaxed the flames higher. It took a few minutes, but eventually the metal began to melt, and it dripped down into the mold. Although some of it didn't quite make it into the mold. There were globs of metal all over the table and floor.

"What are you doing to my forge, girl!"

I swung around to see Hephaistos, huge hammer in his hand, glaring at me.

"Um, making a helmet."

He limped over to the table to see what I was doing. His scowl deepened. "You're making a mess and destroying my work station."

I really examined what I'd done and he was right. Sort of. I was definitely making a mess, but I didn't think I'd destroyed the table. I might've burned some holes into it with my molten metal, but I was sure it could be repaired.

He picked up the mold, glaring at me. "Did Hades put you up to this? Did he tell you to come wreak some havoc in my forge?"

I shook my head vehemently. Hephaistos never really scared me in the past. I'd always thought of him as some old, frail God past his prime, but I realized right there and then he could've ended me if he wanted to. Despite his weathered and aged appearance, he was still a God with fire at his disposal in a blink of an eye.

"I'm trying to make a helmet for myself."

His eyes narrowed. "What kind of helmet?"

"A helm of darkness, like the one Hades has."

"Why in the blazes do you need a helmet like that?"

"To be invisible." Then it all came pouring out. I told him about the earthquake and about seeing my adopted mother buried in the rubble and about what Hades had told me about it not being natural—that someone had released a Titan to do the dirty work. I kept Aphrodite's involvement out of it, for now. I had a feeling that despite her cheating ways he still loved her.

"You know you can't believe everything Hades tells you. He can be manipulative and conniving. There's a reason why he was banned from the academy until now."

"Yeah? And why was that?"

He gave me a long look and then dropped his gaze, busying himself with cleaning up the mess I'd made. "It's complicated. He has a long and arduous relationship with his brothers. Especially Zeus."

"I figured as much, but it doesn't matter to me. All I care about is finding out who killed Sophie. If someone in this academy is responsible, I want to know."

"And if you find out, what are you going to do about it?"

I shrugged. "I don't know yet. But something has to be done."

"I don't think it's going to be as easy as that."

"We're training here to be in an army to protect the people of the Earth, aren't we?"

He didn't say anything.

"Then that's what I'm trying to do. I want to protect those people from future situations. What if what Hades says is true? And that earthquake was just a test for something bigger, something nastier."

He sighed, shaking his head. "I'll make the helmet for you. It won't be as fancy as Hades's, but it will work the same."

I perked up. "You will? Why?"

"Because I sense you want to do the right thing. That's a rare quality, especially in someone so young."

I resisted the urge to embrace him, knowing he'd hate it and would probably shove me away. "Thank you." I hung my head. "You might be the only one who thinks that about me right now."

"But be careful, girl. There is a lot going on in this place that you have no clue about. Not everything is as it seems and that includes Hades. I don't think he means you any harm, but he's not your friend. You are a means to an end for him, despite what he tells you or tries to make you believe."

I didn't want to believe that. I felt something spark between me and Hades. I wasn't sure exactly what it was. Friendship? Probably not. Attraction? For me, yes, although I'd been trying to fight it. And for him? He did look at me differently lately. Sometimes, I'd catch him watching me, when he thought I hadn't noticed. But I had. His gaze was potent and would sometimes make me shiver. More nights than I cared to admit, I had dreams about him.

I pushed the thoughts away as I concentrated on what Hephaistos asked me to do. Together, we cleaned up the mess I'd made and started the process over again. This time the right way. By the time I travelled the shadows back to my room in Hades Hall, I was exhausted.

I stripped out of my clothes, as they stunk of fire and burned metal, put on my pajamas, and climbed into bed. But before I could close my eyes, the alarm bell started to clang. It was time for me to get up and get ready for another long day of training.

Sighing, I rolled over onto my side and crammed a pillow over my head. I wasn't moving. Hades was going to have to come in here and yank me out of this bed by my leg. I wouldn't put it past him to do just that. But until then, I shut my eyes in protest. I was going to get some damn sleep even if it killed me.

CHAPTER FIFTEEN

MELANY

*A*fter Hades found out I'd gone to the forge to make my own invisibility helmet, he loosened the chains binding me to the hall and allowed me to return to the academy to do some more group training. I was equal parts excited and nervous. What if my friends didn't want to see me again after what I'd done? What if Lucian didn't feel the same way about me anymore? I couldn't just pop back into their lives like last time; I needed to ease my way in gradually. So instead of appearing in the middle of the dining hall like a rock star, I opted to humbly walk back in through the front doors.

But first, I decided on a little detour to get my mind right.

I emerged from the shadows into the center of the giant hedge maze. I took in a deep, greedy breath of fresh, cool air. Being underground all the time was hard on the lungs. I raised my face to the light shining down. I hadn't realized how much I missed sunlight until now. When I got back to the hall, I was going to ask Hades for one of those light therapy lamps, so I didn't get depressed.

When I stepped out of the gazebo, I thought I was alone, so I was surprised when I spied a lone figure sitting on one of the stone benches next to one of the statues of a male soldier brandishing a spear and holding a shield. I was stunned to see Medusa leaning back, her long legs stretched out in front of her, with her arms spread out along the back of the bench, her face raised to the sun. She didn't wear sunglasses and had her white eyes wide open.

I suspected I was intruding on a private moment, so I quickly turned to jump back into the shadows, but my foot accidentally crunched a small twig. The cracking sound was like a bullhorn in the relative silence of the maze.

"Trying to sneak away?"

I stopped and turned back. "I didn't want to disturb you."

"Too late." She blinked at me with those stark white eyes and then slid on her dark sunglasses. "Hades let you out, I see."

I didn't know how to answer that so I just nodded.

"I heard what you did to Enyo the other day." She smirked.

"It was an accident," I heard myself say, knowing full well that was bullshit.

She shrugged. "I'm the last person who's going to

judge you. Everyone makes mistakes. Some mistakes are just more severe than others." Her head titled up to the stone statue beside the bench.

Her sympathy surprised me. "Thanks."

She got to her feet, towering over me by a foot at least. "Oh don't mistake me. We're not friends. And if you ever did to me what you did to Enyo, you wouldn't be breathing. You'd be as solid as this guy next to me." She turned to leave, her snake hair lifted up to hiss at me, one of the little vipers even snapped its jaws, and then she disappeared into the maze.

Despite her threat, I felt buoyed by what Medusa had said. People made mistakes. I'd made one. Surely, my friends would forgive me for it. I left the maze and went into the academy through the main doors.

The hallways buzzed with activity. Heads turned and conversations stopped when I was spotted. I didn't let it get to me. Instead, I streamed along with them, looking for a friendly face. I spotted Georgina up ahead. I jogged to catch up to her.

"Gina."

She spun around, her eyes wide. "Mel?" She jumped and hugged me. "Oh my Gods, we all thought we wouldn't see you again."

"What? Why?"

"I don't know. You just disappeared."

"I was ashamed of what I did to Enyo. I didn't think you'd want to see me again."

She hugged me again. "Are you kidding? We've been missing you badly."

People walked quickly around us. A couple of them eyed me with suspicion.

"Where is everyone going?"

"Weapons training on the field with Ares and Heracles."

"Can I come with you?"

She smiled and grabbed my hand. "Of course. Jas and Ren and Lucian are going to be so excited to see you."

Together, we pushed through the crowd out the side door and onto the training field. I spotted Lucian instantly. He was standing at the front of the group helping to organize cadets into various training squads.

His gaze met mine and he smiled. All my nervousness and doubt melted away when I saw that radiant grin. Seeing him like this, being here out in the open, made me realize just how much I missed the light. Obviously, in more ways than one.

I walked toward him. "Do you have room for one more?"

I heard the whispers around me. "I can't believe she came back after what she did."

"Why does Lucian even like her?"

"She should be kicked out."

Lucian met me halfway and pulled me into his arms. I sighed into his chest, inhaling him. Gods, I'd missed him. I missed this level of human contact. I'd been yelled at, chased, smacked, sparred with, insulted, pushed for long enough, that I'd forgotten what a simple hug felt like and how much I needed it.

"Gods Blue, don't disappear like that again." He nuzzled his face into my neck.

"I'll try not to but I can't promise."

When he drew back and looked me in the eyes, I sensed he wanted to kiss me. If we were in private, I knew he would have.

"Break it up." Ares marched across the field glowering at us. "It's time for training." He pointed at me. "You line up with the other spearmen. I want to see if you've gotten any better."

I did as he suggested, grabbing a spear from the weapons rack, and then got in the front line along with ten other cadets, including Mia and Revana. Revana gave me the nastiest look I'd ever seen, and I hoped I had a chance to wipe it off her face.

Ares stood in front of us and then counted off. "One, two, three, four, five." Then he started counting again. "One, two, three, four, five. Now, line up and face off against each other."

We all moved into our positions and as luck would have it, I faced off against Revana. The Gods smiled down on me today, and I couldn't stop the grin blossoming across my face. I was very pleased to see that my smile made her nervous.

"I've been waiting for this for a long time," she said.

"Me too."

Ares raised his arm in the air and then brought it down. "Begin!"

I took a step back, the spear in both hands, and then spun it around like a windmill. Allecto had shown me how to do it. It was a display of aggression and skill, and I loved how wide Revana's eyes got when I spun it over my head, around my back, and then ended it with a grunt, in a side squat with the spear thrust out across my waist. I straightened then brought the spear back to my side in the ready position.

I was showing off, but I couldn't help it. From day one, this girl had thought she was better than me. She'd gone out of her way to bully me, insult me, and do everything in her power to put me down. She would've had me kicked out of the academy, which would have made me one of the lost—I'd be a person without memory of this place, my friends, or my family—if she'd had her way.

I owed this girl nothing. Not even my mercy.

So when she thrust her spear at me, thinking she could spar with me, that somehow she was even in the same league as I was, I knocked it away, spun, and had the tip of my spear pressed against her neck. Just like that, I had bested her. If this had been a real battle, out on the field, it would've taken me no more than a minute to end her life.

The tip of the spear was blunted, so I couldn't jab her through the neck but I wanted to. I could feel the bloodlust rising up inside of me. Megaera spoke in a low whisper against my ear, "She's not worthy to be called a warrior. You're better than she is. She's had it good her whole life while you suffered." Tisiphone's voice was low and seductive in my mind. "She wants you to fail. She wants you to suffer. She's trying to turn Lucian against you. She's trying to steal him for her own. You can't let her win." Allecto's voice was the loudest of them all. "Kill her. Kill her now!"

After pulling my spear back from her throat, I swept her leg, and she fell onto her back on the ground. I spun my spear over my head again and then thrust it toward. Ares snatched the pole away from me before I could jab her in the gut with the blunted tip.

"It's done. You won. Time to walk away."

I raised my head and stared Ares in the eyes. An uncontrollable fury surged through me and I wanted to lash out at him, but I couldn't show my hand like that. Not yet. Not until I had proof. "You're the one who should walk away."

He met my gaze, and it was hard and menacing, but I didn't back down. I was never going to back down ever again.

"You've been in the Underworld too long, cadet. You're starting to say some crazy stuff."

I opened my mouth to fling an accusation his way, but Lucian was beside me, guiding me off the field.

When we were alone, he sighed and shook his head. "What is going on with you? This isn't you. You're out of control."

Anger still swirled around in my belly, but it was starting to fade. I took in a few deep breaths and tried to clear the bloodlust from my mind. Every once in a while, it flashed like a strobe light. In the light were visions of blood and chaos and mayhem. And I had caused it.

I glanced down at my hands and swore I saw they were painted red with blood.

Lucian grabbed them. "Tell me what's going on. Why go after Revana like that?"

"She deserved it. She's a horrible person."

"We all know that, but we're supposed to be on

the same side. We have to be able to trust each other, not turn on one another."

I shook my head, trying to clear my thoughts. "Since when did you stick up for Revana? Are you two friends again?"

He sighed. "No, we're not friends, but we've learned to work together."

I didn't say anything about that. I hated that it made me jealous to even consider that they could be friends.

"And what did you say to Ares? I've never seen him that intense before, which is saying something."

"Someone killed Sophie."

His frown deepened. "It was an earthquake, Blue. You saw it."

I shook my head. "Someone released a Titan to destroy my town."

"You think Ares did that?"

"Aphrodite. Ares. Both of them. All of them." I shook my head and put my hands over my face. "I don't know. I'm confused."

"What is Hades doing to you down there?"

Instead of speaking, I just lunged into his arms. I buried my face in his chest and squeezed my eyes shut against the wave of anguish threatening to surge over me. Threatening to drown me in its violent deluge.

"Just hold me. Please, just hold me."

He did. He wrapped his arms around me and held me tight. He nuzzled his face against my head and whispered that everything was going to be okay, that he was there for me. The anger and hate started to dissipate as I anchored to him. He was my rock.

My safe place. I had to remember that so I didn't dive off the edge.

Something was wrong with me. That much I knew. But I didn't know how to stop it. I was changing, morphing into someone else, something else. I was scared of what it was. But what was worse was that I wanted it to happen. I craved it. Because whatever was happening to me made me stronger, smarter, better. I knew it. And soon enough, the others would know it, too.

CHAPTER SIXTEEN

MELANY

*L*ucian and I didn't spend too much time together, as he had to get back to the training field. He wanted to stay with me, but I told him to go. I opted to leave while I still could. Every time I got around the others, something happened to me. I got enraged. All I wanted to do was fight and hurt people. It was obvious group training wasn't going to work for me any longer. Hades would be happy about that.

Although I didn't want to train with the others, that didn't mean I wanted to return to the hall. So I decided to check in at the forge to see if my helmet was finished. Hephaistos had told me it would take a few days for him to hammer it into submission.

Since everyone was outside in the training field, I had the halls of the academy to myself. I decided this was the perfect time to practice my stealth skills. When I heard the footsteps of someone approaching, I slunk into the shadows and stayed hidden.

Two students ran by the first time. Neither of them noticed me lurking along the wall shrouded in darkness. When they were gone, I stepped out again and continued on my way down to the forge. Right before I reached the stairs leading down into the bowels of the academy, I heard voices coming my way. I gathered the shadows to me like a cloak and hid underneath it.

Demeter and Dionysus came around the corner deep in conversation.

"I heard she attacked another person," Dionysus said.

Demeter gave him a discerning look. "We both know it isn't her fault."

"You have a soft spot for her," Dionysus said.

"I know. She reminds me so much of—"

"She's even starting to look like her. I imagine he's outfitted her entire wardrobe to his liking." They stopped walking, halting in the hall close to where I hid. Dionysus took out a metal flask from the inside pocket of his jacket, opened it, and took a sip. He handed it to Demeter. She took it and chugged a drink.

"I wish I could tell Melany that she has friends here in the academy." She handed the flask back to Dionysus, her gaze sweeping over where I was cloaked. "That she could talk to me if she needed to."

"You worry too much. She won't end up like Persephone."

"I hope you're right."

They moved on down the corridor. Once they turned to the left and disappeared, I came out of the shadows. It was obvious they'd been talking about me, but I didn't know what they'd meant about my attack on Revana not being my fault. And who the hell was Persephone? Was it the young woman who had been in the painting on Hades's wall in his suite?

I had a lot of questions for Hades when I returned to the hall, but right now I needed to see if my helm of darkness was ready for me. I descended the stairs and pushed open the giant doors to Hephaistos's foundry. I crossed the floor, up the stone stairs, across the bridge arching over the rivers of molten metal, and then up to the main forge.

Hephaistos was there, striking his hammer against a red-hot glowing blade of steel. He stopped when he saw me and then dunked the raw new sword into a bucket of water. It hissed as steam billowed from the bucket. He pushed his goggles up onto his malformed head.

"I wondered when you would be back."

"I came for my helmet. Is it done?"

He set the hammer and pincers down onto the table and then moved over to the shelves behind the main forge. It was the place he kept the shadowboxes he made. I followed him over. He grabbed the black helmet on one of the shelves and handed it to me.

I grinned with pleasure. It was beautiful, sleek and not bulky like Hades's. The front plate dipped down over the forehead, but there was a butterfly-shaped opening for my eyes, nose, and mouth. Etched into the side plates were wisps of feathers. It looked like wings sprouted from the sides.

I ran my fingers over the carvings. "It's spectacular, Hephaistos. It's better than anything I could have ever hoped for."

My compliment seemed to please him, as he puffed up his chest. "You always reminded me of a bird. A hawk maybe, or a falcon. And when I heard you'd sprouted black wings instead of white, it didn't surprise me." He tapped the helmet with his finger. "Put it on. See how it fits."

I slid it over my head. It fit snugly, but not too tight. It was perfect. "How do I look?" I purposely unfurled my wings and spread them out around me. My shadow cut an impressive image on the stone floor.

Hephaistos took a step back. I didn't know if it was because my wings were taking up too much room, or he saw something that startled him. "You look all right." He moved back to his work. "Time for you to go. I'm busy."

I took the helmet off and followed him back to the forge. "Hey, what do you know about someone named Persephone?"

His scowl deepened. "Where did you hear that name?"

"I heard it around. Who is she?"

"She's not your concern. I suggest you head back to the Underworld and quit asking dangerous questions."

"I think she's the woman I saw in one of Hades's paintings."

"Go away now." He picked up the long steel piece that was going to make an impressive sword and set it back into the hot coals.

"Do I look like her? Is that why Hades picked me?"

Hephaistos sighed then looked at me. "I don't perceive to know why Hades does anything. But what I do know, girl, is that you need to be careful. Protect yourself."

I resigned myself in the knowledge that he wasn't going to tell me anything. I nodded a goodbye, wrapped my hand over the amulet around my neck, and returned to Hades Hall.

The second I appeared in the corridor, I marched over to the library and went inside. Hades wasn't there sitting by the fire as he usually did, so I stomped down the hall to his suite. The door was shut.

Carefully, I turned the knob, pushing the door open and entered. On first look, the room was empty. The drapes were drawn on the big canopied bed, and Hades wasn't lying there, thank the Gods. I crept over to the big painting on the wall and looked up at it. I studied the woman on the ground, searching for a resemblance. It was hard to tell from a painting, as some things could've been distorted, but the shape of her face was a little familiar.

Setting my helmet down, I went over to the book-shelves on the far wall. Maybe there was something that could tell me who this woman was and her signif-icance. I pawed through books, finding nothing.

There were a couple of decorative boxes on the shelf. I opened them to find them empty. I pulled open one of the drawers to find a stack of rolled scrolls each tied with a red ribbon.

I took one out. I knew I shouldn't read his private correspondence; it was a huge breach in trust, but I had to know what was going on, so I slid the ribbon off and unrolled the parchment. The writing was cursive and flowy and very feminine.

My dearest…

I quickly perused the letter, a few names jumped out at me: Demeter, Aphrodite, Zeus. Then I looked down at the bottom to read…

Always yours,

Persephone

I was going to go back and start the letter again and really read it when the door opened and Hades came in. Startled, I tried to shove the letter back into the drawer, but I wasn't fast enough.

"What are you doing?"

"Who's Persephone?"

He strode toward me, his eyes flashing with fire. He snatched the letter from me, rolled it back up, and put the ribbon around it.

"Who's Persephone? Is that her in the painting?"

He put the scroll back into the drawer then pinned me with a hard look. "How dare you invade my privacy."

Frightened, I said, "I'm sorry, but I need to know who she is, and I knew you wouldn't tell me if I just asked."

"Well, we'll never know now, will we?"

"Please, I have a right to know."

He smirked. "A right to know? What makes you think you have any rights here?"

"People are saying I look like her. That you're dressing me up like her."

His eyes narrowed as he clenched his jaw. "What people?"

"I heard Demeter mention it. And I saw her name in the letter, so she must know the truth."

He glowered. "Demeter wouldn't know the truth if it bit her in the ass." He took me by the arm and started to pull me toward the door. "Get out of my room."

"Who is she? Obviously, it was someone you loved. I deserve to know, especially since—"

He whirled on me, his eyes flashing. "Since what? Because you quickly read some random letter you think you know anything?"

His hand still gripping my arm, he backed me up into the wall. My hip hit the drinks table along the way. He loomed over me with a heated menace that brushed over my skin and made me shiver. My heart thudded hard in my chest. My lungs burned with each rapid breath I took. He was so close to me I could feel his hot breath against my cheek.

"N-n-no," I stammered.

"No, what?"

"No, I don't know anything."

His lips twitched upwards slyly. "Do you think because you might have a resemblance to her and I loved her, that I have feelings for you? Do you have some school girl crush on me, is that it?"

I shook my head so hard my hair flew around my face.

"Oh, I think maybe that's the truth." He leaned in closer to me. "I can hear your heart going pitty pat just thinking about it. I imagine your belly clenches in anticipation of what I might do to you. Right here. Right now." He reached with his hand and lightly encircled me around the waist. I took in a ragged breath.

I lifted my hand and set it on his chest, intending to shove him away, but I didn't. I left it there. I felt his heart racing under my palm. Panting hard, he licked his lips. His gaze raked my face, lingering on my mouth.

Oh my Gods, I couldn't breathe. It was too hot in the room. The air was thick and cloying. I should've pushed him back and gotten out of there, but the truth was I didn't want to move. I wanted him to do something. Anything. To put me out of my misery.

Then he crushed his mouth against mine. The kiss was hot and hard and frantic. Nothing like the gentle, loving kisses I'd shared with Lucian. No, this was all heat and passion and anger. Every nerve ending in my body flared to life.

Then it was over and he pulled back. My lips tingled from his absence.

"Persephone was a strong, smart, spectacular woman. She was the woman of my dreams. And you… are nothing like her." He took a couple of steps back and turned away.

It was a punch to the gut. I'd never felt anything as acutely as I did those words. Tears pricked the side of my eyes, but I wouldn't let them fall. He didn't deserve to witness my pain.

"Leave your helmet. I'll infuse it with shadow to make it work. Then you can do what I told you to do." He waved his hand toward the door. "You can go now. And if I ever find you in my room again, Melany, you will be punished. And it will hurt."

Swallowing, I pushed away from the wall and ran out of his room. I fled to mine, shut and locked the door, and then leaned back against it. Tears pushed past my eyelids and rolled down my cheeks. I'd been so foolish thinking Hades felt anything for me. I was obviously a means to an end for him. He didn't look at me like a woman; he only saw a solider, an instrument in whatever plot he was brewing. I knew that now. And I wouldn't let my guard down again.

CHAPTER SEVENTEEN

MELANY

*D*espite having a terrible sleep with horrific nightmares, I threw myself into my training the next day. I did the twenty-five pullups, fifty pushups, and hundred crunches without complaint. I ran ten laps around the arena and did the obstacle course three times without being prodded to do so.

When I suited up for combat sparring in silence, Allecto was in my face. "What's wrong with you?"

"What do you mean? I'm getting ready to spar with you."

"Yeah, but you're doing it without some pithy remark or sarcasm. So something must be wrong."

"I'm fine. Let's just get on with it." I picked my sword from the training wall, then got into position to parry.

Tisiphone, who had been flying around overhead, fluttered down to the ground near me. "You're not upset because of what happened at the academy yesterday, are you?"

Shaking my head, I considered telling them about my confrontation with Hades, but decided against it. They would think I was whining, and that was one thing the Furies hated above all else: a whiner. They thought it was a sign of weakness to complain.

"Good. Because you should never be sorry for being badass." She chuckled. "I heard you laid out that bitchy girl like that." She snapped her bony fingers.

Caught up in Tisiphone's obvious glee, I couldn't stop the smile blossoming on my face. "She had it coming."

"Of course she did. They all do." She smacked me on the back. "Keep focused and you'll be the greatest warrior the academy has ever seen. Your foes will fear you. They will fear even the thought of you."

"Like us." Megaera dropped down from the ledge she'd been sitting on, landing right beside me and making me jump.

Tisiphone and Megaera smiled at each other while Allecto continued to glower. I'd never seen her smile. She had two facial expressions—glower and scowl.

"Can we spar now?" Allecto twirled her sword around with her wrist. "I'm getting bored with the chatter."

I raised my sword and faced her. "Bring it."

She did.

Shrieking like a harpy, she attacked, swinging her sword from the right. I dodged and blocked, then thrust at her side. She blocked, danced back a few steps, and brought her sword up and around, aiming for my head. I ducked under her swing, spun around, and kicked her in the side of the leg. When she stumbled and fell, I brought my sword down on top of her. My blade struck the armored cowl around her neck. If that hadn't been there, I would've cut her through.

For the first time since I'd started my training, I got a hit on Allecto.

"Nice!" Tisiphone clapped.

I lifted my sword and took a step back, allowing Allecto up off the floor. She didn't smile, but she gave me an appreciative nod. "Keep channeling that anger. It'll serve you well in the future."

After another hour, I was released from the training arena. I decided that it was the perfect time to test out my helmet. When the bell had woken me up earlier, I noticed my helmet sitting on a table near the fireplace. The note with it simply said: *Use it wisely*.

I decided to take Allecto's advice and channel my anger. I was done worrying about what Hades's motives were and concentrated on mine. Regardless of the reasons why I was here, I needed to find out what happened to Sophie—who did it and why. Those were my reasons.

After showering, I dressed in a sleek black jumpsuit perfect for spy work. I settled my helmet onto my head. An icy chill rushed over my body. I wondered if it was the shadows wrapping around me to make me invisible. Then I walked into a shadow, visualizing the corridor just outside of the dining hall.

Traveling through the shadows was getting easier. It only took me a matter of seconds to get where I wanted to go now. I heard voices inside the hall and walked through the open doors cautiously, still unsure if I was truly invisible. I stood at the front of the room and looked around. No one noticed me. Not even Jasmine, Mia, Georgina, and Ren, who sat at one of the tables together eating dinner, glanced my way.

Smiling, I wandered over to their table to listen to their conversation.

Jasmine snagged a French fry from Mia's plate. "Medic training was tough today."

"Yeah, watching Chiron field dress a pretend amputation of Diego's leg left me feeling sick." Mia pushed her plate away toward Jasmine.

"It was definitely hard," Ren said, "but something we're going to have to face at some point."

"Do you really think we'll have to go into battle?" Mia played with the cap on her water bottle. "I know that's why we're here, but it just seems so impossible."

"I heard Demeter say there have been some grumblings from Tartarus. It sounds like some of the Titans aren't happy," Georgina said.

"But they're locked away. No Titan is getting out," Mia said.

Jasmine and Ren shared a look, and I wondered if they were thinking about the destruction we'd seen when we went to our hometowns. They knew, as well as I did, that those earthquakes weren't normal.

"Mel said that maybe a Titan had been released by someone," Jasmine said.

Mia gave her a look. "I don't think we can trust Melany's word anymore. I mean, she's really changed. She could've killed Revana the other day. That's just not cool, even if Revana's a bitch."

Jasmine, Ren, and Georgina looked at each other but didn't say anything.

I hated that they weren't sticking up for me. Maybe Mia was right, and I'd changed and didn't deserve their loyalty anymore.

I was about to take off my helmet and reveal myself, so we could talk about it, but laughter at the doors got my attention. I turned to see Revana and Lucian walking into the dining hall together. Revana laughed at something Lucian said. Obviously, they were closer than Lucian had let on. Anger instantly swelled inside my belly like a wildfire.

They parted, and Lucian joined the others at the table. He sat beside Ren. "What's on the menu? I'm starving."

My whole body started to shake. I wanted to smack the smile off Lucian's face. Instead, I hit Mia's water bottle, sending it sailing across the table. It landed on Lucian's lap, soaking his pants.

"What the hell?" He jumped up from the table.

Everyone kind of snickered nervously and looked at each other.

I didn't wait to see what the verdict was. I marched across the room and out into the corridor.

I hurried through the academy, my strides long, my fists clenched. I imagined if anyone had seen me, they would've jumped out of the way. As it was, I nearly ran into two people as I rounded the corner into the main foyer.

I stopped and sagged against one of the walls to get myself together. I couldn't walk around here so angry; I was going to do something irrational. Something I'd probably regret in time. I considered taking off my helmet, but when I spotted Aphrodite coming down the corridor, I was glad I hadn't. Here was my chance to follow her.

When she walked past, I got in behind her a few paces. Although I was invisible, I knew that I could still make all kinds of noise, so I employed all I learned from Tisiphone and crept on silent feet behind the Goddess. Once she went around another corner, I knew where she was headed—her hall.

As she approached the tall golden doors, they opened for her as if sensing her presence. I had to bridge the gap between us if I was going to get inside before the doors closed on me. I jogged a little on my tiptoes, so I was maybe four feet behind her.

She sailed through the doors and I followed. For a brief second, her head turned to the right just slightly, and I thought she figured out she was being followed. But she continued on through the golden tiled corridor and into her private rooms.

Once inside, she went to a tall metal stand near one wall. Several crystal decanters of liquid sat on top along with tall crystal glasses. She picked up a pitcher of amber liquid and poured some in two glasses. Obviously, she was expecting company.

I didn't have to wait long to see who that particular company was. Ares strode into the room, wearing the same clothes I'd always seen him in— shorts and a T-shirt. I didn't understand why she was with him; he looked like an angry gym teacher when she was married to a really strong, intelligent man like Hephaistos, who I suspected would do anything for her if she asked. Sure, he wasn't nice to look at, but that couldn't be the only important thing in a relationship, could it?

"Sorry I'm late. Some of those mortals are so weak and whiny. Sometimes, I wonder why I don't just slaughter the lot of them and be done with it." He came to her, and she handed him the glass of liquid. He took a sip.

"Because we need them for now. Like cattle, they're being raised for the impending slaughter."

Startled by her admission, I took a step backward. The bottom of my boot scuffed against the pristine tile. I wasn't sure if I made a sound.

"I heard from Cottus, and he said the release of the chimera would be eminent—"

The air around Aphrodite suddenly blew up, twisting around her, then where she had been standing, now a giant snake sat coiled, ready to spring up any second. It had her golden eyes.

It was my cue to get the hell out of there. But before I could turn to find a shadow to dive into, the snake shot forward and twisted around me. She constricted around me so tightly that I couldn't breathe, and my helmet literally popped off from the pressure she placed on the rest of my body. It clattered to the floor.

Ares's eyes widened at the sight of me. "Well, that's a surprise."

She kept squeezing me tighter and tighter. My bones ground against each other. I heard the cracking noise of my joints as my shoulders dislocated. Pain zipped through me and I cried out.

"Careful, babe. You don't want to make a mess in your nice, clean room."

I squeezed my eyes shut as the pressure mounted in my chest and head. I didn't want my eyes popping out of my head. Then the compression lessened until I was a panting, sobbing, quivering mess on the pristine white tiles. I opened my eyes to see Aphrodite, back in her perfect, pale form, leering down at me.

"How dare you spy on me?! I've killed mortals for less."

I gasped for more breath, hoping it would stop my lungs from burning. It felt like I'd swallowed hot coals. Tears kept rolling down my cheeks as the pain from my dislocated shoulders nearly incapacitated me. I couldn't think beyond the agony.

Ares joined her to loom over me. "What should we do with her?"

"Kill her."

"We can't, you know that. She has Hades's backing. It would be a dangerous move to do that."

"She's invaded my privacy."

Ares gave Aphrodite a gentle pat on the shoulder. "I know, my love, but killing her is not an option." He toed me in the arm with his shoe. A bolt of agony stabbed me in the side and I gasped. "You dislocated her shoulders. It must be extremely painful judging by the tears and the screams. She'll think twice about spying on you again."

That seemed to placate Aphrodite, as she sighed and walked back to the table with her drink on it. She picked up the crystal glass and took a sip. "Fine. But please do something with her; her tears are staining my tile."

Ares crouched and grabbed me around the ankles. He dragged me across the room, out the door of her private chambers, and to the main doors of her hall. When the main doors opened, he proceeded to drag me out.

The pain was constant as I slid along the floor, and there was nothing I could do to stop him. As I passed through, I looked up to see Revana and Eros smirking down at me as I went by their feet. I was in such agony that I couldn't even muster enough concern for it to matter that she saw me like this.

Once outside the main doors, Ares dropped my legs to the ground. "Have a good night." He then left me there like yesterday's trash and returned to the hall. The doors shut behind him.

"Blue. Oh my Gods, Blue!"

I cried harder then as Lucian and Jasmine and Georgina and Ren all gathered around me. I blinked up at them through the veil of tears. My friends had come to save me. I wasn't alone.

Then I passed out.

CHAPTER EIGHTEEN

LUCIAN

"Good Gods, what happened to her?" Georgina crouched next to Melany and checked her pulse. "Her pulse is strong, but she looks and feels feverish."

I got on my hands and knees next to her. "Mel? Can you hear me?" I looked her over, to assess her injuries. Her arms didn't look right. They were lying at an impossible angle. My stomach churned at the thought of what could've happened to her for that kind of injury. "I think her shoulders are dislocated."

"We need to get her to Chiron," Ren said.

"How do we move her?" Jasmine paced the corridor. "What if we make it worse?"

I glanced at Ren; he was the most proficient in healing than the rest of us. "Can you put her shoulders back? Then I could carry her."

He rubbed his mouth and frowned. "I don't know. What if there is a tear? I could really mess her up."

"Can you try?"

Ren kneeled down next to Melany. He placed his hand gently on her shoulder and moved it around. His brow furrowed as he assessed the damage. Because of his affinity to water, he found that he could sense injuries inside a body because we were made up of sixty percent water. I remembered how surprised he'd been when he learned he could feel inside the body.

He rocked back on his feet. "Yeah, it's just dislocated. I couldn't sense any tears of muscle or tendons."

"What do you need me to do?"

"You'll need to hold her down while I pop it back in."

We made sure she was laid out perfectly straight on her back. While I pressed down on her chest, Ren picked up her right arm and brought it down to almost her side and then gripping her wrist, he pulled it up to a ninety degree angle, shook her arm up and down. Then he held it up to a one hundred and eight degree angle and shook her arm up, then down. I winced when I heard the pop of her shoulder going back in.

With a gasp, her eyes sprang open, and she tried to sit up. I wanted to cradle her in my arms but knew that wouldn't be good for her. So I kept her pressed to the ground, but damn she was strong. She'd gotten stronger over the past few months. "Stay still, Blue. Ren is fixing you up."

She turned her head to look at me; there was a wild look of horror in her eyes, then she sagged into the floor, and her eyes flickered closed again.

Ren met my gaze over her body. "Need to switch positions, so I can do the other arm."

We moved around her, and Ren popped her other shoulder back in. Once that was done, I carefully picked her up into my arms, and as a group we marched through the academy and to the infirmary. If we'd been alone, I would've kissed her face and whispered to her that everything was going to be okay. Even when I wasn't sure it would be.

There were whispers and stares as we passed our peers in the hallways. Mia found us right before we arrived at the infirmary; she said she heard rumors Melany had been injured when she attacked Aphrodite in her private room.

"Bullshit," I said. "I don't believe that for one minute."

"Lu, we did find her outside Aphrodite Hall," Jasmine said, as she linked hands with Mia.

"So, that doesn't prove anything. We don't know why she was there or what happened."

I carried her into the infirmary. Chiron was across the room talking to Dionysus when I placed her on one of the cots. They both hurried over.

"What happened?" Chiron did a quick visual inspection of Melany.

"We're not sure, but we found her on the floor with two dislocated shoulders."

Chiron pressed fingers to her shoulder and then frowned.

"Ren put them back in," I added.

Chiron nodded and then looked at Ren. "Good work."

"Is something else wrong with her?" I noticed some bruising starting to blossom along her jawline.

Chiron pulled down her shirt and inspected her collarbone and sternum. I could see more bruising.

"Looks like she's had lots of trauma on her muscles."

"From what?"

His eyes narrowed. "Not sure, but it almost looks like she's been squeezed in a vice." He straightened and waved his hand at us. "Get out so I can do a thorough exam of her."

"I want to stay," I said.

Dionysus gestured to the door. "Let's all go and have a nice cup of tea. Let Chiron do his thing, and then you can come back. Okay?"

We followed Dionysus out and down the hall to his "office." There was literally no room as we all filed inside. Just about every surface was piled high with books and papers. All the shelves were crammed with herbs and glass bottles of this and that.

He pointed to a sofa that was covered with books and a couple of animal skulls. "Just push that off and sit."

Georgina managed to makes some space for us, and the four of them sat while I paced around the room.

"This is Hades' fault." I paced, spun, and paced some more. "He's put her up to something."

"You don't know that, Lucian," Mia said.

"How did you even know she went to Aphrodite's Hall?" Jasmine asked. "How did you know she was here in the academy?"

"I smelled her perfume in the dining hall." I sighed. Her scent was so distinctive to me I'd recognize it anywhere. Like lilac wood smoke. A bit sweet and a lot fiery. "And when the bottle went flying across the room, I didn't think that was magic."

"You think Mel did that?" Georgina frowned.

I shrugged. "I don't know for sure. But she was there in the dining hall when we were talking."

"Why go to Aphrodite?" Mia asked.

"Mel's looking for answers," I said.

"About the earthquake." Jasmine glanced at Ren, who swallowed.

Mia grabbed Jasmine's hand. "Do you really believe her that it wasn't a natural disaster, that someone orchestrated it?"

Jasmine nodded. "I do."

"I do, too," Ren agreed.

"Mel is many things, but a liar isn't one of them," I said.

Dionysus was quiet during our conversation, busying himself making a pot of tea, but I knew he was listening. He reacted a couple of times to what we said.

"What do you think, Dionysus?" I asked.

He shrugged, as he poured tea into four cups. "I try not to." He handed me a cup. "I find it can be extremely dangerous to have opinions."

"How can you be so indifferent? Shit is happening around here."

"My dear boy. I've been around for a few millennia and been involved in several wars. I've seen more bloodshed than you could even imagine. The shit, as you say, that is happening around here is just family politics. It doesn't even raise a blip on my 'this shit matters' radar." He took out a flask from his pocket and tipped it toward me before taking a healthy swallow.

After we finished our tea, we returned to the infirmary, but Chiron would only let one of us in at a time. I didn't even give anyone else a chance to go first. I barged inside, and saw, thankfully, that Melany was awake.

Her smile was soft and hesitant when I pulled up a chair to her bedside. "Hey."

"You're really just going to say 'hey' to me and that's it?"

She shrugged, but I could tell it caused her pain.

"What were you doing at Aphrodite Hall? The rumor is you attacked her."

She smirked. "Let me guess who started that one. Revana?"

I didn't say anything because she was right; it was Revana spreading that story, which made sense, as Aphrodite was her patron.

"Tell me the truth, Blue. Tell me everything."

"Hades believes me about the earthquakes. He suggested that possibly Aphrodite had something to do with it, as she possesses the golden rope of truth. Anyone who wears it will do her bidding." She winced a bit, obviously in more pain than she would ever let on. "Like the piece of golden rope I found where my mother was killed."

"I know you have a… I don't know, a thing for Hades—"

She sputtered. "I don't have anything for him."

There was something in her eyes when she said that, but I didn't want to acknowledge it. Hades had some kind of power over her, and maybe she didn't even realize it. I didn't know for sure.

"But he has his own agenda. They all do."

"I know that." She coughed and winced again, and I helped her adjust the pillow under her head. "Aphrodite and Ares are planning something." She put up her hand to stop me from saying anything. "I was right there when they were talking. I overheard them mention something about releasing a chimera."

That didn't sound good, but maybe there was an explanation.

She continued, "You should've heard what they said about us, about the cadets at the academy. They said we were being raised for the slaughter." She grabbed my hand. "They're planning something big. Something that's going to take us into battle, I'm sure of it."

"Who hurt you? Was it Ares?"

She shook her head. "Aphrodite. She shifted into a giant snake and nearly crushed me to death. I think she would have if Ares hadn't stopped her."

I swallowed and squeezed her hand, but not too tight. I didn't want to hurt her any more than she hurt now. The thought of her pain, of her dying, made my chest throb and my stomach roil. I brought her hand up to my mouth and pressed my lips to the back.

"I'm sorry if I've been—,"

I shook my head. "Nope. Not going to hear it. You don't need to apologize, Blue."

She gave me a sly smile. "Okay."

"We should go see Zeus. He'd listen to you. If they're planning something, it goes against everything Zeus has been working for."

She licked her lips and then nodded. "Okay, but I think you're going to have to carry me."

I grinned. "Any time."

Then she looked at me for a long moment, as if she was searching for the words she wanted to say. She touched my hand. "I wished we hadn't parted that night during the celebration. That we'd…" Her cheeks flushed a little.

I leaned forward and brushed my lips against hers. "Me too. But we'll have our time."

She didn't say anything, just gave me a soft sad smile. My heart clenched in response.

After promising Chiron that we'd come back, I helped Melany to her feet. I slung an arm around her waist and helped her walk out of the infirmary. Jasmine was the only one left outside the doors waiting. The others had returned to their clan halls.

She rushed to Melany's side. "Are you okay?"

"I will be."

"Where are you going? Shouldn't you be resting?"

"I'm taking her to see Zeus. Something is definitely going on, and he needs to know."

We made our way across the academy campus

and to the spiraling ramp that led up ten floors to
Zeus's Hall. At the top of the highest tower in the
academy was where I stayed with others in Zeus's
clan, which wasn't too many of us.

At the bottom of the ramp, I looked up. It was
going to take a bit for Melany to make it all the way
up. I didn't want to wait, so I picked her up in my
arms, unfurled my wings, and flew us up to the top.

She laughed when I set her down. "Did you just
sweep me off my feet?"

"Yup, looks like."

I wrapped my arm around her again as we
walked down the wide main corridor, which was
aglow with golden light shining down from the
domed ceiling to Zeus's private chambers. When we
reached the prettily painted tall double doors, which
seemed to be the norm in the academy, I knocked.

There was a booming, "Come in." Then the
doors swung open.

I helped Melany inside.

Zeus stood in the middle of the room, dressed in
long, white robes that he often wore. But he wasn't
alone. Aphrodite stood beside him. She looked as
regal and elegant as she always did, except for her
face; it was pinched in anger, and if I wasn't
mistaken, worry.

When she saw us, she smiled, and it was like
facing a viper with poison dripping from its fangs.
"Oh good, I was just talking about you, Melany."

I had to hold Melany back as she charged
forward, her face a mask of fury. I'd never seen her

like that before. Her face contorted into something vicious and malevolent. The look scared me. And in that moment, she did as well.

CHAPTER NINETEEN

MELANY

"*Y*ou bitch!" I tried to get to her, but Lucian held me back. It was easy, too, as I wasn't in good enough shape to break free of his strong hands. Pain still rippled through me; my entire body ached.

"You see," Aphrodite addressed Zeus, "it's like I told you. She's unhinged. I think all those months with Hades have warped her poor little mind." She touched her face, where now I could see three red scratches marring her cheek. "You see what she did to me. If Ares hadn't been there, who knows what she would've done."

"Melany is not unhinged," Lucian said. "She has something to tell you Zeus, and I think you should listen to her."

"She's just going to tell you lies—"

Zeus held his hand up toward Aphrodite. "Let the girl speak." He gestured to me. "Go ahead."

"She"—I pointed to the smirking Goddess—"and her lover Ares are planning to release a chimera onto the Earth. They want to start a war."

"Ridiculous." Aphrodite frowned. "Why would we want to do that? There would be no purpose."

"Because you want to take over. You want more power than you have."

She laughed. "Girl, I'm one of the twelve Gods of Olympus. I have more power than you could possibly imagine." She moved toward Zeus, turning her back to me. "I hope you aren't entertaining the lies this girl is spewing."

Zeus looked at me. "Do you have proof of what you're saying?"

"I heard them say it. I was in her room. I was invisible. They didn't know I was there."

Aphrodite swirled around and rolled her eyes. "You were in my room and attacked me. I have a witness to that. You scratched my face. Here's the evidence."

If Lucian hadn't been holding me up, I would've charged across the room and done more than just scratch her face. I'd gouge out her eyes and feed them to Cerberus.

I looked imploringly at Zeus, sure that he could smell her falsehood just as well as I could. "Aphrodite is a Goddess, and I'm merely a mortal cadet. Do you really think I would be able to injure her like that? She's as quick as a striking snake. There's no way I could even get to her before she crushed me."

Lucian squeezed me around the waist and leaned into my ear. "Good one."

Zeus sighed, looking at Lucian. "Did you see or hear this exchange?"

Lucian quickly glanced at me, and I could see the war of conscience on his face. He was probably the most moral person I knew. When society talked about an innately good person, they were talking about Lucian.

He shook his. "No, but I believe her."

Aphrodite chuckled meanly. "Of course he does. He's in love with her. We all know the things men will do for love."

Zeus stroked his beard and then walked around the room. He went to the huge window along one wall and peered out over the immense academy grounds. "I'm afraid since you have no proof, I'm going to have to side with Aphrodite. Therefore, you will be punished for trespassing in her private chambers and for attacking her."

"That's bullshit!" I pulled away from Lucian this time and was about to cross the room, when a dark mist swirled out from under the doors, twirled up like a mini tornado, and then fell away, leaving Hades standing there, looking fierce and dangerous in a black suit.

"There will be no punishment."

Aphrodite nearly bared her teeth. "You can't just pop in whenever you want and demand things."

"I can and I will." He mounted the steps to where Zeus stood. "Melany was acting on my behalf. She went to Aphrodite's chambers to deliver a message from me. I highly doubt any attack happened. Aphrodite probably scratched her own damn face— her nails are long enough."

Before I do anything else, I listed to the right. Hades zipped over in a flash and caught me before I fell. Lucian had also moved toward me, but Hades had gotten there first.

"I got her, son. You can stand down."

Lucian's hands started to glow as electricity swirled around his fingers.

Hades's eyes turned jet black. "I wouldn't if I were you."

Zeus clapped his hands together sending a crack of thunder through the room. The windows shook. "Enough! All this bickering is giving me a headache."

"If we're done then, I'll be taking my charge with me back to her room, and no punishment will be doled out." He looked me over, seeing that I quivered. He noticed the bruises blossoming along my neck and chest. "It looks to me that Melany has suffered enough. Honestly, if anyone should be charged with a crime, it should be Aphrodite. I'm sure there's some rule or law that states a professor at the academy shall not harm a cadet. And if there isn't, there should be." He clucked his tongue at Zeus. "Just what kind of school are you running here, old man?"

Aphrodite glowered at him. "You are insufferable."

"I'm aware." He nodded to Lucian. "See you later."

Before I could say goodbye to Lucian, Hades

touched the amulet hanging around his neck, and we zoomed into the darkness. A few seconds later, Hades half carried me out of the shadows and into my bedroom.

He helped me to my bed and sat me down on the edge of the mattress. "You are a lot of trouble, you know that?"

"I'm aware."

His chuckle sent a pleasant vibration over my body. And I hated that I reacted to it.

"What did she do to you?"

"She shifted into a giant snake and—"

"Yes, I've seen what she's capable of." He took a step back and regarded me. "I'll run you a hot bath. I have some healings salts that Apollo made me. An hour in the water and you'll be good as new."

Before I could reply, he strode into the en suite. Seconds later, I heard the water rushing from the tap. Then he came out.

"It's all ready for you."

"I, uh, I left my helmet in Aphrodite's room…"

He smiled and shook his head. "No, you didn't. It's right over there." He pointed toward the hearth. I leaned forward and looked, and sure enough my helmet sat on the table where he'd put it the night before.

"I made a quick pit stop before floating into Zeus's place. I thought you might need it again sometime."

"They're planning something. Aphrodite and Ares."

He nodded. "Not a surprise. They are schemers,

those two. Always have been. The stories I could tell you." His gaze dropped, and he appeared a bit sheepish to my surprise. "Have your bath and I'll make sure Charon prepares your favorite meal." He frowned. "Which is?"

I chuckled softly, touched he was making an effort to make me feel better. I wouldn't presume to think this was some kind of apology for being a dick the other day, but I hoped it was the beginning of one. "Pizza."

His frown deepened and he shuddered. "Pizza? Really? Out of everything in the world you could possibly eat, your favorite thing is pizza."

"My adopted mother Sophie used to make the best pizza."

"Ah." He tapped a finger to his mouth. "Pizza it is. Do you have a preference? If you say pineapple and ham, I'm going to have to drown you in that bathtub."

"Greek, with extra olives and feta."

He tipped his head. "Greek it is." Then he walked out of my room, so I could bathe.

I limped into the bathroom. After stripping off my clothes, I stared at myself in the mirror. I was a hideous collection of scars and bruises. The only parts of my body that weren't currently disfigured were my right breast, my right hip and buttock, and the small patch of skin at the back of my knees. Everywhere else was pretty much a horror show.

Eventually, the bruises would fade, but I'd always be scarred. Looking at myself, I thought I'd gotten used to them, but I think I'd just been avoiding mirrors.

I turned off the tap on the tub, slowly stepping into the steaming water. I sunk down into the tub, gripping the sides to keep my head above water. The moment I was completely submerged all my muscles relaxed. Sighing, I leaned my head back, closed my eyes, and let the healing bath do its thing.

I wasn't sure how long I lay there with my eyes closed, but when I heard a noise near the entrance of the en suite, I opened my eyes and sat forward. Hades leaned causally in the doorway, his gaze averted.

My hands came up to cover my breasts. "What the hell are you doing?"

"I've come to wash your hair."

"What? Are you insane? I'm naked for Gods' sake."

He waved his hand toward me, and a layer of dark mist formed over the water, covering me.

I sunk back into the tub. "Okay, that's fine, but why are you washing my hair?"

"Because quite frankly, it's dirty." As he strolled across the floor, he rolled up the sleeves of his shirt. He grabbed the wooden footstool from under the sink and set it near the tub, behind my head. Before I could protest some more, he ran his fingers through my hair. Then using a small clay bowl, he dumped water over my head. It sluiced over my face, and I reached up and wiped it from my eyes.

I didn't know what to do. This was the oddest situation I'd ever been in. Not only was it odd, but I found the whole thing... pleasant and surprisingly tender. I didn't have the strength to just jump out of the tub, especially since I'd be naked and exposed, so I just went with it. I mean, when else was a person going to get their hair washed by a God?

I closed my eyes and sighed as he squirted shampoo onto my head and started to massage his hands over my hair. I didn't realize how tense I was until his fingers worked magic along my scalp.

"Why are you doing this?"

"Because I'm a nice guy."

I snickered. "But you're not, really."

"Maybe nice isn't the best descriptor, but I'm not this terrible, monstrous dark God."

"I know you're not."

"I care about… things and… certain people. And I feel a certain responsibility for you. Your injuries could've been avoided."

"I'm stronger than I look." I opened my eyes, struggling with the urge to turn and look at his face.

"You look pretty strong to me."

My heart picked up a beat, and I was acutely aware my breathing had intensified. I wondered if he noticed. My teeth bit down on my lower lip. It was so hard not to turn around, to look at him, to see his eyes, and to read them. What would he do if I just stood up in the bath, stepped out, and curled into his lap? Gods, I ached to do that so badly I felt it between my thighs.

But I wouldn't succumb to it. Hades was my teacher, my mentor, thousands of years old and a God, and then there was Lucian. I wouldn't hurt him like that. Even if somewhere deep inside, that cold, selfish part of me wanted to.

Instead, I swallowed down my deepest and darkest desire, and rested my neck against the tub as he washed and stroked my hair.

"Tell me one of those stories."

"What?"

"About Aphrodite. You said 'the stories I could tell.' Tell me one."

"Thousands of years ago, she became infatuated with a mortal named Adonis. He was the son of the Princess Myrrha, who actually despised Aphrodite and refused to worship her. Anyway, it got pretty heated between them, and Zeus had to intervene. He turned poor Myrrha into a tree and then Ares transformed into a bull and killed poor Adonis in a jealous rage. It was quite the scandal for decades."

"That's horrible."

"Yup, it certainly is. Then there was this other time…"

For the next hour, as the water ran cold, Hades regaled me with sordid tales of the Gods. It was both informative and entertaining, and by the time he'd finished, my body felt a hundred times better, even if my heart stayed unsure and confused.

CHAPTER TWENTY

MELANY

$\mathcal{A}$fter Hades left—it was an awkward kind of departure that had us both bewildered, but I imagined for different reasons—I got out of the bath, dried off, put on my robe, and padded back into my room. The smell of pizza hit me the moment I entered. My stomach growled in anticipation.

I saw a large pie sat on the table by the hearth. I was a bit disappointed Hades wasn't going to join me but I made do. I grabbed a couple of slices, put them on a plate, and took them to my bed, crawling in under the covers. As I devoured the food, I wished I had Netflix to watch, or a few friends that I could text.

In that moment, I was aware of how alone and lonely I was.

The feeling was so bad I almost considered taking

the pizza with me and going to find the Furies in the training room to share it with them. I couldn't imagine any of the sisters eating pizza. Their meals probably consisted of baby chicks with their downy feathers still on and freshly caught eel still alive and wriggling.

After eating, I yawned, feeling pretty relaxed, and my body healed. I snuggled down into bed, drawing the blankets up to my chin. I knew I would sleep like the dead.

Except the dead came to see me in my dreams.

In the expanding twilight, I stood alone on a dirt path in a dense forest. I sensed I knew the way to go, so I started to walk deeper into the trees. After walking for some time, the air around me became denser, cloying, as if it grew fingers that brushed along my skin. I shivered but kept walking.

I came to a fork in the path; both ways looked equally daunting. Weeds and flowers grew over both trails, neither of them too visible in the growing darkness. One path curved upward toward the mountains, and the other twisted downward into the deep gorge. I glanced down at my bare feet; they were already covered in dirt and stinging from the cold, so I didn't think it mattered what route I chose..

Before I could choose which trail to take, the sound of breaking branches came from the surrounding brush. I whirled to my right to see Sophie coming out of the trees toward me. Her usually coifed, grey-streaked hair was in disarray; her face was pinched and paler than normal. Her cheeks had black streaks across them, and there was a dusting of ash all over her and her torn dress. Her feet were bare and bleeding.

She reached for me. "Melany…" Her voice was hollow and cracked.

I backed away from her. I didn't want her to touch me. If she did, I was sure I was going to die.

She kept walking toward me, her hand outstretched. I saw that two of her fingers were twisted unnaturally, and her nails had been torn off. "Melany… you must choose…"

"No. Stay away!"

I tried to run back the way I'd come, but there wasn't a path there anymore, just trees, lots of trees and bushes, foliage so thick I couldn't walk through it.

Then she was right in front of me, her face mere inches from mine. Her deformed hand grabbed the front of my shirt, so I couldn't escape. "Choose! Or die!"

Then she burst into flames.

I screamed as her body disintegrated into ash. Flames licked over the grass and trees around me until I stood in the middle of a fiery tornado.

I jerked awake and bolted up in bed. Sweat slicked my face and body. The sheets stuck to my wet skin. My heart pounded painfully in my chest, and I had trouble controlling my breathing. I jumped out of bed and rushed into the bathroom. I vomited into the sink.

I wiped my mouth and saw black streaks on the back of my hand. I looked into the sink. I had retched up ash and soot and charred chunks. At first I didn't know what it was, and then I saw a finger. It was Sophie's hand.

Screaming, I backpedaled away from the sink, tripped over the step stool, and fell onto my ass on the floor. I stayed there until I caught my breath. When I looked at my hand again, it was pale and pink as it normally was. I scrambled to my feet and gazed in the sink. It was empty. No ash, or soot, or Sophie's hand. No vomit, either.

"Gods Mel, you are losing it."

I ran the cold water and stuck my head under the tap. I was wide awake now.

I went back into my bedroom just as the bell clanged.

I got dressed into my training clothes and headed straight to the training arena. The thought of eating made me want to vomit. Allecto, Tisiphone, and Megaera all looked surprised to see me so early.

"Aren't you the eager beaver?" Tisiphone laughed then smacked me in the shoulder. I winced as I was still sore.

We were about to get ready to do some sparring when Hades strode happily into the room.

"Change of plans. There won't be any training today."

"What's going on?" His look of pure glee made me nervous.

"Training is over; it's time for the main event. There's a huge forest fire raging right now, and the government there has asked for help from the academy. I know Zeus is sending out the troops, and you are going with them."

"I'm not sure why you look so happy about that. It's just a fire."

"Is it?" His eyes shone with excitement. "After all that you went through, do you think this is just a fire?"

I frowned. Surely, after what I'd found out, Aphrodite and Ares wouldn't go through with their plans. Not unless they were confident they would get away with it.

"Besides that, I want to see a test of your powers."

"I'm not your weapon."

"Of course you're not." He strode out of the room just as jauntily as he'd entered, calling over his shoulder, "I'll meet you in my library in twenty."

Gone was the man who had treated me tenderly and lovingly last night. In his place was the tactician, the God with a chip on his shoulder and an agenda that I could only hope to guess.

Tisiphone smacked me in the shoulder again. "Remember to always be ready for anything. Have your wings out at all times. You never know when you'll need them."

I turned to go back to my room to pull on my lightly armored jumpsuit.

"Have fun." Megaera finger-waved to me.

After changing, I went into the library as Hades instructed. He was there waiting for me, dressed in his God-like best dark purple suit.

"Ready?" he asked.

I nodded, although nerves fluttered around in my belly. I wasn't sure why I was apprehensive. We were just going to help the local people to fight a fire. Somehow though, it felt like an audition, and I was up for the role of leading lady, although I was sure a lot of people in the academy would cast me as the villain.

In an instant, the shadows swallowed us up. It was a lot easier now to walk through the darkness, but it still made my stomach flip over, like riding a roller coaster. After walking for maybe five minutes, I could see light and hear voices. Then we stepped out into a parking lot where everyone had gathered, demigods, cadets, and firefighters, still a mile out from the actual fire.

The sign just beyond the lot read Victory National Park. I'd come here a couple of times with Sophie for a picnic near the falls. It was an hour drive from Pecunia.

All heads turned at our arrival, including the three or four camera crews and reporters on the scene.

"What are you doing here?" Heracles approached us, but I was sure he addressed Hades, as he looked horrified.

"Just dropping off the kid for play time." Hades had the nerve to pat me on top of the head. I glared at him, but he ignored me.

"You can't be here, Hades." Heracles looked around as cameras were swung our way and photos were being snapped. "Gods just don't show up and do interviews."

"Why not?" Hades asked. There was a playful arch to his eyebrow.

I looked past Heracles and saw Lucian, Jasmine, Georgina, Ren, and the rest of my peers immobilizing. I noticed that Revana and her cronies were noticeably absent. Leaving the Gods to squabble, I unfurled my wings and lifted into the air, flying over to my friends. Several reporters, mouths agape, filmed me as I gracefully drifted back down to the ground.

"What's the plan?"

"Nice entrance." Jasmine shook her head but she was smiling.

I shrugged. "It was Hades's idea. He has a flair for theatrics."

Lucian came over and hugged me, his face pressed in my neck. "I'm glad you're here," he murmured against my skin.

"Me too." If it had been a different moment, I would've kissed him long and hard, not caring who was watching, especially Hades. But as it was, the moment wasn't right for that, or for lots of things. I promised myself that after we did what we came to do, I was going to grab onto the moment, onto Lucian with both hands and never let him go.

I checked out the familiar faces standing nearby and the lack of some. I'd expected the entirety of the second year class to be present. "Not everyone is here."

"We're basically a test run. Only a few cadets from each clan that have abilities to utilize," Lucian said. "Zeus thought just having a select few to manage this crisis would be enough to show that the academy is doing what he said it would do."

One of the firefighters walked over to us; he had a

captain badge stitched on his heavy yellow jacket. "It wasn't my idea to have you here. I think you're going to get in the way, but if you want to help, then do what I tell you."

We all nodded.

"Yes, sir," Lucian said, taking the lead for the group. "There are a few of us who have water powers and can help with the water dumps."

He surveyed our group and didn't look too impressed. "I'm sure our helicopters can handle that…"

Ren stepped out of the group, raising his hands out in front of him. Within seconds he had twin, basketball-sized water balls balanced on his palms. He threw them at the surrounding trees, soaking the trunks.

The captain nodded. "Impressive. But we're going to need more water than that, I'm afraid."

"I'm pretty sure a few of us could actually move the water from the nearby lake and dump it onto the fire," Ren said proudly. "No buckets required."

The captain stared at Ren. "Ah, okay."

Ren gestured to Marek and a couple of others from Poseidon's clan.

"Be safe," I said to him.

"You too." Then he and the others flew into the sky and disappeared behind the treetops.

The captain's eyes were so wide and his head tilted back so far I thought for sure he was going to fall over from shock. It took a minute for him to snap out of it, and then he gestured to the rest of us. "So, what else can you do?"

"Um, I can move the earth." Georgina's voice came from behind me.

He frowned. "Not sure what that means, or how that will help."

She stepped forward, crouched, and placed her hand on the pavement of the parking lot. At first nothing happened, and then the ground beneath us shook a little. Then a crack erupted in the cement, splitting the parking lot, as a ton of soil spilled out of the fissure, like a dirt volcano.

The fire captain had to jump back before a wave of dirt covered his boots. He gaped at her. "Okay, so, I think you would work well with the hotshot team to make firebreaks to stop the fire from spreading." He pointed to a group of firefighters getting ready to jump into a truck. "Go with them, they're getting ready to head in."

"Be safe." I hugged Georgina.

"You too."

She and a few others ran over to the waiting group at the trucks.

The captain glanced at me. "So, what can you do, Twilight?"

I started to balk at what he called me, but as nicknames went, it wasn't bad.

I flicked out my hands to my sides, flames instantly erupting over them.

"We want to stop the fire, not make more," he said.

I shot out a hand, tossing a fireball onto the grass. It immediately took hold and the flames grew. Then I held out my hand toward the fire and slowly made a fist. The flames grew smaller and smaller. Then I shut my hand, and the fire extinguished in a puff of black smoke.

"Can you do that on a large scale?"

I shrugged. "Don't know. Haven't tried to yet. But as a team," I said, glancing at Lucian and Jasmine and the others, "I'm positive we can do something worthwhile."

"All right. I have a team inside about five miles near the gorge. Do you know where that is?"

I nodded.

"I'll radio in, tell them to expect you." He rubbed his face and sighed. "They're not going to believe it when I tell them a group of flying kids are coming to save the day."

With a nod to the others, I lifted into the air, Lucian and Jasmine beside me. The last two, which included Quinn and a girl name Su, who were both in Hephaistos's clan, also followed suit. Once we got into formation, we flew up over the trees. It was then we saw what we were flying into. It resembled the bowels of hell.

CHAPTER TWENTY-ONE

MELANY

*I*t didn't take us long before we were flying through the thick, black smoke. I felt the heat from the fire down below rolling up over my body. Sweat popped out on my forehead and upper lip. I looked over at Lucian and saw the same horror on his face that I was feeling.

Because the air was so thick with blinding smoke, it was difficult to see where the gorge was. After about ten minutes searching, Jasmine pointed out a break in the fire about one hundred feet from the edge of the gorge.

"There!"

We swooped down to the ground where there were about eight firefighters in yellow gear and helmets, digging in the already burnt ground and knocking down blackened trees to stamp out any embers. When we landed, there were some startled looks and some curses, but since they'd been warned of our arrival, it was minimal.

One of the men approached us. "I've been told you can control fire."

"We're going to try," I said.

"Where do you want us to hit?" Lucian asked.

The firefighter pointed to the fire line to the left of us. "If we can keep making strides this way, we can pinch the fire off. From what I've heard, your people with the water are doing some good damage on the main fire."

My heart lifted at those words.

The five of us—me, Lucian, Jasmine, Quinn, and Su—moved toward the fire line on the left. The heat was oppressive this close to the flames. We were a good fifty feet away, but it was like putting your face right into a bonfire.

"Okay, we need to try and gather the fire and snuff it out."

Everyone nodded. Then as one, we stretched our hands out toward the flames.

I concentrated on one flame at a time. It was impossible to think about it all at once. We wouldn't be able to control it like that. I closed my eyes and focused on one of the burning trees, trying to gather the fire to me. But it was hard to distinguish one flame from another. I needed to get closer. I took a few steps forward.

"Mel! What are you doing? You can't get too close." I heard the worry in Lucian's voice, but I knew what I was doing.

The fire wouldn't hurt me. It was part of me. I glanced over my shoulder to Quinn and Su. They were part of Hephaistos's clan; they were part fire, too. "Move closer. The fire won't hurt you."

They glanced nervously at each other.

"Trust me."

Then Quinn took a couple steps forward; Su followed his lead. Eventually, they got in line with me.

I saw that Lucian and Jasmine were going to follow, but I shook my head. "You stay there. Keep trying to control it from where you are."

I urged Quinn and Su to go with me right to the edge of the fire. I could see the fear on their faces, but there was no time to coddle them. They either trusted in their power or they didn't. I trusted in mine. I felt it surging through me.

Flames bent toward me, flicking fiery fingers at me. I suspected I'd have red skin and singed hair by the time the fire was done with me. It was difficult to breathe this close, so I tried not to gulp in the much-needed air, as it was mostly smoke.

I stretched my hand out toward the flames. I pulled and plucked at the fire until I had a handful, then I crushed it in my fist, snuffing out its life. Now, I had the fire's attention. Bolstered by what they'd seen me do, Quinn and Su both drew out the flames and extinguished them.

It was a long, involved, painful process, but after an hour, we had a football-field sized part of the forest doused. The fire was angry though, and some of the flames tried to leap over us, aided by the sudden gusts of wind. Two small fires erupted behind me and in front of Lucian.

I whirled around to snuff it out, but Lucian used one of his other powers to douse it. He gathered the water molecules from the air and from deep in the ground, creating a mini waterspout. He sent it spinning over the small fires, and they were immediately smothered.

We came back to talk to the firefighters who were extremely grateful for our help, and they told us that the fire was getting under control in other parts of the forest. Ren and Marek had completely put out a hectare to the right of us, and Georgina had single-handedly created another gorge effectively cutting the fire off from jumping into another part of the park. Maybe they would name it after her.

All in all, we'd done one hell of a job. Zeus and the other Gods would be proud. I hoped Hades would be proud, too.

The firefighters shared their water with us, and I used a wet cloth to wipe the soot from my face and hands. I suspected that I'd have a few blisters on my skin by the day's end. It was worth it, though. Together, we'd done a great thing and helped the community.

Taking one of the water bottles, I walked toward the gorge. It was the deepest gorge in the world at sixteen hundred feet and a marvel to see. Luckily, the fire hadn't dived down into the crevasse and burned away all the rich vegetation growing along its rock walls. Lucian and Jasmine joined me.

We stood near the edge, each taking turns

drinking the water. I glanced at Lucian and saw he still had soot on his cheek. I reached over and tried to rub it away. He grabbed my hand and held it to his face.

I was happy standing here with him and with Jasmine. It felt like the past three months hadn't happened and I hadn't changed. Maybe there was still hope for me. That I hadn't turned into an angry instrument for Hades. I could just be me. Melany. A girl who had hoped to find a new life at the academy, and found friendship and belonging and maybe love, as well.

I moved closer to Lucian, so he could put his arm around me. As we stood there, a strange thudding sound rose from the gorge.

Jasmine frowned. "What do you think that is?"

"I don't know. Maybe it's one of the helicopters bringing water over—" Lucian's voice trailed off.

The sudden violent rush of air blowing over us cut me off.

A prickling sensation erupted over my scalp as the hairs on the back of my neck lifted.

I knew what was coming.

"Run!" I screamed at Lucian and Jasmine, but it was too late. It was too late to run, too late to do anything.

The chimera rose from the gorge, a monstrous creature, twelve feet in height, with a yellow lion's head and body, a second head of a goat protruded from between its shoulder blades, and large black dragon wings flapped to keep it hovering above us. A hissing sound escaped it as its tail reared around; a tail that was a ten-foot long green snake with four-inch long fangs, dripping venom onto the rocks beneath it.

I heard the shouts and screams from the men behind us, but it was too late for them. There was nowhere for them to run. The beast opened its lion mouth and a stream of fire spewed out, aimed right at the startled and frightened firefighters.

It was their shrieks of pain as they burned that finally knocked me into action.

"In the air!" I shouted, as I shot up above the chimera. I formed a fireball in each hand and flung them at the creature.

One ball smashed into its side, but it did nothing but singe its fur. It dodged the other ball with ease. By this time, Lucian and Jasmine had joined me in the air. Jasmine tossed fire at it as well, while Lucian formed a lightning bolt and hurled it like a spear toward the chimera.

The beast maneuvered out of the way, but only barely. The tip of the bolt seared the head of the snake. It shrieked and hissed, but it wasn't injured.

We weren't going to win this fight. We were unarmed and outmanned. There were already four or five dead men on the ground, burnt to cinders, and if we didn't do something, that would be our fate as well.

"Keep it distracted!" I shouted to Lucian, as I dropped to the ground.

"Where are you going?"

But I didn't answer; I didn't have time. I ran for the nearest shadow, sinking into it. The trip back to the Underworld took seconds, and I ran out of the darkness in the corridor and into the training arena.

"Help me!" I shouted even as I dashed to the weapons wall and grabbed a sword and back scabbard for myself, a bow and arrows, and a spear. While I grabbed a shield, the Furies jumped down to the floor from the rafters they usually rested on.

"What's going on, princess?" Tisiphone tried to grab my sword.

I smacked her hand away. "The fire was just a diversion. The real threat is a chimera. And I need your help."

Megaera rubbed her hands together. "We haven't fought a chimera in a thousand years."

Tisiphone grabbed a sword. "Finally. We get to have some fun."

Without a word, Allecto armed herself and then took a few extras.

Together, we went back into the corridor. Before we disappeared into the shadows again, I put my fingers in my mouth and whistled. It was a matter of seconds before I heard the thump-thump-thump of very large feet on the stone floor. The doors to the hall burst open and Cerberus trotted inside, his head ducked down, but his tail thudding against the ceiling.

"Want to go for a run, boy?"

His excited panting was all the answer I needed.

All four of us climbed onto his back, and I guided him into the darkness.

When we came out on the other side, the chimera razed the tree line with another stream of fire.

Jasmine was on the ground, one of her wings burnt to a crisp. Lucian was still in the air, zipping around the creature and trying to electrocute it, but having no luck.

Su and Quinn attempted to get the other firefighters out of harm's way. Quinn picked up one of the men and flew him to safety while Su tended to another's injuries.

Everyone turned toward us as we emerged from the darkness. The Furies were airborne in an instant. And with triple shrieks, they shot toward the chimera. Cerberus charged toward the hovering beast, but it flew up out of his way. He let out a loud, earth-shaking triple bark.

I took to the air, even as I nocked an arrow on my bow. "Get the others out of the forest," I shouted at Cerberus. He obeyed and ran over to Su and the injured firefighters.

I let the arrow fly at the chimera. It maneuvered out of the way but ended up in Allecto's path. She sliced the creature across the back leg. It let out a roar. I smiled. It was a small victory, but at least I knew the beast wasn't impenetrable and it could bleed.

As I flew toward Lucian, I threw him the spear. He caught it and dove toward the chimera the Furies had circled. I nocked another arrow, aimed at its goat head, and fired. It was confused now, and cornered, and this time it couldn't dodge away. The arrow pierced its left eye socket.

The Furies let out a collective war cry in celebration and then went in for the attack.

The chimera turned its lion head as Tisiphone

dove at it. It opened its mouth, blasting fire. She didn't have a chance to duck. Fire caught her wings, burning them to ash. She dropped from the sky.

Allecto swooped after her and was able to catch her before she plummeted into the gorge. Allecto set her down on the ground, and then shot back into the air, twice as angry, twice as determined to bury her sword into the chimera's flank.

"Cut its wings," I shouted.

I wasn't sure if she heard me, but then she swooped under the chimera and veered up, sword tearing through its right wing. The creature banked to the left nearly colliding with Lucian. But he was able to evade it, going into a roll toward the ground. Right before he reached the rocky side of the cavern, he pulled out of his tuck and soared upwards, his wings spread wide.

Gods, he was magnificent. Like a golden eagle, powerful and majestic. I was lucky to have him in my life.

Megaera flew at the chimera's other side, Jasmine with her, and swiped high then low with her sword. Her blade caught the left wing, tearing a hole in the leathery webbing. The beast listed to the side again, and I could see it was having trouble staying aloft.

It was now or never.

Bolstered by seeing Lucian's power in the air, I slung my bow over my shoulder and unsheathed my sword. As I flew upwards, I met his gaze and smiled at him. I knew it wasn't the most appropriate time to feel joy, but I did. It raced through me like the fire raced through the trees. I felt empowered. I felt invincible.

I swooped toward the chimera, avoiding the stream of fire spewing from its mouth. The attack had been desperate, a last ditch effort to kill someone before it fell from the sky. On the ground, the beast wouldn't be as efficient and it knew that.

I dove down, spun, and then came up again. As I shot directly toward the chimera, I feinted to the right, the beast turned to the left, but I whirled at the last second and brought my sword down. I closed my eyes, knowing my blade struck true.

The chimera dropped to the ground, its lion's head rolling across the blackened landscape. Its blood stained the soil. The body landed with a loud thud. The Furies descended on the beast to finish the job.

I floated down to the ground then looked for Lucian. He was descending slowly near the chimera, a look of triumph on his face. I grinned at him again and he returned it.

Then his body convulsed and he cried out. He flung out a hand toward me, reaching for me to save him.

"Noooo!" I ran toward him, swinging my sword and slicing the snake tail that had struck him in the back in two.

But it was too late. The damage had been done.

Lucian fell the last few feet from the sky.

I caught him before he could hit the rocky edge of the gorge. As gently as I could, I lay him down onto the ground. His body quivered in my arms. I dared not look at his back, knowing full well that the snake's bite had pierced his flesh and shot venom into his body.

He looked up at me, his face paler than I'd ever seen it. "Blue…" He gasped.

I pulled him closer in my arms, rocking him. "Don't talk. Save your energy. It's going to be okay." Tears rolled down my cheeks as I looked around in a panic for help.

The others started to gather around. Allecto, Tisiphone, Megaera. They looked down at us, faces blank.

Jasmine crouched down beside us.

"Help him," I whispered.

She pressed her lips together as tears ran down her face. "I don't know what to do."

I heard more flapping of wings, and others started to land nearby. Ren ran to our side.

He knelt down and touched Lucian's face, which was sallow and slick with sweat. "What happened?"

I opened my mouth to tell him, but the words wouldn't come. I could feel Lucian's body growing cold in my arms.

"The chimera's snake bit him in the back," Jasmine said, her words wobbling.

Without letting Lucian go, I let Ren roll him a bit, so he could examine his back. The look on his face told me everything I needed to know. Everything I would ever know.

I ran my hand over Lucian's face. "It's okay, baby. You're going to be okay."

"Blue…" He lifted his hand and cupped my cheek. "I love you."

I swallowed down my sobs. "Someone help me!"

Then his hand fell away, and he slumped in my arms. Slowly, his eyes fluttered closed.

That was the last thing I remembered before my whole world fell into darkness.

DEMIGODS ACADEMY
YEAR THREE

CHAPTER ONE

MELANY

*A*s we crouched on the dirt and rocks on the edge of the gorge, the air around Lucian and me prickled on my skin as I unconsciously pulled the darkness closer, concealing us from the others. I heard Jasmine and Ren's voices calling out to me, but they eventually faded to silence.

Frantic, I looked around grasping for something in the shadows to make it better, to make Lucian better. I could no longer feel the heat of his body as I held him in my lap. His beautiful blue eyes, black pupils dilated, stared vacantly up into mine.

"You can't leave me." I leaned down and brushed my lips against his. They were cool, turning blue with every passing second that I couldn't help him. "I won't let you go," I murmured.

Tears poured down my cheeks. I was powerless to

stop them. They streamed along my neck and dripped onto Lucian like spring raindrops. If only they were raindrops and could awaken him with their life-giving force. But nothing in this world was that just.

I gathered him in my arms, pulling him up to my chest, and buried my face in the side of his neck. I inhaled his scent of pine and sunshine, knowing it would be replaced with death and decay.

It wasn't fair that he was being taken. I'd done everything I was told to do. I followed the orders; I did what was expected of me. So why was I being punished like this? I could rally against the Gods for the injustice of it all, but I knew they wouldn't care. We were instruments to them, to be used for their purposes, playthings and pets, at best, to be coddled and prettied up when trotted out to the public. Just like Hades had done to me.

I hated them all for this. Lucian's death wouldn't go unanswered. Someone was going to pay for it. I made the vow deep in my soul, sealing it with the tornado of pain and rage inside me.

Gently, I lowered Lucian's body back to my lap. I kissed his lips, his cheeks, his brow. His eyes were still open, staring into nothingness. With the tips of my fingers, I closed them, leaving red prints on his lids. Tears still trickled down my cheeks, and I wiped at them with blood-stained hands.

I felt the weight of the dark amulet hanging around my neck as I shifted position. It was hot against my skin. I reached up and wrapped my bloody hand around it. I closed my eyes and whispered into the darkness.

"Take me instead."

The air instantly chilled, and I shivered. The shadows surrounding me began to move, swirling around like ink in water. The rushing sound of wings flapping echoed all around. I looked up to see a dark form with giant black wings hovering above me, then slowly lowering to the ground. At first, I thought it was Hades coming to take me back to the underworld, but the closer it got I realized how wrong I was.

Draped in a black shroud and carrying a long heavy-looking silver scythe, the tall figure drew near. Then it looked down at me with no face. Only darkness filled the space under the hood. It spoke, its voice a harsh and raspy buzzing in my ears.

"Do you wish to trade places with the fallen one?"

Before I could respond, another figure appeared in the sky also flapping large black wings. Hades landed beside the shrouded figure.

"She's not for you, Thanatos," he said.

"She summoned me."

Hades made a face. "No, she didn't. She summoned me. You were just looking for an excuse to take her."

Thanatos pointed a skeletal finger at Lucian. "I will take him then."

Hades sighed. "Not today."

Thanatos roared, his voice echoing painfully in my ears. "You cannot have both."

"I can and I will."

"You will pay for this Hades."

Hades nodded. "Whatever."

Thanatos roared again, then he exploded into a million black feathers. They drifted down to the ground and on top of my head. I swiped at them and frowned up at Hades.

"I didn't summon you."

"You did with your tears."

He crouched next to me and reached for Lucian. I held onto him. "What are you doing?"

"Just give him to me."

My heart leapt into my throat as I slapped at his grasping hands. "No! You can't take him from me!" I burst into uncontrollable sobs, not caring that tears gushed from my eyes and my nose ran.

He looked at me for a long moment, his face softened. He lifted a hand and touched the tears on my cheeks. "Your pain is powerful. I can feel it inside."

"He's dead and it's my fault." I looked up at Hades, pleading for him to do something to take my pain away. I didn't care how he did it. I just wanted to be free of it. He should have let Thanatos claim me.

He reached for Lucian again. "Just give him to me before I can't do anything for him."

I relinquished my hold on Lucian, and Hades gathered him in his arms. He closed his eyes and pressed the palms of his hands down onto Lucian's chest. At first nothing happened, then a dark purple glow emanated from Hades's hands and slowly enveloped Lucian's body until he too glowed like amethyst.

The hair on the back of my neck rose as I

watched Hades pour dark energy into Lucian. A prickling sensation whispered over my scalp and then down my arms until it crept throughout my body, making me shiver. I didn't know what to expect from this. How could a person be brought back from death? It was a type of magic I was unfamiliar with. I held my breath, eyeing Lucian's body for any twitch or flinch, any indication that it was working.

Hades's eyes snapped open, and he scowled. He looked down at Lucian's body, and I saw the confusion in his face. "It's not working."

I shook my head. "Keep trying. Please!"

"He's too far gone. His soul has already left his body."

"No! I won't accept that." I leaned forward and placed my hands down on top of Hades's. I closed my eyes and pushed everything I had forward. Every spark of energy, every flicker of flame, every molecule of water, every speck of earth, every tendril of shadow. Every aspect of who I was, I forced through my body and out of my hands and into Hades.

I opened my eyes as I heard Lucian's small gasp and watched as his face contorted. Was it in pain or something else? I couldn't tell. The purple glow grew brighter. I had to squint to look at Lucian. And then I saw it. The rise of Lucian's chest. His mouth opened and he sucked in air. Hades fell back, the dark glow shattering like purple glass, shards of it sprinkled onto the ground around us. Then Lucian took in another breath, then another.

I touched his face. His skin was cool and clammy but warming under my fingers. "Lucian?"

I could see his eyes moving around, then slowly, they opened, and his gaze fixed on me. He blinked several times, then licked his lips. "What...what happened?"

Smiling, I leaned down and pressed my lips to his brow, then I looked up as Hades got to his feet, brushing at the dirt on his black pants as if he'd not just brought back a person from the dead.

"Hades, I—,"

He waved his hand toward me. "I'll see you later in the hall." Then he turned and stepped into the darkest part of the shadows still surrounding us and disappeared. The moment he vanished, the darkness fell away.

Jasmine, Ren, and the others who had gathered around the injured firefighters ran toward us.

"What happened?" Jasmine demanded. "You just disappeared."

Ren's eyes grew wide as he spotted Lucian sitting up and rubbing at his face. "How...but he was..."

"Hades saved him," I blurted in a rush of laughing and crying at the same time. My emotions were so conflicted that it felt like one big ball of chaotic energy inside my belly.

Ren helped Lucian to his feet, then he turned him around to look at his back. His shirt was torn away and bloody, but his back was clear of any wound. The only marks were from where his wings emerged. "It's like you never got stung."

Lucian rubbed his head again. "I have the worst headache." His knees buckled, and he would've fallen again if it hadn't been for me and Ren grabbing hold of his arms and body.

"You need to go to the infirmary," Jasmine said.

Lucian nodded.

I put my arm around his waist to support him then looked around, noticing the glaring absence of the dead chimera that was supposed to be on the ground. "Where's the chimera?"

"The Furies took the body away." Jasmine grimaced. "They said they had a use for its parts."

I didn't even want to think about what the sisters would use the chimera for. I pushed it out of my mind as I considered the best way to get Lucian back to the academy and to the infirmary where Chiron could look him over. There was no way he could fly. We'd have to go my way. Although I was positive none of my friends were going to be comfortable with it.

"Where's Georgina and the rest of crew?" I asked.

"They've already been evacuated," Jasmine said.

"Okay, everyone, gather around me. I'm going to take us back to the academy."

"How are you going to do that?" Ren narrowed his eyes at me.

"You'll have to trust me."

As everyone looked sideways at me, I wasn't sure they trusted me entirely. That hurt a bit, but it couldn't be helped. And I wasn't about to beg them to.

Jasmine and Marek moved in closer to me, Lucian, and Ren, who was still helping Lucian stand.

When everyone was grouped closely, I sent out feelers toward the nearest shadows. They were hard to find in the bright sunlight, but eventually I caught onto a few near the treeline and drew them toward me. After a few more minutes, we were covered in darkness.

"Follow me." I stepped forward into the dimmest part of the shadows. I could sense the others' hesitation, but eventually they did what I asked, and we all sunk into the black abyss. A few seconds later, I led them out of the darkness, and we emerged into the corridor just outside the infirmary.

Ren and I half-carried/half-dragged Lucian inside. Chiron turned to see us come in and shook his head. "Now what?"

"Lucian was stung by a chimera's snake tail," I said. "He…he died."

Chiron's eyes narrowed as he looked from to Lucian then back to me again. "He doesn't look dead."

"Hades healed him."

Chiron's eyes widened as he gaped at me. Then he took Lucian from us and lay him down on one of the cots. "Okay, you got my attention. In two thousand years, I've known of only one other person that Hades ever brought back from the dead. You're a lucky guy."

As Chiron started his poking and prodding at Lucian, he pointed to the door and told us to leave.

I didn't want to go. I'd lost Lucian, and I felt like if I walked through that door, I'd never see him again.

Jasmine put her hand on my arm and guided me out. "He'll be okay. He's safe now."

Once we were outside in the hall, I could feel my anger building again. The chimera had been released on purpose. Its intent was to kill as many of us as possible. I had no doubts about that in my mind. And I knew who released it—Aphrodite.

If she wanted a war, she was going to get one.

Without a word, I stepped into the nearest shadow to find out exactly where she was so we could have a little chat about that.

CHAPTER TWO

MELANY

I emerged from the shadows just outside of the tall golden doors leading to Aphrodite's Hall. I grabbed the door handle, twisted it, and threw the door open. I was surprised it didn't bang against the wall. Marching inside, I was fully aware of how I must've looked in my battle gear with arms and hands stained with Lucian's blood. A couple of people leapt out of my way, with looks of fear and terror, as I whirled down the hall like a black and red tornado.

At first, I wasn't sure Aphrodite was in the hall, but then I heard her shrill laugh through the open door of the side rooms. I entered to see the Goddess holding court. She lounged on one of the white sofas that were synonymous with her gilded hall, her long golden dress draped over the edge. She had a glass of red wine in one hand and a bunch of grapes in the other. She looked like one of her paintings that plastered the walls.

Her sculpted eyebrows went up when she spotted me. "Melany. How delightful. We were just discussing the success the academy had fighting the forest blaze. Well done, you."

Those who had been sitting on the floor in rapture of her—Revana among them—stood as I stomped toward Aphrodite. The Goddess didn't bother to rise. She was obviously very comfortable right where she was. She gave nothing away. I wasn't surprised. She'd had thousands of years to perfect the art of denial and Machiavellian schemes.

"We were successful. No thanks to you," I said, my voice low and growly.

Her gaze raked over me. "Is there a reason you're in my hall covered in blood? It's quite disgusting."

"This blood is on your hands."

"How so? I've been here the entire time." She took a sip of her wine and popped a grape into her mouth.

The others in the hall were getting quite a show, their heads turned from Aphrodite to me, to her again with each verbal volley.

"We encountered a chimera in the forest. A chimera you released to start the fire."

She made a face, feigning shock. "A chimera? How awful. Was anyone hurt?"

"A couple firefighters died, burned to death, and Lucian…"

Revana stepped forward. "Lucian's hurt?"

I didn't look at her. I just kept my gaze on

Aphrodite. "He died. Stung by the chimera. And it's your fault." I pointed at her.

This time she got to her feet. Slowly, lazily, as if I wasn't accusing her of killing people and had just come for a social visit.

"Lucian's dead?" Revana moved toward me. Her hands were clenched at her sides, although I sensed that if she could have gotten away with it, she'd have used those hands on me.

"Hades healed him." I looked at Revana. I knew she had feelings for Lucian, so I threw her a bone. "He's in the infirmary."

Aphrodite moved toward me. It was so smooth and effortless. It looked like she was floating. "I'm offended that you'd come into my hall and accuse me of releasing a monstrous creature into the world." She stood right in front of me with a snide smile just dripping with venom. "What proof do you have?"

"I heard you and Ares conspiring."

She rolled her eyes. "Didn't we already go over this with Zeus? You already accused me of conspiring, and it got you nowhere. Zeus didn't believe you and rightly so."

"Zeus is blind to your treachery."

"Careful now." She ran her finger over the rim of the wineglass in her hand. "Saying such things about the all-powerful could get you into some serious trouble."

I met her gaze with my own spitefulness. "I know what you did. I know that you and your lover Ares are planning something." I spoke the word lover with such rancor it left a sour taste in my mouth.

Her eyes flashed with fire, and she leaned down to me. I could smell the wine on her breath. We were so close. I could see the gold flecks in her eyes glow with power. "The only reason I don't reach into your mouth right now and rip out your heart is because you're Hades's little pet. And he is sentimentally attached to his pets. I mean, he lets that dog of his run loose sometimes." She straightened and took a step back, turning away from me. "Revana, please escort Melany out of this hall. I'm tired of her silly false allegations. They're boring me."

Revana looked from Aphrodite to me. I could see some hesitation in her face. Was she hesitating because she was afraid of me or her Goddess? Eventually, her misplaced loyalty won out, and she nodded toward the door, her eyes narrowed with a fierce intensity.

"Time to go."

I didn't move. I came for a fight, and I wasn't leaving without one.

Revana reached out to grab my arm to guide me to the exit. It was a mistake on her part as I was ramped up for any kind of fight.

Lightning quick I wrapped my hand around her wrist and twisted her arm around until I could've easily broken it with just a bit more well-placed pressure. She tried to break free, but every movement she made just put more strain on her arm, and she winced from the pain I imagined zipped up to her shoulder.

"Aphrodite is lying to you, Revana. She doesn't give one shit about you, or any of her disciples.

You're playthings to her. Like dolls manipulated for her amusement."

"She's just rambling." Aphrodite waved her hand toward me. "Everyone knows she's gone crazy. That's what happens to girls when they go to Hades's Hall. All those months down in the underworld with no one to talk to. It would drive anyone mad."

"I'm not crazy," I hissed at her.

"Oh, my dear, you have no idea what he's turned you into. He did it to poor Persephone and now to you. I'd feel sorry for you if you weren't pissing me off so badly with your lies about me and Ares."

Hearing the name Persephone gave me pause, and I relinquished my hold on Revana's arm. She stepped away from me and rubbed at her wrist and forearm.

"What happened to her? To Persephone?"

Aphrodite's grin sent a shiver down my spine. "She went crazy, tried to leave the underworld, but Hades wouldn't let her. Zeus had to intervene to save her life. If you're not careful, the same thing is going to happen to you." She flicked her hand toward me. "Now leave. My patience is wearing thin, and I won't be held responsible for what could happen next."

I wasn't afraid of her, or what she could do to me. I'd already survived one attempt on my life when she tried to squeeze me to death while she was a snake, but I wasn't going to gain the upper hand this way. I had to get proof of her treachery and expose her in front of the whole academy. If I went to Zeus again, he could just sweep it under the rug as if it never happened.

"This isn't over."

Aphrodite chuckled. "Do get some sleep, Melany. You look beyond ragged."

I marched out of the room and back toward the main doors. Revana was right on my tail. I could've told her she didn't have to escort me, that I knew the way. Right before I left, she grabbed my arm and spun me around.

"Is Lucian really okay?"

My first inclination was to grab her hand and crush it in mine, but the look on her face wasn't one of confrontation but of concern and worry. It cracked through my fury and seeped through to my core. Our feelings for Lucian were the only thing that united us.

I nodded. "He is now. He died in my arms, until Hades brought him back from the dead. He's in the infirmary if you want to see him."

She let her hand drop from my arm. She seemed almost sheepish for grabbing it in the first place.

"I know you don't believe me, but Aphrodite is not your friend. She's dangerous."

Revana's eyebrow lifted. "She says the same about you."

"Well, she'd be right." I turned and walked away, finding a shadow to dissolve into to travel back to the infirmary.

Before I stepped out of the darkness, I heard Jasmine and Georgina talking just outside the infirmary doors.

"You should've seen her, Gina. She was magnificent but terrifying." Jasmine shook her head. "I'd never seen anyone fight like that. I was just happy that we were fighting on the same side."

"She's still Melany. She's still our friend."

"Is she? I don't know. It feels like she has her own agenda that has nothing to do with us. When she came out of the dark riding Cerberus with the Furies at her side…" She sighed and shook her head again. "My whole body shook in fear. I don't know. Maybe I'm just tired and being overly sensitive."

Georgina put her hand on Jasmine's shoulder. "You should go back to your dorm and sleep. We all should. What we did today was good, Jas. We saved lives."

"I know, I just wish I wasn't afraid of Mel. Maybe I'm just afraid for her. I saw how she was with Hades. There's a connection there, and that terrifies me."

"It scares me too."

I'd heard enough. I stepped out of the shadows right next to them. They both jumped.

"Mel? Where did you go? We were worried." Jasmine tried to reach out to me, but I avoided her touch.

"It's not me you need to worry about." I walked into the infirmary toward Lucian's bed. Chiron was there, and he crossed the room to intercept me.

"He needs his rest. Come back in a day or two when he might be up for visitors."

"Just tell me one thing: is he going to be okay?"

Chiron nodded. "Yes. I don't know exactly what Hades did to him or for him, but he'll have a full recovery."

"Thanks."

I left the infirmary, and Jasmine and Georgina ambushed me.

"Is Lucian going to be okay?"

"Yes."

"What exactly happened?" Jasmine asked.

"Hades brought him back from the dead."

"How?"

I shrugged. I didn't know how to answer her because I really didn't know myself. He'd said that he couldn't do it, and it wasn't until I laid my hands on his that Lucian started to breathe. I had done something but didn't know exactly what that was. Had I made some subconscious deal with Thanatos for Lucian's life? Or had I made that deal with Hades? Did he own me now?

I had to find out.

"I've got to go," I said as I started for the nearest dim corner.

"Can't you stay longer? Have dinner with us in the dining hall like old times." Georgina eyes pleaded with me.

"The old times are gone, Gina." I moved toward the shadows. The second my boot touched the darkness, I wrapped my hand around the dark amulet at my throat and was immediately sucked into the abyss.

CHAPTER THREE

MELANY

My entire body shook as I stepped out of the shadows and into Hades's Hall. I was running on pure adrenaline. But I needed answers and a long hot shower before I could even think about getting any amount of sleep.

I marched into the library to find Hades. He sat in one of the large chairs by the fire sipping an amber liquid in a short glass and reading a book. When I approached, he casually bookmarked his page with a thin red satin ribbon and set the book down on the table beside him. He arched an eyebrow at me.

"I take it this is going to be some long tirade." Before I could say anything, he stood and moved toward the table with the crystal decanters of water, wine, and other liquids. "Let me pour you a drink."

"I don't want a drink. I want some answers."

He poured me a drink anyway, the same amber liquid that was in his glass. He offered it to me. I grabbed the glass and took a sip. It was strong and burned in my throat, but it warmed my belly the moment it hit, chasing away the exhaustion. I took another drink and drained it in one gulp, then set the glass down on the table with a loud clink.

"Why did you save Lucian?"

Hades shrugged. "It seemed like his death would've been a waste of a good fighter."

"Bullshit. I don't believe you."

"Believe what you want, girl, it's of no consequence to me." He tried to move away from me, but I stepped in his path. His gaze narrowed intensely as he stared down at me.

"You did it for me, didn't you?"

His lips twitched into a wry condescending smirk. "Your schoolgirl crush on me is flattering, Melany, but you really need to rein it in if I'm going to continue to teach you. I'd hate to relinquish my claim on you. You'd probably end up in Zeus's clan or, gasp, Hephaistos's. Talk about a waste."

He tried to go around me again, but I braced my hand against his chest. He looked down at it then back at my face. His eyes narrowed, darkening to pitch. It was now or never. With adrenaline still pumping through me along with the alcohol I'd just consumed, I fisted my hand in his shirt, perched on my tiptoes, and kissed him.

At first, I thought he was going to succumb to me and deepen the kiss, but when it was over and I naturally pulled back, licking my lips where a jolt of electricity still sizzled, he had the nerve to tilt his head indulgently and pat me on the head.

"Run along, Melany. You had a long emotional day and you clearly need some sleep."

"Argh! You're an asshole!" I stomped out of the library, across the hall to my room. Once inside, I slammed the door shut, locked it and cursed a blue streak all the way into the bathroom.

I stripped off my dirty clothes and stepped into the huge glassed-in shower stall. When I turned on the hot water tap, I was instantly hit with a hard spray from overhead and from the sides. I stood there, my face lifted to the scalding water, and let it wash away the conflicted emotions that were assaulting me.

Anger and fury mixed with grief and longing. I supposed those feelings were connected in various ways. I just didn't know how I felt at that moment. Anger still rippled inside me from having been forced to deal with the chimera while trying to save lives. I could still hear the screams of the firefighters as they were burned alive from the monster's fire. I was still grieving for Lucian's loss while trying to grasp onto the relief and joy that his return from the dead should have filled me with.

Then there were the emotions for Hades swirling around inside me making things very difficult and uncomfortable. Those confused me the most. I was angry at him for being so arrogant and superior all the time and grateful to him for healing Lucian and bringing him back to me. I burned so hard for him it was almost painful.

It was that last one that gave me the most trouble.

I couldn't desire Hades. It was wrong on so many levels. He was my teacher, my mentor, an arrogant jerk, a dangerous God. He wasn't nice or thoughtful or caring like Lucian. But I wanted Hades anyway. That probably said more about me than it did about him.

After I finished washing and rinsing, I turned off the tap, opened the door and reached for the towel on the heated rack, thankful for the warming sensation on my body. I dried off, slid on the black fuzzy robe that I'd been given when I first got here, and walked out of the bathroom fully intending to climb into bed and sleep.

I pulled up short, stunned, when I spotted Hades sitting stiffly on the edge of my bed.

When he stood, my racing heart leapt into my throat and butterflies fluttered deep in my belly. I didn't know what to do as he moved toward me, his gaze everywhere but on me. For the briefest moment, the word RUN screamed in my head, but I didn't move. I couldn't. And honestly, I didn't want to.

He stopped a mere foot in front of me and lifted his gaze to mine. I couldn't stop the flustered gasp that sprung my lips.

"You're playing with fire, girl. You know that, don't you?"

"Yes." My voice was raspy, thick with desire.

He took a step forward, and I took one back. "I'm not some boy you can tease and taunt." His gaze raked me from head to toe. The tip of his tongue poked out to wet his lips.

"I know." The ache in my belly deepened. I

nearly groaned as every muscle in my body quickened in anticipation of what I hoped he'd do to me. I had a very vivid imagination.

"If you truly knew, you'd run as far and fast as you could go." He closed the small distance between us, as my back hit the wall. He dipped his head, so his lips were mere inches from mine. "Beg me to take you, and I'll fulfil every desire you've ever had."

I pressed my lips together, then whispered, "Please. I want you—,"

His hands dove into my hair and his lips were on mine. He kissed me until my head swam. All I could think about was him pressed against my body, the heat he gave off, the scent of his cologne, and the taste of him on my lips. Everything about him was fire and passion, and I was a match just waiting to be struck and burned.

Then he pulled back, his eyes lowering to the tie on my robe. He reached out and slowly undid it. I swallowed as the robe parted just enough to show a sliver of my body. Licking his lips, Hades kept my gaze, then he took the two edges of the robe, eased them apart and slowly pushed the robe over my shoulders.

I stood there, fully naked, exposed, vulnerable, my entire body quivering as he stared at me. His gaze was hot and hungry, and I wanted to slap my hands over my breasts and between my legs, but he gripped my arms and pressed them against the wall so I couldn't. I took in a ragged breath and gnawed at my bottom lip with my teeth, so I wouldn't cry out from frustration and desperation. I needed him to touch me; I was sure I'd wither away to dust if he didn't.

Finally, blissfully, he kissed me again. He pressed his body against mine, the fabric of his suit rubbed over the sensitive tips of my breasts, and I could feel how much he wanted me. There was no mistaking it, and I was empowered to know I could do that to him.

When he pulled back again, I mewled in protest. His lips twitched into a sly smile, then he moved away from me, letting his hold on my arms drop. I was about to tell him to stop, when he slid off his jacket, then unbuttoned his shirt.

When he was shirtless, I admired the cut of his pecs and the ridges along his flat stomach. His skin was pale and smooth like marble except for a thin line of dark hair that led to the band of his trousers, which he was undoing. He looked as strong and fierce as I knew he would be. He was a God and a gorgeous one at that.

He stripped his pants off; the rest of him was as hard and beautiful. Then he moved toward me again, predator-like. I was both excited and scared. I couldn't stop shaking. I'd had sex before, but this was beyond anything I'd ever experienced. Hades was beyond any man. Was I truly ready for this?

Pressing up against me, his lips nibbled on the side of my neck while his hand slid up to my breast, caressing it with his fingers playing over the sensitive tip. I let out a long low groan. He trailed his tongue and teeth along my jawline and over my mouth. A hand dipped down over my hip, then he pulled up my leg, hooking it up over his waist.

Gasping, I bowed my back as he entered me. Although I was ready for him, he had to go slow. He gritted his teeth; the muscles along his jawline clenched. I knew he wanted to thrust into me but restrained himself so he wouldn't hurt me. When he was finally seated inside me, he kissed me again, his tongue dipping inside my mouth, and started to move.

I dug my fingers into his back and held on as he took me beyond the limits of pleasure.

At first, we were screwing up against the wall, the rough texture of the stone wall scraping along my skin. Then, we were on top of a large bed with black silk sheets. I could feel the satin caressing my backside as Hades thrust into me again and again.

We weren't in my room though, or Hades's room, but a vast rock cavern, a large fire with flames as high as the stone ceiling crackling nearby. Our bodies were slick with sweat, the glow of the fire cocooning us in orange and red. The place matched how I felt inside.

I grabbed onto him, one hand in his hair the other on his ass, as his strokes became harder and faster. Every muscle in my body clenched and quaked. My heart raced so fast I could barely breathe as my body was pushed to the edge of bliss.

With one final deep thrust, Hades cried out in a language I didn't understand.

My entire body convulsed as an orgasm rippled through me. "Oh, Gods!"

Light burst behind my eyes, as sound roared in my ears. I bowed my back and crushed him around the waist with my thighs as every nerve in my body snapped. I was a swirling tsunami of sensation as I came. I bucked against it, both pushing and pulling Hades, as he continued to coax more pleasure out of me with every slight movement of his body inside mine.

He nuzzled his face into the side of my neck. He licked me, then his mouth covered mine and he kissed me until both our bodies stopped quaking. Panting hard, he peppered kisses along my chin and neck, then he rolled off me and onto his back onto the bed.

I blinked up at the canopy overhead and realized we were back inside my room. I turned my head to look at him. His eyes were closed, and he had an arm flung up over his head. I watched the quick rise and fall of his chest. Hesitant, I reached over and touched him, making sure that this had been real and not a dream.

He covered my hand with his own then opened his eyes and looked at me. I wasn't sure what I saw in those dark depths. I wanted to believe there was affection there; I'd felt it as he made love to me. I wasn't a fool to think there was love. I didn't know if he could even feel that way about anyone.

But for one moment, I fantasized that he felt it about me as I felt it for him.

Hades sat up briefly to pull up the blanket to cover us both. Then he pulled me up onto his chest and brushed his fingers through my hair until we both fell into a blissful deep sleep.

CHAPTER FOUR

LUCIAN

$\mathcal{I}$ dreamt of fire.

I was running through a cave, and flames flickered along the stone walls bathing everything in red and orange. Behind me, running just as fast, loped a large black beast with teeth as long as my forearm and breath that stunk of brimstone and ash.

As I sprinted over the rough, uneven rock floor seemingly for my life, all I could think about was Melany. She was here somewhere in the cave, and I had to get to her before the beast consumed her alive.

Sweat coated my body as I ran, my arms and legs pumping mercilessly. My lungs burned, and my heart throbbed from the effort. I could hear screams all around me. Female screams. Melany's screams. But at one point, I wasn't one hundred percent sure if they were cries of pain or agony or of extreme pleasure.

That made it worse and sent sickly shivers up and down my spine.

I kept running, glancing over my shoulder to see how close the beast was getting. That had been a mistake, and I tripped over a stubby protruding stalagmite. I fell to my knees onto the hard, rocky surface, pain shot up my legs from the impact. A thick dark shadow crawled over me, and I knew I was doomed.

I flipped over as Cerberus cornered me, three sets of glowing red eyes glaring at me. He snorted and smoke curled out of his nostrils. But the worse part was the man who had been riding the hound. Hades slid off the beast's back and loomed over me like a dark specter.

He smiled, and I felt like a knife slid between my ribs and into my heart. "Don't worry, boy, I can't kill you. I'm a part of you now."

"Where's Melany?" I demanded with more bravado then I felt.

"Can't you tell by her screams? She's with me. In the underworld. In my bed."

His words made me nauseous, and I felt like I was going to retch. I scrambled away from him and got back onto my feet. "I don't believe you."

"Yes, you do. You knew this day was coming. You sensed the changes in her. You knew she was no longer the girl that awkwardly stumbled into the academy with a stolen shadowbox." He looked amused, and it made my stomach roil. "You saw how she looked at me. Hungry for the darkness."

I shook my head. "I don't care what you say. She'll never be yours."

"She already is." Hades swirled his hand in the air, and the shadows curled around him like a black opaque curtain. Within those shades I saw Melany with her arms around Hades. She turned her head ever so slightly toward me, and she was laughing.

I jolted out of the darkness. I didn't quite wake up but was floating in the space between sleep and consciousness. It was pleasant, warm and non-threatening. Safe. Then I heard voices nearby. I couldn't tell who they belonged to, or whether they were male or female even.

"The girl knows too much. I suspect Hades is feeding her all kinds of stories."

"She won't know what is truth or fiction."

"Some will listen to her. She has supporters in the academy. Not only students but professors."

"She needs to die."

"We can't get to her. She's under Hades's protection."

"We have to get her out into the open."

"She'll be guarded in a battle, like she was in the fire."

"Then it has to be during another event. Some place and time she won't expect."

"It has to be soon, before she finds out the truth about the academy and…"

The voices faded. I tried to focus my energy on getting them back, but it was too hard. Slowly my warm place was becoming cold and unwelcoming. I struggled inside that space, punching and kicking my way out, my way up to the surface.

Light pierced my eyelids, and I cracked one then the other open. Blinking away the drugged-sensation, I turned my head to survey my surroundings. I was in a bed in the infirmary. I turned my head again to see several faces looking down at me.

"Welcome back." Zeus smiled at me.

As did, Ares, Demeter, Dionysus, Aphrodite, Heracles, and Chiron who were all gathered around my bed.

"Chiron wasn't sure if you were going to come out of it so soon."

"We all heard about your heroic deeds and had to come down to see how you were doing." Aphrodite patted my hand.

I licked my lips which were dry and cracked. "What happened?"

While Chiron helped me sit up to drink some water, Dionysus gleefully said, "Well, you died. What did it feel like? Do you remember?"

Ares nudged him away. "Leave him alone. He's a great warrior. A hero."

I closed my eyes for a moment and remembered the pain that surged through me from the chimera's sting. I shuddered. I also remembered being on the ground in Melany's arms. After that, it was all a bit fuzzy. Hades had been there, I could feel his dark cold touch on my chest, and I remembered waking up and my friends helping me to my feet and coming here.

"Okay, time for everyone to leave," Chiron said. "Lucian needs his rest."

Zeus squeezed my shoulder. "When you are feeling better, son, the academy is going to host a grand ceremony for you and the others who battled the great fire and saved many lives. You are all heroes, and we're going to celebrate your bravery."

"Melany…"

Zeus nodded. "Oh yes, she will most definitely be invited."

"Hades…," I said, trailing off, unsure of what I wanted to say about him.

"We'll invite him, too. We'll make it so he can't say no." He gave me a little wink, as if we were sharing an inside joke. He leaned down closer to my ear. "I'm proud to have you as part of my clan, Lucian. One day I could see you leading my army."

He tipped his head to me, then followed the others out of the infirmary, leaving me with Chiron who forced a disgusting tincture down my throat claiming it would help me get my strength back. Then, he left me to rest.

But I couldn't rest. I had to find Melany and warn her. Someone was out to harm her, but I didn't know who. I could've easily assumed it was Ares and Aphrodite, as Melany had already accused them of treachery, but there had been others in the room. I wouldn't like to believe that Demeter, Dionysus, or Heracles would want to hurt Melany. They were friends, but I couldn't be sure about anything anymore.

I sat up all the way. I had to stop and breathe deeply as a wave of nausea overtook me. Once it passed, I swung my legs over the edge of the bed, my feet touching the floor. That was then I noticed that I was dressed only in a hospital-like gown with no pants and no socks. I stood, felt faint, but moved past it. I looked around to find my clothes but didn't have any luck in finding them. I was going to have to do this as is.

I started across the room toward the exit when a searing burn zipped across my chest. I put my hand up to my sternum, but it hurt when I pressed there. I pulled down the neckline of the gown and spotted several dark purple marks on my chest.

I moved to the dressing mirror in the corner of the room near the sink. I yanked down the gown so I could fully see the bruises that marred my skin. There were several dark blotches. Some were small, the shape and size of a dime, others were inch-long streaks, then there was a large square-shaped bruise below the others. Frowning, I studied them in the mirror. My stomach roiled as I took a step back, and I could see that all the marks together made up the shape of a handprint.

It was Hades's hand that had healed me.

I thought about the dream I had. There were only remnants left in my mind, nothing was too clear. Only whispers of sensations and sounds. The echo of Melany's passionate screams still faintly buzzed in my ears. But I did recall Hades's words. "I can't kill you. I'm a part of you now."

If that was true, maybe then I could use that to travel to the underworld and find Melany.

I shuffled over to the dimmest area of the infirmary where the shadows seemed to gather as if in a meeting. Erebus had taught us how to hide inside the darkness, using it as camouflage, but maybe I could use it like Melany did to travel from here to Hades's Hall.

With my hand, I reached into the shadows and tried to pull them over me, the same way I'd seen Melany do it. At first, nothing happened. I was just grabbing at air. Then a chill enveloped me and slowly I became surrounded by the dark, the infirmary fading away to nothing.

"Now what?" I sighed, unsure of what to do next.

I thought about the trip to the underworld that Jasmine, Georgina, and I took, after I gave blood to that witch, Hecate. I pictured the river that we needed to cross, and the cave beyond that. Had that been the cave I'd encountered in my dream?

I concentrated on that river and that cave, then took a step forward. I thought for sure I was going to walk right into the wall of the infirmary with every small step I took, but I didn't. I sensed I wasn't in that room any longer but somewhere else. Some strange place between corporeal planes.

Still with that image in my mind, I kept walking in the hope that I wasn't just going to be lost in the shadowy spots for an eternity with no way back. I had to believe I was going to end up somewhere.

For what seemed like hours, I kept walking, putting one foot in front of the other, until finally I could hear the rush of water. Buoyed by the sound, I walked a bit faster. Then I felt cold wet stone on the bottom of my foot. The shadows dissolved and I was in the cave. In front of me, looming like a castle tower, were black stone doors.

I made it. I was at the doors to Hades's Hall.

I tried the door handle. It wouldn't turn, so I knocked. The sound echoed around me like thunder bouncing off the stone walls.

"Who's there?"

I whipped around toward the voice and saw Hades sitting atop his three-headed demon hound. I hadn't even heard them approach, which was insane considering the size of the beast. His paws were as big around as a kitchen table.

"Now you're supposed to say Lucian."

Cerberus dipped his head toward me—his nose was the size of my head—and took in a large whiff of me. I wondered if he just smelled his lunch special of the day.

"I need to see Melany," I said.

Hades jumped down from his hound and stepped toward me. "Why?"

"She's in danger. I have to warn her."

"About what?"

"Tell her not to come to the hero ceremony. It's a trap. Someone wants to kill her."

"Who? Zeus?"

I shook my head. "I don't know. I didn't see faces, just heard words about that fact that she knows too much and that they want to draw her out into the open."

Hades rubbed at his chin. "I suspected as much."

"It's your fault." I took a step toward him despite shaking inside. "You put her in danger."

Hades's gaze focused on me. It was direct and intense and sent a shiver down my spine. But I didn't back down like he wanted me to. I wouldn't. Not when it was Melany's life that balanced on the edge.

"I admire your courage to come down here, Lucian. I really do. But don't make the mistake of thinking I won't hurt you. I may not be able to kill you, but there are other inventive ways to inflict pain and suffering."

"I want to see Melany. She deserves to know."

"Oh, I'll tell her to be sure." He smiled. "But she's sleeping right now. All worn out, I'm afraid." That grin again that made my stomach roil. "I'm sure you can imagine why."

I thought about my dream again and realized maybe it hadn't exactly been one. Melany's cries of passion filled my mind again.

"You've done your duty. You've brought the warning now go back to the academy where you belong."

"You can't keep me from her forever." I lifted my head and kept his gaze.

"Oh, I can try." He reached out and pressed a finger against my chest. The burn was instant, and I went sailing backward into the darkness as if hit by a sledgehammer. Seconds later, I landed in a heap on the infirmary floor.

A lot more unsteady than before, I got to my feet and made it back to my cot. I drank more of the tincture that Chiron had made me, vowing that I would do whatever it took to get stronger because I knew without a shadow of a doubt that Melany was going to need me to protect her. Not only from those who would seek to harm her but from Hades. He posed the most danger.

CHAPTER FIVE

MELANY

*A*fter I woke, I lay in bed on my back and stared up at the canopy wondering if I had dreamt the whole thing. I lifted the covers to see I had my sleeping clothes on and that I wasn't still naked. I turned my head and looked at the other side of the bed, trying to picture Hades sleeping there. I ran my hand over the dark sheets. They were cold to the touch.

I touched my lips with my fingers. His taste still lingered there. I could still feel the electricity of our coupling all along my body. My muscles ached a little, especially the ones between my thighs. We most definitely had sex. I hadn't dreamt it. It had been real.

And so amazing.

The bell above my bed jangled, and I rolled out of bed. I got washed and changed and wandered down the hall to the dining room for breakfast. My belly flip-flopped in anticipation of seeing Hades. But he wasn't at the table. I was alone again for breakfast with only the little serving robot for company. I ate quickly then went down to the training room.

When I stepped inside, Megaera and Tisiphone were flying around in the air sparring with swords, and Allecto was throwing knives into the wooden training dummies in the corner. When they spotted me, Tisiphone clapped.

My cheeks flushed. I really hoped it wasn't because she knew I'd had sex with Hades. I would be mortified.

She drifted to the ground as did Megaera, then came over to me. "There she is. The mighty chimera slayer."

Relief surged over me, and I smiled and nodded. "Well, technically you three finished it off."

"True." Tisiphone unsheathed a dagger at her waist. "I made a blade out of the chimera's fangs. Isn't it cool?"

She handed it to me, and I made all the appropriate noises, then handed it back to her. I had to suppress a shudder to think she had actually removed its teeth and fashioned a weapon out of them. When Allecto joined us, I noticed she wore a new fur cape. I swallowed when I realized it was from the hide of the chimera.

She must've noticed my disdain because she said, "It honors the enemy and the battle when you create something new from their death."

I shuddered even more, thinking about what they

would make out of me, if we were ever on opposite sides of a battle and I lost to them. Would Allecto be wearing a Melany cape made from my pale skin and blue hair?

"We heard the golden-haired boy survived," Megaera said.

I nodded.

"That's good. He's a good fighter."

"And pretty to look at, too," Tisiphone added with a leer. "Does he belong to you?"

I frowned. "What do you mean?"

"Is he, you know, yours?"

"What she means is, are you two having sex?" Allecto interrupted.

"No."

"So, you won't mind if I indulge—,"

"I do mind, actually." I couldn't believe we were even discussing this.

Megaera sneered. "What do you care? You've got the darkness. Don't be greedy and take the light as well."

I visibly pulled back, feeling attacked. "I don't have the darkness. What does that even mean?"

Hades took that moment to enter the training room, dressed impeccably in his black and purple suit. My cheeks instantly turned red and all three of the Furies smirked.

"You know what it means," Tisiphone murmured under her breath.

"How goes the training?" he asked, looking at the three sisters.

"We haven't yet started," Allecto said. "We were just showing young Melany here our spoils of battle."

"Ah yes, Charon informed me that we would be having chimera soup for dinner. It's been a long while since we've enjoyed such a delicacy."

All three of the Furies nodded and smacked their black lips together.

My stomach churned at the thought of eating anything remotely related to that dreadful monster.

"I have business to discuss with your trainee," he said to them.

One by one they left us alone, but both Tisiphone and Megaera gave me snide sideways glances before flying away.

Finally, Hades looked at me. But nothing in his face or eyes gave any indication that he was thinking or had thought about our coupling last night. "I trust you slept well."

"Yup. I sure did." If he wasn't going to address it, then I wouldn't either. What a jerk!

"A courier arrived earlier with a message from the academy."

I perked up at that.

"It seems Zeus plans on hosting a grand ceremony to celebrate the cadets who fought back the fire. I think there might even be medals." He sneered. "Tacky, but that's my brother for you. Of course, we are invited to the event, since we really did most of the work."

My eyes narrowed at him. "We? Don't you mean, me? I was the one who put out most of the fire and fought the chimera."

"If I recall, you used my hound and my Furies along with my weapons to make that fight."

I couldn't believe we were having this conversation. It was ridiculous.

I shook my head and smirked. "You're a jerk." Then I stomped out of the training room.

It may have been childish, but I was feeling a bit raw. Last night was an important moment, I thought, between us. But he was acting like nothing had happened, that it was just another ordinary day in hell.

I didn't want to go back to my room and look at my bed and be reminded of our incredible sex session, so I went to the library. When I stepped inside the room, Hades was already there waiting for me. He must've zipped through the shadows, anticipating my destination.

"What's the problem?" he asked.

Pressing my lips together, I lifted my chin and met his gaze defiantly. "Nothing. Everything is just perfectly peachy."

He sighed and rubbed a hand over his face. "Are you angry I didn't stay and sleep in your bed?"

"No." Was I angry about that? Maybe. I didn't want to be some random hook-up.

"I'm no good at this...stuff." He shuffled from one foot to the other. It was the first time I'd ever seen him flustered. "I'm still your patron. We still must maintain a professional relationship, especially in front of others who work for me. You do understand that, right?"

I dropped my gaze, feeling foolish. I hated the

emotions surging through me. I never thought I would be one of those girls, who pined away for any kind of attention or affection from the guy who they found attractive.

Hades was so not just some guy. We didn't just hook up. Our relationship went beyond anything normal or usual. This wasn't high school or college. This was Demigods' Academy, and I was being trained to defend the world from monsters. I needed to get over my needy bullshit.

After a moment, I nodded. "I get it. I'm sorry for being—,"

His fingers caressed my chin, and he lifted my head to look me in the eye. "No, don't apologize. We are in a precarious situation, which I fear neither of us knows how to maneuver."

I gave him a small smile, and his hand dropped away from my face. I wanted to reach up and cover his lips with my own, but I knew it wasn't the right time or place for that to happen. Instead, I turned away and asked about the invitation we got from the academy.

"Tell me more about this award ceremony or whatever it is."

"It's to be a week from now, but for us that means in two days."

"What do you make of it?" I looked at him again.

He looked at me for a long moment. I sensed there was something he wanted to tell me, but he turned away and walked to the table along the wall and poured water into two glasses.

"I'm not sure. On the surface it seems like a way

to congratulate those who fought the fire, but knowing Zeus it will be something else altogether. A way to make him look good, I imagine. He is a glutton for the spotlight." He handed me the glass of water.

I drank it even though I wasn't thirsty. "Why do you dislike each other so much? What happened between you?"

He chuckled. "Oh, it's a long and involved story. Let's just say that Zeus and I have a very contentious relationship. We have different ideas about what it means to be a God."

I wanted to ask him if it was about Persephone and what exactly happened to her, but I knew he'd get angry if I did. I set the empty water glass on the table.

"I should get back to training." I moved toward the door.

"Let's play hooky today."

I turned and made a comical face. "Really?"

"Yeah. If you could do anything, anything at all, what would you want to do today?"

"Are you being serious right now?"

His eyebrow went way up. "I'm always serious."

"Okay. I really miss carnival season."

His eyebrow stayed up as he stared at me.

"You know, Ferris wheels, cotton candy, stupid games to win big stupid stuffed animals. Pecunia always had a great spring carnival. I would go with Callie and her friends, even though they didn't like me. I'd walk down the midway and eat all the different foods until I was almost sick. Then, I would go on the Ferris wheel when it turned dark and look out over the whole town."

"All right." He set his water glass down then offered me his hand. "Take my hand."

I frowned. "What? Why?"

"Just trust me."

Did I trust him? I looked into his dark eyes, then reached out and joined my hand with his. He linked his fingers with mine and smiled. "Hang on. This is going to be a wild ride."

Together we stepped into the shadows. My heart dropped into my stomach as we whooshed though the darkness. It was like the one time I went skiing in the Alps with the Demos family and I lost control and almost went over a jump. I concentrated on the feel of Hades's hand to keep me grounded.

A couple of minutes later, we stepped out into the showroom of what appeared to be a small costume shop. A short plump man scurried out from the back room. He bowed his head.

"Lord Hades, a pleasure to see you again so soon," the man said in a heavily accented voice.

"Francois, please outfit the lady in proper attire for the season."

The man rushed toward me and took my hand. "I am thinking something dark and fierce."

Hades smiled. "Naturally."

"What's going on?"

"Just go with him. You'll thank me later."

I let Francois lead me into a dressing room. A half hour later I walked out in a short yet puffy dark blue and black dress with fishnet stockings and knee-high black boots. On my head was a large hat also dark blue and black with feathers and lace. I looked like a cross between Marie Antoinette and Pink.

Hades waited for me in the showroom. He was dressed stylishly in a dark blue suit jacket with a long tail and high collar, his shirt was frilly, his pants tight, his boots pointy toed and polished to a shine. His dark hair was slicked back, and he wore a lacy black half mask on his spectacular face. It made his cheekbones pop. He nearly stole my breath when I looked at him.

But it was his grin when he saw me that made my belly clench.

"You look extraordinary."

I blushed. "Thank you."

"Turn around."

I did as he asked, and he came up behind me and gently affixed a lace mask like his over my face. When I turned around, his gaze lit up. "Perfect."

"What is all this?" I asked, still completely confused.

He offered me his hand again. Francois opened the door, and Hades led me outside and into a massive buoyant crowd of people in colorful costumes and masks. Lively music filled the square.

"I can't promise you there's cotton candy, but there is a Ferris wheel." He gripped my upper arms and turned me to the right where I spied the tallest Ferris wheel I'd ever seen over the tops of the stone buildings.

"Where are we?"

"Nice."

"France?"

He nodded and looked out over the huge colorful crowd. "Yes, it was the only carnival I could think of to take you to." He tugged on my hand. "C'mon, let's see if they have some cotton candy."

CHAPTER SIX

MELANY

*H*ades led me through the square. We stepped on the mass of colorful flowers that were strewn over the ground by people on the parade floats. It was part of the Battle of the Flowers, which Hades explained happened every year at the carnival. Regardless, it was like walking on rainbows and I laughed.

In the square, there were several musicians and dancers and street artists to entertain the crowds. It was all animated and vibrant and loud, and I loved it. I stopped to watch an artist, wearing a gas mask and gloves, use spray paint and various metal objects to paint the most spectacular picture of the moon and stars reflected in a quiet pool of water. It was the most beautiful thing I'd ever seen. When he was done, everyone clapped. Hades stepped up and handed him a wad of money to buy the painting for me. I didn't know how much money it had been, but the guy's eyes widened and he kept thanking Hades and me while bowing his head.

When Hades gave me the painting, I was stunned. "You can put it up on the wall in your room. It would match the décor," he said with a twinkle of humor in his eyes.

While we continued strolling around, I had to keep readjusting my grip on the painting. Although I loved it, it was awkward to hold. "Is there somewhere I can drop this off and pick it up later?"

"I have something better." He grabbed my hand and pulled me into a narrow alleyway between two old stone buildings. He found a dim corner and leaned into the shadows and shouted. "Charon!"

No more than thirty seconds later, the skeletal butler hovered in the shadows. "Yes, my Lord?"

He handed the painting to Charon. "Take this to Melany's room."

Skeletal hands clutched the paper. "Right away, my Lord."

"But don't you dare hang it on the wall without her permission, like you did with that portrait Pablo painted of me a hundred years ago. You have no sense for decorating."

Charon nodded, then vanished inside the darkness.

I laughed, which seemed to please Hades. He grabbed my hand again and led me out of the alley and back into the frivolity. We came across several food stands. There was no cotton candy unfortunately, but Hades bought me something even better—a ganses. It was a deep-fried pastry, much like a croissant, served warm with a light sprinkling of powdered sugar. It melted in my mouth. It was the most delicious thing I'd ever tasted. After finishing one, I demanded another. He obliged me with a chuckle.

For the rest of the day and well into the evening, Hades indulged my every wish. We ate and drank, listened to music, and watched the different street artists including a magician and juggler. I even danced with a man with a huge papier-mache head. I felt lighter and freer than I'd ever been in my life, which was so surprising considering my company. Who would have thought I would have the most delightful day of fun and frivolity with the God of darkness? It seemed impossible, but it was happening.

And to top it all off, when the sun set and the colorful lights of the carnival glowed over the old city and sparkled on the clear blue water of the Mediterranean, Hades took me on the Ferris wheel.

My stomach did a few flip flops as the wheel spun us up to the very top and stopped. I could see everything. The dancing lights of blue and red and green, the vibrant costumes of all the revelers as they converged into the square and started to dance to the lively music coming from the sound stage constructed in the market. I looked out over the sea; several boats and yachts had strings of white lights twinkling over their bows and masts.

I looked over at Hades as his gaze swept the scenery. The look on his face was as soft as I'd ever seen it. "Thank you for this."

His gaze swiveled onto me and he smiled. "You're most welcome."

My belly clenched, and my heart skipped a few beats. *Shit.* I was falling in love with him.

"We should probably return home soon," he said. "We will both need some sleep before the ceremony at the academy tomorrow. We'll both need to be in fine form."

I was about to ask him why we needed to be in fine form when a sudden drop in temperature sent a shiver over my body. Our passenger car started to rock back and forth as wind whipped around us.

Over the water, I could see thick dark storm clouds rolling in like an avalanche would move snow down a mountain. The unusual sight made the little hairs on the back of my neck rise. Down below, I saw crowds of people stopping to stare at the incoming storm.

"That doesn't look normal," I said.

Hades's expression matched what I felt inside. "No, it doesn't. We need to get out of this pod." He stood to inspect the door. "There aren't enough shadows in here, so we'll have to go out the old-fashioned way." He pressed his hand against the metal and pushed. The lock didn't stand a chance and the door swung open. Violent wind instantly whipped inside and yanked at my hat, pulling it off and blowing it outside. I watched as it swirled around then dropped to the ground.

Hades positioned himself at the opening of the pod. His wings broke through the back of his suit jacket but didn't fully unfurl. There wouldn't have been enough room inside if they had. "Come behind me and wrap your arms around my waist."

"I have wings. You don't need to carry me." I urged them out just a little.

"I know, but it will be easier for you to unfold them once we are in the air."

Seeing the logic, I wrapped my arms around him from behind. Just as he took a step out, the wheel started to move knocking us both into the side of the pod. Obviously, the attendants understood the need to get the people off the ride as soon as possible. The storm was nearly here. The wind had picked up, and it was making waves on the water. I could hear people shouting on the boats, trying to get to dock before it was too late.

Hades held onto the metal spoke, trying to get balanced again. I nearly slipped down his body and fell. Lightning quick, he snatched my arm and held me up until I could unfurl my wings.

I did, which proved to be a little harder in the violent wind, but eventually I was able to let go of him and get airborne. Hades pushed away from the wheel and flew after me. I struggled to fly straight and kept getting blown sideways. I collided into Hades, and he had to put an arm around me to help me stay in the air.

As we flew down beyond the square and to the shore of the harbor, people shouted and pointed up at us. I imagined we looked like harbingers of death, both wearing black with our large black wings, to the regular people below, compounded by the turbulent storm blowing in. In my mind, we looked wicked and fierce as hell.

We landed on the boardwalk overlooking the water, as waves crashed over and soaked our feet. I could see the waves were getting higher and more powerful with each passing second. But where was the rain? Surely the black clouds should've let loose already. And where were the lightning and thunder? I expected the sky to be lit up by white bolts zigzagging across the black backdrop.

I glanced at Hades. He stared out over the water, his brow deeply furrowed. "This isn't a storm, is it?"

"No. It's something else entirely."

A booming sound arose from the water. It wasn't the crack of lightning but the whoosh of something large emerging from the depths of the sea. A wave, twenty feet high, surged toward the shore, but inside that wave I swore I saw a monstrous form, just as high, with horns and scales chopping at the water.

"What is that?" I had to speak up over the roar of the approaching wave.

"Not what, who." Hades grabbed my hand, and we shot up into the air as the water crashed down on the boardwalk, smashing the wooden planks. Horrified I saw several people swallowed up by the wave and tossed out to sea.

"We have to save them."

Hades nodded, and together we swooped toward the water. I spotted an elderly man thrashing about, his head going under with every roll of a wave. I dove for him, not caring about getting wet, grabbed him around the waist and pulled him out of the water. He screamed as I flew him over to the safety of land and dropped him there. A few people who had witnessed what I'd done ran over to the man and helped him. Next to him, Hades set down a girl, no older than six. The old man opened his arms to her, and I realized that she was his granddaughter.

Hades hovered above them. "Go! It isn't safe here. Get as far inland as you can. Tell others!"

They heeded his warning and ran for the square, shouting at other people to run and get away from the harbor.

He turned back to the turbulent water. I hovered next to him. "Is it a Titan?"

"Yes. It's Oceanus. He's been locked away in Tartarus for over a thousand years. There's no way out of that prison."

"He's obviously been released, just like before, with the earthquake in Pecunia," I said. Then something occurred to me. "Who knew we were here?"

"I told no one. I didn't even know we were coming here until we left."

"I don't believe in coincidences. Do you?" I asked.

"No, I don't."

"What are we going to do?"

"Find out why Oceanus is here."

Hades flew out over the water, I joined him. More waves crashed onto the harbor, breaking it apart and surging out into the town square. Thankfully, the crowd had dispersed, heeding Hades's warning, but a few stragglers remained, taking cell phone videos.

"We're going to need weapons," I said. "How do we fight a water entity?"

"With the darkness." He slapped his hands together and rubbed them. When he pulled them apart again, a black form forged between them. Long, narrow, eventually I could make out a shape. He'd constructed a sword from shadow and night.

He tossed it to me. I caught it surprised how substantial it was. I'd expected it to be as light as air, not heavy like steel. I sliced the air in front of me with it, testing its quality. It seemed to be as expertly crafted as a sword from Hephaistos.

"How is this going to damage a creature made of water?"

"Shadow is devoid of light. The dark is without warmth. Darkness is cold and unyielding. It will freeze the water even as it cuts through it." After making himself a sword, Hades dove toward another thirty-foot wave. But this wave moved around and flailed a giant serpent-like tail into the air.

I followed Hades into battle.

As we neared the Titan, Oceanus opened his muzzle, revealing rows of razor-sharp teeth, and roared. The closer I got the more of the creature I could see. Oceanus looked like a dragon standing upright with four curved horns protruding from his heavily scaled head. His barrel chest also looked armored with thick dark scales. The creature appeared to be impenetrable. I didn't know how our shadow swords were going to do anything but piss him off.

When Hades swooped toward him from the side, he turned and swiped a very large, very muscular arm at the God. Claws as long as my arm came close to taking Hades's head clean off. Instead, Hades swung his sword, and the blade hit the Titan's bicep. I saw the tip freeze the creature's flesh. He roared again, this time in pain.

Buoyed by what I'd seen, I flew at the beast from the opposite side, hoping Hades was distracting him enough. I drew in close and swung my sword at his head, aiming for one of the horns. My blade struck, reverberated up my arms, but my blow broke his horn in half. It cracked apart like ice.

He swung his head toward me and roared again. The blast of his breath blew me backward. I dipped down toward the water, and I spied a bit of gold around the Titan's neck. I knew what it was instantly.

I flew over to Hades, close enough for him to hear me over the rush of water and roar of the Titan. "He has a golden rope around his neck. He's being controlled."

He nodded. "Then we have to cut it off. It's the only way to stop him."

"You distract him and I'll go—,"

"No. It's too dangerous."

"He won't be expecting me, I'm smaller than you are. And honestly I'm quicker." I smirked.

He shook his head, but I could see that he knew my plan made sense. "Come at him from under his head. He won't be able to see you. He'll be glaring at me."

Before I could fly off, he snatched my hand. His gaze searched my face, as if he was trying to memorize what I looked like. I thought he was going to say something, but he let go of my hand and swooped toward Oceanus.

As Hades hovered near the Titan's face, I could see his lips moving. He was talking to him, but I couldn't hear what he was saying. The water beast was distracted, and I needed to make my move. I dove down toward the water. Right before I was swept up in the waves that the Titan made with his huge body, I arched upward. I flew so close to him that I could see the intricate patterns on the scales that surrounded his ribs. I could see the rise and fall of his chest as he breathed.

I raised my sword just as Oceanus swiped at Hades again. A wave as high the beast himself surged toward Hades. The water was going to swallow him up. There was nothing I could do about it. I had to cut the rope. It was the only way.

When I was right under his muzzle, I swung my sword at the rope around his neck. The blade hit but didn't cut the golden threads. One blow wasn't enough. I reached for the rope with my left hand as I hacked and slashed at it. The Titan shook his head trying to dislodge me, but I hung on with all I had. Positioning myself against the rigid scales just under his chin, digging my feet into his flesh, I kept swinging my sword. I was like a mad woman as I hacked over and over again. Until finally, the threads gave way.

I fell into the surging water, but at least I had the rope clutched in my hand. I'd stopped the Titan and I had the proof of Aphrodite's treachery.

CHAPTER SEVEN

MELANY

The second I hit the water I got sucked under in a tide pool caused by the erratic movements of the Titan. Flailing my arms, I kicked hard to push myself upward, but I got sucked back down again. I tried to calm my mind so I wouldn't panic. Luckily, I could hold my breath for a long time.

I kicked my legs again to propel myself away from the beast's thick powerful legs, but he moved and I smacked my head right into him. The blow obscured my vision in the murky water, and I couldn't see where I was going. I reached out my hand. My fingers brushed against hard scales, and I brought my feet up and tried to kick away from him again.

I didn't get very far before I was scooped up by a large clawed hand. I thought about fighting against it but realized when I came sputtering out of the water that Oceanus was saving me. He held me up toward Hades who hovered near the Titan's head.

"Thank you, my friend," Hades said.

"Your human is plucky." Oceanus's voice boomed all around me. It was like a foghorn, deep and air rattling.

"Yes, she is." I was about to argue that I wasn't *his* human, but Hades turned away from me and put his attention on the giant water dragon. "Do you remember how you got here, Oceanus?"

He shook his big head. "No."

"Do you know who put this rope around your neck?"

I held up the golden tie for him to see.

His dragon eyes narrowed as he studied the rope. "No, but it must've been one of you, as you are the only beings with the keys to Tartarus."

"Well, it wasn't me," Hades said.

"I know. You are not like your brothers who only care about power." Oceanus's gaze fixed on the shore and the destroyed harbor. "Did I kill anyone?"

Hades shook his head. "No. But it was lucky that we were here."

He nodded. "Yes. Lucky." His other hand went up to his head and I realized he was feeling for any damage we'd caused him.

"I'm sorry about your horn," I yelled up at him.

His dark eyes fixed on me, and I realized he could squish me into goo if he wanted. "It will grow back."

"I fear that there will be more Titans released soon. Someone is trying to start a war," Hades said.

"I cannot return to Tartarus to warn my

brethren, but I will find a place to hide and wait. If you need my assistance when the time comes, you only need to call me back."

Hades flew over to me and dropped onto the Titan's hand. "Thank you. I wish you well." He grabbed my hand and pulled me up into the air. The feathers on my wings were still damp, so I appreciated Hades's help to stay airborne.

The moment we were away, Oceanus sunk back down into the water. From up above, I could see him swimming down into the depths of the sea. When he was gone, the black clouds overhead dissipated to reveal the bright moon and a twinkling carpet of stars.

Hades flew us back to shore. The second my feet touched down, I was looking for the shadows to take us to the academy. "We need to take this to Zeus. He'll have to believe me now about Aphrodite's scheme."

"No."

I frowned. "What do you mean no? We have to tell him and the others about this."

"We will, but not now. We need to wait for the right moment, the most opportune moment." He took my arm and directed me toward a dark grouping of shadows. We stepped into the darkness, and within seconds we emerged back in the hall.

"I don't understand." I held up the thick golden rope. "We have proof."

"That could belong to anyone, Melany."

"But it's made from Aphrodite's clothes—,"

"Do you know how many ropes and belts and chains she's made for others over the past thousand years? Hundreds. She made me a rope once over four hundred years ago. It proves nothing except that Oceanus was compelled to destroy."

My shoulders sagged. I thought this was undeniable proof, but now I realized why Zeus hadn't done anything before when I showed him the rope that I found in Pecunia next to the destroyed Demos's estate. I felt like an idiot. Had I been wrong about Aphrodite and Ares all along? Had I attacked her for no reasons except for my uncontrolled fury toward her?

Hades took the rope from me. "Let me hold onto this until it's time to use it."

For a moment, I considered snatching it back from him and jumping into a shadow to go to the academy on my own. But I resisted.

"The best way to snare a fox is to lure it out into the open, then whack," he slapped his hands together, and I flinched, "pull the rope tight around its throat to snap its neck."

"I take it Aphrodite is the fox in this scenario?"

"Yes, and others."

I regarded him curiously. "I didn't realize that you were close with the Titans. I was surprised by your conversation with Oceanus."

"The Titans are not the monstrous violent beings that you've been taught. History is always written by those in power, and it's not always the actual truth."

"So, what is the truth, then?"

Instead of answering, he reached out and feathered his fingertips down my cheek, then tucked some stringy strands of my blue hair behind my ear. "You should shower and change. We need to be at the academy in a few hours."

My heart fluttered from his light touch. I had to stop myself from breaching the distance between us, grabbing him by the shirt front and kissing him. My entire body thrummed with desire.

Then he dropped his hand and walked away. He went into the library and closed the door. I went to my room and did as he suggested. My clothes were still damp, and I smelled like brine and seaweed. As I stood under the hot spray of the shower, I half-expected Hades to walk into the bathroom and join me. I wanted him to. Even now, even though I knew he was keeping things from me, I ached for him.

Since it was going to be some kind of award ceremony according to the courier who sent the message to Hades, I opted for an elegant dress, dark purple with spaghetti straps and a slit up the side. Charon helped me with my hair. Over the months, I'd learned that the scary butler was an expert stylist. He did a Dutch braid bun that I couldn't even begin to understand. I did some heavy makeup, a smoky eye and dark lip. When I looked in the mirror, I thought "Damn! I'm smoking hot!"

That was confirmed when I walked out into the hall where Hades waited for me. His eyebrows lifted, and his lips twitched upward into a long lazy grin that sent shivers down my back. He licked his lips while his gaze lingered on the leg teased by the slit in the dress, then up to the plunging V neck that clung seductively to my breasts.

"You…" He licked his lips again, and I reveled in the fact that I'd made him speechless. "You look delectable."

I couldn't stop the smile or the color in my cheeks. His choice of words sent a very vivid image of sex in my mind. "You do, too."

And he did. The man could wear the shit out of a suit. It fit in a way that was elegant but also sexy. There was no mistaking the lean powerful body under the black fabric of his pants and shirt. This time he opted for a dark blue jacket. It gleamed in the firelight when he stepped closer to me.

I lifted my head toward him, hoping he would kiss me. He stopped a foot away from me, raking his gaze over me again. My lips parted with a sigh of desire. Kiss me! I wanted to scream at him. He was teasing me. Just being near him, like this, was torture. And he knew it.

Finally, blissfully, he dipped his head down. His lips brushed against mine. It was just a soft caress, but it stole my breath, and I felt faint afterward. When he pulled back, he traced his finger over my cheek again. Then he took a step away and offered me his arm.

"Shall we? We're just the right amount of late to make a memorable appearance."

Chuckling, I took his arm, and we stepped into the shadows.

When we came out of the darkness and appeared

in the great hall, there was a collective gasp from those in attendance. A surge of arrogance filled me, and I lifted my head and met the gazes of my peers and the other Gods gaping at us.

"Are we late?" Hades's playful grin was full of spite.

Zeus greeted us with his own poisonous smile. "Of course not. We've not even started the festivities yet." His eyes went to me. "Melany, you look stunning. Your friends have been anxiously awaiting your arrival." He waved his hand toward Jasmine, Georgina, Ren, and Mia who were grouped together gaping at me. "Why don't you join them while Hades joins the professors."

Hades took my hand, kissed the back, then gave me a little bow. I knew he did it to get a reaction. And he most definitely got one. I saw many shocked faces and I heard someone in the crowd whisper the word, "Slut." I scanned the crowd, certain it was Revana who spoke, but was surprised to see it was someone I didn't know.

Hades walked away with Zeus, while I joined my friends. Or at least, I hoped they were still friends. The way Jasmine looked at me put that in question.

Georgina approached me first, grabbing my hands, as if months hadn't passed and we were still roommates trying to survive our first year at the academy. "You look incredible."

"Thank you, Gina. So, do you." And she did. The green dress she wore, short but flirty, accentuated the muscles she'd developed over the past term. Her earth powers emanated from her and her skin seemed to glow with vitality.

Jasmine's gaze wasn't as complimentary. "You look like him."

I knew the "him" she meant. Hades.

The well-aimed barb hurt, but I tried to keep it from my face.

"Thank you," I said with a sardonic arch to my eyebrow. I looked past her, letting her know I was pissed at her. "Where's Lucian? Is he out of the infirmary?"

"Blue?"

I turned toward his voice. He crossed the room toward me, a smile on his face. He looked amazing in a royal blue tunic and white pants. His blond hair was slicked back from his face. Despite his trip into death, there was a radiance that shone through his eyes.

He looked me up and down. "You look like a Goddess."

It was the perfect thing to say.

I went to him and hugged him close, inhaling his warmth. "I'm so happy to see you."

"Me too." He nuzzled his face into the side of my neck. "I didn't think I'd see you here."

I pulled back. "Why not? It's supposed to be a celebration, isn't it? You didn't think I'd be invited?"

He shook his head. "It isn't that."

His gaze drifted across the room and settled on Hades who was talking to Dionysus. He turned slightly, his eyes meeting Lucian's and he tipped his head. Something passed between them. I didn't know what it was, but I could tell Lucian was angry about it.

"What is that all about?" I demanded. "What is going on between the two of you?"

Before he could answer though, Zeus lifted his hand to quiet the soft violin music that had been playing, then he began to talk.

CHAPTER EIGHT

MELANY

"Welcome all." Zeus's voice boomed throughout the room. "Tonight, we celebrate the achievements of this academy and honor those who have brought great glory and recognition to our institution."

That brought a round of applause throughout the room.

"The fire at Victory National Park was handled quickly and efficiently by our cadets with very few casualties. Our friends in the country's government were very thankful for our assistance and assured us that this was just one step closer to an integration of our warriors into their system."

I frowned. I didn't know how Zeus could consider it a success when there had been loss of lives. Several firefighters had died from the chimera's attack. Lucian had died, technically. I couldn't keep silent.

"What about the chimera?" I said loudly, stepping away from my friends and toward the Gods who stood up on the dais at the front of the room. "It was responsible for several human casualties."

I could hear Hades sigh. He wasn't subtle about it. I also was keenly aware that Aphrodite was shooting daggers from her eyes my way.

A wave of animated murmurs surrounded me.

"The chimera's appearance was unexpected," Zeus said. "But was handled with the utmost delicacy and candor by those on the frontlines. We have you to thank, Melany, do we not? For the quick dispatchment and disposal of the creature." He smiled at me as if I was supposed to be delighted by his praise.

I took another step forward, intending to lambaste him for his complacency and to demand that an investigation be mounted to find out who released the beast into the park.

Hades also stepped forward. "The chimera's appearance was indeed a surprise, and I know I can speak for the rest of the professors that we will find out how the creature arrived in the forest and why." His gaze swept over the Gods in attendance, lingering a little longer on Aphrodite and Ares I was happy to see. "It will not go unanswered, I assure you."

Zeus nodded. "Quite right."

I was about to speak again, but Hades glared at me, telling me to stop before I put my foot into my mouth again. I did but only because Lucian moved in beside me. I didn't want to drag him down into what I was sure was going to be my downfall.

But I couldn't hold my tongue. "I expect that the families of those fallen firefighters will be fully compensated for their loss. A year's favor from all the Gods wouldn't be too much to ask."

There were gasps from my fellow cadets at the gall I had to demand such things from the Gods. I knew I was pushing my luck, but I was tired of the games they were playing. They were all culpable, even Hades. It was obvious that he was playing his own game and not letting me in on the stakes or rules.

Lucian set his hand on my arm and whispered, "What are you doing?"

Aphrodite smirked. "Your request comes with the assumption that we had something to do with the chimera."

I could hear Hades's voice in my head. "Don't you dare do it."

"The chimera is a creature of your world. It's your responsibility, isn't it?" More gasps from my peers and a few stunned faces of the demigods in attendance. Heracles looked like he wanted to hide in a cave on my behalf. "As are the Titans who you locked away in Tartarus. If one were to escape, that would be your responsibility too, wouldn't it? I mean, you're the only ones with the key."

I saw Dionysus shake his head and say, "Oh, shit."

Demeter covered her face with her hand. I could

just imagine the words she mumbled under her breath.

The other Gods all looked like they wanted to kill me, even Hephaistos. Before any of them could react though, Hades flew off the dais and scooped me up and flew us out of the room. He set me down just outside the looming doors.

"What are you trying to do?" he demanded. His eyes flashed with his inner fire.

"More than what you're doing. I'm rattling cages to see what falls out."

"An axe to your head is what is going to fall out if you're not careful." He scrubbed at his chin. "Zeus is not a patient man. He'll only put up with so much insubordination."

"Is that what happened between you two? You lipped him off one too many times?"

His gaze raked me over the coals. "You need to stop talking about things you know nothing about. You're being a stupid girl here. You need to learn when to keep your mouth shut."

His tone made me shake. I bit down on my bottom lip to keep from either screaming or crying; I wasn't sure which I wanted to do more. I hated that he talked to me like I was some child, one of his students that he needed to be chastised for doing something wrong.

I thought I was more to him than that.

I kept his gaze, refusing to give him the satisfaction of my compliance. He stared back at me, breathing hard out his nose. I fully expected to see smoke curling out of his nostrils.

Gods, I wanted to kiss him right there and then. What would he do, if I did? Grab me? Slam me up against the wall? Kiss me until I couldn't breathe? Rip off my panties and thrust himself inside me until I screamed in ecstasy?

Before I could respond to him, we were interrupted. Lucian came to my side.

"Is there a problem, here?"

Hades gaze briefly flitted over to Lucian, then he sniffed and shook his head. "Maybe you can put some sense into her head. I'm going to go back and try to save her life. Again." Without looking at me, he marched back into the great hall to talk to Zeus.

After he was gone, Lucian touched my shoulder and he noticed that I was shaking. "Are you okay, Blue? What did that asshole do to you?"

I let go of a shaky breath. "Nothing."

"I don't believe you." He cupped my face in his hand. "You can talk to me, Blue. You can tell me anything."

But I can't, Lucian. Don't you see? I was sure he wouldn't want to know how much I wanted Hades, how I was falling for him, even as I wanted Lucian, right now. He wouldn't be able to understand how I could feel so much, so intensely for them both.

"Can I have a hug?" I finally said.

"Always." He gathered me into his arms, and it was like embracing the sun. Warmth surged over me, through me. My body stopped shivering. I no longer felt like I wanted to cry. Lucian was calm and comfort for me, the exact opposite of what Hades represented. Light to his dark.

And I hated myself for it, but I wanted, no needed, both in my life.

I lifted my chin and found his mouth. Reaching up, I sunk my hands into his soft golden waves and kissed him hard. I knew I'd taken him by surprise, so he was unsure at first, but it didn't take long for him to grip me around the waist and kiss me back. Just as hard, just as eager, just as lost as I was, searching for something to make sense.

And Lucian made sense. I knew he did. But it still didn't stop me from wanting Hades to return from the great hall to wrap me up in darkness and spirit me away down to the Underworld, back to his bed.

How despicable would I be if I enticed Lucian to make love to me right here, right now, to help me purge the darkness from my mind, body, and soul?

I decided not to test the limits of my immorality and pulled back to nestle my head against his chest and find solace in the strong vibrant beat of his heart. I sighed into him, wrapping my arms even tighter around his waist.

He ran a hand over my hair. "I'm worried about you."

"I know and I appreciate it."

"I can see his influence on you."

"And I can see Zeus's on you." I raised my head to look him in the eyes. "And Ares's on Jasmine, and Demeter's on Gina. It's inevitable, isn't it?" I took a step away. "I mean we have their blood running through our veins." I rubbed a hand over my wrist. "It's what makes us special."

"You were special even before Hades came into

the picture." He reached for my hand. "He is not what makes you special at all."

I linked my fingers with his. Gods, he was sweet. I didn't deserve him. Here I was making of mess of everything, and Lucian just wanted to make every-thing right again. I knew I said Zeus had influence over him, but the truth was Lucian was superior and more just than Zeus could ever hope to be. He was the best of us all.

"Why are you so good to me? I've been such a bitch lately."

His grin was quick, and he pulled me closer. He dipped his head and brushed his lips against mine. "Because I know its not your fault." Another light dusting of his lips making my belly clench. "And because I love you."

My heart swelled at his words. I stared him in the eyes, searching for a response in them. But I knew the truth, deep down inside. "I love you, too."

He kissed me again, a bit more playfully, as his hand snuck down to caress my backside. "We could go find a dark alcove and finish what we started all those months ago. Forget the ceremony." His lips trailed down to my neck and nibbled at my skin. "This dress of yours is giving me all kinds of inter-esting thoughts."

I was tempted. It would be easy to just sneak away down the hall, thumb our noses to duty and obligation, and just give into each other. But that wasn't who Lucian was. And I supposed that wasn't how I was either. We'd both worked hard to be in the academy, to find out respective places in the pantheon of eventual demigods. Lucian had literally died fighting that fire to save the park and the town nearby from being destroyed. He deserved to be recognized for that. I wouldn't get in the way of that, no matter how good it would feel to have his body entwined with mine.

Zeus's booming voice coming out of the great hall announcing the cadets who had risked their lives battling the inferno and the chimera kind of made that decision for us.

I pulled back from him, gave him a smile, and linked my arm around his. "Let's go get our medal, or whatever they're presenting us with, then we can have our way with each other."

Lucian laughed. "Sounds like a plan."

Together, arm in arm, we walked back into the great hall to get what we deserved. A shiver rushed down my spine as I suspected my reward wasn't going to be what I expected.

CHAPTER NINE

MELANY

I was fully aware of the way Hades glared at us when Lucian and I walked into the hall together, our arms around each other. I hated that I got pleasure out of his obvious jealousy. I glanced at Lucian and saw that he was grinding his teeth as he glared in return.

We joined Jasmine, Mia, and Georgina who were standing to the right of the dais waiting for their names to be called. Ren, Marek, Quinn, and Su had already been called up and were now standing on the stage as Hera and Aphrodite did the honors of draping gold medals hanging on silk ribbons over their heads.

Jasmine shook her head as we approached. "You're unbelievable," she said to me.

"What's your problem?" Lucian had to restrain

me from getting in her face. I had sensed this confrontation was some time coming. "If you have something to say to me, say it."

For the past few months Jasmine had been looking at me differently. I could feel our friendship drifting apart. I couldn't deny I was partly responsible for that, but she'd been displaying animosity toward me ever since my sojourn to the Underworld where I'd been training with Hades and the Furies. It was almost like she was jealous, but I didn't know why. She had Mia, and I didn't think she wanted to be with Lucian.

"Jasmine Walker," Zeus called her up to the stage.

She turned away from me and walked up the steps to join the others. Hera draped a medal around her neck, and our peers in the crowd clapped and cheered. Georgina was called next. She got louder applause led by my hands, as Aphrodite draped her medal around her neck.

"Lucian Perro."

I gave his hand a squeeze, and then he went up the steps onto the stage. Hera placed the medal around his neck, and I cheered the loudest. I thought he should get all the medals as he had died fighting the chimera. There should be something more than a silly medal for that kind of bravery.

For a moment, I thought Zeus wasn't going to call me up as punishment for speaking my mind, but then he did.

"Melany Richmond."

I wasn't sure what kind of reaction to expect from my peers, but it most definitely wasn't the silence that accompanied me up the steps and onto the stage. I stood next to Lucian, who gave me a reassuring smile. Unfortunately, it was Aphrodite who was to put the medal around my neck, although I imagine she would've much rather have wrapped her hands around it instead.

With a saccharine smile, Aphrodite stepped in front of me. "Congratulations," she said with all the sincerity of a narcissistic psychopath.

I bent my head forward a little so she could slip the silk ribbon over it. As she did, she leaned in close to my ear. "Beware the snakes all around you. Their venom just might be the death of you some day." When she finished, she stepped back and gently clapped her hands.

There was a smattering of applause in the room. The Gods on the stage were more enthusiastic. It was obvious my peers didn't feel all that warm toward me anymore.

"Congratulations to all our heroes," Zeus said. "You are the leaders of this academy, and I look forward to seeing where you will lead us in the future."

More applause, some cheers. I spied Revana in the crowd and her deep scowl nearly made me burst out laughing. Now, she was probably regretting not volunteering to fight the fire in Victory Park. I wanted to shout out to her, "Suck it up, buttercup!" But I refrained.

"Now we celebrate!" Zeus clapped his hands together, and the main lights dimmed while a variety of colored lights flared to life. Loud dance music blasted from the speakers strategically placed around the hall. It sounded like Dionysus was in fine form again.

Hephaistos's little serving robots zoomed into the room, carrying trays of drinks and food to everyone's delight. My stomach rumbled. I hadn't eaten since the ganses from the carnival in Nice. Thinking about that, I looked for Hades on the stage. I didn't think it was right that we hadn't told anyone about the Titan's attack. Regardless of who released Oceanus, I still thought it was prudent that we inform Zeus of what happened so the academy could prepare for another attack. Because I had no doubt, that an even bigger threat was imminent.

I caught his gaze; he was across the dais talking to Artemis. She didn't look very happy with what he was saying. I started toward him when Lucian hooked an arm around my waist and spun me around.

"Dance with me," he whispered into my ear.

I considered rejecting his request, but something about the way Hades looked at me, pissed me off, so I draped my arms around Lucian's neck and kissed him. "Let's dance."

We stepped down from the stage and joined the others who had already made space for dancing in front of Dionysus's DJ setup. Smoke was drifting across the floor and flashing strobe lights pierced the dark. It reminded me of the first night in the academy, and that first dance with Lucian when I hadn't been sure about him.

I was sure about him now.

I molded my body to his, and we moved as one to

the rhythmic beat of the music. Others danced around us, but I was oblivious to them. All I could see, all I wanted to be with was Lucian. When the music slowed a little, I draped my arms over his shoulders and pressed in close to him. One of his hands gripped my waist, the other pressed against my lower back. We swayed like that, in sync, our eyes locked on each other for what seemed like an hour. I was perfectly happy to stay just like that until my stomach got the better of me and I desperately needed some food.

"I need to eat," I said to Lucian. "I'll be right back."

He kissed me on the cheek then I set off to find a plate and pile it full of food. Unfortunately, I ran into Revana and her new minions while doing so.

She looked me up and down and sneered. "Now I guess we know why you're being treated so special."

Peyton and Klara both snickered with her.

"How does it feel to be Hades's whore?"

I flinched surprised by the true malice in her voice. I clenched my hand into a fist fully intending to use it on her when both Peyton and Klara's eyes widened and they both audibly swallowed.

"Here, I brought you something to eat. You looked ravenous." Hades slid in next to me and handed me a plate with a couple of finger sandwiches and pastries on it. His gaze swept over Revana and the others, as if they were inconsequential.

"Are you going to be teaching at the academy now?" Klara asked him eagerly. I saw the dreamy look in her eyes and wanted to scratch it out.

"Gods no." He shooed them way with his hand. "Go away. You're boring me."

I had to bite my tongue to stop from laughing, as the three of them scurried away. When they were gone, I chuckled. "That was priceless. Did you see their faces?"

"What are you doing?"

I plucked one of the sandwiches from the plate. "Eating. I'm starving."

"You shouldn't be running around here on your own."

I frowned. "Why not? This is a safe place."

He didn't answer but continued to glower at me.

"We should tell Zeus about the Titan attack," I said after eating both sandwiches.

"I will when it's the right time."

"When will that be?"

He rolled his eyes. "You ask too many questions, it's exhausting."

"Maybe I'll just go back and dance with Lucian."

"Yes, maybe you should."

My eyes narrowed at him. "Why are you acting like this?"

"Like what?"

"Like you don't give a shit about our relationship."

"Relationship?" His eyebrows shot up and he smirked. "We don't have a relationship, Melany. We've had some fun, but that's about as far as that goes. I'm your teacher and you're my student."

Stunned, I flinched back as if he'd actually slapped me across the face. Tears pricked my eyes, but I refused to let them fall in front of him. He didn't deserve them. "I can't believe you said that to me."

"I don't know why."

"You're an asshole."

He shrugged. "Yes, I've been told. You should really return to Lucian. I'm sure he's worried about where you've run off to." He looked away from me and surveyed the crowd.

I shoved the plate he gave me back at him, not caring that the cream-puff pastry smooshed onto his shirt and pants. I stormed away, found Lucian at a table near the dance floor sitting with Georgina, Ren, Diego, and Rosie. When he saw me, his eyes lit up and I wanted to cry.

Instead I grabbed him by the shirt front and smashed my lips to his. I wrapped my hand in his hair and deepened the kiss until we were both breathless. When I pulled back, I was acutely aware of several sets of eyes on us. I looked for one particular set, hoping he had seen. I found him standing with Demeter and Heracles staring. For someone who didn't give a shit, he sure seemed to be angry.

I wanted to scream.

Lucian ran his hand over my arm. "Are you all right?"

I looked at him, a forced smile on my face. "I'm fine. Where's Jasmine? I think the two of us need to have a talk." My anger was swirling, and I needed it go somewhere. Not that I wanted to lash out at Jasmine, but it was obvious we needed to hash some things out. I didn't want her to hate me.

"Last I saw her she was talking to Dionysus about music." Lucian gestured with his head. "Here she comes."

I turned to see Jasmine walking toward us, carrying two drinks. When she neared, she smiled, and I felt relief surge through me. "Hey, I'm sorry about earlier. It's none of my business what's going on between you and Hades—"

"No, don't apologize. There's nothing going on, I assure you."

She nodded then offered me a glass. "A peace offering."

I glanced inside the cup, expecting soda or juice, but I was pretty sure it was wine.

She leaned in. "It's got some kick. I thought we could party a little together. We've earned it."

"We certainly have."

We tapped our glasses then I took a big swallow. It was indeed wine and definitely had a kick. I felt it the second it hit my stomach. A heat swelled inside like a tsunami. It reminded me a bit of the whiskey Hades had given me in his library. Except the whiskey hadn't burned like this did.

I swallowed, trying to subdue the burning sensation but it just seemed to be growing. My mouth now was on fire.

Lucian frowned as he looked at me. "Blue?"

I pointed to my throat. "I need some water." I could barely get the words out as my throat seemed to be constricting.

"What did you give her?" Lucian demanded of Jasmine.

"Just some wine." She was now looking at me with concern as well.

Georgina came to my side with a glass of water. She took the wine away and handed me the water. I swallowed it down. It did nothing for the blistering pain in my body. I shook my head. "Something's wrong."

I couldn't stand anymore. I sagged in Lucian's arms and he carefully laid me down on the floor. By now, a bit of a crowd had gathered, murmuring to each other.

"What's wrong with her?"

"Is she sick?"

"She doesn't look good at all."

Searing pain rippled through me and my body convulsed. I curled into a protective ball to relieve the pain, but it didn't work. The pain was all through me. It felt like my insides were melting.

"Help!" Lucian called. "Someone get Chiron!"

There was a commotion around me, then the crowd parted, and Zeus and Chiron pushed through. Chiron crouched next to me. He put his hands on my head and chest. His cool touch was a relief to the burning on my skin. He then pried open my mouth and looked inside. He winced.

"She's been poisoned."

Lucian glared at Jasmine. "What did you give her?"

"Just some wine. I swear it."

Georgina held out the glass toward Chiron. "This is what she drank from?"

Zeus snatched it from her and whirled on

Jasmine, who was starting to cry. "Where did you get the wine from?"

"Dionysus," she stammered.

Everything around me started to fade. I couldn't make out distinctive voices or faces. It all became just one loud buzzing in my ears. Pain was the only thing I knew. It ate at my body and my mind. It consumed me entirely. And I realized this was what it was like to die.

CHAPTER TEN

MELANY

I woke in a field of yellow flowers with the sun beating down on me. I sat up, shielding my face from the glare of sunlight. Blinking spots from my eyes, I wondered how long it had been since I felt the warm sun on my skin. Months? A year? It felt longer than either of those.

I stood and stretched out my arms. I heard the satisfying pop of my bones aligning. I glanced down at where I was laying and wondered how long I'd been there. By the way my muscles cramped and my bones ached, it had been a long time. Longer than a night's sleep, that was for sure.

After bending and cracking my body, I surveyed my surroundings. The field of yellow stretched out in all four directions as far as I could see. I spun around in a circle, trying to get my bearings. I couldn't be sure which way was north or south or east or west. I looked up at the sun starting to arc downward, and figured I was facing west. I'd walk that way for a lack of a better plan.

As I walked, I realized I wasn't wearing any shoes. I looked down at my bare feet, wriggling my toes in the dirt. I was sure I'd recently had high heels on. Pretty fancy shoes. I also noticed I was wearing a plain white sheath dress with short sleeves. In my mind, I pictured a purple dress with a long slit along one leg. But why would I have been wearing that kind of dress? It seemed like something way too sophisticated for someone like me.

I kept walking, running my fingertips over the petals of the wildflowers. Soon, I came to a slight rise. I crested it, and at the top I stared out over a stunning valley with more flowers of every color imaginable and a narrow stream that meandered like a snake through them. Beyond that were several high rock formations, greenery wrapping around the stone like a blanket, with waterfalls cascading down the sides. On top of the middle structure was a building that looked very much like one of the Gods' temples back home.

Home? For a minute, I wondered where home was. I couldn't quite picture it. I just had flashes of darkness and fire that seemed to contradict each other but somehow felt right together.

I continued to walk through the field of flowers. When I came to the stream, I imagined a pathway through the water, then it appeared. A dirt path cut right through the stream. It seemed impossible, but I stepped onto it just the same.

After I crossed the water, I was magically at the bottom of the highest rock formation. That was how things worked in dreams. And this most definitely had to be a dream. It had that floating sensation like one. I looked up at the rock wondering how I was going to get to the top. I thought that I could use my wings.

I looked over my shoulder at my back wondering where my wings were. I was sure that I possessed a pair. Then I thought, *Why I would have wings.* That didn't make any sense. While I was debating the merits of having wings, a path erupted from the rock, winding around and around all the way to the top.

I stepped up onto the path, thinking it was going to take me a long time to reach the top, then I watched as my foot stepped onto a white cobblestone platform. I looked up to see I'd reached the top of the rock and the white stone temple loomed ahead of me.

A shudder of fear rushed through me as I mounted the steps to the temple. I didn't know why I was afraid. This didn't seem like a place to fear. It was welcoming, a place to reflect and pray. Once I mounted all the steps, I passed between two massive stone pillars and entered the building.

Inside there were plants growing out of large painted pots that were surrounding a grand stone fountain of a siren sitting on a bed of rocks. Water gushed out of her mouth and up into the air. At first, I thought the temple was empty, but then I spotted a woman, dressed in a gauzy white toga, lounging on a sofa in the corner. As I approached her, I saw she was beautiful with long black hair and vivid blue eyes. Her full lips were painted blood red, and her eyes were coaled in gold.

She smiled when she spotted me, and there was something about her that seemed familiar to me. I'd seen her before, but I couldn't quite place where or when. Maybe I'd dreamed about her before.

"Hello," she said, her voice like a musical interlude.

"Hello."

She lifted a slim hand toward me. I took it, and she gently pulled me down to sit next to her on the sofa. "I'm happy to see you, but I don't think you're supposed to be here."

"Where is here?"

"Elysium."

The sound of the word made me giggle. "I'm dead?"

"No, you're not dead."

"I must be lost then."

"Yes, you are very lost, Melany."

I frowned. "You know my name."

"Yes, I know everything about you." She grabbed both my hands in hers and smiled at me. "I've been watching over you." I liked her smile, it made me feel comforted.

"What is your name?"

"Persephone."

I smiled and repeated her name, enjoying the way it felt on my lips.

She placed a hand on my cheek. "You must listen to me, child."

My head felt floaty and drugged. "Okay," I whispered to her.

"You are the key, which is why I sent you the shadowbox during the Demos girl's birthday, since your original one was intercepted. You will be the one to end the battle. You have control of all five elements, but they must be freely given to you."

I didn't know what she was talking about, but I liked the sound of her voice. It was so melodic and silvery. I reached up and touched her hair. "You're so pretty."

"Melany, you need to hear what I'm telling you. You need to lead them. Without you, they don't stand a chance of stopping the war."

Before I could respond, two other people entered the temple from another doorway. An older man and woman. When they spotted us, they ran over, their voices and faces animated with excitement. The woman hugged me tight.

"Oh, my darling. My sweet girl."

Confused, I pulled away from her, searching her face for something. Then I saw it. Her eyes were the same as mine. The shape of her face, the cadence of her voice. It came back to me in a distressing rush, and I cried out.

"Mom?"

Tears streamed down her face, as she nodded. "Yes, my darling. I'm your mother."

I looked up at the man, hovering right behind her. He too had tears. "Dad?"

He crouched and wrapped his arms around me. "Oh Melany. I can't believe you're here."

Persephone stood. "She's not supposed to be here. It's not her time. And you need to let her go, she has work to do."

Then like a sledgehammer to my mind, my memories surged back into my head.

My parents' death.

Sophie adopting me.

The shadowbox.

The directions to the academy.

Meeting Lucian.

The trials.

Hades.

Dying…

Gasping, I jolted to my feet, nearly knocking my dad onto his butt. He got up with me, as did my mom. They both reached out to grab one of my hands.

I started to sob. My whole body shook with them. "I miss you so much."

My dad kissed my hand. "We miss you, my darling. You have no idea how much. We never wanted to leave you. Ever."

"Our car accident wasn't an accident." My mom squeezed my hand. "They knew about you. They knew how powerful you'd become."

"Who's they? What are you talking about?"

Persephone pulled me away from my parents. "It's time for you to go back. You've been away from your body too long already."

I grasped at my parents' hands. "No, I want to stay here."

As Persephone led me out of the temple, my

parents remained where they were. They clutched each other, both crying.

"I don't know what's going on. Who would want to kill you?"

"Look into the past, Melany," my mom said. "Look into the history of the academy. You'll find us there."

Outside the temple, Persephone continued to lead me away, toward the cliff's edge. I tried to struggle against her, to go back to the temple, back to my parents, but she was strong, and something else, something unseen, compelled me to let her pull me away.

Persephone stopped at the edge of the cliff, still holding onto my arm. "It's time for you to go back."

"I don't understand what's going on. I know my parents are dead. Am I? Are you?"

She cupped my face again with her hand. "Dead is never really dead. We will see each other again."

Then she backed me up another step and pushed me off the cliff.

"Tell Hades I never left him. I was taken against my will. Tell him Zeus…"

But I didn't hear the rest of what she said as I fell from the mountain.

***

LUCIAN

Melany's whole body convulsed on the floor. Foam bubbled out between her lips. I didn't know what to do. I held her in my arms, feeling completely useless.

"Help her!" I shouted at Chiron.

He shook his head. "I can't. She's too far gone. The poison has done too much damage."

So many faces stared down at us. Jasmine had collapsed on the ground beside us, crying uncontrollably. I could hear Georgina's quiet sobs behind me. And Ren's and the others. I looked up to see Revana staring down at me, her face unreadable.

I saw some of the Gods crowd around. Demeter looked upset. Heracles, too. The looks on the others' faces were hard to make out. Unconcerned. Upset. Annoyed. I couldn't tell. Then there was Hades. He stood apart from everyone else.

Our gazes met, and something passed between us. I could hear his voice in my head.

I'm a part of you, Lucian. Remember. My power is in you.

Frowning, I looked down at Melany as she convulsed once more then slumped against me. I swallowed down my tears, my sorrow. As I did, I felt a heat along my chest. It was reminder of what Hades had done to me.

He left a scar on my chest. A scar in the shape of his hand.

Setting Melany down flat onto the ground, I lifted my hand over her, then placed it down upon her chest. I closed my eyes and poured every ounce of power I had in me into her. I poured all my thoughts, all my love, everything that made me, into her body.

I concentrated on her healing. I pictured each organ, each piece of her, and enveloped it with a power to counteract the poison. Purification to counter the decay. I poured all my positive energy into every cell of her being.

At first, I didn't think it was making a difference, but then I felt her heartbeat. It was faint at first, then strengthened with each beat. I opened my eyes to watch her face for some sign that she was healing. Her eyelids fluttered, then she coughed. I rolled her over onto her side, and she coughed up some liquid. It was the wine she drank.

There was a collective gasp throughout the room as she opened her eyes.

Relief surged through me, and I wiped the tears from my face. I rubbed a hand over her back as she hacked up more of the poison.

"Get it out, Blue. That's good."

Chiron crouched next to us. His gaze was wild as he took in Melany and me. "What did you do?"

I shook my head. "I'm not quite sure." My guts started to cramp up. A terrible taste erupted into my mouth. I leaned over and retched. Red wine, just like what Melany had drunk, spewed from my mouth.

"You drew the poison out of her body."

I looked up to see Hades leaning over Melany. He reached for her, and his fingers brushed against her cheek.

I jumped to my feet and got right in his face. "I wouldn't have had to save her if you'd done what I told you to do. To keep her away from the ceremony."

There was a murmur in the crowd around us. I could sense everyone staring, wondering what we were talking about.

Melany coughed some more, but she was awake and lucid now, looking at me and Hades. She frowned, and with Chiron's help she got to her feet.

"What's Lucian talking about?"

Hades didn't answer. "Now that you're feeling better, we should return to the hall."

Melany turned to me. "What's going on?"

"I told Hades that there was going to be an attempt on your life tonight. I told him not to bring you here. To keep you safely away."

Melany's eyes narrowed as she regarded Hades. "Is this true?"

"I knew Lucian would save you if something were to happen. That's why I told you to stay by his side. As usual, you didn't listen." He waved a hand toward me. "But look he saved you. With my power, mind you."

She blinked at him and made a face. "Are you actually blaming me right now?"

"Of course, I'm not blaming you. You're being overly dramatic." He reached for her arm. "We can discuss it later."

She pulled away from his grasp. "No. I'm not going back with you. I'm done being your little pet project." She wrapped her hand around the amulet around her neck and tugged. The chain broke, and she tossed at him. It hit his shoe before landing on the floor.

"Oh burn, dude," someone said from the crowd hovering around. A couple other people snickered.

Hades bent to pick up the amulet. He tucked it into his jacket pocket. "Now that the show is over, I bid everyone adieu." He waved a hand in front of him, and tendrils of darkness seemed to appear from thin air. Before he disappeared, he looked at Melany. "You are part of the darkness, Melany. You'll never be done with that. You'll never be done with me." Then he was gone.

As I cradled Melany into my side, more commotion erupted around us. Uniformed guards pushed through the crowd and grabbed a hold of Jasmine. She struggled against them, but they were strong.

"What are you doing?" she shouted.

Zeus stepped forward. "I'm sorry, but we need to know who tried to kill Melany."

Melany tried to rush toward Zeus, but she was still weak. "Jasmine wouldn't try to kill me. We're friends."

Beyond the crowd, I saw more guards escorting Dionysus out of the hall. Melany must've seen it as well because she shook her head. "No way. I won't believe it."

"One way or another, we will find out the truth." Zeus turned and walked out of the room. The other Gods following in his wake.

I saw Aphrodite and Ares whispering to each other as they walked away. And I was sure Aphrodite was smiling.

CHAPTER ELEVEN

MELANY

After Jasmine and Dionysus were taken away, naturally the party ended. Zeus instructed everyone to return to their respective clan hall. I couldn't return to mine. I refused to.

"You can stay with me," Georgina said as if reading my mind. "Demeter won't mind one bit."

I nodded my thanks.

Lucian rubbed a hand over my back again. "You should let Chiron check you out to make sure you're okay."

The aforementioned healer nodded in agreement. "I concur. Although I'm getting tired of the two of you always being in my infirmary."

"Hey, if we weren't dying all the time, you'd be bored." I gave him a small smile to ease the tension in the room, although I didn't feel like smiling. I was exhausted. My trip to Elysium tired me out. And I wanted answers.

As Lucian, Georgina, and I walked together across the academy to meet Chiron in the infirmary, I started asking questions.

"How did you know someone was going to try and kill me?"

Lucian grimaced. "When I was recovering in the infirmary, I heard someone talking about it."

"Who?"

He shrugged. "I couldn't be sure. I was in a place between awake and asleep and couldn't tell who was in the room or who was speaking. I just heard the words spoken. When I finally woke up, there were quite a few people in the room."

"Tell me who."

"Zeus, Chiron, Ares, Aphrodite, Demeter, Dionysus, and Heracles."

"It has to be Aphrodite and Ares. The others would never conspire against me." Wincing, I rubbed my forehead. I was starting to get a headache. A bad one. "They would have no reason."

"You need to sleep," Georgina said.

"I need to get Jasmine out of wherever they took her. It's not right. She was obviously set up to take the fall."

"We will." Lucian put his arm around me. "You don't have to do all of this alone."

After Chiron did a thorough examination and I refused his offer of convalescing in the infirmary, I marched out of there hell bent on finding out where Jasmine was. But when I stormed down the hallway, I collapsed. My legs didn't work all that well. My entire body was trying to heal the damage the poison had inflicted on me.

Lucian picked me up. "You're going to go with Gina and get some sleep."

"But—"

"I will do some snooping around and find out where Jasmine is and what is going to happen to her."

I nodded when I what I really wanted to do was to slide into one of the shadows and find Zeus to demand that he release Jasmine. But I could hardly move. Dying was catching up to me. Georgina took over the holding me up duties and led me to her hall, while Lucian set off to find out about Jasmine.

We walked to the far east corner of the academy. The doors to Demeter's Hall were tall like all the other halls, but they were made of white wood instead of stone or metal with intricate patterns carved into them. I had sense if I touched them, they would pulse with the power of nature. When we neared, they opened, and Georgina helped me to hobble inside.

I was immediately struck by the beauty of the hall and the floral scent that perfumed the air. Flowers of every color sprouted from small pots, big pots, long planters, and some even seemed to be growing right out of the floor. Other flowers and vines hung down from upside down planters sweeping along the ceiling. A waterfall cascaded down one wall, filling a lagoon populated with more plants, fish, and frogs. The domed ceiling seemed to emanate sunlight. I raised my face to it and smiled; it reminded me of my dream.

I must've gasped, because Georgina chuckled. "It's amazing, isn't it?"

"It is. I think it's my favorite hall in the academy."

Georgina squeezed me around the waist. "I'm so happy you're here. I know it's under crappy circumstances, but I'm pleased just the same."

"Me too."

And it was nice to have a moment's reprieve just to relax with my friend.

She led me to her room, which was a small alcove just past the waterfall. "You take the bed. I'll sleep on the floor."

"I can't put you out like that, Gina."

She grabbed another blanket and put it on the floor. "You aren't. Besides that, out of the two of us, you died. So, you kind of win on who deserves the bed more." She opened one of her dresser drawers and took out a pair of sweatpants and a T-shirt and handed them to me. "Thought maybe you'd want to change. You can't possibly sleep in that gorgeous dress."

I hugged her close. "I've missed you."

"Me too."

After I changed, the pants were a bit short and the T-shirt a bit loose, but I was thankful for them. I sat on the bed and regarded my friend. She'd really blossomed in the past six months. She wasn't the timid girl I'd tripped over on the dorm room floor. "You look happy here."

She sat cross-legged on the blanket. "I am.

Demeter has been an incredible mentor. She's taught me so much."

"That's awesome." I brought my knees up to my chest and hugged my legs.

For a moment, it felt like we were back in our dorm room, and it was the first week of being at the academy. We were both so unsure and scared of what we'd been drawn into. Now, we were on the cusp of fulfilling our destinies as soldiers in the Gods Army. Except it wasn't as simple as that. And I started to question exactly what we'd been conscripted to fight for.

I didn't think the Gods were all on the same page. There were conflicting goals. It felt like everyone had an agenda.

"I'm worried about Jasmine," I said.

"Me too. You don't think she had anything to do with poisoning you?"

"Gods no. She may have been angry at me, but I know she loves me, as I love her. Like I love you. You're my best friends." I could feel tears welling in the corner of my eyes. It was strange how many emotions I had bubbling up to the surface since being away from Hades's Hall. I hadn't realized how much that place had influenced me, how much it and Hades had changed me.

"She wasn't angry with you, just worried. You know how she gets."

I nodded. "I know."

Georgina reached under her bed and pulled out a big bag of chips. I laughed as she ripped them open, ate some, then handed it to me. "We can't have a girls' night without snacks."

I took some chips and ate them. It had been a long time since I'd just hung out with anyone. Maybe back home. Despite the animosity between Callie and me over the years, we did have a few nights of just sitting around, eating junk food and watching a movie. Callie would paint her toenails, and on a rare night she would paint mine for me.

It had been a long time since I thought about her and about Pecunia. I pushed most of it down, so I wouldn't have to think about losing Sophie that night in the earthquake.

"I'm glad to see you and Lucian together," Georgina said between chip crunches.

I smiled. "I've missed him, too."

She looked at me for a long moment. "Are you in love with him?"

"Yeah probably." I chuckled.

"No, I meant Hades."

I sobered a little, but said wistfully, "Yeah probably."

"You're different around him."

"I'm aware." I laid on the bed. "It's just he makes me feel things that I don't feel with anyone else."

"Like what?"

"Strong. Fierce. Powerful. Like I could pick a fight with the world and win."

"Lucian doesn't make you feel those things."

I rolled onto my side and looked at her. "No, but he makes me feel strong in other ways. Like I'm important. Does that make sense?"

She laid on her side as well, propped up on her elbow. "I don't know. It's not like I understand guys at all."

I narrowed my eyes. "I have a feeling there's a story in there you're not telling me."

She shook her head, but I caught the shy smile. "Ha! Not a story at all. A paragraph maybe."

"Uh-huh, what's his name?"

"Everett."

I made a face thinking. "Isn't he that really stalky guy with the longish brown hair. He wears it in a ponytail."

She nodded shyly.

"Oh, he's cute. Well done, Gina."

She shook her head. "He's not my boyfriend or anything. We've just, had a few…moments."

I laughed. "Moments. Uh-huh. Like kissing moments?"

She tossed her pillow at me. "Shut up."

I tossed it back, and we started talking about other things. By the time we both rolled over to sleep, I was feeling lighter. Georgina had taken the weight off my shoulders. I knew it was temporary, but I appreciated the reprieve her friendship had given me.

An hour later, I heard Georgina's soft snores. Although my body was beyond exhausted, I couldn't sleep. I had too much on my mind. I sat up and decided a short walk through the hall might spend the rest of this nervous energy.

Everyone must've also been asleep, as I was alone in the hall. I walked through the meandering paths around the plants and lagoons. I found a door that led to an outdoor garden and decided some air would probably do me some good.

The moment I went outside, the skunky scent of weed hit me in the face. I walked around the corner to find Demeter sitting cross-legged on the grass smoking. She coughed on her next hit when she spotted me.

"Melany. You startled me."

"I'm sorry, I'll just go."

She lifted her hand toward me. "No, don't. Come and sit with me." I did and she offered me a hit. "I know I shouldn't offer it to the students, but you know what, you're an adult. You're perfectly capable of making decisions for yourself."

I shook my head. "No thanks."

Demeter took another hit, then snuffed it out. "Fun night, huh?"

I snorted. "Yup, can't remember a better ceremony."

"Dionysus didn't poison you."

"I know. I think it's ridiculous that he was taken or arrested, or whatever happened."

She leaned back onto her elbows on the grass. "Makes sense though, as he's the poison master and the wine maker."

"Lucian told me he overheard someone planning to kill me."

She frowned. "When? Who?"

"When he was recovering in the infirmary. He didn't know who it was."

She nodded. "Ah. So there is a small list of suspects. I'd be on that list."

"I don't think you want to kill me."

"No?" She smiled. "And why not?"

"You're way too chill."

She guffawed, then choked on her laughter. "That's good. I like that." She sobered, then regarded me. "So, who do you think it was?"

"Aphrodite for sure. I suspect she is planning something with Ares. Twice now I've heard them conspiring, and twice now I've found golden rope near sites of disasters."

She frowned. "I know about the earthquake, but—"

Hades would kill me if he knew I was about to tell her what happened to us, but I knew I could trust Demeter. There was something about her that made me feel secure, something familiar. "Hades and I encountered Oceanus in Nice the other night."

She sat up. "What happened?"

"He started to flood the city. We attacked him, and I saw there was a golden cord around his neck. When I cut it off, he came to his senses. He wasn't sure how he got there or who put the rope around his throat."

"Have you told Zeus?"

I shook my head. "Hades didn't want to. In fact, he'd probably be pissed that I told you. But I'm tired of being told what to do. He hasn't been completely truthful with me, either."

Demeter gave me a side-eyed glance. "None of the Gods are completely truthful."

"Not even you?"

She rubbed at her face. "Nope, not even me. We

have thousands of years of practice of twisting the truth. It becomes as natural as breathing."

I studied her profile. "I met Persephone."

She turned her head then to look at me. "How?"

"When I died. She met me in Elysium."

She nodded. "That makes sense."

"Why? Who is she? What does she have to do with me? With Hades? Just tell me one truth. I'm tired of everyone lying."

"Here's your one truth Melany Richmond. You are a direct descendant of Persephone. You have her blood in your veins. And you have my blood in your veins."

I gaped at her as a heavy feeling filled my stomach.

"Persephone is my daughter."

I sprang to my feet, too anxious to sit still. "But, if that's true, why don't I have powerful earth abilities? Why am I not a part of your clan?"

She also stood, as I paced around her. "You do have powerful earth abilities and water and fire and electric. But it's your affinity to the darkness that holds you sway. It's what seduced Persephone and took her from me."

"You mean Hades."

"Yes, but he and the darkness are one in the same." She reached for me. "And I know he's seduced you, too. It reads all over you."

I pulled away from her touch. I didn't want it right now. "I think you're wrong about Hades taking Persephone. I think she went willingly." I searched my own mind, my heart, my soul, and I knew that I had gone willingly. "She told me to tell Hades that she didn't leave him. That she was taken away from him against her will. She didn't have time to say, but I'm sure Zeus had something to do with it."

Demeter shook her head, as if she didn't want to hear the truth. I supposed after thousands of years of lies and mistruths, that honesty was like a slap in the face.

"She told me other things as well. About a war, that I would be the one to end it."

The Goddess grabbed my hands, forcing me to look her in the eye. "There is so much you need to know, and I don't know how to tell you, or what to tell you. If Persephone has indeed prophesized this, then you must know the truth."

"Then tell me."

"Go into the maze. There you will find a portal that will lead you to the Hall of Knowledge and everything you will ever need—"

"Am I interrupting?"

I swung around to see Aphrodite walking across the garden toward us.

Demeter dropped my hands and stepped away from me. "Melany and I were just having a little girl time."

"I'm sorry I'm late for our meeting, Demeter. I had a few things to take care of, as I'm sure you know." Her smile was full of maliciousness, and I wanted to scratch it off her.

I glanced at Demeter, but she gave nothing away. Could I even trust her? Now, I didn't know.

Aphrodite looked me over. "You look pretty lively for someone who died."

I took a step toward her. "I'm surprised you care."

"Oh, I don't."

"Go back to the dorm, Melany," Demeter warned. "Get some sleep. You've had a long eventful day."

I considered mounting an attack on Aphrodite, but I was still exhausted, my body still not fully healed. It would be foolish to do so, as it would just give her an excuse to kill me in self defense. No, I had to gather my strength, and my will, as I knew that one day soon, we would be on opposite sides of a battle, facing each other, and I'd need everything I had to defeat her.

CHAPTER TWELVE

MELANY

J managed to get a few hours of sleep when I returned to Georgina's room. She was still asleep when I tiptoed back in thankfully, so I didn't have to explain where I'd been or what happened. Everything was still swirling around in my head when I woke up. I still wasn't sure how to sort out my emotions about what I'd learned.

I wanted to trust Demeter, everything inside told me I could, but her meeting with Aphrodite gave me pause. Especially since Aphrodite seemed smug about it. Although she always appeared smug, so maybe it was just my paranoia getting the better of me.

My stomach rumbled loudly, so I was happy to accompany Georgina to the dining hall. I still wore the clothes she gave me; I didn't think my dress would be appropriate early morning breakfast wear. There was a lot of mumbling and whispering when I entered the room. I ignored it and got in line to get some eggs, bacon, and toast. Some of my peers visibly flinched as I neared. Did they think I was cursed or something? Or I had some disease that could be transmitted?

As I carried my tray to the table where Ren, Mia, Rosie, and Marek sat, I heard some of the whispers buzzing around.

"I can't believe she'd blame Jasmine."

"Jasmine wouldn't hurt anyone."

"I heard they were fighting over Lucian."

"I heard it was over Hades."

"She's such a slut. Did you see the dress she wore?"

"She totally had sex with Hades."

"Yeah, but who wouldn't? He's hot."

"Poor Lucian. He so doesn't deserve her bullshit."

"I wish Lucian hadn't saved her."

I sat at the table, the urge to cry and the urge to punch someone in the face battling for supremacy in my head. No one at the table said much to me except for a brief greeting, which also hurt. I started to eat, but I could still hear the whispers. They were getting louder and bolder and painful.

I set down my fork, stood, stepped up onto the seat, then onto the table. I turned to address the room. "I didn't arrest Jasmine. I know she wouldn't hurt me. No, we weren't fighting over Lucian or Hades. Jasmine has a very nice girlfriend named Mia. I'm sorry if my dress made you uncomfortable, but I looked hella good in it. It's none of your Gods damn business if I had sex with Hades! I'm an adult I can do what I want. And, bitches, I am alive and well. So, get used to it!"

Every face turned my way looked surprised. Including Lucian's, who I hadn't noticed had come into the room. I'd wished he hadn't heard any of that.

Georgina stood and clapped. "Well said."

I got down from the table just as Lucian came over. "What was that all about?"

"Some things I had to get off my chest."

He didn't look happy. I imagined hearing about the possibility of me having sex with Hades bright and early in the morning wasn't the best wake-up call. I'm sorry it had come out at all, as I didn't want to hurt him.

"Do you still want to see Jasmine?"

"Yes, of course I do."

"Then we need to go now."

Georgina hugged me. "I'll see you later. You can crash with me again if you need to."

"Thanks."

I followed Lucian out of the dining hall to the main foyer, around the corner and down the spiraling stone steps.

"We're going to the forge?"

"Hephaistos is going to help us."

"How?"

"He's the one who built the cells. He devised a back way inside."

We went into the forge and found Hephaistos shaping a piece of metal into what I was sure was a new sword. I noticed he had several new swords in various stages of creation. He set the metal into the cooling bucket, then pushed up his face protector to look at us.

"Thank you for helping us," I said.

"I'm doing it for the academy and the cadets. I don't like what's being going on behind closed doors." He gave me a death glare as if I was the one causing the problems. Then he mumbled under his breath. "I should never have gotten involved."

I frowned. "What do you mean? How are you involved with this, with me?"

"Stop pestering me. There's been no peace since you arrived."

"Hey, that's not my fault. I'm not the one trying to kill me."

"I know, girl. Don't get all riled up. I've just prided myself on staying out of the bullshit politics."

I so wanted to ask him about the bullshit politics he was trying to stay out of, but I knew he wouldn't discuss it. Hephaistos was the strong, silent, grumpy type. Emphasis on grumpy.

He set his tools down and motioned for us to follow him. He led us across the bridge, down a set of stairs, over another bridge that crested the river of molten metal, and to a stone wall in a darkened corner. Mind you, all the corners here were dark.

Hephaistos ran his hand along the wall, then one of the stones moved, and he pulled it out, handed it to Lucian then stuck his hand into the hole, and the stone slid away to reveal a dark passage.

"At the end of the passage, take a right, you'll come to a locked door. Use fire to open it."

We stepped into the tunnel.

"Oh, you'll have to find another way out. You can't come back this way. No one can know I helped you."

I met his gaze. "You know one day soon you're going to have to take a stand. A war is coming, Hephaistos. You can't hide in your forge forever."

Without a word, he slid the wall shut, plunging us into complete darkness.

A few seconds later, we both formed fire balls in our hands so we could see.

"You have a funny way of thanking people for their help," Lucian said.

I frowned at him as we moved down the passage. I had a feeling he wasn't just talking about Hephaistos. "You're right. I never truly thanked you for saving my life."

"I wasn't talking about that."

I set my hand on his arm and got him to look at me. "Thank you. You've saved me in multiple ways."

He caressed my face. "I'd do it again without hesitation."

"Good, because I have a feeling that won't be the last time someone tries to kill me." I smirked.

"Well, you do seem innately skilled in making enemies."

"It's because I'm so damn charming."

He laughed, and we continued on our way.

At the end of the passage, we took a right and almost immediately came to a locked wooden door. Lucian examined it, frowning.

"Knowing Hephaistos, it will take some kind of fancy fire and smoke to find a way to open it."

"Yeah, we don't have time for that." I set my hand on the door handle and created a fire so hot that in seconds the metal reddened like hot coals then started to melt. The result was a hole in the door and a destroyed locking mechanism. I put my hand through the hole and easily pushed the door open.

Lucian shook his head. "There goes our sneaking in advantage."

I shrugged, then peered around the corner into a long empty corridor dug out of the stone with curved archways. I had no idea where the cells were or if there were guards. For the most part, we were operating on blind faith that we were going to get away with this.

Before we went marching through the prison, I grabbed Lucian's hand and gathered the shadows around us for camouflage. If we did happen to run into anyone, we'd be practically invisible to them. Together we ventured out into the corridor.

I led the way, Lucian right behind me. We passed a couple of empty cells. The crisscrossed bars were thick iron. Then I stopped in front of one, eyes focusing on a dark form in the corner lying on the floor. I stepped out of the shadows and went to the bars.

"Jasmine?"

The form looked up. I could see then that it was indeed my friend. She stood, stumbled, then came to the bars. I nearly wept to see that she'd been hurt. There weren't obvious bruises on her face, but I spotted the scorch marks on her hands and feet, where I imagined electric bolts had been used.

I reached my hands through the bars and took hold of her arm, careful not to harm her. "I'm going to kill whoever did this to you."

"They tortured you?" Lucian's voice was incredulous. I wasn't sure why he sounded so surprised. They'd been torturing all of us in the name of training. In the trials, they even pitted us against each other to see who could endure the most torture.

Jasmine nodded. "They kept asking what side I was on."

"Why would they ask you that?" Lucian asked.

She shrugged and sobbed. "I don't know."

I pulled her closer to the bars, so I could cup her face. "I'm so sorry, Jas. This is all my fault."

"How? You were the one poisoned."

"This is about more than an attempt on my life. There are factions being developed in the academy. I think the Gods are starting to pick sides."

"For what?" she asked.

"A war."

"Over what?" Lucian asked.

"I think over the academy itself."

"That doesn't make sense," Jasmine said.

"I'm not sure, but Demeter told me to find a place under the maze that would tell me everything I need to know." I pulled back and wrapped my hands around the bars. "But first I'm getting you out of here. Stand back. I'm going to melt these bars."

"I tried that," Jasmine said as she stepped back.

"It doesn't work. I think our powers are muted in here."

Concentrating on the metal, I pushed all my kinetic energy into my hands. Flames erupted over my fingers, curling up to my wrists. I could feel the fire burning, but it wasn't having any effect on the bars. They remained black and cold.

"Lucian, put her hands over mine and direct your lightning into them."

"What if I electrocute you?"

"I handled Zeus's bolt, remember?"

He did as I asked and settled his hands over mine on the bars. Within seconds, I could see the sparks zipping off his hands. An electrical current shot over my fingers and up my arms. The pain was immediate and sharp, and I gritted my teeth, but I refused to let go of the bars. But after a few minutes, the metal still wasn't heating up and most definitely wasn't melting.

"Damn it." I released my grip on the bars, and Lucian dropped his hands.

"What are you doing here?"

I whirled around to see two guards, wearing leather armor and carrying spears, running down the passageway toward us.

For a brief second, I considered tossing some fire balls at them, but the last thing we needed was a battle that wasn't going to get us anywhere except possibly thrown in the cell next to Jasmine.

"I want to see Zeus," I demanded.

I didn't think the guards were expecting that because they looked at each other curiously.

Fifteen minutes later, we were escorted up to

Zeus's private chambers. It helped that Lucian was part of his clan because the guards didn't argue with us. He had access to the hall anyway.

Zeus greeted us with a warm smile. "Melany, it's good to see you up and about. How are you feeling?"

"I'm fine, thanks to Lucian."

Zeus beamed at Lucian and put his hand on Lucian's shoulder, like a father to a son. "Yes, quite heroic. I had no idea you possessed that kind of power."

"Nor did I," Lucian said. I could see that he looked a bit uncomfortable.

"Well, it worked out for the best." He moved away from us, his long white robe dragging on the floor behind him.

"I want Jasmine released. She had nothing to do with poisoning me."

"Technically, she did. She gave you the glass of wine."

"She was used. She didn't know that the wine was poisoned."

"Yes, I surmised that. She has no motive for your murder." Zeus waved his hand. "She will be released."

"When?"

He turned, and I saw the annoyed sparks in his eyes.

Lucian grabbed my hand and squeezed it in warning. "Thank you, Zeus," he said.

I refused to thank him, as Jasmine shouldn't have been detained to begin with, but Lucian nudged me in the side.

"Yeah, thank you." I figured it wouldn't hurt to keep the all-powerful God on my side.

He walked toward us again, his brow furrowed. "I didn't realize the two of you were close. An item? Is that what the term is?"

"We're good friends," I said. "Strong allies."

Zeus nodded. "That's good. It's important to have...friends here. The academy and the training we do can be a very isolating thing for cadets. Especially when one stands out among the others. Sometimes friends are hard to keep."

I had a sense there was a warning in there somewhere. But I wasn't sure to whom. Me or Lucian?

CHAPTER THIRTEEN

MELANY

*A*fter we left Zeus's hall, Lucian suggested we go flying together like we used to before all the shit happened, before the trials, before Hades. We went outside toward the maze to unfurl our wings. I pushed mine out, a tension in my back releasing, and spread them out around me. Shivers rushed over my body at the anticipation of taking flight. I smiled at Lucian then took off into the sky.

I'd forgotten how it felt to soar through the open air. For the past few months, all my flying had been done in the training room in Hades's Hall. This was freeing in more ways than one. Laughing, I did a corkscrew up, then dove back down toward the ground, swooping up at the last moment. That move always made my belly flip over.

Lucian flew in beside me, and we swooped

toward the woods and lake. Together, we soared over the treetops. I lowered my hand and brushed my fingers against the highest branch of leaves. Then we glided over the lake. I stared at our reflection in the water, watching as my black wings flapped, the tips touching the water, and Lucian's beautiful red ones doing the same. We made quite the impressive pair.

After flying over the lake a bunch of times, we jetted back to our favorite spot—the top of the tallest tower of the academy. Once I landed, I folded in my wings and walked to the edge to look out over the grounds. I could see the training field, the maze, and the cobblestone path to the academy that I remembered walking when I first arrived. I couldn't believe how much had changed since then.

Lucian came up to my side. "The view from up here will always be awesome."

I nodded. "Yeah. I've missed it."

"I've missed you." He grabbed my hand.

"I've missed you, too."

"Have you?"

I turned to him. I knew what he was really asking me. Hearing about Hades this morning must've been hurtful. I wanted to tell him that being with Hades hadn't meant anything, that I didn't have feelings for him, but that would be a lie. I had very real, very strong emotions for the God of darkness, just as I had feelings for Lucian.

I reached up and traced my hand over his brow, down his cheek to his lips. He kissed the tips of my fingers. I stepped into him, wrapping my other hand around his waist. Slowly, he dipped his head down and pressed his lips to mine.

My heart leapt into my throat as he cupped me around the neck and deepened the kiss. Holding me tight, he walked me back into the stone turret wall. His face nuzzled my neck, then he brushed his lips over my chin, then up to my mouth again. He swept his tongue over mine.

A little moan escaped my throat. I couldn't stop it. I was too swept up in what he was doing to me with his kiss. My body was on fire for him. I fisted my hands in his shirt and kissed him back just as hard, just as frantic.

His hands moved down to my waist, his thumbs pressed into my hips. My belly fluttered. Then that flutter lowered between my legs, and I moaned again. Louder this time. I couldn't keep it in. I wanted Lucian so bad.

Pulling back, he rested his forehead against mine, his breath coming in short hard gasps. His thumbs were still pressed into my hips, and I so desperately wanted them to slide down lower, to be bolder.

"I don't want to stop this time," he murmured.

My throat was dry, but I managed to say, "Then don't."

Covering my mouth with his again, his hands moved upward, slipping under my shirt. He palmed my breasts, and I gasped in pleasure. As he tweaked my nipples with his fingers, he nibbled on my bottom lip, then pressed kisses to my chin, over my neck to my ear. With his tongue, he made little circles just under my earlobe. A pleasant shiver rippled over my skin.

Heat rushed over my entire body as he lifted my shirt to expose my breasts to the cool air. Lowering his head, he pressed his lips to one nipple, then licked it with his tongue. I gasped, as he moved over and lavished the same attention on my other breast.

I was burning up. I didn't think I could stand his delicious teasing. My hands raced down to the waistband of his pants and unbuttoned them. Once undone, I slid a hand down and over his erection. He groaned against my skin, the rumble of it sending a rush of shivers over my belly and straight down between my legs.

He pulled back, and I thought he was going to tell me this wasn't a good idea, or we shouldn't, or some shit like that.

He rested his head against mine. "Not here. I don't want to take you against this wall out in the open where anyone can see us." He did up his pants, and the grabbed my hand. "C'mon."

Together, we lifted into the air, and Lucian guided us to another tower, to one of the windows. He pushed it open and climbed inside. I followed him to see it was his room in Zeus's Hall. Still holding my hand, he led me to his bed.

He guided my arms up over my head and pulled off my shirt. His gaze swept over me, there was a hunger in his eyes, but also appreciation and love. I scooted back onto his bed and lay back as he knelt beside me and hooked his fingers into the waistband of my sweatpants and slowly drew them off.

Then I was completely naked lying on his bed, but I didn't feel exposed or vulnerable. I was proud of my body even with its tattoos and scars, and Lucian's admiring scan of me sent heat blossoming all over. He got off the bed and quickly took off his own clothes. I watched him, enjoying the sight of his powerful yet lean body. He was beautiful to look at. Then he lay beside me on the bed and began his exploration.

He touched and kissed every part of me. He trailed his tongue along the branches of lightning that marred the side of my neck and down my side. His slow worship of my body turned me into a quivering hot mess. Then I couldn't stand it anymore. I needed him to be inside me. I craved release and only Lucian could give it to me.

I reached for him, burying my hands in his silky golden waves, and pulled him down. He positioned himself between my parted legs, and I could see the restraint he used to stop from completely losing himself. But I wanted to see him lose control. I needed him to.

"You won't hurt me," I said as I hooked my legs around his waist. "I'm not fragile."

"I know." He leaned down and kissed me. "But you deserve to be worshipped."

Then finally, blissfully, he guided himself between my legs and in one quick thrust was inside me. I cried out as my body squeezed around him. A tsunami of heat surged over us, and we were swept away by it.

Then it was all panic and heat and hunger as our bodies melded together.

It wasn't long before I lost all control and came, digging my fingers into his back and crying out.

Collapsing on top of me, Lucian buried his face into the side of my neck and followed me over the edge of orgasm.

After his body ceased quivering, he rolled over onto his back. We were both sweaty and breathing hard. It felt like I'd been through a three-hour work-out. My heart was still racing. Eventually, I turned my head to look at Lucian. His eyes were closed, and he had a wide silly grin on his face. It made me giggle. I never giggled.

His eyes opened and he turned to look at me. "That was incredible. I feel like I could dead lift the world with one hand."

"Ha! You'll be asleep in fifteen minutes, I bet."

"Nope." He reached for me and rolled me up onto his chest. Then he lifted me up into the air. "See!"

I squealed. "But I'm not the world."

He lowered me down and wrapped his arms around me. "You're my world."

I pushed up onto my elbows and looked into his eyes. His love for me was evident, and I swallowed against the well of emotions flooding inside of me. I feathered my fingers over his face, his nose, his cheeks, his chin, his lips, memorizing each part of him. My feelings for him were huge, but I didn't know how to express them in a way that he'd know how much he meant to me. How important he was.

"I'm scared that I'm going to lose you."

He tucked some hair behind my ear. "You're

never going to lose me, Blue. No matter what happens I'll always be there for you."

"Why? I'm not a good person."

He smiled and searched my face. "You're better than you'll ever know."

I shook my head. "I've done some things…Hades and I—"

"I see the darkness in you. I know it's a part of who you are, and I don't care." He cupped my cheek with his hand. "I love you for who you are, not for who you think you should be to make other people happy."

"But it's not fair to you."

"I'm a big boy. Let me decide what's fair or not."

Tears slipped down my cheeks. I didn't deserve this man. He had a heart of gold and a soul to match. Maybe that was why we fit together. His light complimented my darkness. Together we made sense.

I leaned forward and pressed my lips to his. He brought his hands up to my hair. Deepening the kiss, he rolled me over onto my back, and for the next couple of hours we just loved each other in the best possible ways we could.

Afterward, we slept. Well, Lucian slept. I laid on my back staring up at the ceiling. There were too many thoughts whirling around in my mind. I needed to get under the maze and find the room Demeter told me about where I'd find answers. War was coming, and I needed to be fully prepared. I needed to know who I was fighting against and who I was fighting for and what the outcome was meant to be.

As silently as I could, I got out of the bed and

found my clothes. I quickly put them on but felt greatly underdressed for an adventure underground in only a pair of sweatpants and thin T-shirt. I opened Lucian's closet and found training gear much like I wore in the underworld. I didn't think he'd mind if I borrowed a pair of pants and a long-sleeved shirt and socks. I'd have to make do with the sneakers that Georgina had lent me as Lucian's boot would be too big.

I also pilfered one of his knives he had stashed away. I took it and a holder that wrapped around my leg. I got outfitted, then after a long look at Lucian still sleeping, I gathered the shadows around me, and zipped down to the maze.

CHAPTER FOURTEEN

MELANY

$\mathcal{I}$ stepped out of the shadows right beside the gazebo in the middle of the maze. Thankfully, no one else was here. I found that not a lot of my fellow cadets came into the maze. There were rumors that it was haunted by Medusa's ex-lovers who she'd turned to stone. I assumed they thought all the stone statues outside and around the maze were once people. I was pretty sure those rumors were started because everyone was afraid of the snake-haired demigoddess. Not that I didn't blame them. She was frightening, but I kind of liked that about her.

I stepped up into the gazebo and looked around. Demeter had said I'd find a door in the maze. She didn't necessarily say in the gazebo, but where else could there be a door? I needed more light as the sun was setting, casting darker and deeper shadows around the hedges. For a moment, I considered stepping into them to return to Hades, but I was still angry at him. And with Lucian's scent still on my skin, his taste on my tongue, I didn't want to rub me and Lucian's reunion in his face. Not that I thought he'd care.

I held my hand over one of the four big cauldrons set around the gazebo and set it ablaze with fire. I did the same with the other three. Just as I finished lighting the last one, I sensed movement behind me. I unsheathed the dagger on my leg and swung around, my arm up in defense.

Georgina yelped. "Don't stab me. I like my insides where they belong—inside my body."

Sighing, I lowered my weapon and shook my head at her and Lucian, who had come up behind her. "The both of you move too quietly."

"So do you or I would've woken when you snuck out of my room."

I blushed a little since Georgina was there and probably knew what we'd been doing in his room. "You looked too peaceful to wake."

His lips twitched up as he did a once over. "Are you wearing my clothes?"

I shrugged. "Yes. The T-shirt and sweatpants I had weren't up to code for an adventure."

"They look good." There was a humor-filled glint in his eyes.

My eyes narrowed. "How did you know where I was?"

"When I woke, saw that you were gone, I figured

you were up to something. So I tracked Georgina down, thinking maybe you might have told her something. She didn't really know but knew you'd talked to Demeter."

"She told you I'd be here?"

He nodded. "When are you going to learn that you don't have to do these things on your own?"

I shrugged. "Probably never." I chuckled.

"What are we looking for?" Georgina asked.

"A door of some kind."

"Well, we can probably assume it's not going to be some ordinary door," Lucian said as he inspected the floor of the gazebo.

"Did she say door?" Georgina asked.

I stopped to think for a moment. "Hmm, I think she said portal actually."

"Okay, tell me exactly what she said." Georgina put her hands on her hips and gave me a look.

I closed my eyes for a second to recollect the conversation I had with Demeter. "She said…go to the maze. There you will find a portal to the Hall of Knowledge and—"

"Hall of Knowledge, are you sure?"

I nodded. "Yes."

"I think I know where the portal is." Georgina took off into the maze.

Lucian and I followed her, having no choice. Because it was dark, I created a ball of fire to give us some light. After a few twists and turns in the maze, Georgina stopped in front of one of the stone statues. I came closer to see that it was of an owl and not a man.

"Okay? What are we supposed to be seeing?" I asked her.

"Whose symbol is the owl?"

"Athena," Lucian answered.

"And what is she the goddess of?"

"Wisdom." I slung my arm around her shoulders. "You're a genius, Gina."

"No, I just listened during history of the Gods class while you were daydreaming about fighting hydras and minotaurs."

I scrutinized the owl statute. "Okay, so how do we get this to work?" I reached for it and tried to pry it off the stone pillar it sat on. It didn't budge. Then I tried pushing the whole thing over thinking there'd be some kind of secret entrance underneath. That didn't work, either.

I stepped back and looked at the stone statue again. "What do we know about owls and Athena?"

"The owl is said to be the Goddess's companion. It's supposed to help her see all," Georgina said.

See all? How do owls see? With their eyes. I crouched down to look at the stone bird's face. The flames from my hand flickered over the statue to reveal two large round orbs where its eyes would be. I looked at my hand again, and the light of the fire. Owls could see in the dark.

I put my other hand over the fire and snuffed it out.

"What are you doing?" Lucian asked.

The moment we were plunged into darkness, light glowed from the owl's eyes. I looked into it but didn't see anything. Then I stood back and saw that the light made twin beams that shot forward.

"Move out of its way." I pulled Lucian aside, and we stood beside the statue.

Then I saw a pool of light hovering in the air about six feet from the statue. When I moved, it glimmered.

"It's a portal," Georgina said in awe.

One by one, we walked toward the shimmer in the air. I stuck my hand into the pool of light. A prickling sensation went up my arm as my hand disappeared. I pulled it out again to make sure it was still intact, and I hadn't disintegrated.

"Fortune favors the brave." I took in a deep breath then stepped into the glimmering portal.

I immediately appeared in a circular room, made from marble with giant pillars and a domed prettily painted ceiling. There were several lit torches in sconces around the room. The warm orange glow illuminated shelves upon shelves of rolled scrolls and large yellowing tomes. The place looked old. Not just old but ancient.

Lucian and Georgina appeared beside me. "Wow, it's a library," Georgina said as she gaped at the surroundings. "*The* library. The Library of the Gods."

Lucian ran his hand over one of the pillars. "What are we supposed to be looking for?"

"My parents said to look into the past of the academy. That I would find answers."

Surprised, Lucian whirled toward me. "Your parents? I thought they died when you were young."

"They did. But I saw them when I died and went to Elysium." I moved toward one of the shelves and pulled out one of the scrolls.

"Mel, I think there's a bunch of stuff you haven't told us."

I proceeded to tell Lucian and Georgina about being in Elysium and meeting Persephone and my parents and what they told me. I also told them about what Demeter had told me as well about my connection to Persephone and to herself.

"Whoa." Georgina looked stunned. "Demeter is like your great-great-great-great-great times hundred grandmother."

I shook my head. "I don't think it works like that."

"I don't know. I think it does. You have her blood running through your veins. As do I, that's why I'm in her clan and have an affinity to the earth. So technically we're like sisters." Laughing, she grabbed my arm and pulled me in for a hug.

I hugged her back, shaking my head.

"So, we're looking for anything about the history of the academy?" Lucian asked.

I nodded, then we got to work.

I wasn't sure how long we pulled out scrolls, unrolled them, read them, and put them back, but it was most definitely hours. I'd just gotten my third papercut on the skin between my thumb and index finger, when Lucian called out from the far side of the library.

"I found something."

Georgina and I gathered around him and the scroll he had rolled out on one of the stone tables. He pointed to a paragraph of text. "It says that the academy was founded in 700 BC."

"Whoa. I didn't think it was that old. Our history texts say that the academy was created during the New Dawn in the early 1900s to protect the world from the Titans." Georgina shook her head. "Why would the historians lie about that?"

"I'm pretty sure it wasn't the historians who were lying. They can only write about what they know to be true," I said.

"There's more," Lucian said. "The academy was founded by Prometheus and Hesiod as a place for higher learning for Gods and humans alike."

I couldn't believe it. This was what Hades had been alluding to, when he said that the academy didn't belong to Zeus.

"Holy crap," Georgina sighed. "Prometheus was a Titan. The story goes he gave fire to mortals and cared for their wellbeing. And the rumor is that Zeus didn't like that Prometheus favored mortals over the Gods, and, therefore, cursed Prometheus to an eternity of torture."

"Why would the Gods lie about the nature of the academy?" Lucian asked.

"Because it's no longer a place of learning but a place to learn to fight and kill." I rubbed at the scar on my cheek. It was throbbing a little, as a reminder of Zeus's penchant for torture.

"But to fight against the Titans, right? To keep the world safe." Georgina frowned.

"Are we so sure now that it's the Titans who are a threat to our world?" I stormed back to the shelves and pulled out more scrolls and books. "There has to be more here. My parents said they were part of the academy. They said they were killed protecting me."

"Protecting you from what?" Lucian rolled up the scroll.

"From who, maybe." I flipped through the giant tome I pulled from the shelf. "Someone is trying to kill me."

"To keep you from being 'the one to end the war?'" Lucian came to my side.

I shrugged. "Yeah, maybe. I don't know." I continued to flip pages.

"Do you still think it's Aphrodite and Ares?" he asked.

I swallowed and shook my head. "I'm starting to think maybe it's bigger than the two of them."

He frowned. "You can't possibly think—"

"I don't know. He's the head of the academy. He's the all-knowing, the all-powerful. I can't imagine anything goes on without his knowledge." Then, I found the information I was looking for.

Right there staring at me was a photo, a recent one by the looks of it, maybe ten years old. It was of my parents. They were smiling, they looked happy, and standing between them with his arms over their shoulders was Zeus.

They had been part of the academy, and Zeus had known them both.

I pushed away from the table, my heart racing. My throat went dry and I found it hard to breathe.

"Holy shit." Lucian stared down at the picture. "Is that your parents?"

I nodded but pulled at the collar of my shirt. I couldn't get any air.

Georgina rushed toward me and rubbed a hand over my back. She bent me over. "Take a deep breath, then let it out slowly."

I did as she instructed. It was helping even though my heart felt like it was going to burst out of my throat.

"I can't believe this." Lucian started to pace the room, rubbing at his face. "It's all been a bunch of lies."

I straightened and rubbed at my mouth. Georgina still ran a hand up and down my back to soothe me. I was about to say what we should do about the information we'd obtained when something out of the corner of my eye drew my attention.

I swirled around just as one of the stone statues from the maze came through the portal. And he was holding a sword and a shield.

CHAPTER FIFTEEN

MELANY

"*I* think we have a problem."

Lucian and Georgina looked to where I pointed as three more stone soldiers armed with weapons came through the portal.

"It must be a security system for the library," Georgina said.

"You'd think it would've been activated the moment we got inside, not hours later." I unsheathed my dagger, although I wasn't sure it would be any good against stone. "No, I think this is something else."

By the time we lined up side by side, two more stone statues entered the library. There were now six of them in front of us, blocking our exit. I didn't know if they were here to detain us or kill us, and I supposed it didn't matter. One was as bad as the other in my opinion.

"Can you shadow us out of here?" Lucian asked.

I shook my head. I'd already tested the shadows, and they were blocked. We couldn't travel through them. I wasn't surprised though because I didn't even know where the library truly was. We could've been anywhere. Underneath the academy or a thousand miles away, maybe even another dimension parallel to this one. It was hard to know. Nothing about coming to the academy to train had been comprehensible. It had all been cloaked in secrecy and lies.

"Maybe I can reason with them."

"They're made of stone, Gina. It's not like they have fully functioning brains."

Georgina stepped toward the soldiers. "We didn't come here to steal anything." She took another step forward with her hands out to prove she wasn't a threat.

One of the stone statues carrying a spear and shield, moved forward, while advancing its spear. Georgina had to back up to avoid being poked in the chest with the tip.

"Okay. I guess that didn't work." She moved back to stand with us.

"This is crap." I took a few steps forward. "Let us pass. Now."

They all moved like they were preparing to attack. I didn't like this situation one bit.

I sheathed my dagger, then gathered the shadows to me. Although I couldn't use them for travel, I could use them to make a weapon just as Hades had when we fought Oceanus. I wrapped my hands around the darkness and drew them upward like the way I'd seen Hades do it. It took a couple of tries, but eventually I managed to fashion a short shadow sword.

"What are you doing?" Lucian asked.

"Getting us out of here." I lifted the sword into a ready position. "Use your lightning to blast them."

"Maybe we should wait to see who——" Georgina started.

"It doesn't matter who sent them. We're going to be detained just like Jasmine. I refuse to be anyone's prisoner."

I advanced on the soldiers, expecting that Lucian and Georgina were behind me ready to attack. The statue in the middle with the sword came at me. He swung toward my head, but because of his bulkiness, his aim was off, and I was able to duck under it, and then come up with my sword. The shadow blade struck the statue across the chest. It didn't do what I had hoped, but I was rewarded with a fissure across the stone. A few more hits like that, and the solider would crumble.

Lucian blasted the soldier with the spear, breaking the weapon in half. It fell to the floor and shattered into pieces. Georgina managed to pick up one of the pedestals that were scattered decoratively around the library and threw it at the soldiers. It broke across one soldier's helmet and managed to chip off a few pieces of its face. When it turned toward her, to attack, I saw that it no longer had a nose. Score one for Georgina.

I wanted to turn toward her and give her a high

five but thought maybe it wasn't prudent in the middle of a battle. I grinned instead. If we kept hacking away at them piece by piece, we'd definitely win.

The swordsman came at me again, backing me up into the marble table. I leapt onto the table just as it swung its sword. I jumped over the blade. The air vibrated just under my feet as it whizzed by me. The sword came down on the table and cracked it in half. I kicked the statue in the head, it didn't do any damage, except maybe to my big toe, but the blow got its attention. As it turned toward me, I curved my shadow sword toward its midsection and swung.

When my blade hit the stone, it vibrated up over my arms. It nearly rattled my teeth, but I hit my mark, and the stone solider cracked in half, the two pieces falling to the floor, where it broke even more. One down, five to go.

Two of the soldiers advanced on Lucian. He sent another blast of lightning at one, as he ducked under the other's spear as it was thrust at him. The bolt did the job and cracked the solider along the midsection and arm. It would take one blow to shatter it into pieces. I tossed my shadow sword to Lucian, as I attempted to make another one while running.

Lucian swung at the spearman, aiming for the visible fracture, and hit the target. The soldier's arm broke off and shattered on the floor. The rest of it crumbled into pieces as it tried another attack at Lucian.

Georgina got cornered by the other two statues.

She'd run out of podiums and heavy stone vases to toss at them.

"Use your earth powers, Gina! You're stronger than they are!" I shouted at her as one solider drew back with his sword and was about to cut her across the shoulder.

She caught the sword in her hands. It was amazing. Then she proceeded to squeeze it in her grip. I could hear the stone breaking apart from where I launched an attack on the last two soldiers guarding the portal. It was time to bail and get out of the library. Once we were out, I could jump us into a shadow and get us somewhere safe.

I hit one of the stone guards in the shoulder, cracking its armor. It stumbled sideways giving us a very small window of opportunity.

"Get to the portal!"

Lucian ran toward Georgina, sent a blast of lightning at the last soldier near her, then grabbed her hand and pulled her toward the portal. I was already on my way there but stopped. I wasn't leaving without some sort of proof of the lies Zeus and the others had been telling. I rushed back to the broken table, snatched the big tome, hugged it to my chest, and ran back to the glimmering doorway. I swung my shadow sword at the other stone statue as it turned toward me. The black blade hit it in the head and took it clean off. It bounced onto the floor and broken into several pieces.

Lucian and Georgina jumped into the portal, and I followed right behind them.

We popped out right back into the maze by the

owl. Lucian ran toward the path to the exit of the maze. Georgina and I were right on his heels.

"The second we're out, I'll take us into a shadow. Be ready."

We ran as quickly as we could. A few twists and turns later, I could see the exit to the maze right in front of Lucian. He ran through, then Georgina and I came out side by side. We all stopped short as another line of stone soldiers stood in our way. And right in front of them stood Athena, in all her glory.

"Stop!" she commanded. Her voice vibrated all around us.

We did. There was no denying that we were outnumbered and outgunned. We'd never be able to fight our way out of this situation. Not with Athena leading the charge. She was a fierce fighter; some would say she was even better than Ares when it came to battle.

Panicking, I surveyed the area, looking for the closest shadows to pull toward me. Maybe I could still get us out of here without having to fight.

"You will come with me," Athena said.

"Why? What did we do wrong?" I demanded, taking a step forward.

Lucian frowned at me, in warning. He hated it when I smack talked to the Gods.

"You have entered a forbidden area of the academy."

"Why is a library forbidden?" I was pushing, I knew, but I refused to go quietly.

"You can discuss that with Zeus in the detention center," she said.

"Prison cells, you mean."

Her eyes narrowed at me. "The academy doesn't have a prison."

"Right. Tell that to Jasmine, who is still in there after being tortured for something she didn't do."

Athena frowned. "I'm sure that isn't what happened."

I took another step forward. I could see that the Goddess was having doubts. She probably didn't know about what exactly, but there were obviously some things going on that she wasn't aware of. Maybe I could convince her to take a stand, to pick sides, to learn the truth.

"Were you aware that the academy was founded by Prometheus, a Titan, and a human named Hesiod?"

"Of course. We were all there when it was founded."

I frowned. Huh. I obviously wasn't as smart as I thought I was.

She waved her arms toward the stone soldiers. "Escort these three to the detention center."

The statues marched toward us, fanning out, and coming around to the sides to flank us. We were trapped in the middle of them. I didn't see a way out of this. Lucian's gaze met mine. He was just as conflicted as I was.

A couple of the stone soldiers lowered their spears. We had no choice but to march forward or risk getting a stone spearhead through the heart. I looked around, there had to be a way out. That was when I spied a dark mist swirling around on the ground as we walked.

Before Athena could escort us into the academy through the back entrance near the training field, Hades drifted out of the darkness, as if he was out for a nightly stroll over the grounds. He looked like an eighteenth-century gentleman in his dark suit with the long tails, just like the one he wore for our impromptu trip to Nice, and silver tipped cane.

"Hello, Athena."

The Goddess immediately drew the sword holstered at her waist and stepped back into a defense position. "You have no business here, Hades."

"Yeah, I kind of do. You're making a mistake."

"These three violated the rules."

"By seeking information?" He clucked his tongue and twirled his cane. "Is that really what we're all about now? Keeping knowledge away from mortals. What happened to our enlightenment? Isn't that what the academy used to be about?"

She didn't respond, and I wondered if she was questioning the validity of what she'd been tasked to do. At least, I hoped she did. She was the Goddess of Wisdom. Surely, she had been questioning what was going on in the academy.

"Zeus said you'd come for Melany."

"My dear brother knows I always come for what is mine." He grinned, tapping the cane on the ground with a click, click.

I didn't have time to be angry about the "mine" quip before everything erupted into chaos.

More stone soldiers appeared from every corner.

Two of them carried what looked like a fisherman's net, but it wasn't made out of rope or twine, it looked to be made from thick, heavy metal. They threw it at Hades. But he was quick. He moved quicker than anyone I'd seen before.

One moment he was in front of Athena, and the next he was beside me, grabbing my hand. I knew what he was about to do.

"No, wait!"

But it was too late. We dissolved into the shadows before any of the soldiers could react.

Before I could grab Lucian and Georgina and take them with us to safety.

CHAPTER SIXTEEN

MELANY

$\mathcal{W}$e came out of the shadows and into the hall.

"We need to go back for Lucian and Gina." I whipped around, hoping to jump back into that portal, but Hades closed his hand and the black hole vanished.

"Nope. It's too dangerous."

I glared at him. "When is anything too dangerous for you?"

"I'm not talking about me." He walked into the library. I followed right on his heels. "If you go back, you'll be detained. And detained will lead to imprisoned." He stopped at the drink table and poured amber liquid into two glasses. He handed me one. "Look at poor Dionysus. He's still in one of those cells, even though they know he didn't try and poison you."

Hades tossed back the drink, then his eyes narrowed. He reached for my face. "You're hurt."

I pulled back from him and touched my cheek. Blood stained my fingertips. "Must've been a piece of rock that cut me when I smashed one of the stone soldiers."

"I'll get something to patch you up." He moved toward the door.

"Don't bother. I'll do it myself." After setting the drink back down on the table, untouched, I marched past him, out the door, then toward my bedroom.

He followed me. "I take you're still angry with me about the other night."

Not answering, I went into my room. After setting the big book onto the table by the fireplace, I went into the bathroom to wash and find a bandage if I needed one. Hades leaned up against the doorway and watched me as I wet a cloth and dabbed at the cut on my face.

I tried not to look at him, so unaffected, so cool and casual. So frustratingly sexy.

I hated that even now, maybe even more so, I reacted to him. He didn't even have to be doing anything. He just had to exist for desire to surge through my body like wildfire.

I whirled on him. "You knew there was going to be an attempt on my life. Lucian told you, and you still let me go to the ceremony." I stomped toward him and hit him in the chest with a closed fist. "You used me as bait, and I died."

He rubbed at the spot where I hit him but didn't back up. "I'm sorry you were poisoned, but I knew Lucian could bring you back. I'd given him the power to do so, and it was obvious he'd use it. He's completely in love with you."

He said that last bit as if it was a fatal flaw to love me. Maybe it was.

Chin lifted, I met his gaze but had to tamp down the urge to ask him if he loved me, too. It was a silly question, by a silly girl, who couldn't help the abundance of emotions she had swirling around for him.

I turned and went back to the sink to finish doctoring my battle wound. "Did you find out then who really tried to kill me? Since we both know it wasn't Jasmine or Dionysus. Did you get an answer worth risking my life for?"

"I have my suspicions."

"Yeah, who?"

"You won't like the answer."

I turned toward him again. "Tell me. I think I've earned an answer."

"I'm sure it was Demeter."

I gaped at him. "No way. I don't believe that. Did you see her drop the poison in the wine?"

"No, but she has a vendetta against me. She'd do anything to destroy me."

I stared at him for a long moment. "So, hurting me would destroy you?"

He made a face, probably realizing what that insinuated and that he hadn't meant to go down that path. "It wouldn't destroy me. I mean, obviously, I don't want you to get hurt. I care what happens to you…"

"Well, isn't that nice." I tossed the cloth. Thankfully, I didn't need a bandage on the cut. It wasn't that deep. I moved to the bathroom door to leave. Hades wouldn't get out of my way, so I had to brush past him. When I did, his scent filled my nose and I suppressed an inner groan. I hated that even the smell of him sent ripples of desire through me.

He snagged my arm, forcing me to stop. "You have to know that I do care about you, Melany."

"Do I have to know? How? You don't really show it. I mean apart from our hookup—"

"You're more than a hookup." He frowned. "It's just…complicated in ways you couldn't understand."

"Oh, I'm not an idiot. I understand quite a bit actually." I pulled out of his grip. "I know that we're like thousands of years apart in basically everything. I know how much you loved Persephone and that when she left you, it devastated you. And now I know that I'm connected to Persephone, that I'm somehow her descendant."

His eyes widened at that. Either he was astonished that I knew about the connection or that I was connected. Maybe he didn't know. Shit. If he didn't know, that would've been a huge punch in the gut. I guessed I'd already put my foot in my mouth, so I might as well continue.

"I also know that Persephone is Demeter's daughter and that you blame Demeter for turning her against you. But you know what? She didn't. Persephone loved you, and she didn't leave you on her own. She was taken against her will."

He looked angry as he stormed toward me. "What did you say? How do you know this?"

Sighing, I rubbed my good cheek. "When I died, I was transported to Elysium. I met Persephone there."

He gasped under his breath, then he turned away from me. He slowly lowered himself onto my bed, mumbling to himself. "She's dead then."

"She said, dead is never really dead."

"What else did she say?"

I shook my head. "She was going to tell me something about Zeus, but I came back before she could."

He clenched his hand on his lap. "I'd long suspected Zeus had something to do with her disappearance."

"I don't know if that's what she was going to say…"

He looked up, and I saw the fury in his eyes. Flames flickered violently around like a blistering tornado. Not only could I see the rage in him, I also saw the anguish. There was a sorrow and desolation to him that I hadn't really understood before now. I felt sorry for him, and I knew he'd detest it if he ever knew that.

I moved to stand in front of him, and I reached out and gently set my hand on top of his head. I ran my fingers through his hair. At first, I thought he was going to push me away with anger, but instead he hooked me around the waist with an arm and pulled me closer. He nuzzled his head against my chest and closed his eyes.

As I stroked his head, he clung to me with a sort of desperation that broke my heart. I knew that he'd hate being so vulnerable and open with me. That it was costing him so much by exposing himself like this.

But I'd never betray him. I'd never deliberately hurt him.

Soon, he turned his face into my chest and sighed into me. His hands slid down my back to my hips. He pressed his thumbs against them, which sent a quick jolt down my legs. He tilted his head up and looked at me. The flames of anger had died in his eyes, to be replaced by a longing.

Swallowing, I dipped my head down and gently pressed my lips to his. He pulled me into him and deepened the kiss. Then he flipped me around and pushed me up onto the bed, as he crawled up beside me, his body covering mine. I wrapped my arms and legs around him and let him take what he needed from me.

A couple of hours later, Hades was asleep beside me in my bed, but I couldn't sleep. My mind was racing too fast about too much. I couldn't languish here, safely in Hades's Hall when my friends were being tortured for all I knew. It wasn't right, as they wouldn't have been in trouble if it wasn't for me.

I sat up and quietly got out of bed. I went into my closet and dressed appropriately, in full combat wear. I strapped a second knife to my leg to match the one I'd taken from Lucian. I smiled when I noticed that they looked alike.

I crept out of my room and went into the hall. I

located the shadows near the walls and pulled them to me. Once I cloaked myself, I took a step forward. Except all that happened was I walked out back into the hall again. I tried it again and got the same result. Hades had obviously shut the shadow portals, so I couldn't travel through them.

Since I couldn't leave that way, I was going to have to go the old-fashioned way. This time I was better prepared to venture out of the hall and to the River Styx.

The moment I opened the doors, I whistled with my fingers in my mouth. Seconds later, I felt the ground shake beneath my boots as a big old three-headed puppy lumbered over to me. Three tongues slicked me with saliva. It was really gross, and I wiped it off my face with the sleeve of my shirt.

"Hey, boy, I've missed you."

His tail wagged, thumping against one stone wall. It echoed off the rock, and I worried he was going to wake up Hades.

"Can you take me for a ride?"

His tail wagged even faster. I took that as an affirmative answer, and I reached up, grabbed hold of his spiked leather collar and pulled myself up onto his neck. Holding onto his ears, I steered him down the cave tunnel to the river.

When we got to the river, Charon stood on the bank waiting for us. His black cloak fluttered in the brisk cool wind that blew down the river. Cerberus pulled up short and whined. Considering the size difference, I nearly laughed at the dog's fear of the skeletal butler.

"You cannot cross the river." Charon's raspy voice carried on the wind and sent a shiver down my back.

"I need to leave, Charon. I have to get back to the academy."

"Lord Hades forbids it."

I blew out an angry breath. I was tired of being bossed around by everyone. "You know what? Lord Hades can kiss my ass." I pressed my heels into Cerberus's sides, like I would a horse, to urge him forward. He obeyed me for a change and lifted his giant paw to step forward.

All of a sudden Charon sprouted upward. He grew into a giant until his head nearly touched the cave ceiling, fifty feet above. Yelping, Cerberus jerked backward, and I nearly tumbled off his back. It was like Jack and the Beanstalk, and I was little ole Jack.

Charon was so big that we couldn't even go around him. We were effectively blocked from going anywhere but back to the hall.

"Argh! This isn't fair!"

I turned my canine mount around, and we returned to the big double doors of the hall. I slid off Cerberus. He whined and I gave his head a good scratch.

"It's not your fault, buddy."

The doors swung open, and I dragged my ass inside. Hades, dressed provocatively in a black silk robe, stood in the middle of the hall to greet me.

"I told you, you can't go back. You're too valuable. Too important."

"I'm going back somehow. I must rescue my friends. They would do it for me. I can't leave them there for Zeus or whoever to do what they want with them. It's not right."

He shook his head then rubbed his chin. "Fine." He sighed and rolled his eyes.

I went to him and hugged him tight. "You're a good man."

"Don't tell anyone. I don't want to ruin my reputation."

CHAPTER SEVENTEEN

LUCIAN

I couldn't stop pacing the cell. And that's what it was—a prison cell—despite Athena's assurances that it was just a detention room, so they could hold me until they could figure out an appropriate punishment for breaking the rules. It was all bullshit. I saw that now. I was in this cell because we uncovered the truth about the academy.

Georgina and I had been separated and put into different areas. From being down here before, I knew I was only a couple cells away from Jasmine. I'd called out to her the second the guards slammed the barred doors shut on me. But she hadn't responded and that worried me.

Maybe they'd released her, like Zeus said he would, but I wasn't confident in that. Zeus had been lying to all of us from the very first moment we stepped through the academy doors. Actually, it had all been lies the moment, as children, when we were told about the shadowboxes and the great honor it would be to be chosen at eighteen to train as part of the Gods Army.

I didn't know how long I'd been in here, but it felt like hours. I couldn't sit still, though. I had too much angry energy coursing through me. I was glad that Melany had been able to get away, even if I hated the fact that it was Hades who saved her, and only her. Despite that, I wouldn't be able to stand knowing that she was in one of these cells waiting to be tortured.

After I paced enough to nearly make a divot in the floor, I opted for some push-ups and crunches. Then I tried my powers to see if I could use them to get out, but like before when I was here with Melany, whatever was in the room dampened all my abilities. I managed some pretty useless sparks on my fingertips but that was all.

After the sixth, seventh, eighth hour, I didn't know, it was hard to tell time down here, I heard footsteps coming down the tunnel. Several guards stopped at the bars to my cell. One of them opened the door.

"Come with us," he said.

"Where?"

He didn't answer, just stared mutely at me until I moved.

I walked out of the cell, and they surrounded me then escorted me down the tunnel. I looked into the other cells as we passed hoping for a glimpse of Georgina and Jasmine to let me know they were okay.

Three cells down from mine, I spied a motionless lump in the corner. The lump had red hair.

I pushed out from the guards. "Gina!" I wrapped my hands around the bars. "Gina!"

She stirred. When she lifted her head, I saw bruises and blood on her pale skin.

"What did they do to you?"

I struggled against the guards and was rewarded with a fist to the gut and the hilt of a sword to the head, which made my knees buckle. I was dragged away before she could answer.

The guards led me out of the underground prison, through a secret door. We ended up in a part of the academy I'd never seen before. The corridors were devoid of life, no art on the walls, no color on the floors. It was all very stark and sterile and utilitarian. Not at all like the vibrant parts of the academy.

I was led into a circular room with only a chair in the center. I was forced to sit, and then the guards left, shutting and locking the door behind them. After only a few minutes, the door opened again, and Zeus, Aphrodite, and Ares entered. Apollo followed behind them. I was surprised to see him here. By the look on his face, I thought he was just as confused about what was going on.

"Why am I here?" I demanded.

Zeus gave me that fatherly smile of his. "We just want to ask you some questions, that's all, Lucian."

"What did you do to Gina? I saw her face."

"Nothing that won't heal." Aphrodite waved her hand. "She's a lot stronger than she lets on."

I glared at them. "You won't get away with this."

"Get away with what, exactly?" Aphrodite titled her head to look at me. "What do you think is going on here?"

"Let's not confuse the boy." Zeus moved toward me. "Now, Lucian, what were you and Georgina and Melany looking for in the library?"

I shrugged. "Something to read. Sometimes it can get a bit boring."

Aphrodite sneered. "I know he's your favorite, Zeus, but he's obviously under her influence."

"Who told you about the library?" Zeus asked.

"I'm pretty sure it was in the academy welcome guide."

Sparks lit up in Zeus's eyes. He came around behind me and set his hand on my shoulder. I swallowed down fear.

"I know you're protecting your girlfriend Melany. I understand your motivations. Love is a very complicated thing. We're all capable of doing surprising things when we're in love."

The spot where he touched me heated as if someone had pressed a clothes iron to my skin. It grew hotter and hotter by the second, until the burn was so painful, I couldn't stand it any longer. I tried to get out of the chair, but he held me down and the burn got worse. Grimacing, I bit down on my lower lip to keep from screaming.

Zeus lifted his hand and the relief was instant. I slumped against the chair.

"I know you think she loves you back, Lucian, but she doesn't." He walked around and stopped in front of me. He had that sad fatherly look about him, like he was just giving me some sound advice and not torturing me. "She belongs to Hades. She's his whore. Everything she's doing and saying is for him. She's turning you into a traitor for him."

I looked at the other Gods while this went on. Aphrodite looked positively gleeful. Ares looked as stoic as ever. Apollo was the only one who seemed a little uncomfortable.

"What were you looking for in the library?" Zeus asked again, as he walked around me.

I hated that I flinched when he moved behind me again. "I don't know about the others, but I was looking for the new James Patterson book. I heard it was really good."

This time Zeus put both his hands on my shoulders, and a jolt of electricity surged through my body. I convulsed in the chair. The heels of my boots hammered against the floor. The pain was indescribable. I bit my tongue before I screamed.

"Zeus…" Apollo stepped forward.

The pain stopped, and I tumbled off the chair and onto the floor. I could barely catch my breath as I struggled to stop my body from shaking. Zeus reached down and grabbed me by the arm and put me back into the chair.

"This pains me dearly, son, to do this," he said. "I had high hopes for you. But I won't allow Hades or anyone to jeopardize what we've built here in the academy. We're doing good work. We're protecting the world. And Hades would see that destroyed. My brother has always been jealous of me. He's always wanted what I have." He turned toward the others and nodded at Apollo. "Help Lucian with his memory, will you?"

Apollo knelt in front of me and set his hands around my head. "It'll hurt if you fight me." He closed his eyes.

I didn't feel anything at first. Then it was like getting an ice pick in the temple. I could feel Apollo rooting around in my brain looking for something. I tried to push him out, but that just made him dig in deeper and harder. I gritted my teeth as pain seared in my head. Blood filled my mouth.

"They found a scroll about the academy," Apollo said. "The founding date and founders. Melany found a picture of her parents in a book of their time at the academy."

I could feel him reaching for my memories of what Melany had told us about what she learned from Persephone. I tried to pull away from him, but I couldn't move. It was like I was frozen to the chair, my limbs paralyzed.

"Melany spoke with Persephone in Elysium. She knows she's the one," Apollo said, then dropped his hands and stood. I slid off the chair like a puppet without strings and onto the floor again. "That's all I could find."

"Thank you, Apollo," Zeus said. "This was very helpful."

"What does that mean? Melany is the one? The one what?"

"You may leave now."

Apollo glanced down at me. "What is going on, Zeus? Why did you torture him?"

Ares stepped forward and got in Apollo's face. "He said to leave, pretty boy. I suggest you do that."

I thought for sure Apollo was going to do something, but he took a step back. Then after a last glance at me on the floor, he walked to the door, opened it and left. I was on my own, and there was nothing I could do.

"Maybe we should reschedule the strike," Ares suggested.

"Absolutely not," Aphrodite said. "Everything's been planned. Everything's in place."

Zeus stroked his beard. "Aphrodite is right. We should go ahead with the plan. If we want full destruction, we need to do it now. We can't give Hades time to coordinate a defense or warn the mortals of the ruse. We need to solidify our position as protectors of the world, so we can take control of it all."

I realized as they talked about their plans of destroying my world, and gaining more power, that I wasn't getting out of this alive.

Aphrodite peered down at me, like she was looking at a lame pet that needed to be put down. "What do we want to do with him?"

Ares nudged me with the toe of his boot. "We could use him as a sacrifice to the kraken. Get things started."

Aphrodite shook her head. "We don't need another Perseus situation."

"We'll take him back to his cell, until we can figure out the best use of him." Zeus crouched next to me and stroked a hand over my head. "You had such potential. It's such a shame."

Aphrodite snorted. "They're a dime a dozen, Zeus. They'll be another shining golden boy in the next batch of recruits. Loyal families are piling up the tributes for a chance to get their sons in the academy. You can take your pick after we solidify our dominion over the mortals. They'll be forever grateful once we save their lives from the Titans. War is necessary to keep the peace."

The guards came into the room and yanked me to my feet. I couldn't stay on them, my legs were like jelly, so they had to drag me out and all the way back down to the cells. After they tossed me onto the ground and shut and locked the door, I crawled into the corner and propped myself up against the wall. I didn't know how I was going to do it, but I refused to die in this cell. One way or another, I was going to get out of here, get my friends, and together we would make them pay for what they'd done.

CHAPTER EIGHTEEN

MELANY

I pushed away the plate of food that the serving robot set in front of me. "I'm not hungry. We're wasting time."

"You can't save the world on an empty stomach. It's unheard of." Hades cut off another piece of the rare steak and popped it into his mouth. He happily chewed, regarding me from across the long table in the dining room.

Although he'd agreed to help me to save my friends, it was one thing after another. First, he took his sweet ass time having a shower, then getting dressed, only to be outfitted in the same thing he always wore. Then, it was a trip to the training room to collect a couple of weapons, and then it was to the dining hall to eat. Hours had passed, and I feared what Lucian, Georgina, and Jasmine had already gone through. What if I was too late to save them?

"Fine. If it will make this all go faster." I pulled the plate to me, picked up the steak with my hands and tore into it, purposely chewing like a cow with its cud. I swallowed and ripped off another piece.

Hades rolled his eyes. "Being childish isn't helpful."

"I'm not the one being a child here. You're stalling on purpose because you're jealous of Lucian. You don't want to save him."

"Jealousy is for foolish mortals." He picked up his napkin from his lap and patted his puckered mouth. "Besides that, I don't wish your...friend any ill will."

I smirked. "Yeah right. You Gods perfected jealousy into an art form. From all the stories I've read growing up and from firsthand experience, that's all you guys seem to do. You bicker and fight and plan your revenge plots against each other. You change sides and alliances as often as I change my underwear. It's exhausting, to be honest."

He laughed. It was the most honest reaction I'd ever seen from him, and it made me grin.

"My dear, no truer words have been spoken. It is exhausting." He balled up the napkin and set it on the table. He stood, pushing his chair back. "Let's go get your friends from Zeus's clutches."

We walked out into the main corridor. I was beyond ready to go. I was still dressed in my combat gear and had a dagger strapped on each leg. Hades had several knives hidden under his jacket, and one strapped to his ankle. He also carried his cane, which I found amusing.

"Why are you taking that? We're not going to a fancy dinner party."

Holding it up in his right hand, he ran his left along it, and the ends elongated until it was no longer a cane but a bo staff with sharp silver-tipped ends. His eyebrow arched sardonically as he spun the staff with his hand then did complicated overhead spins. He was just showing off to prove a point—that he may look like a gentleman all dressed up for a ball, but he was in fact a lethal weapon. And a sexy one at that.

Done showing off, he tapped the staff on the floor, and it shrunk back into the cane. "Satisfied?"

I grinned. "Yes, very."

"Good." He raised his left hand and instantly the shadows swooped across the room and enveloped us in a black cocoon. We took a few steps forward in the pitch then walked out onto one of the stone bridges in the forge.

I frowned. "What are we doing here?"

"Forming one of those alliances that affront you."

"I didn't say alliances are bad, just that you tend to make and break them rather quickly."

"What in the hell are you doing here?!" Hephaistos stomped toward us, a big hammer in his hand and a deep scowl on his haggard face.

"Access to the prisons," Hades said.

"No. Not going to happen." He pointed at me. "I told you that I wasn't getting involved."

"Sides have been drawn, Heph," Hades said. "You need to pick one."

He kept twirling the hammer in his hand. For a brief moment I thought he was going to use it on Hades or me.

"Aphrodite and Ares and Zeus are planning something awful," I said.

"They're always planning something awful."

"Your wife is a horrible person and basically wants to kill me," I said.

He sniffed. "You don't think I don't know that. Who do you think was behind *your* birthday shadowbox going missing? She convinced the Demos's to intercept it before it could ever reach you. She promised them riches beyond the imagination, which they received."

I gaped at him. I'd always wondered why I never received a shadowbox on my eighteenth birthday. I had always found it strange, and when I'd asked Sophie about it she'd been confused about it too. The Demos's though, never batted an eye over it. And why would they, when the Gods made them wealthy.

"Then do something about all of it, man. For over a thousand years, she's played you for a fool. Grow a backbone. Join us and get back at her." Hades smiled. "I promise, you will have a chance to go head to head with Ares. Prove once and for all who's the better man."

"Spoiler alert. It's you!" I said, hoping to alleviate a bit of the tension building.

Hephaistos glowered at me and grunted. Then he stormed toward the wall where he'd shown us the door to the prison earlier, lifted his hammer and smashed it apart. The stone fell away in broken chunks to reveal the tunnel Lucian and I had gone down.

"I guess he's picked a side," Hades said with a chuckle.

Kicking away the bits of stone, we entered the dug-out tunnel. At the end, we turned right and ran abruptly into another wall where the door should have been.

"The door's gone."

Hephaistos ran his hand along the wall. "After you and Lucian came through here and wrecked the door, although I told you how to open it, I was tasked to build another wall." He seemed to have found a good spot because he backed up and lifted his hammer. "Good thing I know how to destroy them as well." He swung his hammer and broke a huge hole in the stone, big enough for us to step through.

I ran ahead of Hades and Hephaistos, anxious to find Lucian, Georgina, and Jasmine. When I came to the first cell, I wrapped my hands around the metal bars and peered into the dank and dark cage. At first, I thought it was empty, but then I spied a lump on the ground in the murky corner move slightly.

"Jasmine?"

I heard a groan.

"Jasmine? It's Mel. I'm going to get you out." I rattled the metal crossbar on the door. I had tried to melt it before and it hadn't worked, so maybe just breaking it down would work.

Hades and Hephaistos joined me at the cell. "What are you doing?" Hades asked.

"Trying to break it down."

He nudged me over and put his hands around the metal. "Together." His brow furrowed as he pushed power into his hands. Soon I could see a red glow. I added my hands to the same metal bar and concentrated on creating heat. Hephaistos got in line beside me and did the same.

At first, I didn't think it was going to work, but then the metal started to glow orange, then red. Drips of iron splattered on the ground as we melted the bars of the cage. When enough had melted, Hades and Hephaistos pried the door apart, and I ran inside to crouch next to Jasmine.

"Jas?" I stroked a hand over her head.

Slowly, she raised her head to look at me. Her face was sunk in, she looked skeletal. Her usual silky dark curls were in knots on top of her head. Her lips were cracked, flaking off as she tried to speak. Angry tears welled in my eyes, as I hooked an arm around her and pulled her to her feet. She limped against me, as I walked her out of the cell.

As a group we moved down to the next cell, which turned out to be empty, then curved around the corner and stopped when we spotted Demeter at the bars of another cell. Surprised, she whipped around, her hand going to the handle of what looked like a sickle hanging from her belt.

She frowned as she looked at me, then Hephaistos. Her frown turned into a deep scowl when her gaze locked onto Hades. "What are you doing here?"

"We could ask you the same thing," Hades said as his hand went to his jacket. I imagined he was going for one of his daggers to throw at her.

I stepped ahead, getting in between them. "We've come to rescue my friends."

"I've come for the same reason." She turned back to the cell. "Gina's in here." When we approached, she glanced at Hephaistos. "I'm surprised to see you here. You're not one to get involved."

He just grunted at her. "Neither are you."

"I never really had a reason to until now." Her gaze fixed on me for a moment, then she turned back to the cell.

I propped Jasmine up against the wall, then joined Demeter at the metal bars. Georgina got to her feet and shuffled toward us. Her face was cut up and bruised, and one eye was nearly swollen shut. It looked like someone had beat on her for hours.

I reached through the bars and grabbed her hand. "Oh, hon. I'm going to kill whoever did this to you."

She nodded. "Okay."

I nudged Demeter aside. "We can melt the bars."

But she held firm. "That'll take too long." She knelt in front of the bars, nodding to Georgina to do the same. She did. Together, they placed their hands flat on the ground. Within seconds, the floor beneath their feet began to shake. Then the earth fell away from the bars, and Demeter stood and was able to pull the whole metal lattice work out of the floor. Georgina walked out of the cell.

I hugged her. "I'm sorry I left you."

"It's okay. I'm pretty sure you didn't have a choice." Her gaze flitted over to Hades, and she gave him a lethal look.

He had the decency to look abashed and didn't crack a sarcastic comeback.

"Where's Lucian?"

"I think he's three cells down." She pointed to the right.

"Do you know where Dionysus is?" Demeter asked Georgina.

She shook her head.

"After we get the boy, we will look for him," Hephaistos said, then glared at Hades.

He rolled his eyes. "Yes, fine, we'll rescue poor Dion. I can just imagine what my brother has done to him."

As a group, we moved down to the next cell, then the next, then to Lucian's. He was already waiting at the bars. He must've heard us coming. I imagined everyone could hear us coming, and it wouldn't be long before a deluge of Trojan soldiers in red kilts and funny metal helmets came after us.

"Blue!" Lucian reached a hand through the bars. I gripped it hard in mine.

I took him in. He looked weak and broken down. There were scorch marks along the shoulders of his shirt. I immediately felt rage. I shook with it. "What did he do to you?"

"It's okay. I'll live. But hurry. I know they were planning to kill me sometime soon."

Demeter and Georgina stepped up to the bars. "Move. We'll get him out." They crouched and put their hands on the ground. A minute later, Hephaistos lifted the door and Lucian stumbled out into my arms.

He cupped my head and kissed me. It was a good kiss, a strong one. When we broke apart, I shyly glanced at Hades. He wasn't looking at us but tapping his cane on the ground.

"We need to leave before we're ambushed by guards," he said.

"Can you shadow us out of here?" I asked him.

He shook his head. "No. We'll have to go back the way we came."

"What about Dionysus?" Demeter asked.

Hades sighed then shook his head. "Hey, Dion! You here?" His shouts echoed down the stone corridor.

I glanced at him. "So much for discretion."

"We were noticed the moment we came through that wall."

Then a faint voice came back. "Get me the hell out of here. I need a Gods damn drink!"

Hades and Demeter chuckled. Hades gestured toward the way we came. "He must be down the other corridor."

As one group, we turned to go back toward the hole in the wall. But as we rounded the corner, we were met by a set of guards armed with spears and swords. And Ares standing at the front. "Well, if this isn't convenient. All the rebels in one spot. Lambs to the slaughter. Let's start with little girl blue."

With a smile that sent a shudder down my spine, he drew his sword and charged toward me.

CHAPTER NINETEEN

MELANY

*B*efore I could react, Hades jumped in front of me, his hands moving in circles to form a shield out of the shadows. Hephaistos also moved; his hammer raised. Beside him, Demeter pulled out her sickle and was already swinging it by the time Ares's sword arched toward me.

Everything seemed to happen at once.

Ares's blade sunk into the shadow shield, as he ducked under Hephaistos's hammer and kicked Demeter in the stomach. She went sailing backward and hit the wall while Hades pushed me to the side. Hephaistos spun around and swung his hammer again. This time the anvil met Ares's sword. A vibrating clang echoed through the corridor, setting my teeth on edge.

"Go!" Hephaistos said. "Get out of here! I'll deal with Ares!"

Hades led the charge toward the Trojan guards. He protracted his cane into a Bo staff, tossed it over to me, as he reached under his jacket for a couple of knives. He fired them at the guards, hitting one in the side of the neck, and another in the leg. The shock of seeing the blood and pain nearly stunned me into inaction. I'd never been in a real battle before, not against other people, but I knew it was us or them. Taking two of them out made a small hole in their line for the rest of us to go through.

I made a run for it with Lucian at my side. Hades scooped up the fallen guard's spear and tossed it to Lucian. He caught it and then used it against another guard as he advanced on us. I knocked another guard in the side with the staff, then spun it and hit him in the face.

Behind us, Georgina carried Jasmine through the line. Demeter brought up the rear. A guard charged at her, and she swung her sickle in a figure eight. The blade caught the guard in the arm and nearly severed it. Blood gushed over the floor. The sight made my stomach roil, and by the horrified look on Demeter's face, I'd guess her guts were churning as well at the carnage she created.

As we took out six of the guards, I could hear the metal clanging and grunts of effort as Hephaistos and Ares clashed. When I looked that way, I saw Ares slice the blacksmith God across the chest. Blood flowed down from his wound, staining his shirt and pants red, but it didn't slow him down and he mounted another attack. Ares blocked him and spun around. It almost looked like he was playing around.

"Gods, you're an ugly bastard," Ares taunted. "I'm surprised Aphrodite never slayed you in your sleep. I even begged her to a few times over the past millennia."

"Maybe because she was too busy in my bed to even think about it."

Good one, Hephaistos!

Yelling, Ares ran at Hephaistos, his sword overhead.

I never saw the outcome as I was pushed through the line of guards and ushered along the corridor. Once we were past the guards, most of them were injured, one or two dead I was sure, on the ground, Demeter stopped in the middle of the corridor.

"Gina. Stand with me."

Lucian took Jasmine from Georgina, then she rushed to stand next to her Goddess patron. They crouched together and put their hands flat onto the ground. Seconds later the ground began to tremble. Then, an explosive crack reverberated all around as a fissure five feet across erupted along the ground, effectively separating us from the guards.

And from Hephaistos, I sadly thought.

Hades led us forward again, Demeter bringing up the rear. When we reached the hole in the wall that led back to the forge, Demeter gestured to the other corridor branching off to the right.

"I'm going to get Dionysus."

"Be quick," Hades said. "Once we're in the forge, I can transport us to safety through the shadows. But

I won't wait long. Zeus will send more soldiers. And eventually others like Apollo and Athena and Artemis. We won't stand a chance against them."

She nodded and ran down the passageway.

The rest of us stepped through the hole in the wall, down the tunnel, and out into the forge. Lucian gently set Jasmine onto the ground so she could rest. While we waited for Demeter's return, I crouched next to Jasmine and checked her injuries.

In the flicking orange light of the forge, I spied several holes in my friend's neck. I counted nine in a circle. "What did they do to you?"

She swallowed audibly before she spoke and licked her cracked lips. "Zeus asked me about you and Hades, and what you were planning. I didn't tell him anything, but then…" She shuddered, and I rubbed her back. "…the door opened, and a pretty woman walked in. I didn't recognize her from the academy. He said her name was Lamia. At first, I thought she might be like Apollo and be able to read my mind or something, but when she opened her mouth there were these needle-like teeth inside, and she bit me on the neck and all I could feel was pain. It felt like I was dying, like my life was being sucked out. I told him whatever he wanted to know." She started to cry.

I hugged her to me and rocked her in my arms. Zeus was going to pay for what he'd done. I didn't know how I was going to do it, but I vowed I would stop him from hurting anyone else.

Persephone's voice echoed in my mind… *You're the one to end the war.*

I had no idea what she meant by that, but if it was an opportunity to get back at Zeus, Aphrodite, and Ares, I'd take it.

Hades paced in front of us. "It's foolish to stay here. We should be going *now*."

Before I could respond, Demeter, holding Dionysus up, emerged from the tunnel. Out of breath, she set him down for a moment.

Hades gazed down at the poison God. "So, what did Zeus do to you?"

In answer, Dionysus bent his head and vomited wine all over the ground. The stink of it nearly had me retching. I put my hand over my nose and mouth to stop from breathing in the stench.

"Ah, the old gluttony curse." Hades shook his head. "Zeus is getting boring in his tragically old age."

Dionysus wiped his mouth. "It's a lot better in than out, that's for sure." Then he gagged again.

"Okay, time to go." Hades started pulling the shadows around us.

I jumped to my feet. "We're waiting for Hephaistos."

"There's no point. I assure you Ares ripped him apart."

"How can you be such a jerk about it? Isn't he your friend?"

"It's complicated, Melany. Aren't you the one who just gave me a lecture about the complexity and absurdity of God politics?"

"We're waiting. Five more minutes. Please?" I hated begging, but I would. Hephaistos had been an ally to me from the moment I'd arrived at the academy, and I hadn't realized how much of one until that moment. I wouldn't abandon him.

He sighed. "Fine." He turned on his heel and continued pacing around the forge and watching the tunnel.

Lucian came to my side and put his arm around me. "I knew you'd come for me."

I leaned into him and sighed. "I wished it had been sooner."

He folded me into his arms and kissed the side of my head. I relaxed into him, enjoying the way he made me feel. I reveled in it, even if it was just for a moment. For that brief time, I could imagine we were just two people who'd found each other and fallen in love. That it wasn't any more complicated than that.

Then the sound of a barrage of footsteps coming from the main entrance of the forge smacked me back into reality.

Hades's head whipped around toward the main doors. "That's our cue to leave." He raised his arms, splaying his fingers wide, and drew the darkness to him. Like a dog to its master, the shadows scudded across the room toward Hades until the forge started to fade to black.

"I'm here, you impatient ass."

Hephaistos lumbered out of the tunnel, his face bloody and bruised, his right arm hanging uselessly at his side. The gash across his chest still oozed with blood and gore. I was surprised he was still able to stand let alone walk. But walk he did, right over to Hades, scowling up a storm as usual.

I grinned.

"Now, that we're all here. One big happy family." Hades waved his arms around, swirling the shadows into a huge swirling tornado. They whipped arounds us, howling like storm clouds. The noise reached a crescendo that nearly popped my ear drums, then it all just stopped, and you could hear a pin drop. The shadows dissipated and we were now in the middle of the corridor in Hades's Hall.

"Welcome home, my Lord." Charon, dressed in his usual black flowing robe that seemed to float at his feet, bowed to Hades.

"Thank you, Charon. Make sure all the portals are slammed shut and put security measures at the River Styx."

"At once, my Lord."

Lucian, Georgina, and Jasmine were all startled to see the skeletal figure as he turned to me. He inclined his head. "Good to see you, my Lady."

"You too, buddy. Oh, Charon this is Lucian, Georgina, and Jasmine. My friends."

"Any friend of Lady Melany's is a friend of mine," Charon rasped.

I looked at our motley group and realized everyone was injured and needed tending. They also were going to need somewhere to sleep. "Do we have room for everyone?" I asked Hades.

"We'll make room." He waved a hand at the far wall, and then it moved as if on a roller. Where there had once been six rooms branching off the hall, there were now ten. He pointed to the new one just past the library. "That's the infirmary. You'll find everything you need to patch yourselves up. Charon will help you. He is an accomplished healer."

The butler inclined his head. "You humble me, my Lord. It's only because you taught me so well."

"That's true."

Dionysus threw up again, making a huge mess on the dark purple rug that rolled down the middle of the corridor. Hades grimaced. "I guess I'll have to take care of your curse for you." He gestured to Demeter. "Drag his ass into the infirmary."

In the infirmary, everyone got doctored up. Charon stitched up Hephaistos, ointments were applied to small cuts and bruises and burns in Lucian's case, and Hades removed the curse on Dionysus and he was sleeping off what was now just a horrific hangover. I helped Georgina put Jasmine to bed in one of the new rooms. She climbed in beside her. Then I sat with Lucian in his room sharing a large pepperoni pizza that Charon had specially made for me. He was the weird skeletal uncle I never knew I needed in my life. When I said as much to Lucian, he laughed so hard he nearly fell off the bed we were sitting on.

After we stopped laughing, Lucian told me everything he learned from Zeus and the other Gods. War was coming. And soon. We needed to be ready for it.

"Do you think Ren and the others are safe in the academy?" Lucian asked as we finished the last two pieces of pizza.

"I don't know. If the Titans are released, then Zeus will call the cadets to arms to fight against them under the pretense of saving the world. Ren and

Diego and Mia and Rosie and Marek, and all the others will be tasked to join the fight. They'll have no choice and won't know any better."

"And what are we going to do? How can we fight against the Gods, save our friends, and keep the Titans from killing thousands? We'll be caught in the middle."

"I don't know, but we're going to have to try."

There was a knock on the doorway of the open door. We looked over to see Hades walk in. I was surprised he'd bothered to knock.

"I've come to check if either of you needed anything."

I made a face, knowing he didn't mean it and was just intruding to be a jerk. "That's kind of you."

"I know."

I shook my head at him.

Lucian rolled off the bed and approached Hades. "I wanted to thank you for coming to get me despite our differences. I appreciate it." He stuck out his hand.

I was surprised when Hades took his hand to shake but wasn't at all shocked when he tugged Lucian nice and close. "I did it for Melany." He let Lucian's hand go. "Don't get too comfortable, boy. You won't be here long." Then he strolled back to the door. He waved a hand. "Night. Better get some sleep because we have a war to get to in the morning."

I got off the bed and hugged Lucian. "I'm sorry about him."

"Don't be. It's not your fault he's an asshole."

I laughed.

"Will you stay with me?" he asked.

I nodded and we climbed onto the bed. I snuggled my back into his chest, and he wrapped his arm over me. His fingers stroked my arm, then up to my hair. I sighed as he nestled his face into my hair and kissed my head.

"I don't know what's going to happen tomorrow, but I want you to know that I love you, Blue. Always will."

I swallowed down the well of emotions that threatened to spill out. "I love you, too." And I did with all my heart. But a cold shiver of dread washed over me, as I knew I was going to have to do something that could destroy that love. But if we wanted to win the war, it was going to have to be done.

CHAPTER TWENTY

MELANY

*A*s usual, I couldn't sleep. Especially not with a million thoughts swirling in my head. So, when I knew Lucian was deep in dreamland—he mumbled a little, it was so cute—I crawled out of the bed, careful not to wake him, then returned to my room. I could pace in there without disturbing anyone.

I walked around the room going over everything that I'd learned in the past couple of days. I wasn't sure it was enough to win. There had to be something I was missing. I went over Persephone's words again and again.

You are the key. You will be the one to end the battle. You have control of all five elements, but they must be freely given to you.

Given to me by who? I shook my head. I just didn't understand.

Finally, tired out, I sat in the chair near the fireplace. I grabbed the book I'd taken from the library and opened it. Maybe it would give me some insight into the academy and the Gods, and a way to beat them.

I flipped through the pages reading more about how the academy was meant for higher learning of both demigod and mortal and not a place for war. For thousands of years, it was a place of enlightenment and fellowship. But when the Gods fell out of favor with the mortals and their temples were replaced with other places of worship, they started to lose their powers and that made them angry.

For another thousand years, the Gods tried to integrate themselves into the academy, but Prometheus and the other Titans didn't trust them. And after reading some of the things the Gods had done over the years, I didn't blame them. When I was younger, I'd read some fables about the Gods, stories with not so happy endings, but the reality was way worse.

Zeus was the worst of them with his punishments on mortals he thought had insulted or wronged him in some way. One story told of a mortal named Ixion, who had the unfortunate favor of being caught hitting on Hera. So, Zeus basically chained him to a burning wheel that would spin forever. I shuddered thinking about it. The cruelty of it.

It looked like there were some decades of the academy's past missing, but then it seemed to jump back into the limelight right after the earthquakes of 1906 and 1908, caused by an escaped Titan. This gave rise to the New Dawn, and new temples for the Gods were built and mortals went back to worshipping them. Now, I wondered if the Titan had escaped on its own or if it had been released on purpose. Zeus had locked all the Titans and other monstrous beasts away in Tartarus. It was convenient to have all of one's foes locked away forever.

I loathed to think about what happened to Prometheus and Hesiod after Zeus and the others had taken over the academy. Although Hesiod would've been long dead by that time since he was mortal.

I shut the book. It was obvious some of the Gods weren't happy with what had happened. Hades namely. Obviously, Demeter and Dionysus and Hephaistos had their concerns. I wondered who else in the pantheon wasn't happy with Zeus's leadership and the direction he'd taken the academy. Could there be more allies out there?

Zeus had Aphrodite and Ares for sure. Hera most likely, since she was his wife, and big brother Poseidon I imagined. He most definitely hadn't been happy to see Hades show up. Jasmine said Apollo had been the one to pull her memories, and Athena had arrested us in the library. But what of Artemis and Hermes? Were they on Zeus's side?

I also thought about Heracles and Erebus. Heracles had always been kind to me, and once told me I had friends in the academy. Could he be persuaded to join our side? I also thought about Medusa. She wasn't necessarily a friend to me, but the last time I saw her in the maze, there seemed to be something there between us. And if the stories were true, she'd have a grudge against Athena, since the Goddess was the one who supposedly cursed Medusa with snakes for hair. Would it be enough to lure her over to our side?

As it was, I wasn't sure if we had enough power to overthrow Zeus.

He had the majority of the fighting Gods, along with the best demigod champions like Achilles, Bellerophon, Antiope, Helen of Troy, Enyo, and Phobos and Deimos. Mind you, we had the Furies; the three sisters were the equivalent of nine skilled fighters. And Hades, of course. I imagined I hadn't seen even a third of his powers.

But would it be enough? Would I be enough? How could I be the one to end the battle? I was one woman with limited powers. I wasn't a God. I wasn't even a demigod.

Before I could despair even further, a loud bang echoed out from the main corridor. I left my room to see what it was. Hades had also come out of his room. Charon floated out from the library.

The banging came again.

"Is someone knocking on the doors?" I asked, surprised. "Is it Cerberus?"

Hades shook his head. "No, he's in his kennel happily chewing on a couple of chimera bones."

"I will see who it is, my Lord." Charon swooped toward the doors, then vanished. I hadn't realized he could move through doors and walls. He returned a few seconds later. "Hecate wishes entrance. She and her companions had to vacate their oak tree as Ares and his cohorts were cutting them down looking for the gateway to the underworld."

By now, others had come out of their rooms. Lucian and Georgina came up behind me. Demeter leaned up against the doorway to her room.

"Shall I let her in?" Charon asked.

Hades nodded. "We need all the power we can get and Hecate is very powerful."

Charon waved his hand at the tall dark stone doors, and they slowly opened. A whoosh of wind from the cave beyond came in and blew my hair back, as a tall, willowy woman with long black hair walked in, followed by three small, bald women who seemed to glow. I could see a ball of light literally floating inside their bodies through their translucent skin.

"Thank you for the sanctuary, Hades, my darling."

They kissed each other's cheeks.

"You are always welcome, Hecate. I wish it was under different circumstances."

"As do I." Hecate's gaze flittered from one person to another, then fixed on Lucian. She smiled. "Lucian. How lovely to see you again."

I glanced at him, as his cheeks flushed red. Hmm, obviously there was a story there that I wanted to hear.

"You too." He nodded, then ducked his head.

"So it seems you are gathering an army." Hecate glided over to Demeter and the two Goddesses embraced and kissed. It looked like a chaste kiss, but I sensed it was from years of intimacy. That took me by surprise.

"Zeus has outstayed his position at the academy," Hades said.

"I don't normally bother myself with the battles of others. One is usually the same as the other, but in this I will fight by your side. I was never okay with how Zeus manipulated Persephone."

Hades's face changed as she talked about her.

"It didn't sit right with me one bit."

He inclined his head to her. "I appreciate that."

"Is Dion here?" she asked.

Demeter nodded. "He's in his room, recovering. I'll take you to see him."

Together, arms hooked, the two women strolled down the corridor, the three glowing women following close behind.

"Who else do you think would fight on our side?" I asked Hades. "Erebus? Heracles?"

"Erebus isn't much of a fighter, I'm afraid. He'll stay out of the fray, I'm sure. As for Heracles…he's always struck me as a dutiful and loyal man. He'll fight for the academy, however that plays out."

I sighed, frustration starting to settle in. I knew the others weren't quite ready to go. Jasmine had yet to wake up, but I was eager for a fight. Hades must've sensed my anxiousness because he moved in closer to me and set a hand on my shoulder. His touch energized me, as it so often did.

"I'll go do some recon topside. See if I can find out where and when."

I almost asked him if I could join him, but I knew I needed to stay here with my friends and allies to prepare.

"While I'm gone, you make sure Allecto is doing her job. She's supposed to be actively acquiring our weapons and armor."

I snorted. "As if she's going to listen to me."

"I know, but at least it will keep you busy." He gave me one of his rare sly grins that made my insides quiver, then he vanished in a haze of black mist.

"Where's he going?" Lucian asked.

"I want to say he's going to check things out, but I have a feeling he's going to go pick a fight."

Lucian, Georgina, and I went to go check on Jasmine. Out of the three of them, she seemed to have suffered the hardest at the hands of the Gods. Thankfully, she was sitting up in bed, when we came into her room.

"Hey, how are you feeling?" I asked.

"Better. Skeletor gave me some powerful tea."

I chuckled at her use of a name from Saturday morning cartoons for Charon.

She scanned the room, which looked similar to mine. "I can't believe this is where you've been for the past six months. It's like a goth five-star hotel."

"You should see the training room."

"Okay," she said with a wry smile.

Fifteen minutes later, I led them into the dojo. Their collective eyes bugged out as they took in the wooden dummies, and ropes and obstacle course. They bugged out even more when Allecto, Tisiphone, and Megaera dropped down from the rafters where they had been perching.

"Are these guests or did you bring us lunch?" Tisiphone flapped her bat wings and licked her black lips while gawking at Lucian.

He started to back up, but Tisiphone slapped him on the shoulder. "Just kidding. We already ate."

Jasmine immediately went to the weapons wall and pulled things down to test them out. Georgina went with her.

"Where's Hades?" Allecto grunted.

"He went to do some recon——"

I was interrupted as Hades walked out from a deep shadow in the corner, a deep scowl on his face. "It has begun."

All of us gathered in the training room to arm ourselves. As we picked weapons and armor, Hades told us of what he'd seen.

"Zeus has released the cyclopes onto Pecunia."

Hephaistos perked up. "Cyclopes? Who?"

"Arges, Brontes, and Steropes."

The forge God shook his head. "Damn it. I can't believe it."

"Remember," I said, "they aren't acting on their own. They're being controlled. I guarantee there is a golden rope around each of their necks. Cut off the cord and that should eliminate the threat."

Demeter sniffed. "Yeah, and getting close enough is going to be painful."

Hephaistos hefted his hammer. "Do what you will to Zeus and Aphrodite and Ares, but no one dare kill my friends."

"Our goal isn't to kill anyone," I said. "It's to release the monsters from Aphrodite's influence and to stop Zeus."

"Oh, is that all?" Tisiphone snorted. "Easier to just kill everyone."

"I agree," Megaera said, slapping her sister on her back.

I was about to argue again, but Hades spoke up to my surprise.

"Melany said there will be no killing. The cadets who fight for Zeus are innocent. They don't know any better. It's the Gods who fight with Zeus who will be the problem. Aphrodite and Ares are for sure complicit. The others, I'm not sure."

"So, basically," Dionysus said from his spot on the floor where he sat cross-legged and drinking, wine most likely, from a canteen. "We're going to try and make an omelet without breaking any eggs." He tipped the canteen to his lips again. "Perfect. I've already lived too many years already."

CHAPTER TWENTY-ONE

MELANY

*A*s we waited in the corridor to coordinate our arrival in Pecunia, nerves zipped through me. I had no idea how we were going to pull this off. One little thing could go wrong, and that could set off a domino effect and ruin everything and get all of us killed. Well, not the Gods. They'd survive. But the rest of us wouldn't.

I looked at Lucian who stood beside me, shuffling from one foot to the other. He looked like a golden lion, fierce and proud. He carried a sword at his waist and wore black armor, as Hades didn't have anything in any other color. Lucian made a comment about that while getting outfitted and it had made me laugh.

Demeter and Dionysus had given the four of us some energy balls, like the one Georgina had made me last year when Ren, Jasmine, and I had snuck out of the academy to find out about the earthquakes that had rocked our hometowns. I remembered it smelling like old cheese and tasting just as bad. But it had been effective and gave us super energy.

Charon had also given me a canvas bag of healing supplies, like bandages and alcohol swabs, and special healing potions and ointments. I handed it over to Georgina, as out of the four of us, she would most likely be on the ground where her power lay. She wasn't as good as flyer as the rest of us, so she needed to be where she'd be most effective.

Lucian turned his head and met my gaze. He smiled, and I felt like I wanted to cry. What if this was it? What if this was the last moment we were going to have together? I cupped him around the neck, brought his head down and kissed him long and hard until we were both breathless. After, he rested his head against my mine.

I could tell he wanted to say many things to me, but I couldn't bear to hear them. So when he opened his mouth, I put my fingers to his lips and shook my head. "Tell me later."

When I pulled back, I caught Hades watching us. I couldn't read the look on his face, and that broke my heart a little.

"I'm unsure if I can take all of us through the shadows at once," he said.

Hephaistos made a face. "I'll make my own entrance." A wall of fire erupted in front of him.

When Hades taught me how to use shadows to travel, he told me that there were other types of portals that the Gods used. Seeing it in front of me was startling and awesome. Hephaistos just went up to a hundred on my wicked cool scale.

"As will we," Demeter said, her hand on Dionysus's shoulder.

Hades nodded. "Okay, that should work—"

He was interrupted by loud scratching and an ear-piercing whine at the big doors. With a wave of his hands, the doors opened, and Cerberus lumbered in.

I laughed at the hang dog expression on all three of his faces. "Did you want to come, boy?"

His tail wagged.

I glanced at Hades. "Do you want to take him, or can I?"

He gestured to the hound. "Be my guest. I think he likes you better anyway."

I nodded to Lucian, Georgina, and Jasmine. "You guys want a ride?"

After we climbed on, securing ourselves, Hades waved his hands around drawing the darkness to him. "Be ready. We're going to be walking into a war zone." The shadows enveloped us, plunging the world into the black.

I gripped Jasmine and Georgina's hands. "I love you guys."

"We love you, too," Georgina said.

Then we bounded out into daylight. The sounds and smells of blood and death assaulted my senses. Screams from townspeople blasted my ears as Cerberus growled from all three heads. I patted him on the side so he wouldn't react to the chaos all around. And chaos it was.

We'd come out onto one of the busiest streets in Pecunia, the one that cut through downtown. Buildings had been destroyed, powerlines lay on the street, and bodies of men, women, and children littered the parking lot in front of the shopping mall. They weren't all dead, some of them moved obviously grievously injured, but they were in immediate danger as one of the thirty-foot tall cyclopes hefted a huge chunk of cement wall over his head and was about to toss it.

The giant's limbs were stubby compared to the rest of him, and his skull was misshaped like an egg with tufts of dark hair right on top and around his chin, which I guessed was some sort of beard. He had one large multicolored eye right in the middle of his wrinkled forehead, and it was focused on the injured townsfolk on the ground.

I saw three, winged academy cadets flying his way, all armed, all ready to take the cyclops out. Unfurling my wings, I lifted into the air. I pointed to the injured people and shouted to my friends.

"Help them!"

Then like a shot, I zipped through the air toward the cyclops. The Furies were right on my tail. Before I reached the cyclops, a circle of fire erupted on the ground below me, and Hephaistos emerged from the flames, his big hammer in his hands. His eyes bugged out when he spotted the cyclops about to throw the piece of wall.

"Brontes!" he shouted. "Stop!"

Either the cyclops didn't hear him or didn't care, and he tossed the chunk of cement.

I had to veer to the right to miss being hit. Horrified, I watched as the wall segment smashed onto the ground. Luckily, I saw that Lucian, Georgina, and Jasmine had managed to get a bunch of the people onto Cerberus's back and out of the way.

I flew toward Brontes again. One of the cadets fired a couple of arrows at him. One struck him in the cheek and the other in the shoulder. Neither even caused him to react. I imagined it was like getting a tiny splinter in your finger. A bit bothersome but nothing to worry about.

As the archer lifted her bow again, I swooped toward her and saw that it was Mia under the armor. She lowered her weapon when she saw me.

"Melany!"

We clasped arms in greeting.

"Don't shoot him."

She frowned. "What? Why?"

"See that gold cord around his neck?" I pointed to it as the cyclops turned to smash another building. "He's being controlled. Someone released him from Tartarus. He didn't escape like you've been told."

I could see that she wanted to believe me, because we were friends, but it would mean going against everything she'd been told by the Gods.

"Who released him?"

"Zeus." Or Aphrodite, but I didn't have time to explain that. In my mind, Zeus was responsible for it all.

Her frown got deeper, and she shook her head. "Are you sure? I don't know…"

"It's true. This all a power play. Help me cut the

cord off and you'll see. If I'm wrong, I'll help you kill him."

"Is Jasmine with you?"

I nodded and pointed to where Jasmine and the others were helping the injured. "I broke her out of the cells. Zeus tortured her for information against me."

Mia still hesitated, and I didn't have time to coddle her about it. "Go. Talk to Jasmine. I'll try and break the cord on my own." I didn't give her a chance to respond and flew away, trying to figure out how to get close enough to Brontes to cut the rope.

I didn't recognize the other two cadets trying to attack the cyclops. One of them, a girl with black hair, shot toward him, swinging her sword. She was kidding herself if she thought it was going to do any good. It would be like a paper cut to the giant. Sword first, she dove toward his chest, but Brontes swiped at her like hitting a bug, and she dropped toward the ground unconscious. I dove after her, hoping I could get to her before she hit, but I didn't make it in time, and she landed in a heap on the street. By the sickening angle her landed in, I suspected she broke both legs and an arm.

"Ow, that's got to hurt," Tisiphone said.

Megaera gave a little laugh.

"Try and stop the others from shooting at him," I said to the sisters. "But don't kill anyone."

They flew off to intercept the other flying cadets.

While I flew up toward Brontes's head again, I spotted Hephaistos down below at the cyclops's feet, swinging his hammer and yelling at him to get his attention.

"Brontes! This isn't you! Stop what you're doing!" His hammer met Brontes's big toe, smashing it flat. That most definitely got the cyclops's attention and he focused his one big eye on Hephaistos and roared.

This gave me a chance to fly around behind the giant and grab hold of the golden rope around his neck. As I neared, someone else flew up beside me. I glanced over to see Lucian as my wingman. Together, we were able to fly close enough to his neck to grab the cord. The second I had a handhold, I unsheathed one of my daggers and started to saw at the gold threads.

I cut through a few threads, while Lucian did the same. Gearing up to slice through some more, an arrow zipped by my face and sunk into the back of the cyclops's neck with a sickening thunk. Another arrow whizzed by me, narrowly missing my leg. If I hadn't have moved, it would've embedded itself in my thigh. I glanced down to see Ares nocking another arrow in his bow.

I glanced at Lucian to make sure he saw what I did. He did and pushed off Brontes's neck to shoot down toward Ares.

"Don't! He's too strong!" But he didn't stop.

I had to get this rope off now more than ever. I grabbed hold of the cord again and started to saw at the threads. Brontes shook his head, and I nearly fell off. Then his big hand came up to his neck and swiped at me. I was able to let go of the cord, hover in the air and avoid his massive hand. Lucian returned to my side.

"What happened?" I asked.

He pointed down. "Hephaistos has it handled."

I glanced down to see the forge God swinging his big hammer at Ares.

We went back to cutting the cord. I sliced though another few threads, and the rope was starting to fray. As we continued to cut, out of the corner of my eye I spotted two more cadets attacking the cyclops. One of them was Ren.

I waved at him and yelled. "Ren!!"

His head turned our way and he frowned, then his eyes widened when he realized who it was and what we were doing. He flew over to us.

"What happened to you guys? There was a rumor that you left the academy."

"No time to explain," I said. "But don't hurt the cyclops. Help us cut off the cord. He's being controlled."

Dawning showed on Ren's face when he realized what that meant. He was there at the Demos estate when I found the remnants of a golden rope near Sophie's body. He nodded and flew in closer, but shouts and screams and loud thuds drew our attention.

Another cyclops ran into view; I didn't know his name. He was followed by several cadets flying after him in the air, shooting arrows and throwing spears and more on the ground, lagging behind because of his immense strides forward. He charged into the downtown square, swinging his arms and smashing trees and another building. I hoped that the building had been evacuated.

"What do we do?" Lucian asked.

"Let's get this rope off. Maybe Brontes can talk his brother down." Another couple of cuts and we'd be through.

"I'll attempt to get the other rope off. I'll tell the others." Then he was off, flying toward the other cyclops.

Then the sound of something mechanical in the distance drew my attention. I turned to see a helicopter approaching the scene. The chuff of the whirring blades intensified as it drew closer. On the side of the helicopter door was stenciled, *Channel 9 News*.

"Shit. That's the last thing we need."

I was about to fly over to the helicopter and tell them to get away, but Brontes swung his big arm around and hit the machine. It lurched to the side and lost control. I shot toward it. Lucian flew in beside me, but it was doing down too fast. It was going to crash.

CHAPTER TWENTY-TWO

MELANY

*B*efore the helicopter hit the ground, something black zipped by underneath us and got under it. Emerging from a cluster of shadows, Hades caught the machine before it could smash into the ground. He set it down on the street in front of the shopping mall, as the pilot powered it off.

Lucian and I flew back to Brontes who was staggering around swinging at anything he could. Blood dripped from minor cuts to his arms and legs, and he still favored his broken toe courtesy of Hephaistos and his big hammer. We swooped up around him again, but he was moving around too much for us to get a proper hold. I had enough.

I unsheathed my sword, lifted it up and swung it down at the cyclops's neck. The blade sliced though the last remaining golden threads and the rope unwound from his big neck and fell to the ground. The second it was off him, Brontes stopped moving and looked around bewildered. His big brow furrowed. His eye focused on Hephaistos on the ground.

"Hephaistos?" he said, his voice like thunder. "What's going on?"

"You're okay, my friend. You were under a spell."

Brontes swung around to his brother, who was busy pulling large oak trees from the ground and using them to swing at the cadets flying around him in the air. He managed to hit a couple of them, knocking them to the ground. Unfortunately, I thought one of them was Rosie.

"Arges!" Brontes reached for his brother. "Stop what you are doing!"

But Arges wasn't listening.

I flew in front of Brontes's face to get his attention. "Tear off the collar around his neck! It's what's controlling him!"

At first, I didn't think he heard me, but then he grabbed his brother, pulled him into a headlock, and put his hand around Arges's neck. The other cyclops struggled, stomping his feet which made the ground shake. Then I saw Brontes break the golden rope and toss it to the side. He let go of Arges, who straightened and shook his head. He looked everywhere, taking in the destruction.

He rubbed at his malformed skull. "My head hurts."

Brontes squeezed his lumpy shoulder. "We were spelled, brother."

Arges then noticed all the broken bodies and demolished buildings. He shook his head, then he collapsed onto the ground. Giant tears rolled down his doughy cheeks. "Nooooo," he moaned.

All the cadets in the air fluttered around, then gently landed on the street in front of the ruined shopping mall. They all looked at each other in question. They were just as confused of what was going on as the cyclopes.

With Lucian, I went to hover above our fellow cadets and uninjured townspeople. I saw a reporter in the mix with a camera and she aimed it at me. "These cyclopes are not our enemies. They didn't escape Tartarus. They were released and were sent here to kill and destroy."

I saw faces turn to others, frowning, brows furrowing in confusion. Murmurs spread through the group.

"Who would do that?" Diego asked.

"Zeus released them. Just as he released others last year to cause the earthquakes in Pecunia and New Haven, and the chimera to burn down Victory Park."

"How?" came another voice.

"The golden ropes around their necks controlled their actions. Those ropes were weaved from golden threads belonging to Aphrodite. She's been working with Zeus and Ares."

The murmur grew louder, along with whispers of, "She's lying." And "He would never do that."

"She's not lying," Lucian said, his voice unwavering, commanding. I looked at him and saw the leader that he'd become. "Zeus has been lying to us for our whole lives. The academy was never supposed to be used for war. It used to be a place of learning and fellowship between demigod and mortal. He's subverted it for his own lust for power."

Georgina, Jasmine, and Mia joined the group but stood apart, just near Lucian and me. Ren and Marek had also arrived and moved over beside Jasmine. A few of the Gods also flew in on white wings. Artemis and Apollo. Hermes and Athena. I wondered if they showed up to take me out on Zeus's orders. If they were, they were taking their time about it and had stopped to listen to what I had to say first.

I could see the confusion on some of the cadets' faces. A few, like Diego, had moved over to stand beside Ren and the others, obviously declaring their decision to believe what Lucian and I were telling them. Apollo and Athena also looked uncertain of what to believe.

Near them, the ground started to vibrate. A hole formed and Demeter and Dionysus emerged. Demeter held another of the golden collars. The reporter's camera swung their way.

"We were able to stop Steropes before he could destroy the dock in Calla." She raised the rope. "We took this off him, a golden cord weaved from the threads of Aphrodite's robes. Everything Melany is saying to you is true. Zeus has lost his way."

"How do we stop him?" one of the cadets in the group asked.

"You can't." I looked up as Hades slowly

descended from the sky to hover next to me. "It's up to the Gods to fight."

Hermes shook his head, his hand going nervously to the bowtie around his neck. "He's too strong. And he has Aphrodite and Ares with him. I suspect Hera and Poseidon as well."

"It wouldn't be the first time we've fought each other," Hades said.

Suddenly, there were flashes of light zigzagging across the cloudless sky. The sizzle in the air lifted the hairs on my arms and on the back of my neck. I could smell the ozone in the air from the lightning. Then a colossal bolt struck the ground searing the grass and the last standing tree nearby, the crack of it reverberated off of every structure within a mile.

From within the flash of light, Zeus, Aphrodite, Ares, Hera, and Poseidon materialized.

Their appearance sent a wave of shock and awe through the crowd. I heard more than a few gasps coming from the townspeople.

"This is quite the little gathering," Zeus said, smiling.

I flew closer to him. I couldn't help myself. Fury rushed through me like wildfire. "We stopped the cyclopes from killing more people."

His grin grew brighter, but I didn't feel any warmth from it. "You're cleverer than I gave you credit, Melany Richmond. But this isn't where it stops. It's just getting started."

"It's over Zeus," Demeter said. "Why continue with the ruse?"

Hades swooped over to Zeus and landed right in

front of him. "Because he wants a war, don't you, big brother? War is a great motivator for worship. He wants the mortals to bring more offerings to his temple to pray to him to protect them from the monsters." He ran his hand over the lapel of Zeus's pristine white robe. "But what does one do when the monsters are in fact the Gods themselves?"

"You were always so dramatic, Hades." Zeus raised his hand and blasted Hades with a bolt of light. It sent the dark God flying twenty feet in the air. He landed with a heavy thunk on top of abandoned car in the shopping mall parking lot.

"Hades!" I flew over to him.

Cerberus bounded into the lot as well, concerned about his master.

Zeus chuckled. "She's just as brainwashed into loving you as your last one. What was her name? Persephone, wasn't it?"

I helped Hades to his feet. His shirt was burned away and the flesh beneath it was raw and singed like a burnt steak. Cerberus tried to lick him, but he pushed his big heads away. The hound turned around and growled at Zeus, his three sets of eyes glowing red.

Then he charged at the God.

Zeus flicked his wrist and sent a bolt of lightning shooting through the air. It pierced Cerberus's chest. The hound reared up, his paws clawing at the air, then he collapsed onto his side, shrieking in pain.

I ran to Cerberus, my heart in my throat. The stench of burned hair, flesh, and blood filled my nose. I put my hands on his middle head and petted him, as he labored for breath. I wasn't sure if he was going to survive, the wound in his chest looked dire.

Hades unfurled his huge black wings and lifted into the air. A dark mist grew around him. The higher he floated the more the shadows gathered until he was a giant dark bird of prey in the sky. I could feel his anger growing. It pulsed inside me just as it pulsed in him. His darkness was part of my soul.

Everyone grew silent, eyes wide, anticipating something horrific to happen. Even the other Gods looked stunned, their gazes going from Hades to Zeus and back again. The usually stoic and smug Aphrodite looked a bit unnerved. She took a few distancing steps away from Zeus. I wasn't sure if she felt fear, but if she did, I hoped it was running through her veins like ice water.

"You have wronged me for the last time, brother," Hades snarled.

"You know your Persephone begged me to let her say goodbye to you." He shook his head sadly. "Right before I squeezed the life out of her." He raised his hand, curling it into a claw, then quickly snapped it closed. He laughed. "I'd considered doing the same to Melany, but it would've been too quick." He reached inside his robe and pulled out a curved horn. "This way will be more satisfying." He put it to his lips, Demeter and Dionysus and Apollo and Athena all cried out and ran toward him, but they couldn't reach him before he blew into it.

The sound that emanated was deep and mournful and sent a shiver of dread down my spine.

"You doomed us all, you stupid fool!" Hades shouted.

I didn't know what he meant, or why the Gods were acting so strangely, but it soon became apparent why they were so frightened. The ground began to shake.

Lucian came to my side. "Is it an earthquake?"

I didn't know, but had a feeling it wasn't something as normal as that. Something caught my eye in the distance. Squinting, I peered at the small mountain range just on the outskirts of the town. Thousands of years ago one of them had been an active volcano, but it had been dormant for just as long. Horrified, I watched as the mountain cracked open and red hot lava spewed out.

The sound it made was terrifying, like thunder, but what was more frightening was the creature that emerged from the rift in the rocks.

I'd read about the Typhon in the storybooks meant to scare little children. But seeing it in reality was a million times worse. It was impossible to tell how tall it was from this far away, but I knew it was taller than the cyclopes we'd just fought. Parts of it looked humanoid, its arms and chest, but its head was that of a dragon, and then colossal black wings unfurled from behind its wide back. Wings flapped, and it lifted into the air to reveal a long serpent body and tail. Then it swooped toward us, each flap of its massive powerful wings creating gusts of wind. The closer it got the redder its eyes glowed.

I looked around for my friends. We had to get these people out of here. I flew over to Georgina,

Jasmine, and Mia. "We need to move these people out of here!"

"Can we move them through a portal?" Georgina asked.

Jasmine looked at me. "You're the only one I know who can move through shadows."

"I can do it." I turned to see Erebus approach us. "I'm not a fighter, but I can do this."

I nodded to him, then grabbed his arm before he could turn. "Could you take Cerberus with you, too? I don't know if he'll make it, but I can't bear it if—"

"I will." He rushed toward the crowd and started directing people toward the fallen hound.

When he was gone, a crowd gathered around me. Lucian, Jasmine, Georgina, Mia, Ren, Marek, Diego, Demeter, Dionysus, Hephaistos, the Furies, Hecate— all looked to me for a plan. Other cadets from the academy moved over, including Revana, and her hangers-on, Klara and Peyton. The Gods started to distance themselves from Zeus. Uncertainty was on all their faces.

Hades continued to hover nearby, his gaze on me.

"It must have a similar golden rope around its neck," I said. "That's the only way that Zeus can control it."

"How the hell are we supposed to get to it?" Mia asked. "It's impossible."

"We have to try," I said.

"We'll do it." Allecto puffed out her chest. "We don't have any fear." Her sisters nodded along with her.

I nodded to them. "Everyone else's job is to help

the Furies get to its neck by whatever means necessary. It's our only hope to win."

Dionysus snorted. "Win? Girl, our only hope is to not die."

"Then that's our goal. To not die."

He laughed, then tilted the canteen he always carried to his lips and took a drink.

"Why are you in charge?" Revana shouted from just outside the circle.

I looked at her. "Do you have something to add?"

"Why don't we just fly out of here? We could go back to the academy."

That caused a ripple through the group.

"You'd leave all these people to die? To let this thing destroy our world?" I took a step toward her. "You think after it's finished ruining this part of town that its going to stop? Where does your family live, Revana? Do you think they're safe?"

She frowned, obviously not thinking about that. "The Gods will save them."

I shook my head. "You're an idiot if you think that. It's up to us. All of us together to fight this thing. Only then does this world stand a chance."

Others in the group nodded.

I gestured to Demeter. "Do you think the other Gods will help us?"

"They'll have to. When the Typhon is done here, it will move on to the academy and to Olympus." She put a hand on my shoulder. "I'll take care of it. You do what *you* need to." Then she ran over to Apollo, Artemis, Athena, and Hermes.

An image flashed in my mind. Wincing I rubbed my forehead, not quite capturing the picture.

Then I glanced over to the volcano. The Typhon was on its way. I could hear the whoosh of its wings. A rush of fear filled me, and I didn't know if I could do what I needed to. I looked at my friends— Georgina, Jasmine, Ren, Mia…Lucian. I wanted to tell each of them how much they meant to me. But there wasn't time.

I took out the energy ball in my pocket. The others did as well. We pinched them all apart and shared them with the rest of the group. The second it was in my mouth, a jolt of energy and vitality shot through me and I grinned.

I thought about making some grand speech to motivate the group, something about blood and glory, but honestly I sucked at putting words together. So, I just looked at everyone. "Let's go kick some Typhon ass."

The Furies whooped, then shot up into the air. They were always up for a good fight.

One by one, the cadets, my peers, my friends turned and ran, some flew, into battle. Only Lucian remained. He cupped my face in his hand. "Forever. That's how long I will love you. Even if I die and go to Elysium, you will always be my everything."

Gently he brushed his lips against mine, then he swooped into the air with two strokes of his beautiful red wings. He glanced at Hades. "You'll protect her?"

"Eternally."

With a final nod, Lucian ascended, sparks starting to sizzle along his fingers, others lined up in formation behind him. Out of all of us he was the most God-like. He had all the qualities that would make a great leader and mentor. When everything was said and done, I hoped Lucian would take over the academy and continue its legacy of a place of learning and fellowship.

I unfurled my wings and joined Hades in the air. Together we soared toward Zeus, who hadn't moved and was just watching, with a dreamy smile on his face, as the Typhon advanced. He turned right before we reached him, and shot a bolt of lightning from his fingers.

Hades shoved me aside just as the sizzling, jagged, fragment of light zipped between us. The tips of my hair melted from the blast of heat. After I righted myself, I shot toward him again, determined to make him pay.

"Daughter, do your duty," Zeus shouted.

Before I could aim a fire ball at him, Aphrodite stepped in front, creating a wall of beaming light as a shield. It blinded me, and I veered off to the side again. Blinking back white spots, I flew back.

Hades had formed a sword from shadow and was trading blows with Zeus and his golden staff. Both white and dark sparks burst into the air each time their weapons clashed. They seemed evenly matched. Maybe I could come up along his side with a fire ball and aid Hades's attack.

But I was stopped again when Aphrodite transformed into a giant harpy with vicious sharp bird claws. She flew in the air and dove at me with her claws first. I drew my sword and swung at her. My blade cut through one of her claws slicing it in half. Shrieking, she swooped around and came at me again. This time I instantly formed a ball of fire in my hand and threw it at her. It lit upon one of her wings and burned half the feathers off.

She dropped to the ground and turned back into her human self. Her right arm was blackened like crispy fried chicken. I smiled, knowing I'd done that even though I knew she'd heal. I created another ball of fire in my hand, readying to throw it at her, when a small cyclone of water splashed over me from the side, putting out the flames and dampening my one wing. When I landed, I spied Revana coming at me, forming another water spout in her hands.

Aphrodite grinned smugly. "You will be rewarded in Olympus, my dear Revana."

Revana threw the water at me, and I countered with a blast of fire. The attacks hit each other and produced a blast of hot steam over us both. I turned toward her, raising my sword. If she wanted a fight, I wouldn't deny her. She drew hers that was strapped on her back and ran at me.

Our steel clashed. The force of it reverberated up my arms. I stepped back, lifted my blade to the side and advanced on her. Again, our swords clanged. I spun to my left, lowered my sword, then back at her. This time I was rewarded as my blade sliced across her side. Blood spilled over the steel and ran down her leg. Wincing, her sword arm drooped and she took a couple steps back.

"I don't want to kill you, Revana," I said. "There's no point. We're in this fight together."

"I hate that you're better than me."

I shook my head. "I hate that you've been made to feel that you're less than your whole life." I remembered what I saw about her abusive homelife during Apollo's trial. "You're a fierce warrior, Revana. You are good enough."

"Fight her, you coward!" Aphrodite screamed at her.

Revana raised her sword, took a couple of shaky steps toward me, then stopped and sheathed her blade onto her back. She shook her head. "I won't."

The whole ground shook beneath us. Typhon had landed on the ground. It opened its mouth and roared. The sound was deafening. I stumbled to the side as the pavement cracked between us, and the earth moved. Horrified, I watched as the crack widened into a crater. The ground fell away from under Revana's feet.

I screamed. "Revana!" and leapt forward, reaching out with my hand.

She tried to unfurl her wings but because of the cut in her side only one would open up. She flung out her arm toward me as she plummeted into the hole. On my knees, I stretched as far as I could...our fingers brushed.

I couldn't grab her.

I watched as she spiraled down into the hole. She hit one side of the rocky slope. She scrambled to grab hold of anything, but her fingers couldn't dig in.

Then she was gone.

CHAPTER TWENTY-THREE

MELANY

I smacked the ground with my hands. "Noooo!" I felt sick to my stomach.

I glanced up to find Aphrodite, hoping she saw what her bullshit had done, but she'd sprouted her wings and was flying away like a coward. Even Ares hadn't run away. He'd put on his armored helmet and charged toward the Typhon with his spear and shield. I was tempted to go after her, but my fight was not with her. She wasn't important right now. Zeus was my target. Taking him down would fix everything else.

But how? He was too strong. Even Hades couldn't hurt him, and he had the power of darkness behind him.

Persephone's face popped into my mind and I could hear her voice.

You are the key. You will be the one to end the battle. You have control of all five elements, but they must be freely given to you.

What five elements?

As I considered this, my peripheral caught Ren in flight, shooting water at the Typhon's open mouth as it formed a fire ball. Steam rose from between its lips and out his nose as the water cooled down the fire. Water.

Then I searched for Jasmine and spotted her hovering near the Typhon's wing trying to burn the membrane between the bones in its wings, so it wouldn't' be able to fly. Hephaistos was there helping her. Fire.

Down below, I saw Georgina with Demeter pushing up the dirt on the ground to cover the Typhon's serpent tail. I could see that they were trying to cement it to the ground, so it couldn't slither away. Earth.

Lucian flew by. He spiraled up toward the Typhon's face, doing some fancy flying to avoid the large fire balls it spewed from its mouth. Sparks flew off his hands as he formed a bolt and hurled it at the creature's eyes. Lightning.

I raised my hands in front of my face and drew the darkness into my palms. Shadow.

The five elements.

I could control them all, but only two were really strong—fire and shadow. I needed to be strong in all of them if I was doing to beat Zeus.

I unfolded my damp wing and flapped it a few times, drying it out, then I unfurled the other and shot into the air. I flew to Lucian. When he spotted me, he came to my side.

"I need your help," I said.

"Anything."

"I need you to get Ren and Jasmine and meet me down there." I pointed to a spot behind what was left of one of the stores in the mall. It was safest place I could think of at that moment.

"Okay." He took off.

I flew down to where Georgina and Demeter toiled away. They'd managed to get some of its snake tail buried under the dirt and rocks, but the Typhon was struggling and looked like it would break it at any moment.

"I need your help, Gina."

She nodded. "Okay."

I grabbed her hand and flew her over to the destroyed building. Lucian, Jasmine, and Ren all landed at the same time.

"What's going on?" Lucian asked.

"I'm going to ask something difficult from each of you. But it's the only way I know of beating Zeus and stopping all of this."

"What is it?" Jasmine had to yell over the sound of the fire balls hitting the ground nearby.

"I need your powers." I looked at each of them. "I need you to give them to me without question."

Frowning, Jasmine glanced at Ren, then Georgina. I could see the hesitation and concern in her eyes. "Will we lose the powers forever?"

I shrugged. "I don't know. Maybe. Maybe not.

But I need for you to decide now. We're running out of time."

Lucian set his hand on my shoulder and gave me a small smile.

Ren placed his hand on my other shoulder.

Then Georgina did, on my back. Her gaze fixed on Jasmine.

Swallowing, and still unsure, Jasmine set her hand on my back as well.

"Thank you." I nodded to each of them, then took a deep breath. "Push your power into me."

At first, I didn't feel anything. Then it was a sharp small pinprick, like when you get a shot at the doctor's. That needle pain slowly grew into something harsh and stabbing. I could barely breathe as water, fire, earth, and lightning power surged into me. Waves and waves of it poured over me, through me, until my body felt like it was going to explode. I slammed my eyes shut as I bit down on my bottom lip until I could taste blood.

Then it stopped. Like a snap of the fingers.

I opened my eyes. All four of them were on the ground, as if they'd been shoved away. Lucian blinked up at me. "Did it work?"

"Yes," I said as I took in deep breath. "I can feel it all swirling around inside me."

Georgina placed her hand onto the ground beside her. "It must have because I can't feel the earth anymore."

They all got to their feet.

"How do we fight now?" Jasmine asked, as she

flexed her fingers, probably feeling the loss of her fire power.

"We still have weapons." Lucian unsheathed his sword. "We're still warriors."

Jasmine pulled the bow off her back.

Ren pulled his blade.

Georgina patted the canvas bag at her side. "I can still heal."

"Thank you, my friends."

I unfurled my wings and lifted into the air. I could feel each element twirling around me, through every organ and muscle, making me strong and invincible.

Lucian's eyes widened. "I wish you could see yourself, Mel. You look like a fiery dark phoenix. With blue hair."

"Go kick Zeus's ass." Jasmine raised her fist into the air.

I flew up higher and over to where Hades and Zeus still battled. I glanced over my shoulder and saw my friends running back into the fight with their weapons raised. I didn't know if by taking all their power away, they were running to their doom. I had to trust that it was the right thing to do, the only thing to do, so I turned back and focused on the task at hand.

As I dove toward Zeus, he landed a powerful blow to Hades which sent him to the ground. Hades's face was bloodied and bruised. There were burns marks on his hands, and his shirt was seared in places, the flesh beneath it blackened.

Rage ignited inside at seeing him wounded and in pain. While I closed the distance between me and

Zeus, I spread my arms out to the side, as fire, water, earth, lightning, and shadow glimmered around me. I saw the elements rippling over my skin in a kaleidoscope of colors. When Hades saw me, his eyes widened, then slowly his lips twitched upwards into a smile…

"This is for my parents, you son-of-a-bitch!"

Gathering everything I had, I flung my hands toward Zeus.

Several flashes of bright light erupted all around. Bolts of lightning zipped in front of me, behind me, everywhere at once. At first, I thought the power was coming from me…but it wasn't. Zeus had sent everything he had at me. I put an arm up over my head to shield my eyes from the glare so I would not be rendered blind, but I knew it was all too late. I hadn't acted quickly enough and now I was going to die.

I braced for the searing agony of being electrocuted. But it didn't come.

I lowered my arm just as Hades jumped in front of me, taking the full impact of Zeus's attack. Light pierced him through the chest, and arms, and legs. He fell like a ragdoll at my feet; I saw white current and sparks coiling around his body, from his feet to his head.

I crouched next to him, reaching for him. Sparks popped off his skin and onto mine. The pain was miniscule compared to the gut-wrenching agony I felt inside. I thought my heart was going to burst. I touched his face, careful not to cause him more pain.

"Why did you do that?" Tears rolled down my cheeks. "Why?"

He grabbed the back of my head and pulled me down to his mouth. "He's depleted. Finish him." He brushed his lips against mine, then pushed me away. Groaning, he curled into a ball, grimacing from the pain.

Zeus loomed over him. "I'm sorry, brother. It was not you I meant to kill."

Calling all the force inside of me, clutching every molecule of fury and rage and despair I possessed, I launched myself at Zeus. Before he could react and knock me away, I wrapped my arms and legs around him, squeezing him tight, and drove my power into his body.

Wailing, he thrashed about, trying to yank me off. But I held on, continuing to force every ounce of energy I had. Eventually he stopped fighting and dropped to his knees. I thought for sure I was going to crush him with the white light of my energy. Instead, I felt him start to fade into the darkness until I was holding onto nothing but air. When Zeus was gone, I quickly turned around to hold Hades to help him heal.

But I found nothing but ash.

I sunk my fingers into it, hoping that I could piece him back together grain by grain. A light breeze picked up and blew the gray soot from my hands. I collapsed onto my side, sobbing.

Through my tears, I saw that the Typhon had stopped spitting fire balls and grasping at people to crush them in its hands. It looked around in a daze, then it turned around, flew up into the air, and returned to the volcano it had erupted from.

I heard people cheering from nearby, and the happy sounds of relief and victory. Then I heard wings flapping in the air, and the sounds of feet hitting the ground. I heard voices calling my name. I rolled onto my back and looked up into familiar faces as they stared down at me.

My hands were clasped. My face touched. My hair smoothed back. I knew these things happened, but I couldn't feel them. I couldn't feel anything but a deep, gnawing black hole in my mind, body and soul.

"She saved us. She's a hero."

"Is she going to be okay?"

"I'll take her to the infirmary."

"Blue?" More touches on my face. "Blue, you're going to be okay. I'm going to make sure you're okay."

Am I? I wanted to say, but no words would come. I closed my eyes and hoped the darkness would come for me. Only then, would I ever feel whole again.

CHAPTER TWENTY-FOUR

LUCIAN

$\mathcal{I}$ walked down the street near the construction site of the new mall that was being built in Pecunia. It had been only a couple of months since the war that ravaged the town, but the townspeople had quickly picked up the pieces, buried their dead and moved on. I wished it had been that easy for the rest of us.

As I approached the construction office, a tall man with a receding hairline waved at me. I waved back and joined him. He shook my hand with enthusiasm.

"I'm so happy to see you, Lucian."

"You as well, Mayor Remis. How goes the rebuilding?"

"Good. Good. I wanted to let you know that when we reopen, we'd be honored if you and your fellow protectors would attend the opening ceremony."

"We wouldn't miss it."

He smiled. "Excellent. The townspeople will be thrilled to know."

We said our goodbyes, and I unfurled my wings and took to the sky. As I soared over the town, I noticed other things being rebuilt with one noticeable exception. The temple to Zeus had been permanently torn down, the stones used to erect a memorial to the mortals who had lost their lives. I thought it was fitting, and I couldn't wait to tell Melany about it. I hoped it would bring her some solace.

It didn't take me long to fly to Cala to the under-water portal to the academy. It was the only portal to and from the academy now. All the other portals had been closed. Even the Gods couldn't just pop in and out anymore.

I landed on dock six and looked out over the bay, remembering my first encounter with Melany. I chuckled to myself picturing her out in the water floundering around looking for the portal to the acad-emy. My hand still tingled from where I'd grabbed hers and yanked her out of the water.

Turning, I walked back along dock six and over to dock nine. I took in a deep breath and dove into the water. I kicked hard, swimming further down to the portal. It shimmered in front of me. I put my hands in and was pulled up into the spout. A few minutes later, I pulled myself up onto the rocky edge of the pool in the cave.

As I walked through the cave to the opening, I

used a bit of my fire power to dry my clothes and skin. I was happy to still have that small ability, as well as some water skill. I could still fight, of course, and fly, but I still couldn't manipulate lightning. That power was gone. Chiron told me it was still possible for it to come back, but I didn't put any hope on it.

I came out of the cave and smiled when I saw the academy looming ahead. Despite of all that had happened, I still called the massive, dark-stone estate home and would for the rest of my life, which now according to the prophecies would be a very long time.

While I walked along the cobblestone path, I spotted Georgina just off to the side tending to the plants and flowers. She was on her knees digging in the dirt with her spade. I admired her for her tenacity. I knew it wasn't easy for her to have lost her earth power. She'd also lost her left arm in the battle, burned off by one of the Typhon's fire balls. Chiron had been too late to save it.

She looked up as I neared and set down the spade so she could wave at me. "Good morning."

"Morning. How's it going?"

She shrugged. "Would be better if I could tell the plants what to do."

I gave her a sympathetic smile. "Chiron says that—"

"I know what he says, but we both know its bull-shit." She wiped her face with her hand, leaving streaks of dirt on her cheek.

"Demeter should be here helping you."

"She's in the hall with Hephaistos, getting those statues up finally. I think Jasmine's with them."

"Where's Mel?"

"Probably the same place she was yesterday."

I glanced at the maze in the distance, and then nodded. "I'll see you later."

"Yup." She went back to her digging.

When I entered the academy, I ran into Ren and Diego. They were busy helping Athena and Apollo with the new passageway to the Hall of Knowledge. Athena decided that all the knowledge needed to be out in the open.

I nodded to them as I passed by, and then continued on to the far wing of the academy. We had construction of our own going on. When I neared the tall golden doors, they were already open, welcoming people to come inside. I heard Hephaistos the second I crossed the threshold.

"That is not where that should go, woman."

I turned the corner to see Hephaistos and Demeter arguing over where one of the new stone benches should go. Jasmine was looking on, hands on her hips and shaking her head.

"Then move it, you big oaf." She looked over at Dionysus who was sitting on the floor, his back to one wall, sipping from his canteen. He shrugged and took another drink.

Hephaistos picked up the bench effortlessly and moved it over to the other side of the hall in between the stone statues of Marek and Rosie.

I watched as the forge God took care of the placement of the bench. He looked up at each statue to make sure they weren't blocked or impeded in any way. He'd constructed the statues to honor our dead. Revana had one as well across the hall and near a window. Melany had insisted on putting it there, claiming that Revana would enjoy the natural light. I didn't question why she was adamant about that. Something had transpired between them before Revana's death and I didn't ask. I knew it was private.

There were other statues in the newly constructed Heroes Hall of other fallen cadets. We'd lost ten people altogether and wanted to honor their sacrifice. It had also been Melany's idea to take over Aphrodite's Hall for that purpose, as the Goddess was no longer in need of it, since she was locked away with Ares in Tartarus alone, as we'd released all the Titan prisoners.

Some of them came back to the academy to resume their teaching, while others like Oceanus went to Olympus to spend eternity in comfort and bliss. Prometheus returned as head of the school, of which I was grateful, because as it was, everyone had been looking to me to take the reins. I wasn't ready for that kind of responsibility. I did agree to take Ares's place though, and take over the training of all the cadets, new and old. If there was ever another threat to the mortal world, I would be the one to lead the battle.

When the idea had first come up to carve the honorary statues for the Hall of Heroes, I'd suggested erecting one of Hades. But Melany claimed he wouldn't want that. So, I didn't press.

Jasmine came up to me. "How was your trip to Pecunia?"

"Good. They're rebuilding, slowly but moving forward. The mayor invited us to the ribbon-cutting ceremony for the new mall when it's done."

She smiled. "Cool. That'll also give me a chance to zip over to New Haven to see my family."

"Have you seen Melany today?"

She sobered a little. "No. I didn't see her at breakfast in the dining hall. I should've gone to her room to make sure she ate."

I nodded. "It's okay. Don't worry about it. I'm sure I know where she is."

The moment I stepped out the back door of the academy, I flapped my wings and shot up into the sky. Flying still gave me such a thrill. One I was sure that wouldn't ever grow old. I swooped over the garden, and the stone statues guarding the maze. I knew exactly where to go.

I slowly dropped into the middle of the maze behind a piece of hedge near the gazebo. I folded my wings behind me and then got onto the path. I spotted Melany just past one of the thick round columns sitting on one of the stone benches in the gazebo. She sort of had this glow about her now. It wasn't bright, just a soft golden aura that surrounded her. Chiron said it was because of all the conflicting energy she still had in her.

"I think they're putting up the statues in the hall today. I'm going to check it out later. I imagine it will be a sight better than all that gold and pink that Aphrodite had up on her walls." She paused, then laughed. "I know, right? Heph keeps asking me to make one of you, but I told him you'd hate that." She laughed again. "I agree. He'd never be able to capture your style." Then she paused again.

I took a step forward and saw her frown. She brought a hand up to her face and wiped at her eyes, then she whispered, "I miss you."

I couldn't stand to see her like this; it broke my heart every day. Ever since we returned to the academy, she'd been coming here to the gazebo every day. And every day I heard her talking to herself. I worried about her state of mind. Maybe taking all the powers of the Gods had broken her. Chiron had assured me that her body was healthy but he couldn't tell me anything about what went on in her head.

I continued to walk to the gazebo, making no attempt at being quiet any longer. She probably knew I was there anyway. Her head came up as I stepped up into the arbor. She smiled.

"I saw you fly in. You look good in white."

I rustled my wings a bit, one white feather stuck out and I smoothed it down. Shortly after the war, my wings had turned white. As had Georgina's, Jasmine's, Ren's, all of those who had fought in the battle. We'd all became demigods in the end.

Except for Melany. Her wings stayed black. And I suspected she was more than a demigod. So much more.

"Did you eat today?" I asked her.

She shook her head, sending her blue hair swinging. It had grown long in the past few months but had stayed blue. Even the new hair had been tinged that color.

"You need to eat, Blue. You're getting too skinny,"

I teased her. She was far from skinny. Her body had grown more muscular and lean and fierce. But I worried because I didn't know what was fueling her. She hardly ate anything anymore.

She reached for me and grabbed my hand. "Are there pancakes?"

I laughed. "Yes, there are most definitely pancakes, and fruit and whipped cream, just the way you like them."

"Okay. Let's go eat some pancakes."

I pulled her to her feet and then swung an arm around her shoulders. I leaned in and kissed her. She kissed me back with more passion than she'd had in the past few months. When she pulled back, she smiled, and it was big and warm and made my heart skip a beat. Maybe she wasn't as lost as I thought she was.

We walked out of the gazebo and started for the path through the hedges. Before we turned the corner, I glanced over my shoulder at the gazebo again. Curls of black mist swirled around the other stone bench. In the exact same place I'd always seen Hades sit in the past.

I shook my head then turned back and gave Melany's shoulder a squeeze. She was going to be okay. I knew that now.

Hades had made a promise to always protect her, and he was keeping it. Eternally.

***

Thank you for reading Demigods Academy! Don't

miss SEASON TWO, now available! And be sure to join our EMAIL and SMS lists below to don't miss any of our future books!

We hope you enjoyed Melany's adventures and can't wait to share more with you. In the meantime, we would love to read your opinion on Amazon and Goodreads.

Sign Up for EMAILS at:

www.KieraLegend.com

www.ElisaSAmore.com/Vip-List

To Sign Up for SMS:

Text AMORE to (844) 339 0303

Text LEGEND to (844) 339 0303

ABOUT THE AUTHORS

Elisa S. Amore is the number-one bestselling author of the paranormal romance saga *Touched*.

Vanity Fair Italy called her "the undisputed queen of romantic fantasy." After the success of Touched, she produced the audio version of the saga featuring Hollywood star Matt Lanter (*90210*, *Timeless*, *Star Wars*) and Disney actress Emma Galvin, narrator of *Twilight* and *Divergent*. Elisa is now a full-time writer of young adult fantasy. She's wild about pizza and also loves traveling, which she calls a source of constant inspiration. With her successful series about life and death, Heaven and Hell, she has built a loyal fanbase on social media that continues to grow, and has quickly become a favorite author for thousands of readers in the U.S.

Visit Elisa S. Amore's website and join her List of Readers at www.ElisaSAmore.com and Text AMORE to 77948 for new release alerts.

FOLLOW ELISA S. AMORE:
facebook.com/eli.amore
facebook.com/groups/amoreans
instagram.com/eli.amore
twitter.com/ElisaSAmore

elisa.amore@touchedsaga.com

***

Kiera Legend writes Urban Fantasy and Paranormal Romance stories that bite. She loves books, movies and Tv-Shows. Her best friends are usually vampires, witches, werewolves and angels. She never hangs out without her little dragon. She especially likes writing kick-ass heroines and strong world-buildings and is excited for all the books that are coming!

Text LEGEND to 77948 to don't miss any of them (US only) or sign up at www.kieralegend.com to get an email alert when her next book is out.

FOLLOW KIERA LEGEND:
facebook.com/groups/kieralegend
facebook.com/kieralegend
authorkieralegend@gmail.com

***

Made in United States
Orlando, FL
04 April 2022

16472363R00421